THE MODERN
OF THE WORLD'S

From Henry David Thoreau . . .

. . . to Hunter S. Thompson

THE MODERN
LIBRARY IS THE
HOME OF THE
CLASSICS IN
HARDCOVER

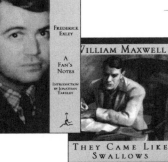

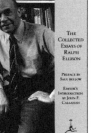

For a complete list
of titles, write to:

THE MODERN LIBRARY
201 East 50th Street
New York, NY 10022

═══════ MODERN LIBRARY ═══════

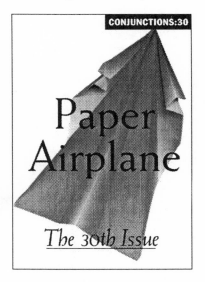

CONJUNCTIONS

Bi-Annual Volumes of New Writing

Edited by
Bradford Morrow

Contributing Editors
Walter Abish
Chinua Achebe
John Ashbery
Mei-mei Berssenbrugge
Guy Davenport
Elizabeth Frank
William H. Gass
John Guare
Robert Kelly
Ann Lauterbach
Patrick McGrath
Mona Simpson
Nathaniel Tarn
Quincy Troupe
John Edgar Wideman

published by Bard College

EDITOR: Bradford Morrow
MANAGING EDITOR: Michael Bergstein
SENIOR EDITORS: Robert Antoni, Martine Bellen, Thalia Field,
    Pat Sims, Lee Smith
ART EDITOR: Anthony McCall
PUBLICITY: Mark R. Primoff
WEBMASTERS: Brian Evenson, Michael Neff
EDITORIAL ASSISTANTS: Anne Dearman, Lauren Feeney,
    Mia Fiore, Blair Holt, Andrew Small, Sadia Talib, Alan Tinkler,
    Karen Walker

CONJUNCTIONS is published in the Spring and Fall of each year
by Bard College, Annandale-on-Hudson, NY 12504. This issue is
made possible in part with the generous funding of the Lannan
Foundation and the National Endowment for the Arts.

This publication is made possible with public funds from the New
York State Council on the Arts, a State Agency.

SUBSCRIPTIONS: Send subscription order to CONJUNCTIONS,
Bard College, Annandale-on-Hudson, NY 12504. Single year (two
volumes): $18.00 for individuals; $25.00 for institutions and overseas. Two years (four volumes): $32.00 for individuals; $45.00 for
institutions and overseas. Patron subscription (lifetime): $500.00.
Overseas subscribers please make payment by International Money
Order. Back issues available at $12.00 per copy. For subscription
and advertising information, call 914-758-1539 or fax 914-758-2660.

Editorial communications should be sent to 33 West 9th Street,
New York, NY 10011. Unsolicited manuscripts cannot be returned
unless accompanied by a stamped, self-addressed envelope.

Cover design and collage by Anthony McCall Associates, New York.

Printers: Edwards Brothers.
Typesetter: Bill White, Typeworks.

ISSN 0278-2324
ISBN 0-941964-45-0

Manufactured in the United States of America.

TABLE OF CONTENTS

TRIBUTES
American Writers on American Writers
Edited by Martine Bellen, Lee Smith and Bradford Morrow

EDITORS' NOTE

IF ONLY WE COULD have paid homage to them all, our forebears and predecessors, all those writers who have gone before us. Mark Twain would surely have been included, and Frederick Douglass. Anne Bradstreet, of course. A few essays had been proposed on Nora Zeale Hurston, Wallace Stevens, Djuna Barnes, Jane Bowles, even Isaac Bashevis Singer and others, but circumstances prevented them from coming into being. Who else is absent and why? Certainly one obvious impediment was limitations of "SPACE," to paraphrase invertedly the opening of Charles Olson's *Call Me Ishmael*, his homage to Melville that largely inspired this issue. And yet, what a brilliant congregation of writers is celebrated by forty-five fellow authors in the pages you hold in your hands.

Surely it is valuable to think of who else is here in spirit. You can compile your own list, maybe starting with Kenneth Rexroth, Richard Wright, Carson McCullers, James Baldwin, Countee Cullen, H.D., Donald Barthelme, Arna Bontemps, Washington Irving, Katherine Anne Porter, Vachel Lindsay, Tennessee Williams, Amy Lowell, Margaret Fuller, Kate Chopin, Jean Toomer, John Steinbeck, Stanley Elkin, Booker T. Washington, Raymond Carver, Claude McKay, Laura Riding, Frederick Jackson Turner, Ellen Glasgow, Robert Frost, Louisa May Alcott, e. e. cummings, Horatio Alger, Thomas Merton, William Inge, Sarah Orne Jewett, Truman Capote, May Swenson, John Dos Passos, Mary Moody Emerson, Harriet Beecher Stowe, Muriel Rukeyser, Thornton Wilder, Chester Himes, Edgar Lee Masters, Frank Norris, Jean Stafford, William Wells Brown, Flannery O'Connor, Paul Monette, Edna St. Vincent Millay, James Jones, Robinson Jeffers, Henry Roth, Nella Larsen, Charles W. Chesnutt, Louis Zukofsky, Sherwood Anderson, Lorraine Hansberry, Jack London, Paul Blackburn, Carl Sandburg, Paul Laurence Dunbar, Sidney Lanier, John Berryman, Eugene O'Neill, Mary McCarthy, James T. Farrell, Paul Goodman, Patricia Highsmith, Charlotte Perkins Gilman, Theodore Dreiser, Thomas Wolfe, Martin Luther King, Jr., Robert Lowell, Haniel Long, James Schuyler, Dorothy Parker, Ted Berrigan, Peter De Vries, Wallace Stegner, Helene Jackson, Delmore Schwartz, Henry Adams, John Crowe Ransom, Marcus Garvey, H.P. Lovecraft, Fitz-James O'Brien, George Oppen, F.O. Matthiessen, Dorothy West, John Cage, Randall Jarrell, Alice Childress, James Merrill, Joel Oppenheimer, Jack Spicer, Charles Henri Ford, Walker Percy, James Fenimore

Cooper, Nathaniel Hawthorne . . . the catalogue might fill pages as it continues to build toward mere incompletion!

Most of the writers honored in *Tributes* are best known as novelists, poets, story writers or playwrights, which is great and appropriate. But in a literature as manifold and hybrid as that of these United States, it would have been equally representative to have included historians (like Francis Parkman) and justices (like Oliver Wendell Holmes), translators (like Mary Barnard) and newspapermen (like Ring Lardner), screenwriters (like Orson Welles) and political leaders (like Malcom X), lyricists (like Ira Gershwin) and inventors (like Buckminster Fuller), philosophers (like William James) — and even an occasional president who could weave ideas with words in exceptional ways (like John Adams, or Abraham Lincoln).

This is all to say that the intention was never to provide a comprehensive accounting of American literature. *Tributes* should be seen as an invitation to begin to have a look at where we have been, as a various and often dissociated fellowship of American authors, in order to see where we might be headed — together and apart — in the future.

The choice of authors honored was happily left up to the contributors. So there are two pieces on Gertrude Stein and nothing on Hemingway. Prokosch is here but not Stephen Crane, nor Hart Crane, nor the creator of Ichabod Crane. There is a tribute to Dr. Seuss but the author of *Old Possum's Book of Practical Cats* is neglected. A number of contemporary writers were invited to pay homage to an American writer, one who made something possible for them, whether that was the act of writing itself, or writing a certain book, or in a particular manner, or living in a way that was consonant with the work of writing. This is an anthology of personal enthusiasms — enthusiasm as Emerson defined it: exuberant and magnanimous — a colloquium Whitman might have seen as a progress of vistas.

And it's with Whitman, of course, along with Emerson, where many meditations about American literature have typically found their source. Still, what is American literature? Emerson believed it must be autochthonous and original, must look to itself for inspiration and resource, and following his criteria it's easy to see why he often doubted its existence. Is American literature no more than the collected products of writers who by accident of birth, or socioeconomic design, or immigration, are by nationality American, citizens for better or worse of the United States? And how long do you have to have been here to count as American? Several generations on a cotton plantation or the time it takes to arrange a green-card marriage? Was Russian-born Nabokov *really* American, though he became a citizen; was Henry James, who became at the end of his life a British subject, ever *really* American? British-born Paul West, who writes so eloquently on Faulkner, has been an American for over half his life, and is living proof that the art itself transcends national and bureaucratic boundaries. In every way it is ultimately temperament that dictates the answers.

Finally, if American writers are supposed to have an original relationship with the universe, like others have had, then how is the relationship original? Is American literature an idea only, then, an idea about one's relationship to the universe? If so, is it available to anyone, Americans and non-Americans alike? (Maybe that's why nineteenth-century Latin American writers recognized Whitman not only as a prophet of personal acquisitiveness and political expansionism, but also as a great poet long before their northern colleagues did.) Is there an American literature, or are there American literatures, each marked by individual idioms, manners, subjects? Or is it fruitless to speak of racial, ethnic, class-based, sexual and geographical distinctions when each writer by necessity must wage her or his own eccentric articulation against and within a culture that tends to devalue the individual voice in favor of consensus? Do such questions begin to erode fundamental purposes of the very activity of asking?

If we can't answer, at least we know where these questions come from, and we honor both the questions and those who would try to answer. If we don't know, maybe never can know, precisely what American literature is, we are quite aware we're not the first to not know. This shouldn't in any way suppress our desire to pay homage to a handful of the great ones who wrote, many of them against all odds, in this country we've inherited. The tributes in this issue are offered in that spirit of magnanimity.

— Martine Bellen, Lee Smith, Bradford Morrow
September 1997
New York City

9

Sterling Brown. Photograph by Thomas Victor. Schomburg Center for Research in Black Culture.

Sterling Brown: A Southern Man
Ntozake Shange

ON SUNDAY AFTERNOONS IN ST. LOUIS, particularly when for-
sythia, honeysuckle and dogwood blossoms were ebulliently infus-
ing the air with scents so different from those of hatred, hunger,
heartbreak and forlorn ennui, my mother would inevitably jump
into "Strong Men":

> *They dragged you from homeland,*
> *They chained you in coffles,*
> *They huddled you spoon-fashion in filthy hatches,*
> *They sold you to give a few gentlemen ease.*
>
> *They broke you in like oxen,*
> *They scourged you,*
> *They branded you,*
> *They made your women breeders,*
> *They swelled your numbers with bastards. . . .*
> *They taught you the religion they disgraced.*
>
> *You sang:*
> > *Keep a-inchin' along*
> > *Lak a po' inch worm. . . .*
>
> *You sang:*
> > *Bye and bye*
> > *I'm gonna lay down dis heaby load. . . .*
>
> *You sang:*
> > *Walk togedder, chillen,*
> > *Dontcha git weary. . . .*
> > > The strong men keep a-comin' on
> > > The strong men git stronger.
>
> *They point with pride to the roads you built for them,*
> *They ride in comfort over the rails you laid for them.*
> *They put hammers in your hands*
> *And said — Drive so much before sundown.*

Ntozake Shange

> *You sang:*
>> *Ain't no hammah*
>> *In dis lan',*
>> *Strikes lak mine, bebby,*
>> *Strikes lak mine.*
>
> *They cooped you in their kitchens,*
> *They penned you in their factories,*
> *They gave you the jobs that they were too good for,*
> *They tried to guarantee happiness to themselves*
> *By shunting dirt and misery to you.*
>
> *You sang:*
>> *Me an' muh baby gonna shine, shine*
>> *Me an' muh baby gonna shine.*
>>> The strong men keep a-comin' on
>>> The strong men git stronger. . . .
>
> *They bought off some of your leaders*
> *You stumbled, as blind men will . . .*
> *They coaxed you, unwontedly soft-voiced. . . .*
> *You followed a way.*
> *Then laughed as usual.*
>
> — from "Strong Men"

No number of bars of Dvořák from my violin, my brother's Frederick Douglass or my sister's Dunbar or the baby's forced phonetic reconstruction of Baker's "La Vie en Rose" compared in stamina or passion with my mother, Ellie's, passionate encounters with Sterling Brown, graced unobtrusively with my father on bongo drums.

Why am I returning to the experiences of a prepubescent Negro child on the banks of the Mississippi, luckily way upriver from Mississippi? This is, as I imagine Jefferson Davis or Thomas Jefferson would say, a matter of honor and authenticity, bloodlines and legitimacy.

While Dvořák (with his *New World Symphony*), Douglass, Dunbar and Baker remain icons in American culture, falling off the lips of the tenuous day, quasars of the Mothership, Sterling Brown is unique: an honorable craftsman whose handling of the voices and feelings, perceptions of our people could only be questioned by the spirits, the ancestors and the collective unconscious of what Henry Dumas called African pageantry.

12

I found me a cranny of perpetual dusk.
There for the grateful sense was pungent musk
Of rotting leaves, and moss, mingled with scents
Of heavy clusters freighting foxgrape vines.
The sun was barred except at close of day
When he could weakly etch in changing lines
A filigree upon the silver trunks
Of maple and of poplar. There were oaks
Their black bark fungus-spotted, and there lay
An old wormeaten segment of gray fence
Tumbling in consonant long forgot decay.
Motionless the place save when a little wind
Rippled the leaves, and soundless too it was
Save for a stream nearly inaudible,
That made a short stay in closewoven grass
Then in elusive whispers bade farewell.

— from "Arc of Sons"

Dvořák reaped his soul from ours, Douglass turned his back in disgust on us, Dunbar resented our language, which created the very foundations of his genius. He even persuaded his wife, Alice Dunbar Nelson, to be ashamed that his sonnets were not the "Talk of the Town." And La Bakaire made up almost as many versions of herself as Brown has characters, women like Clareel, even Frankie.

FRANKIE AND JOHNNY

Oh Frankie and Johnny were lovers
Oh Lordy how they did love!

— Old Ballad

Frankie was a halfwit, Johnny was a nigger,
  Frankie liked to pain poor creatures as a little 'un,
Kept a crazy love of torment when she got bigger,
  Johnny had to slave it and never had much fun.

Frankie liked to pull wings off of living butterflies,
  Frankie liked to cut long angleworms in half,
Frankie liked to whip curs and listen to their drawn out cries,
  Frankie liked to shy stones at the brindle calf.

Frankie took her pappy's lunch week-days to the sawmill,
  Her pappy, red-faced cracker, with a cracker's thirst,

Beat her skinny body and reviled the hateful imbecile,
    She screamed at every blow he struck, but tittered when
        he curst.

Frankie had to cut through Johnny's field of sugar corn
    Used to wave at Johnny, who didn't *'pay no min—*
Had had to work like fifty from the day that he was born,
    And wan't no cracker hussy gonna put his work behind—

But everyday Frankie swung along the cornfield lane,
    And one day Johnny helped her partly through the wood,
Once he had dropped his plow lines, he dropped them
        many times again—
    Though his mother didn't know it, else she'd have
        whipped him good.

Frankie and Johnny were lovers; oh Lordy how they did love!
    But one day Frankie's pappy by a big log laid him low,
To find out what his crazy Frankie had been speaking of;
    He found that what his gal had muttered was exactly so.

Frankie, she was spindly limbed with corn silk on her
        crazy head,
    Johnny was a nigger, who never had much fun—
They swung up Johnny on a tree, and filled his swinging
        hide with lead,
    And Frankie yowled hilariously when the thing was done.

There are literary architectural reconstructions of Shakespeare's England, Dante's hell and Faulkner's Yoknapatawpha County. While Dickens's London and de Maupassant's terrifying yet elegant Paris can be identified, even visited. But to know the worlds of Sterling Brown, I only have to walk a few miles in the South Side of Chicago, the lonely roads outside Allendale, South Carolina, and the byzantine worlds of black ten-year-olds in Red Hook, and Sterling Brown manifests the essence, not maquettes of a people.

THE NEW CONGO

(With no apologies to Vachel Lindsay)

Suave big jigs in a conference room,
Big job jigs, with their jobs unstable,

Sweated and fumed and trembled 'round the table
Trembled 'round the table
Sat around as gloomy as the watchers of a tomb
Tapped upon the table
Boom, Boom, Boom.
With their soft pigs' knuckles and their fingers and their
        thumbs
In a holy sweat that their time had come
Boomlay, boomlay, boomlay, boom.
How can I go back to being a bum.
Then I had religion, then I had a vision
I could not turn from their anguish in derision.
Then I saw the Uncle Tom, creeping through the black
Cutting through the bigwoods with his trousers slack
With hinges on his knees, and with putty up his back.
Then along the line from the big wig jigs
Then I heard the plaint of the money-lust song.
And the cry for status yodeled loud and long
And a line of argument loud and wrong
And "Bucks" screamed the trombones and the flutes of
        the spokesmen
"Bucks" screamed the newly made Ph.D. Doctors
Utilize the sure-fire goofie dust powder
Garner the shekels
Encompass mazuma
Boomlay, boomlay, boomlay, booma.
Bing.
Tremolo, mendicant implorations
From the mouths of Uncle Toms
To the great foundations.
"Jack is a good thing
A goddamn good thing
The only bad thing
Is there ain't enough.
Boom, fool the whitefolks
Boom, gyp the jigaboos
Boom, get the prestige
Strut your stuff."
Listen to the cry of the Negro mass
Down to its uppers, down on its ass.
Hear how the big jigs fool 'em still
With their services paid from the white man's till.
Listen to the cunning exhortations
Wafted to the ears of the big foundations

Blown to the big white boss paymasters
Faint hints of far-reaching grim disasters.
"Be careful what you do
Or your Mumbo-jumbo stuff for Sambo
And all of the other
Bilge for Sambo
Your Mumbo-Jumbo will get away from you.
Your Bimbo-Sambo will revolt from you.
Better let Uncle Tombo see it through,
A little long green at this time will do. . . ."

Not unlike Guillén Leon, and Aimé Césaire, even Luis Palos Matos and Julia de Bargus, Brown was committed to humanity in spite of its denigration of such as evidenced in "Side by Side":

VII. MOB

A nigger killed a white man in the neighborhood
The nigger was shot up and then hung out
For the blood to dry, a black sponge dripping red.
John, you were in the mob, and what did it get you?

The killed man is just as dead as the lynched,
And both busted hell wide, wide open,
And side by side, Lord, side by side.

So Brown recognized the Africanization of our hemisphere long before we as a people, or a nation recognized him. Brown paid homage to the heroes Nat Turner, Crispus Attucks McKoy, in the same breath as Garvey & Du Bois.

I sing of a hero,
Unsung, unrecorded,
Known by the name
Of Crispus Attucks McKoy.
Born, bred in Boston,
Cousin of Trotter,
Godson of Du Bois.

No monastic hairshirt
Stung flesh more bitterly
Than the white coat
In which he was arrayed;

16

But what was his agony
On entering the drawing-room
To hear a white woman
Say slowly, "One spade."
— from "Crispus Attucks McKoy"

This lack of self-consciousness, this visceral and aesthetic commitment to the lilt of our tongues, the swing of our hips and the brilliance of our minds and improvisational acuity is particular to Sterling Brown for his generation. He was bothered not so much by who he was, or who we were, but that we could not see him, we could not hear: I offer a quote from Sterling Brown's own "Honey Mah Love":

We who have fretted our tired brains with fears
That time shall frustrate all our chosen dreams
We are rebuked by Banjo Sam's gay strains,
Oh Time may be less vicious than he seems;
And Troubles may grow weaker through the years —
Nearly as weak as those Sam told us of, —
Sam, strumming melodies to his honey love;
Sam, flouting Trouble in his inky lane.
Oh, I doan mess wid' trouble. . . .

As noted in Neruda's memoirs, the coal miners reciting his poems to him would also have made Sterling Brown's heart sing.

17

Nelson Algren. Chicago, 1973. Photograph by Nancy Crampton.

Chicago Guy: Nelson Algren
John Sayles

I READ A LOT as a kid, indiscriminately. In the fifth grade I might be reading *Treasure Island, The Black Stallion, The Caine Mutiny, White Fang, Fail Safe* and whatever World War II combat memoirs and Readers' Digest condensed novels my parents had kicking around the house, often simultaneously. I wrote stories as well, mostly intentional or unintentional parodies of books I'd read or movies and TV shows I'd seen. But the idea that a writer was something you could be, that I might write something that could get out in the world and be read by other people, was fairly late in coming.

I think I was in junior high school, twelve or thirteen years old, when I came across Nelson Algren's *Somebody in Boots*. Typical of my scattered approach to reading, I picked it up because I saw on the jacket that he had written *A Walk on the Wild Side* and I really liked Brook Benton's title song from the movie (I hadn't yet seen the movie, which falls apart after the opening titles by Saul Bass). I had read *Grapes of Wrath* at this point, and my parents had told me stories about the Depression era, but Algren's book brought it alive to me in a more visceral way — it is an epic of powerlessness. The protagonist — poor, ignorant, small — has some humane impulses, but it is clear they will only be a liability in the mean world he lives in. There are brief glimpses of hope, moments of peace, but then somebody in boots stomps in and the fun is over.

I don't think I set foot in a bookstore or knew such a thing existed (my parents were teachers and brought stuff home from school but I can't remember them buying a book) until I was in college. So I began to dig into the card catalogues of the local libraries looking for more things by Algren. I read his short stories, a few of his essays and reportage. I'd never been to Chicago, never played poker or bet on the horses, but somehow his world was very familiar to me. The books were funny, not because Algren made fun of the characters, but because the characters understood the humor of desperation. A story like "A Bottle of Milk for Mother," in which world-weary cops banter with the night's haul of murderers,

19

drunks and thieves as one by one they face the hard glare of a police line-up, has a bizarre, stand-up comedy feeling, where all the participants, cops and criminals, understand that the joke is on them. Algren was a devotee of Hemingway, but his characters barely kept up the facade of living according to a code. They tried to survive day by day and the best and most compelling of them knew their own weaknesses. There is no second chance in Hemingway, whereas Algren's characters often hit bottom halfway through the book, then have to take a good look at each other and push on.

Reading Algren was not unlike reading Faulkner in that I came to have a geographical impression of the world he created, meeting characters central to one story on the periphery of another, finding themes repeated and expanded upon. But Algren's world, mostly city-dwelling immigrants and small-time operators, was more familiar to me than Faulkner's guilt-ridden Mississippi. The cruelty Algren's characters showed to each other was more venal and immediate, not based on some deep historical sin but on everyday human frailty, deceit, selfishness and longing. He is wise to his characters but not dismissive, his sentiment tempered with irony. When the rough edges he worked so well began to gentrify he moved from Chicago but never really found another home. He is one of those writers, like Faulkner or Cheever or Raymond Chandler or Zane Grey, who owns a piece of turf in the American imagination. You think "Nelson Algren's Chicago" and it's sure, I know exactly — *there.*

Beside entering his world, I got something else from reading Algren. It was the realization that, hey, they let this guy get away with this stuff, recognizable human behavior, people with warts and humor and appetites, and somebody typed it up in a book and got it out in the world. Maybe I could do something like that. I remember reading a book with the dedication "For Nelson Algren — who does not know me from Adam and should not be held responsible." The people who influence you to write aren't necessarily who you're going to write like, but the fact of their existence, of the existence of their characters, the spirit in them, opens up a possibility in your mind. There have been a lot of writers whose work I got into later that really knocked me out, writers who brought me into worlds unknown and opened up areas of style and technique that helped me get my own act together. But the one who jump-started me from reader to writer was Nelson Algren, who I never met and should not be held responsible.

My Willa
Maureen Howard

I HAVE BEEN TRACKING HER for well over fifty years, since the good sisters instructed me that there lived somewhere — in Maine or was it New Mexico? — a wonderful lady who wrote stories for Catholics. In their zeal to lure us away from comics, movies and our favorite radio shows, they elevated Willa Cather to the state of blessed, never suspecting that in *Death Comes to the Archbishop* and *Shadows on the Rock*, it was the culture of Catholicism in America that interested her, the organizing drama of its rituals, the missionary's overlay of European morals and manners on native life. And — shocking to say — Cather, with renewed desire (the secular desire of most writers), was, in these late works, finding her way into new forms:

> In the Golden Legend the martyrdoms of the saints are no more dwelt upon than are the trivial incidents of their lives, it is as though all human experiences, measured against one supreme spiritual experience, were of about the same importance. The essence of such writing is not to hold the note, not to use an incident for all there is in it — but to touch and pass on. I felt that such writing would be a kind of discipline in these days when the "situation" is made to count for so much in writing, when the general tendency is to force things up.
> — Letter to *Commonweal*, November 23, 1927

I see now that Cather was finding her way further into legend, for her novel she would claim as her first real work, *My Ántonia*, is partitioned into tales that have become legendary to the narrator, but I hadn't a clue when I borrowed that novel from the public library and never thought why *my* Ántonia? Because she is the girl, the woman that Jim Burden makes into legend. Because the teller of the tale lays claim, possesses his material — or hers — and this burden may, or may not, be unburdened by the telling. Fitzgerald, who admired Cather, was drawn to this narrative frame

21

when giving Nick Carraway the first and last say in his *Gatsby*. Nick's performance in these passages is grandiloquent. He speaks a rhetoric at once beautiful and defensive. Jim Burden, Cather's early narrator of what is actually a disturbing American pastoral, cannot import his romantic view into the present.

But already I'm writing of rereadings, reevaluations of Cather's sturdy, or was it inspired, career. When I was a kid I would have called her Miss Cather if granted an audience, but in truth she would not have welcomed me in her parlor. Privacy was sacred to her in her later years. No longer William, the flamboyant cross-dresser at Lincoln University, nor Willa of the girlish middy-blouse, nor the celebrated Willa Cather of the velvet opera cape, she wanted no intrusions into her life and very little into the life of her art. In her will she forbade the use of her work in movies or television, so there is no point in discerning the dandy script in *Lucy Gayheart* or the possible docudrama of *My Ántonia*. Cather closed down: nothing mean spirited, just a reaffirmation that good work must be valued for its own sake, honored in its original form like a fine Mimbres pot or the Dutch landscapes she so admired, or like magnificent landscape itself, not sold to the highest bidder.

From her earliest novel, *Alexander's Bridge,* she wrote about the dream of artistic accomplishment, the talent which elevated the artist yet often diminished the human response. The trade-off was real to her. She made it so pressing to the men and women of her invention that the Yeatsian dilemma — "perfection of the life, or of the work" — seems removed by the eloquence of its beat from the compromised lives of her characters. There is no wonder that Cather was rediscovered in our time by feminist critics, or, let's say less academically, by women readers made newly aware of the counterdemands of family and work, of the liberation of self and the loss that it might exact. Who better than Cather to turn to — a woman writer, reputation in decline, misread as schoolroom genteel? Yes, Miss Cather, the poet of passion and accommodation, endurance and loss, yet she has been scolded for her male narrators, for not outing, for a conservative bent that blossomed as the American audience grew, to her mind, vulgar in its tastes.

Does anyone pretend that if the Woolworth store windows were piled high with Tanagra figurines at ten cents, they could for a moment compete with Kewpie brides in the popular esteem? How old-fashioned her complaints in "The Novel Démeublé" (1922), perhaps even a dated view in that year, the year in which she won

Willa Cather. The Granger Collection, New York.

the Pulitzer for her war novel, *One of Ours,* a lesser work, a willed work. A bumper crop that year: *Ulysses, The Wasteland, Women in Love.* D. H. Lawrence arrived in Santa Fe, Cather territory, in September of 1922, quite unaware that in April she had gone after him in this essay on the impoverishment of "realism" for depicting the behavior of "bodily organs under sensory stimuli." *Can anyone imagine anything more terrible than the story of* Romeo and Juliet *rewritten in prose by D. H. Lawrence?* Yes, that can be imagined, as well as the fact that she quite liked Lawrence when they met and that they both were moved by the grandeur of the Southwest to write powerful romantic tales of retreat from the Woolworthian goods of society.

To be fair, though Cather's famous essay is more writer's jotting than theory of the novel, it can be read as a modernist proclamation, a call to move away from verisimilitude and clutter to suggestion. She puts forth the example of modern painting, abstraction, understatement — a more telling simplicity. Art must unfurnish, discover *"the emotional aura of the fact or the thing."* All of her work has a surface simplicity — she was, we must recall, a popular novelist — all, that is, except her masterpiece, *The Professor's House,* which is intricate, bold in its construction and furnished. In the novel, Professor St. Peter refuses to write in his new house, though his writing of history has paid for all its splendid conveniences. A trophy house, we might call it in current lingo: it is literally and newly furnished. Published in 1925, the novel can be read as working through the prescriptions of "The Novel Démeublé." The furnished fiction, that is, the recognizable bourgeois novel of the opening section, "The Family," with its intricacies of plot and politics of family, class and money, is rendered in detail, adorned with many *things* — bathtubs, lamps, jewelry, clothes — which tell of a worthy past and a fashionable present. "The Family" is not so much concluded as abandoned, just as the Professor has departed emotionally from wife, children, affairs of the university — and Cather turns to a simple tale — "Tom Outland's Story."

Or not so simple, for the idyll lived by Tom Outland on the Blue Mesa of Old Mexico is a boy's adventure that is ruined by money and politics, the very stuff of novels, not heroic tales. Tom Outland had appeared at Godfrey St. Peter's house, the *old* house, the shabby house, to propose himself as a student. One of the notes touched on is the irony that the Professor, who has earned his laurels by writing about the Spanish adventurers in America, has never been to the land they explored, has never gone beyond the European story, his material researched in European libraries. In "The Family," the appearance of Tom Outland is magical, the gifts which he brings princely — turquoise stones, ancient pots with the black fire marks still on them. Cather is setting the reader up to witness a rotten deal: Tom's things with their pure aura traded off for the family's things weighted with envy and a smug, even hilarious display of upward mobility.

Troubled by the present, the Professor is drawn to recollection, not only to discover the lost record of Tom Outland's story, but the lost boy and the ambitious young man in himself. All of Cather's novels are narratives of recollection. *The Professor's House* is her one indulgence in, or confrontation with, the present; perhaps even in part Cather's novel is an admission of her disappointment in Isabelle McClung, the great love of her life, who married a middling musician, Jan Hambourg.

The Professor believes:

> Desire is creation, is the magical element in that process. If there were an instrument by which to measure desire, one could foretell achievement. He has been able to measure it, roughly, just once, in his student Tom Outland — and he had foretold.

It is reductive to read the displacement of sexual desire for artistic achievement, to take God-free Saint Peter, a man of diminished ardor whose best work lies behind him, for a wounded Cather. The biographical note is a footnote, as it is so often to great fiction. What's more, the Professor, in voluntary exile from his family, sees that "the design of his life had been the work of this secondary social man, the lover." Second billing was not a role Cather would easily take on. In writing her most complex, to my mind, her great novel, she recollected herself camping in the Southwest with her brother where she was as overwhelmed as Tom Outland by the landscape and exulted in the discovery of the layered history that was still its secret. Look up, look out, increase the field of play. Turn to another less familiar, less familial story. Tom Outland's story (oh, the Bunyanesque names, Cather's draw to tale, to parable) is that of the adventurous orphan, who, to remain our hero, is killed off in the First World War. Though he is engaged to the Professor's most worldly daughter, the design of his life is

25

neatly cut off before marriage.

The Professor's House was out of print when I first read it in the early sixties. So was the novella which followed, the brilliant *My Mortal Enemy*, a love story that is richly spare and brutally anti-romantic. I remember writing against the loss of these works which were quite forgotten while the prairie novels of Miss Cather, as I would properly have called her, were still in textbook editions. And later, having misread, I wrote with some petulance of Willa throwing over the real thing for her "piously researched later works," *Death Comes to the Archbishop* and *Shadows on the Rock*. Misreading *Death Comes*, indeed, for the novel of the two French priests who go from the seminary to the Spanish Southwest is a risky work that finds its structure in tales within tales, nonlinear as the fables of Márquez or Calvino.

The narrative of Cather's great novel of the Southwest is worked like a tapestry or a quilt to tell its many stories. There is, of course, the inevitable chronology — both Father Valliant and Archbishop Latour grow old. The railroad reaches Santa Fe. There's gold discovered in them thar hills and now . . . now I see that it's only my Willa who was smart enough to juxtapose landscape of the tertiary social man, the prospector, with the golden yellow hill in the Rio Grande Valley that will yield the stone for Bishop Latour's ambitious European cathedral bringing two cultures together, chipping away at the land for God and Mammon. A chapter, toward the end of the novel, is titled simply "Cathedral." This is a story of male friendship: Bishop Latour is more attuned to beauty than Father Valliant, the plainer man of the cloth and the more spiritual. Raymond Carver must have read these pages with care, with as much care as he read D. H. Lawrence's "The Blind Man" before writing his "Cathedral."

> Father Latour laughed, "Is a cathedral a thing to be taken lightly, after all?"
> "Oh, no, certainly not!" Father Valliant moved his shoulders uneasily. He did not himself know why he hung back in this.

How smooth the surface of this interchange, how subtle Willa's instruction that Latour's aesthetics, or even the sacred edifice of cathedral, does not quite win the day.

At my parochial schools, the nuns' adulation of Willa Cather seemed to me, even in adolescence, an embrace that would not be returned, that she was given more to the manner of storytelling than to the subject matter of Catholic missionaries. That was perhaps my first understanding of desire as creation, and of the magic that must bring together what medievalists term the *matière* and the *sens*, the material and its meaning. She was rightly annoyed with reviewers who could not classify her late work, the forms which she went on to invent. When she wrote of her writing at all, it was with brief clarity and brought to our attention not the work, but the paintings, music, legends, *contes*, lay of the land and recollections of her Nebraska childhood as well as her European travels, which brought forth her own desire.

I have made her up, my Willa, though I offer no narrative frame to my view of her work. Reading, rereading a writer who has opened the schoolroom window has no end, not even an elegiac — So long! She died when I was seventeen and had outgrown her, then turning the page, a printed page, I see that I called her my mentor. Now, though I am happier than she would ever be to work with the popular goods in the dime-store window, Willa speaks more as my familiar: "The courage to go on without compromise does not come to a writer all at once — nor, for that matter, does the ability" [1920]. A tough statement, something of a burden: all passion not spent.

Ralph Waldo Emerson. Concord Free Public Library, Concord, Massachusetts.

The Emerson Madrigal
Bradford Morrow

I HONOR THE MAN who wrote *My cow milks me.*

I admire the youthful Emerson who proclaimed *I will no longer confer, differ, refer, defer, prefer or suffer* — the Emerson who with those words promised a lifelong resolve against indifference, dullness, detachment, disregard. The man who discovered early on that passionless thought *builds the sepulchres of the fathers.* He who asked *Why should not we also enjoy an original relation to the universe!* as fresh as that known to Plato and Pythagoras, Lucretius and Zoroaster, Buddha and Jesus, Meng Tsu and Marcus Aurelius, Dante and Milton, Goethe and Kant who went before? The radical contrarian who, even as he read over the course of a long life through so much of the world's literature, believed always that the journey is only in the footfall, that the masterpiece is only in the word read now, that *all literature is yet to be written.*

I celebrate the humanist but exacting Emerson who would have read our present mudslide of exposés and confessions, and the same exacting but humanist Emerson who would have read our Gobi of newspaper critiques and academic deconstructions as simply more works *by the dead for the dead.* The man who proposed *The real danger of American scholars is not analysis, but sleep.* The man who thundered *All this polemics, syllogism, and definition is so much wastepaper.* The man who would clear his mind.

I honor Emerson the botanist who took delight in the names of reeds and weeds and grasses, and Emerson the friend whose house was forever filled with the discourse of so many voices, and Emerson the doubting Thomas who often annotated his journals with outbursts of humorous self-deprecation, and Emerson the abolitionist who said in a blistering speech in Concord not only that *black or white is an insignificance* but that *The negro has saved*

29

himself, and the white man very patronizingly says I have saved you (1844). Emerson whose wife Lidian was so ashamed of her country that she draped their front gate with black cambric cloth every Fourth of July until the emancipation was in sight. The Emerson family who were members of the underground railroad in Massachusetts. This same Emerson who protested the illegal removal of the Cherokees from their homeland, who wrote Van Buren that such a crime *deprives us as well as the Cherokees of a country* — who when he recognized his remonstrations were in vain still concluded that *The amount of it, be sure, is merely a scream, but sometimes a scream is better than a thesis.* The angered Emerson who wrote *Abolish kingcraft, slavery, feudalism, blackletter monopoly, pull down gallows, explode priestcraft, open the doors of the sea to all emigrants.* The Emerson that Lincoln and John Brown had good reason to respect, and Polk and Webster to resent.

I celebrate Emerson's fundamental and sacramental congeniality with the earth and its inanimate and animate denizens, his genius for observing a moral precept in the shivering sunstruck needles of a pine, say, or the warm ashen path in the shadow of Etna. Admire him for seeing how nature's individuals — plover, hawk, wood anemone, foxglove, otter, laurel — constitute the divine; how the starlight and wild strawberry are sources of comprehension and revelation in and of themselves. I commend the man who understood nature's transformative clout as when *Frogs pipe; waters far off trickle; dry leaves hiss; grass bends and rustles; and I have died out of the human world and come to feel a strange, cold, acqueous terraqueous, aerial etherial sympathy and existence.* The man who learned his land and house were more than what was measured by the surveyor and stipulated in the deed. Who wrote *When I bought my farm, I did not know what a bargain I had in the bluebirds, boblinks, and thrushes; as little did I know what sublime mornings and sunsets I was buying.* The thoughtful man who looked again and saw more than first met the eye, listened again and heard more than struck the ear. I honor him for his mastery of so many nonverbal and invisible languages, of the syntax of forests, of the grammar of birds and fish and flowers, the rhetoric of embryo and carrion.

I applaud the audacity of the man who wrote *Beware when the great God lets loose a new thinker on this planet*, the same who deduced from Stoic and Quaker and Islamic thought the unhampered personal philosophy that insists *the universe is the externization of the soul*. He who would weave his own religion from the threads, the brambles, the seeded shafts of various others, looking less for differences among mankind's doctrines than the convergences which he found everywhere. Synergies of spirit and thought were his focus, the world *sans murs* and history outside time: the American thinker not as isolationist, but in fact outward bound. And like the osprey willing to build with what is at hand. Writing of Goethe, Emerson revealed himself — where some saw only fragments he saw connections. Here is an Emerson I respect, and there are other Emersons, too.

Such as the bemused Emerson who wrote that *Pirates do not live on nuts and herbs.* The grinning Emerson who admired Henry David Thoreau's credo "If a man does not believe that he can thrive on board nails, I will not talk with him." The scowling Emerson who loathed the faker, the flimsy, the mock, and was always alert to such weaknesses in himself, to such a degree that sometimes he discovered them when they were not there. The manifold Emerson who was private yet public, fond yet cross, discreet yet frank, religious yet antireligion. The Emerson who was compelled to write it all down and who would, despite the many days he spent reading, note once in his journal: *It makes no difference what I read. If it is irrelevant, I read it deeper. I read it until it is pertinent to me and mine.* Who in another year on another day laughed in the face of his very muse: *Books, — yes, if worst comes to worst.*

I honor the secular theology of the declaration *To believe your own thought, to believe that what is true for you in your private heart is true for all men — that is genius.* Such is one of his many convictions that displays Character, which is to say a purity of ends realized by a rigor of means. Whenever I stumble either in choosing an imperfect means to an end, or perfect means to a flawed end, let me be reminded of the more perfect original thought I must have had, and work once more from the private heart to the better consequence: so I wrote in my own notes, a small prayer prompted by the son of a preacher who was himself a lapsed preacher.

I admire the man who remarked of his sentences *I am a rocket manufacturer.*

I celebrate his impudence and his prudence, his certainty and doubt, his exultations and darknesses, his love of home and the exquisite impetuosity that led him to resign his ministry at the Second Church in Boston, give up his house, auction off most of his worldly effects and board the brig *Jasper* (sick with diarrhea) to sail away to Europe. I laud his decision to make the Grand Tour backwards — working his way from Italy through France to England — as he searched out new ideas, new images, new knowledge in the Old World. I am intrigued by his grudging respect for the art he saw in Rome, the gardens he rambled in Paris, the writers he met in London and Ecclefechan in Scotland — his unsentimental education and admission into the larger world of struggle and accomplishment. By the way in which no matter how far from Concord his travels took him (before he was done, Emerson would walk beneath the sequoias in California, touch the pillars of Stonehenge, behold the sphinx in Egypt) he was always renewed upon his return to wife, children, family, friends, even enemies.

His brilliant unapologetic contradictoriness I celebrate. I revere this same wanderer who with customary cheek in the face of contradiction wrote *Let us not rove; let us sit at home with the cause* and wrote again *The soul is no traveller; the wise man stays at home, and when his necessities, his duties, on any occasion call him from his house, or into foreign lands, he is at home still.*

I celebrate the pure élan, the tenacity, the ferment and holy grit of the man!

His dictum *A foolish consistency is the hobgoblin of little minds* with its clarion whoop of invitation to *speak what you think now in hard words and to-morrow speak what to-morrow thinks in hard words again, though it contradict every thing you said to-day* inspired and freed, no doubt, the minds of many readers since it was first published a century and a half ago. I acclaim the simple complexity of such plain insight, the recognition of our mercurial humanity, the philharmonic nature of our lone voice. And acclaim that Emersonian rebelliousness which draws us to him when we are young, and carries forward into later years if our suppleness, wit and fire remain at work.

The force of character is cumulative, he wrote, referring to women and men and the societies they build. Who but the Plato for an unfledged, immigrant nation would declare that the old institutions and their attendant rituals are stinking ghosts we drag behind us in an act whose only magnanimity is the lame aerobics of the backward glance?

I love the Emerson who was unafraid of enthusiasm.

The Emerson who wasn't afraid of making mistakes.

The Emerson who learned from the fieldhand Tarbox.

The Emerson who knew the value of indignation.

To conform or not to conform, this is the question I celebrate in him. *For nonconformity the world whips you with its displeasure,* and yet, isn't it also true that contempt is the malign gift the public eventually bestows upon its conformers? Emerson who thus proposed you act as you will, and let the world go its own way: *What I must do is all that concerns me, not what the people think.* What gives this intimate declaration of independence such greatness, though, is that it does not come with an invitation to retire from society, to seek hermitage, but to walk straight into society with your autonomous head held high. *It is easy in the world to live after the world's opinion; it is easy in solitude to live after our own; but the great man is he who in the midst of the crowd keeps with perfect sweetness the independence of solitude.* Walden Pond may serve as a kind of temporary seminary, a secluded lyceum where student and teacher are one and the same, but the moment comes when we must reenter the world. Walden Pond is a state of being, a grace that soon streams onward.

I honor Emerson who was the first to translate Dante's *La vita nuova,* that liturgy and analysis of love. I celebrate his own love for Ellen Tucker and Lidian Jackson and Margaret Fuller and Caroline Sturgis. And for Henry David Thoreau. I praise the authentic love of and taste for the world shimmering in a dream where he *floated at will in the great Ether, and saw this world floating also not far off, but diminished to the size of an apple. Then an angel took it in his hand and brought it to me and said, "This thou must eat." And I ate the world.*

I toast the boundless appetite of Ralph Waldo Emerson.

How I would like to think he would have embraced the newness of the music of Harry Partch, and that of Leadbelly, too, despite the fact that he seldom mentions music in his journals and essays (in one notebook he does bemoan *prison melodies* and *Jim Crow songs*, calling instead for *the Godhead in music, as we have the Godhead in the sky and the creation*). Coltrane? and Ives? and Amy Beach? Miles? Godhead is present in their measures. I celebrate the idea of Emerson down at the crossroads with Robert Johnson.

His droll self-portrait I honor: *I am awkward, sour, saturnine, lumpish, pedantic, and thoroughly disagreeable and oppressive to the people around me,* just as I admire his response to someone who asked him to describe his life: *I have no history, no fortunes that would make the smallest figure in a narrative. My course of life has been so routinary, that the keenest eye for point or picture would be at fault before such remediless commonplace.* And concluded with the pronouncement *We will really say no more on a topic so sterile.*

I celebrate a mind this rich and unremedial and admire his preference for the tough edge, in himself and in others, to any sophisticated suave: *Hard clouds, and hard expressions, and hard manners, I love.* Emerson was tough on himself even as he allowed himself to ramble and digress, and recognized that such dignified and unadorned hardness was the best way to make the mind limber and the spirit serene.

I celebrate the man who early on championed Walt Whitman.

And the mad Jones Very and unlucky Bronson Alcott.

The Emerson who was admired by Emily Dickinson.

His assiduous routine that began before dawn with hot coffee and cold pie, then the invariable steps to his desk where for seven hours he would work, I admire, and that he attempted to maintain this habit no matter what circumstances of disaster fate visited upon him, I admire — work in the face of a fate which often was truly cruel to Emerson. His life was boundary-stoned by deaths. His first wife he married likely in the knowledge she was dying of tuberculosis (they had three indelible years). His son, Waldo, born to his second wife, Lidian, died young of scarlet fever. *He gave up his innocent little breath like a bird,* Emerson wrote in his journal that winter. His brothers, so promising, met with professional disappointment, or else died young — John Clarke aged eight, Edward aged twenty-nine, his beloved Charles but twenty-eight. And his sisters mostly fared no better — Phebe lived two years, never having met her brother-to-be, and Mary Caroline just three. *Sorrow makes us all children again, — destroys all differences of intellect,* he noted. *The wisest knows nothing.* I honor him in his anguish and his phoenixlike response, his understanding of the value of the tragic flame, his earned words about the enrichments attendant to disaster: *He has seen but half the universe who never has been shown the House of Pain.*

I celebrate the Emerson who might lose this or fail at that, but note the very next day with superb delicacy: *This morn the air smells of vanilla and oranges.*

I celebrate the writer who said outright what most writers think: *No man can be criticised but by a greater than he. Do not, then, read the reviews.*

The Emerson who at once displayed majesty and aloofness and engagement and human-kindness and pluck and flamboyance and knotty radiance and the one who regretted he didn't possess a greater knowledge in the fields of geography, mathematics, astronomy and who wished his German was better, and his Greek.

I celebrate the photographs of him so sadly joyful, so sternly charitable, with almost always the same expression in every frame, a firmness of spirit in the eyes and on the brow but with the mouth drawn out not quite into a smile, nor quite into a frown, but rather toward a magnificent variance of thought. His *I must be myself* — yawping forward toward Whitman and the

35

century of thinkers who had not yet been born — I celebrate not only for the sheer classic weight of the charge, but for how the very proverb formed itself in the countenance of the man who made it. Both Emersons always there in the visage: the Emerson who wrote *I enjoy all the hours of life,* and the Emerson who wrote *The badness of the times is making death attractive.* His face which wore a similar serious benevolence at seventy-four and forty-three and fifty. Scholar, husband, father, friend — the look of one who rarely if ever bothered to invent an excuse.

Emerson the stylist I honor, the maker of phrases immaculate and sound. Emerson the etymologist who proposed that *Every word was once a poem.* Emerson with his unfailing bias for developing an argument through apothegm, pith, maxim, a flurry of gists. I admire Emerson for his knowledge that *utterance is place enough* and how he accorded language its rightful physicality and elemental power. And how his essays are like growing organisms that respond, word by word, phrase by phrase, sentence by sentence, now to this barrier, now to some other, drawing the reader into the spell, seducing us by narrative unpredictability: what facet will be cut next? We cannot guess; we press on. Emerson's great exemplars from Plutarch to Empedocles and Heraclitus, from Eckermann and Dugald Stewart to Montaigne and the Upanishads, from de Staël to Hafez and Swedenborg, had all been gleaned so thoroughly that their necessary ideas and forms became a part of Emerson; or rather blended, coalesced *into* Emerson, so that they were less referents than reflexes, less without or within than *of.* Like a Monroe Doctrine of the mind: You who would have that idea or image, *take it,* for it is your own to begin with. Whoever would simply say what he thinks, name what he knows, is *sovereign, and stands at the centre.* If words are stones that we arrange into cairns and columns and palaces of thought, then Emerson was a master mason.

I cherish the Emerson who found his exemplary self-reliant man in Henry Thoreau. *Insist on yourself; never imitate* — this his confrere Thoreau embodied to a fault. Writing of Plato, Emerson unwittingly sketched Thoreau: *He said, Culture; he said, Nature; and he failed not to add, 'There is also the divine.'* And, in yet another context, not long after meeting this son of a pencil maker, he noted *The one thing of value in the world is the active soul;* in Henry he had his vivid model — *nature vivre* — and rampant doppelgänger from whom he could take his measure, and against whose works and manner he could refine his concept of nature itself, and of wisdom, purity of will, defiance, justice, destiny, health, value, life, death, the rigorous universe *in toto*. His moving elegy for Thoreau exfoliates by its own rationale, just as did the man himself. *No opposition or ridicule had any weight with him*, Emerson remembered. He remarked how Thoreau *chose to be rich by making his wants few*. He even insisted, with a straight face, that as an ichthyologist Henry was so skilled that *the fishes swam into his hand, and he took them out of the water*. The wonder is he didn't claim that they conversed in watery whispers. Thoreau was Emerson's most true brother, and harshest mirror. When they argued they argued with the full force of their affections, and they held each other to high standards of honesty and kinship. *I know not any genius who so swiftly inferred universal law from the single fact . . . wherever there is beauty, he will find a home.*

I celebrate, then, the Emerson who said that *friendship, like the immortality of the soul, is too good to be believed*, and who realized *All lives, all friendships are momentary* and therefore pitched himself heart and soul into the lives of those who called him friend.

I celebrate the man who so simply proposed *Show us an arc of the curve, and a good mathematician will find out the whole figure*. Meaning: *We are always reasoning from the seen to the unseen.*

I celebrate the curiosity that led Emerson, on one of his daily walks to Roxbury to visit the grave of his first wife, to open her coffin and look at her perished body. If thoughts are actions, actions are externalized thoughts. How did what he saw there in the dwarf wooden ketch direct his intellectual voyage thereafter? *I visited Ellen's tomb and opened the coffin* is what he recorded. Was it morbidity, curiosity? Emerson himself, the great analyst of gesture and philosopher of synecdoche, offers no commentary on this singular moment. He wanted to know something. And presumably he found out. If you celebrate asset, you celebrate method. Commentators have, over the years, viewed this incident with solemn disbelief. Some have proposed it never happened, that it was a dream, a nightmare even. It was not a dream. It was a loving scientist gazing upon an undeniable truth in his search for freedom and its own undeniable truths. Of lovers he wrote, *When alone, they solace themselves with the remembered image of the other.* I honor Emerson's breaching the coffin and fathoming Ellen Tucker's corpse.

I celebrate the man who wrote *I admire answers to which no answer can be made.*

The man who wrote *Pretension never wrote an Iliad.* Who wrote of one of his friends who had difficulty writing with any concision that he *should be made effective by being tapped by a good suction-pump.*

The man who predicted *When the rudder is invented for the balloon, railroads will be superceded.*

The man who knew that *envy is ignorance.*

I celebrate his common human fear of being a fraud and that *they would find me out.* The raw mind of the man, its spontaneous sincerity. His vulnerability so tersely bared. I take my hat off to the Emerson who endured unheated winter lecture halls and the sometimes indifferent, hostile and even hissing audiences, as he traveled the circuit for months on end, presenting his talks, reading his work, assaying his ideas before whoever would come to listen. Who carried on despite the mixed notices. Whose physical strength against the witless, withering rigors of the road was admirable. Who asked *What if you do fail, and get fairly rolled in the dirt once or twice? Up again, you shall never be so afraid of a tumble.* I honor the depths of his depressions which made his moments of ecstasy that much more elevated.

The primary wisdom is intuition, whilst all subordinate teachings are tuition, he stated; one of his unveering convictions was that all we can truly know is understood through experience, gathered from the visceral engagement, learned from watching the peony explode into June whiteness and then wither brown under the July sun, eventually to be buried under December snow, and from that seen sequence infer one's own process, mortality, lot.

I celebrate Emerson the intuitionist, the man of seasoned instinct. The man who considered most universities hostile to the development of the minds of the young, insofar as they kept those minds away from primary experience, from the field, where things are really realized.

I respect his Pythagoreanist proposal that fundamental truths cannot finally be stated, but are discovered only through nuance, through metaphor, through natural emblem. In so many of his greatest essays the truth comes forth in this manner: *between* the hard rocky truisms, *between* the immaculate verities, *between* the disparate lines. Emerson who understood that in the synapse the blaze of electric transfer happens.

I commemorate 25th May 1803 when he was born and 27th April 1882 when, having taken his daily constitutional though ailing from a chest cold, and being caught in a sudden rainshower, he arrived home drenched, a fever ensuing, and though his son pled with him to rest in bed he continued to work in his study during the days that followed, maintaining the same unswayable routine by which he'd led his entire remarkable life, until the pneumonia bested him. The bell in the Unitarian Church of Concord tolled seventy-nine times that night, one stroke for each of his generous years, a death-knell embodying the fused contradictories of grief and revelry.

I celebrate the many Emersons and the one Emerson. *What is life, but the angle of vision?* he asked himself. I celebrate the man who would always ask.

Marianne Moore. Photograph by Roger Mayne. Courtesy Special Collections, Vassar College Libraries, Poughkeepsie, New York.

For M. Moore
Cole Swensen

Such animals as
all over   word
             wish
             if
             after
It alters
or: its afters' only altar with such minute meanders
we know it changed her, that she left altered
that she lived altered and left here

is all there is of the animal. It's almost locked in place, a pacing
and a perpendicular heaven that hasn't, that has not, that does
not have

fish   chameleon   wasp   weather   must
winter the horse, the housing of the carp, carapace of concern concerning her concentric love for vermin, the ermine, the asp. Wasp
won't thee but will will:

forgetting that there is in woman
a quality of mind
which as an instinctive manifestation
is unsafe,
           and wonders just for whom, what him, and how soon
                                but that it would

soon
turn.

I think we love people for what they love. Ms. M. and her pocket
zoo, heart made of zippers, opening out like one of those makeup
cases women take travelling that expand in all directions at once.
Consider the opossum. I can't picture Marianne Moore wearing

makeup. Ms. Moore did not wear makeup. Consider the horse, the mouse, the house that gets contorted into a heart. Ms. Moore did not go in much for travel. A few times to Europe, a few times west and her hat there at the end of her hand and her hand, all hasp

to so many perhaps   you know first

what the creature's named and then you hold — how many of them had she held. Not the giraffe, the elephant, the bat in broad daylight, the bat, all mouse with its own elaborated house and its own horse and out there in the sun.

1.: Early on, invented forms. Take, for instance, the fish.: *wade/through black jade/an/injured fan.*

Precise, planned to step like a spine, so rigorous and diligence never counts but exactly knows. To be read whole or first "lines" only or the first two. At times caving/curving in, symmetrically, like the spine of a well-read book seen end-on: "Injudicious Gardening," "To a Chameleon" or steadily, unpredictably laddering, "Critics and Connoisseurs," "To the Peacock of France." Let it precise, pare off any end and in it nip.

"I was trying to be honorable and not steal things."
(is governed by gravity)
"Words cluster like chromosomes, determining the procedure."
(like symmetry)

if honor be
exactitude, an implication of biology and warily, a splice of light that spares the selves, the pares the rest to emergent else. Where then find strife? And what then bind through stealth?

2.: Rhyme, wound tight; spring in the step, fight in the clock and often off: "craven/frighten/certain"; "waist/crest"; they tighten: "star/hair"; "enough/proof"; "faith/death." Again, whose and yes, we get it but whom? (the proof was partial and the faith given conquered:
     God be praised for conquering faith . . .   2.5: *"I like Gilbert & Sullivan."* Inseparable directions
               with unequal determinance and inclinations that will not rest innumerous. Will conquer us. G. M. Hopkins brings in tea.

42

How often do you think she had tea? I've always thought frequent-ly, but now feel I may be or at least must have been entirely mis-trued. She could have done anything with the butt ends of her afternoons.

She haunted the Brooklyn Zoo. This we know. But we don't know what she thought. How much was shock. It should have been all and it was, if nothing else, not.

Octopus.
Snail.
Eight-fold
Owl.
Mouse-skin bellows.
Ostrich.
Ghost.

Cast an own. Come an ox. Add a wild (a feral) truce, a Persian thought, an undefined Bordeaux.

Holding equal court with Ben Jonson, Jackie Robinson, Captain John Smith and Melchior Vulpius.

She was angrier than you would have thought from the pictures. Some spare feminist constructions and "To Military Progress" and perfectly happy in New York.

we've grown all apart

though half the word is after
when asked at the age of 20
what she'd like to be, answered
a painter.

gold thread from straw and have heard men say:
"There is a feminine temperament in direct contrast to ours,

which makes her do these things. shift of chin. the eye
slips on. someone enters the library in a wedge of light,
a shower of dust *(If I, like Solomon, . . .*
could have my wish—

Cole Swensen

"What I write, as I have said before, could only be called poetry because there is no other category in which to put it."

I was recently reading an essay in which the author went to great length to establish Marianne Moore as an "American poet" — or rather was using her particularities, her eccentricities really (which should have defeated his point right there), to sketch a floorplan of "American-ness." I wonder if she would have noticed, thought it mattered, thought it existed. Liked England, it's said. Oh yes. (My brother, the doctor . . .) (My mother, the dead.) It's its hardness, all that solid ground, the concrete both and not metaphorical that's supposed to be so American, the quick twist, brisk thrust, trust. She moved through her world on trust. Who would ever know if this (what am I saying) is truth or just, or if the air in Sweden is sweeter as she says or if the ermine really would rather be dead

than spotted.
> *Chameleon.*
> *Fire laid upon*

She's walking across a room.

an emerald as long as an ire.

She's walking across a room with an inverted glass in her hand and in the glass, a spider, escorting it "home," sealed at the bottom, of course, with a postcard.
From whom.   A three-cornered hat. A hat with three corners that, in my mind

she is always connected with Joseph Cornell. It's the love of things that's common. Or the love of the loss of as well as the loss of and the sense of love as an intransitive verb. Collect cows, dolls, matchbooks, matches, spiders, crows, I think she had a "thing" about "home."

She's walking across a room. It's dinnertime. Who are the logical (the inevitable) guests? Table for four. She says she said: Joseph Cornell, Emily Dickinson, Gerard de Nerval and Marianne Moore. But Marianne is late tonight, more spiders than usual or the

44

elephants uncommonly insistent. Natural habitat: botanical gardens, dimestores (Joe at elbow, suggesting this or that). Definitely the type to poise rubber snakes in cupboards, laundry baskets. Tried it on E. Dickinson, who cried when she touched it and found it wasn't real.
But sound curved
a hand
holding a hand that's holding a hand. What do you call them? *"Experiments in rhythm, exercises in composition."*

and what do you mean by enough. .

Let us.

3.: *for love that will gaze an eagle blind.* If blindness be fusion, there and only there was decision. Note in the above quotation the invention of the verb. Animals with moving fur. The blur of animals in motion. Blinding. If sight incites distinction, discretion, dissection. (Gerard is shaking his head, saying, "no, this is not a pet," and "I think you understand.")

what we have here built

(in which there are hounds with waists
I must not wish
it comes to this
lit
with piercing glances into the life of things

"My interest in La Fontaine originated entirely independent of content."

I have always wanted to enter

a room and find the animals
already there and staring
out the windows.

(Every mind is a house.
(Who did you let
    did you

Cole Swensen

                    answer the
in/door   we invent new animals in our
most desperate moments that dissolve on solid ground
one found
one had fed
and had therefore led the life of

(anything you feed you will come to love) giraffe, antelope,
      egret, absent,
pear
where
are you going my going what are you doing to the door?
What snow? No, let us.

Old Poets, Old Poems: Edwin Arlington Robinson

Robert Creeley

FOR YEARS I'VE HELD to Ezra Pound's insistence, "What thou lov'st well shall not be reft from thee/ What thou lov'st well is thy true heritage . . ." These lines argued a sense of value I found securing to my mind and habits, making the familiar finally an unequivocal place where I might feel both legitimate and welcome. It would be impossible indeed to say that all worlds are in that way made or that we are not a far more complex persuasion of possibilities and tastes, proposing and reacting much as tides ceaselessly increase and ebb. But returning now to a poet and poetry I once must have taken as a benchmark for the art, I find myself, as it were, coming home.

Edwin Arlington Robinson, in fact, came from a town, Head Tide, Maine, where my mother and her sister, my aunt Bernice, used to help their blind grandfather manage the crossing of an often swift brook by means of the stepping stones. Just up on the hill from there is the surviving schoolhouse, still modest and determined in its white paint, and that is where my mother went first to school. I have a photo of her (and wonder who could have taken it) at ten with her lunch pail, backed against the great trunk of a pine tree, before she goes off to learn.

I have never been able to feel at home with Robert Frost, and one of my own memories of school days is the time I am asked to leave the room for mocking his "Stopping by Woods on a Snowy Evening." It's curious that I so distrusted a poet so skilled in his craft and so persuasive in his themes. Yet even his poem "Birches" was suspect to me, not because he didn't know how such swinging of birches is accomplished but for the way he contests the located feeling with ironic homily, an unexpected smugness of ownership as if such lore could be only one's own. In Maine there is a lovely way of avoiding resolution for another person's choices, avoiding the opinion or advice that says simply, "This is the way to do it." Those who have wondered at Robinson's characteristic ambivalence

47

in such a situation, or his persistent demur always, faced with such judgments, might well consider the way persons have long thought in Maine and also spoken.

In my own books surviving there is a mid-century Modern Library anthology edited by Conrad Aiken, which includes Robinson's "The Man Against the Sky." My sister and I were taught to be careful with books, not to mark in them or crease their pages, or to put them face down for fear of breaking their spines. Just so this book has painfully little to tell me now as to what excited my senses of poetry over fifty years ago. Very occasionally there is a modest check against a title (in pencil) and, even more rarely, an underscoring or line in the margin. As I recall, Hart Crane is given attention, and Marsden Hartley, and particularly Robinson and this one poem. I see that I was caught by the image, and the scale of its assertion, somehow more substantial in my thinking than the existential world I otherwise tried then to apprehend. I could find the same ground in Dostoyevsky and Lawrence, a personal, physical sense of things, which provoked even as it evaded all the usual meanings. Robinson's rhetoric, his phrasing, pitch and cadence, had a particularity seeming to come from his own determination, a self-willed, self-taught character which moved me immensely. Of course, D.H. Lawrence had the same tone as did Hardy and Hart Crane. I deeply cared for those who had learned the hard way, so to speak, and for whom writing seemed a necessity against all odds.

The Second World War was a demanding time in which to come of age, and equally so its aftermath. It seemed we were all reading Sartre, Camus, leavened with Kafka and Gide's *Lafcadio's Adventures*. My own delight was also Valery's *Monsieur Teste* — and Defoe's *Robinson Crusoe*, an existential handbook if ever there was one. Then there was Céline, and again Dostoyevsky, whose *Notes from Underground* was first identified for me by Charles Olson.

The world was not very accommodating of "humanness," albeit we seemed to overwhelm it just by our conduct and numbers. My schooling had begun with the Great Chain of Being firmly in place. Now it seemed humans ranked well below cockroaches and rats if literal survival were to be the measure. So, to that person I was, these lines concluding "The Man Against the Sky" seemed very apt and very true:

What have we seen beyond our sunset fires
That lights again the way by which we came?
Why pay we such a price, and one we give
So clamoringly, for each racked empty day
That leads one more last human hope away,
As quiet fiends would lead past our crazed eyes
Our children to an unseen sacrifice?
If after all that we have lived and thought,
All comes to Nought, —
If there be nothing after Now,
And we be nothing anyhow,
And we know that, — why live?
'Twere sure but weaklings' vain distress
To suffer dungeons where so many doors
Will open on the cold eternal shores
That look sheer down
To the dark tideless floods of Nothingness
Where all who know may drown.

A poem of Malcolm Lowry's begins something like, "As the dead end of each drear day draws near . . ." There are also Samuel Beckett's magnificently pessimistic poems. But no one can manage such a curiously vulnerable and shopworn rhetoric as does Robinson and make such ungainsayable sense, all in the determination, it would seem, of a confident depression — but that is not the right word? He is absolutely a writer, and it is the one thing he never yields, despite the circumstances into which, as "Miniver Cheevy," he has been born — the death of his mother, the general despair, it would seem, of the whole family, the insistent pain of his damaged ear, the addicted brother, failing economics, desultory education, the isolation he experiences, somewhat as Marsden Hartley, whether in New York or Boston, or in Maine. The most happy circumstance appears to be his stays at the MacDowell Colony in Peterborough, New Hampshire, to which he returns year after year as to a homestead.

Robinson is five years older than Frost, born the same year as Edgar Lee Masters (1869), and four years younger than Yeats. Hardy is twenty-nine years older although the two are often thought of together. It's Robinson who writes Frost in 1917, "In 'Snow,' 'In the Home Stretch,' 'Birches,' 'The Hill Wife,' and 'The Road Not Taken' you seem undoubtedly to have added something permanent to the world . . ." His own success in the twenties is marked by the publication of *Tristram* (1927), together with the honors variously given him a few years before. His great popularity and the Pulitzer Prize awarded his collected poems (1921) would seem to argue a secure authority. But after his death in 1935 Frost increasingly occupies the situation of the "New England" poet, and Robinson, unfashionable by my generation and presumed as an echo of the late nineteenth century at best, expectably fades from view.

Yet his circumstances were so curious. What other American poet can one think of whose work is reviewed by an American president, who then sees to it that he, the poet, is comfortably employed? Here is Yvor Winters's summary:

> In 1905 Theodore Roosevelt became interested in Robinson's work, which had been called to his attention by his son, Kermit, then a pupil at Groton. Roosevelt, after trying to persuade Robinson to accept several positions, succeeded in getting him a place as special agent of the Treasury at $2,000 per year. Roosevelt invited Robinson to the White House and talked with him at length; he later wrote an article in praise of Robinson's poems, for the *Outlook* and persuaded Scribner's to reissue *The Children of the Night*. For his temerity in writing a critical article, the president was generally abused by the literary experts of the period, and Robinson's poetry was belittled by them; but Roosevelt must have accomplished more toward assisting Robinson at this juncture with regard both to his reputation and to his personal life than anyone else had done. It is curious to note that Roosevelt found "Luke Havergal" and "Two Gardens in Linndale" obscure, although fortunately for Robinson he shared with the critics of a later generation a liking for poetry which he could not understand.
> —*Edwin Arlington Robinson*, 1946

Winters's interest is much to the point. His own adamant standards, both as poet and critic, were the terror of his time, and I well recall how he assayed to cut William Carlos Williams down to size and with confident judgment dismissed Hart Crane's last poem "The Broken Tower" as ill done. His discussion of Robinson, written for New Directions' *The Makers of Modern Literature* series, is compact and provocative, and it is certainly forthright ("... but as I have already said, he devoted himself mainly to long poems, for which even in the years of his greatest achievement he had shown a marked incapacity, and he wrote too much and

Edwin Arlington Robinson. 1930. The Granger Collection, New York.

apparently published all that he wrote").

It is hard to argue with him now. What Winters proposes as Robinson's virtues states my own sense of them very clearly: "the plain style, the rational statement, the psychological insight, the subdued irony, the high seriousness and the stubborn persistence." Fifty years later these qualities are even more emphasized, and a poem which Winters speaks of as "one of the greatest short poems in the language" still intrigues me with its confusing mastery of a nearly frivolous form and rhythmic pattern, together with a pace and rhyming of such absolute and intimate integrity it cannot ever be abstracted or forgotten.

> She fears him, and will always ask
> What fated her to choose him;
> She meets in his engaging mask
> All reasons to refuse him;
> But what she meets and what she fears
> Are less than are the downward years,
> Drawn slowly to the foamless weirs
> Of age, were she to lose him . . .
>
> — from "Eros Turannos"

But I cannot spoil the haunting story. The ending is just that, neither an explanation nor a conclusion — simply there. I find my-self again crying, face wet with tears. Is it Maine I am talking about, or that he's talking about, or a common sound, or feeling, or a way these words echo now in mind, or just that it is, *life* is, like this, an endless ambivalence one will never do more than recognize, at best, far too late? I heard this all so very long ago, and he was the one who told me.

> . . . Meanwhile we do no harm; for they
> That with a god have striven,
> Not hearing much of what we say,
> Take what the god has given;
> Though like waves breaking it may be,
> Or like a changed familiar tree,
> Or like a stairway to the sea
> Where down the blind are driven.
>
> — Ibid.

* * *

Robert Creeley

OLD POEMS

One wishes the *herd* still wound its way
to mark the end of the departing day
or that the road were *a ribbon of moonlight*
tossed between something cloudy (?) or that *the night*

were still something to be walked in like a lake
or that even a bleak stair *down which the blind*
were *driven* might still prove someone's fate —
and pain and love as always still *unkind.*

My shedding body, skin soft as a much worn
leather glove, head empty as an emptied winter pond,
collapsing arms, hands looking like stubble, rubble,
outside still those barns of my various childhood,

the people I still hold to, mother, my grandfather,
grandmother, my sister, the frames of necessary love,
the ones defined me, told me who I was or what I am
and must now learn to let go of, give entirely away.

There cannot be less of me than there was,
not less of things I'd thought to save, or forgot,
placed in something I lost, or ran after,
saw disappear down a road itself is no longer there.

Pump on, old heart. Stay put, vainglorious blood,
red as the something something.
"Evening comes and comes . . ." What
was that great poem about *the man against*

the sky just at the top of the hill
with the last of the vivid sun still behind him
and one couldn't tell
whether he now went up or down?

Herman Melville. Circa 1885. The Granger Collection, New York.

Melville and the Art of Saying No
Jim Lewis

IS THERE A BETTER BOOK that's worse? Is there a masterpiece so unmasterful, so little of a piece? *The Confidence Man* is a catalogue of failings. The true wonder of the thing is not why it was neglected for so long, but how it ever got published at all.

Even the most basic standards of novel-writing are grossly unmet. The plot, such as it is, is gimmicky and simplistic: on board a Mississippi steamship called the *Fidèle*, a man gets himself up in various guises and tries, with varying degrees of success, to con a few of his fellows. The anecdotes that flesh out this minor conceit are episodic, repetitive and incomplete. What's more, the whole thing is lopsided and disproportionate. Some incidents are so brief that they're over almost as soon as they're begun. Others are interminable. The author digresses for chapters at a time, losing himself in allegories without meaning, in disquisitions without argument or conclusion; the result is a tediousness and an obscurity so pronounced that he feels compelled, at various moments in what passes for the book's narrative, to stop and explicitly defend himself against charges of incompetence.

The charges stand. The title character, for example, is entirely protean and inscrutable. His success at self-disguise is improbable and unconvincing. In fact, the elusiveness of his outer life is matched only by the vacuity of his inner one: he has no history, no personality, no motivation, no goal. He is inconsistent, and not even consistently inconsistent: in an early chapter, the Black Guinea, himself the first appearance of the confidence man (unless we count the deaf mute who appears at the book's opening — should we count the deaf mute?), lists eight men on board the boat who will vouch for him. In the course of the book, six of them appear, each one another manifestation of the same wily character. Obviously an attempt at subtle structuring. — But . . . what about the other two? The man in the violet robe? The man in the yellow vest? They're never mentioned again.

The other characters are simple and bland, and they're drawn in the crudest possible way. Each is described according to a single, unmistakable trait, a tic — a habit of coughing, a foppish air, a violent temper. They're straight men, puppets who pop up on the stage, say their little piece, then disappear again.

The prose itself is often bland and mannered, sapped of all vigor by Melville's evasiveness, his perverse indirection. He continually indulges in negatives, double negatives, hedged and qualified double negatives; he backs into every description like a man trying to perjure himself without getting caught. There is a passage in which one of the confidence man's first victims, a merchant named Roberts, reacts to an entreaty: "the merchant, though not used to being very indiscreet, yet being not entirely inhumane, remained not entirely unmoved." Other characters are 'not untouched,' 'not unaware,' 'not unselfpossessed,' 'not uncongenial' and so on. Four years previously Melville had created another voided character in Bartleby, whose perfect and gentle refrain of "I prefer not to" contained a negating power so immense that even Wall Street — especially Wall Street — was helpless before it. *The Confidence Man* is *Bartleby, the Narrator*.

Everywhere Melville flaunts what his book is not, he lavishes attention on characters who don't really exist and dwells rapturously on events that hardly occur at all. He's circular, evasive and flippant, and he can't resist advertising as much. One chapter is entitled, "Worth the consideration of those to whom it may prove worth considering"; another is called "Moot points touching the late Colonel John Moredock"; a third proclaims itself "Very charming," though it's essentially charmless.

And yet he seems completely unembarrassed. He simply pushes on ahead — did he revise the book even once? — until he gets bored, at which point he ends more or less in mid-anecdote, with the line, "Something further may follow of this Masquerade." There's no reason to believe he ever intended to write a sequel.

I love the book, more than *Moby-Dick*, more than any native novel I can think of. Melville is the muse of my America, and *The Confidence Man* is my *vade mecum*. I've read it over and over, and sometimes tried to imitate it. And yet . . .

Is there a more lighthearted and amusing tale that's meaner and more misanthropic? It's a Barnum of a book (the circus man's own memoirs, *The Life of P. T. Barnum, Written by Himself*, had been published just two years before, and was already vastly popular). Hardly a character escapes it without suffering Melville's sly and cheerful contempt: the rich and the poor, businessmen, soldiers, doctors, invalids and Indian-haters. Emerson and Thoreau appear in the guise of a dour mystic named Winsome, and Egbert, his callow disciple.

Only the confidence man himself is allowed any dignity, and then only because he is corrupt. He does not, after all, scruple to gull the weak-minded or the infirm, the credulous or the true. Nor is he motivated by anything so mortal as the love of money; he expends enormous effort and wit in order to cheat a barber out of the price of a shave. No, it's the principle that appeals to him, it's a point he feels like proving: that men are blind and weak and stupid, vain and stingy and easy to rob, and that he is Scratch and made to rob them.

From *The New York Herald,* July 8, 1849:

> ARREST OF THE CONFIDENCE MAN
>
> For the last few months a man has been traveling about the city, known as the "Confidence Man"; that is, he would go up to a perfect stranger in the street, and being a man of genteel appearance, would easily command an interview. Upon this interview he would say, after some little conversation, "have you confidence in me to trust me with your watch until to-morrow?"; the stranger, at this novel request, supposing him to be some old acquaintance, not at the moment recollected, allows him to take the watch, thus placing "confidence" in the honesty of the stranger, who walks off laughing . . .

That is, by the way, where the phrase "con man" comes from; the perpetrator was named William Thompson, "said to be a graduate of the college at Sing Sing." (In times before, such a man would have been referred to as a "Jeremy Diddler"; Poe has a rather wan sketch called "Diddling Considered as one of the Exact

Sciences."] But he bequeathed us more than a tag, because in that passage lies the origin of American humor, or at any rate a substantial strand thereof, and if you listen very closely, you can still hear the original confidence man's laughter, faintly echoing in the city. It is an unmistakable sound; it's the amusement of a man walking away from a mark, the joy of a demon who has just rooked an innocent, and then presented the act as a happy affront to the idea of human will and ability.

To share in that laughter was Melville's great act of brilliance and bravery, the more so because it demolished the myths that had accrued to him over the preceding decades. The author of *The Confidence Man* was not Melville the bear, the adventurer, the bestseller and the purveyor of theodicies, not the mammoth man who made mammoth masterpieces. *This* Melville deserted the first whaleboat he signed onto, and took part in a mutiny aboard the second: he was a Timon of the New World, a court jester in a country without a Court.

It is, then, a very American form of humor that he proposes, underwritten by the pessimism that lurks behind our optimism, by our fatalism and our rage. As comedy it relies — as all comedy does — on a certain surprise, but the surprise comes from what does not happen — from the violence of what does not happen, and with it the sudden realization that nothing is going to get better, that the situation at hand is never going to improve, nothing will change and you will never win. On and on the routine runs, spiraling downwards towards a distant darkness; and just when you think that some form of redemption must be in the offing, just when you allow yourself a little hope — down it drops a little more. You can see that sort of comic abjection in Buster Keaton's face; you can hear it in Richard Pryor's voice; you can find it in the later performances of Lenny Bruce and Andy Kaufman, the ones they did just before they died, where the comedy is so desperate that it's impossible to tell whether they're kidding or not. It's the humor that comes from being hounded by failure in a culture which is notoriously afraid of such a thing, until there's nothing left to do but turn around and laugh.

Failure, of course, was one of Melville's few forms of success. *The Confidence Man* was the last novel he published in his lifetime, and it's hard to argue that he went out with a bang. Foisted on the world on April Fool's Day 1857, it was met with almost uniformly negative notices: I don't know if he was surprised or not. Most reviewers found it incomprehensible; several claimed to have read it, first forwards and then backwards, looking in vain for some sense to it. It was not *Typee,* they all said. In fact it was not a novel:

> *The New York Dispatch:*
> It is not right — it is trespassing too much upon the patience and forbearance of the public, when a writer possessing Herman Melville's talent, publishes such puerilities as *The Confidence Man.*

*

> *The New York Times:*
> Melville has not the slightest qualifications for a novelist.

*

> *Putnam's Monthly:*
> The sum and substance of our fault-finding with Herman Melville is this. He has indulged himself in a trick of metaphysical and morbid meditations until he has perverted his fine mind from its healthy productive tendencies.

Well, it's easy enough to make fun of the blindness of the critics. But I don't think they were really wrong: Melville was indeed being puerile, and inept, and morbid; and not entirely on purpose, though not quite by accident, either. He was after something; he was aiming in some direction so little known to literature that it's taken us all this time — an astounding ninety-two years lapsed between the book's first printing and its second — to bring our own gazes around to follow.

What he wanted, I think, was a story strange enough to capture the strangeness of the country as he understood it; because however long the man may have lived among the Polynesians, he knew of no people as extraordinary and inexplicable as the citizens he might meet on board a Mississippi steamboat, none so ridiculous, so fascinating, so tempting. The rest of the world was peculiar, perhaps, but Americans were insane, they had gone berserk in

Eden, they were not to be believed. They were fair matches for the Devil, so Melville sent the Devil to walk among them.

The book strolls alongside, poking its head here and there, circling back, tossing off grim anecdotes as it goes: a man who hated Indians, a man who reluctantly borrowed money, a bad wife. The effect is effortlessly odd — not merely eccentric, but deeply uncanny. Reading it is an adventure in aesthetic credulity; it feels as if some stricture on intention is constantly being broken, that it's impossible that anyone — especially a man who wrote such carefully tuned dramas as *Moby-Dick* and *Billy Budd* — could mean to do *this*. And yet Melville does, apparently, mean it; in any case, he never lets on otherwise. And he must be doing *something* purposeful, because the themes seem to achieve a kind of consistency, even as they divide and redivide, double up, hide themselves and then jump out unexpected. It's a style and strategy that the film critic Manny Farber described perfectly, in a brilliant but forgotten essay called "White Elephant Art vs. Termite Art." He's discussing movie-making in the early 1960s, but he might as well be speaking of novel writing a century earlier (I have elided a few references to specific films):

> Good work usually arises where the creators are involved in a kind of squandering-beaverish endeavor that isn't anywhere or for anything. A peculiar fact about termite-tape-worm-fungus-moss art is that it goes always forward eating its own boundaries, and, likely as not, leaves nothing in its path other than the signs of eager, industrious, unkempt activity. The best examples appear in places where the spotlight of culture is nowhere in evidence, so that the craftsman can be ornery, wasteful, stubbornly self-involved, doing go-for-broke art and not caring what comes of it.
>
> A termite art aims at buglike immersion in a small area without point or aim, and, over all, concentration on nailing down one moment without glamorizing it, but forgetting this accomplishment as soon as it has been passed; the feeling that all is expendable, that it can be chopped up and flung down in a different arrangement without ruin.

Well yes: *The Confidence Man* is wasteful, ornery and unkempt: the book is a barnacle, a stubborn and inert parasite on the hull of the great, gliding culture above it, fastened there by a drowning man. You can't outsmart it, you can't lose it, you can't even criticize it; it seems to defy every attempt at understanding. It takes you as the confidence man takes his victims: with a patience and tenacity that will wear you down if it can't win you over.

I love the book for its cranky brilliance, its slipperiness and mystery, its refusal to apologize or clarify, its fat humor. I love it for its dissolution and monstrousness. And I love it, as much as anything, because it is such a colossal disaster.

How often have I wished that I could write as badly as Melville did when he was writing *The Confidence Man*. God knows I've tried. It isn't easy; I can't imagine it was very easy for him, either. In a letter he wrote to Hawthorne celebrating the publication of *The House of the Seven Gables*, he says that the novelist's job is to say "No! in thunder." It is a harder thing to say than yes. But to succeed, to build a bomb of a book, in such devious and uncompromising fashion . . . a career-ender . . . to be willing to wait a century, long past the first flowerings of American art and well into one's own death, for the glory of its strange explosion. . . . Has there been any act in the history of our literature more admirable?

W. E. B. Du Bois. Drawing, circa 1910. The Granger Collection, New York.

Black Reconstruction:
Du Bois & the U.S. Struggle
For Democracy & Socialism
Amiri Baraka

BLACK RECONSTRUCTION IS, for revolutionaries in the U.S., particularly for the militants of the Black Liberation Movement, as cogent a work in laying out the history and field of our struggle as the singular works of the great international teachers. Some have carped at the work, because they claim it is not strictly Marxist, others because it did not make a "sharp enough" class analysis of pre–Civil War whites in the South, but to both questions I answer, read it again.

By 1935, when this work was issued, Du Bois had been a socialist twenty years. Though he had joined then unjoined the Socialist Party because, as he said, they tried to push Black folks into the background. This has been a problem throughout the movement, anywhere you look or investigate. That there has been a consistent belittling of the Black Liberation Movement. Ironically, not just from the mostly white, or multinational political forces, but, alas, even from those Negroes and white folks claiming to represent the best interests of the Afro American people.

Certainly, this was true for the NAACP, the organization Du Bois helped found, which was coopted by the bourgeoisie who replaced him with the comedy team of White and Wilkins. The Left too has been outrageously in evidence when such policies and ideological reaction is cited. So that given the fundamental relationship of the Afro American people to almost any segment of the organized U.S. body politic, aside from the identifying jargon that separates them, there has been a stunning similarity.

What *Black Reconstruction* does is present the historic development of the Afro American people, across the U.S. and most pointedly in the South, the area Du Bois called The Black Belt in *The Souls of Black Folk*. It is in *Souls* that we also receive his earliest perceptions and attempts to understand just what the South was and is, to Black people, to white people, to Afro America, to "White America" (the media fiction) and to the world.

By the 1930s, after his first removal from the NAACP, Du Bois had initiated the most scientific and detailed study of the South (Atlanta University Publications on "The Study of the Negro Problems 1897–1910," edited by Du Bois; conferences covered by Du Bois at Atlanta University), from his chair at Atlanta University. But from the time he arrived at Fisk, astonished at the wonderful beauty of the sisters there, and believing he was, indeed, in heaven, there are few people who we will claim studied or knew more about the South than Du Bois. And that was obviously the strength and thoroughness of his analysis, and the penetrating force of *Black Reconstruction.* So that by 1903, when *Souls* appeared, with its millennium shattering force, Du Bois was already deeply immersed in Black southern studies, for, as he said many, many times, "The future of the Negro is in the South."

What *Souls* did was to clarify the present by presenting it as a continuum, politically, socially, economically, culturally, psychologically, of the past. The African past and the Afro American present, both of which were hidden, obscured, crushed, belittled, denied, exploited beneath the Veil of "otherness" which slavery had placed upon Black people, which not only hid us from the world, but hid the world from a great part of itself, its history and its potential for salvation in the real world.

From the outset, those jarring words — "How does it feel to be a problem?" — he goes on for sixty more years to tell us. In *Souls,* he deals with the South before and after the Civil War in a general agitational overview, presenting at the same time a new form of presentation, the multiformed essay, poem, short fiction, analytical work, that Langston Hughes claimed was the single spark of the Harlem Renaissance. This is important in accessing *Black Reconstruction,* because the seeds of all his later explorations and conclusions are there.

First, the surgical dismantling of Booker T. Washington, to clean the slate and announce a new dispensation, a new generation's assault on Black oppression. He speaks at length of the conditions, psychological, social and cultural and political, of the Black Belt, imparts to us a sense of its being, actually, somewhere other than the U.S. but exploited by being inside the U.S. at the same time. This is the thesis of the Veil, and the revelational description of the "twoness" of the Afro American. Being in it but not in it. To see ourselves through the eyes of those who hate us. That "double consciousness." Am I Black or am I American? That double consciousness that we still until this very hour must deal with. And this is the overriding victory of studying Du Bois, because you understand, moving along with him through the years, through the twists and turns and small and substantial victories and defeats, the constant changes and regroupings, the common self-criticism and often sharp criticism of others, you understand the seriousness of the man and his work, but also the infinitely sensitive consciousness and self-consciousness which spurred him to move forward, to go back, to change, to modify, but to continue, always, at the very top of the mind he carried, always to struggle for Black Liberation, as he said, through "Self-Assertion." It is this Self-Assertion that we must understand is at the root of everything Du Bois has ever said, or is moving to say, or why he will dismiss things he has said before. This is personal and intellectual and scholarly Self-Consciousness, which he urged on us — to seek a "True Self-Consciousness."

Souls had to clear Booker T. and the submissionist sector of the Black national bourgeoisie out of the way, because for all that might pass as the practical motherwit of Washington, Du Bois could see that nothing lay in that direction but submission, the emergence of a comprador Black Bourgeois, rich servants of the same white master.

Souls dealt with Afro America, the history and culture of the U.S., but as a context in which Black life, the Afro American people, had developed. His essay on "ATALANTA," the Atlanta, which he had experienced as the site of anti-Black riots, which actually had some part of the early tragic death of his First Born, and his wife's lifelong partial withdrawal from the world, laid out the root of that city's corruption. That it was an artificial thing created by the northern conquerors to control the South, that Atlanta was a city of the bribed. The essay is brilliant and evocative until this day. How prophetic that not only Booker T. Washington gave us back into new slavery there, but in 1988, Jesse Jackson followed suit.

The essay on African religion and the Sorrow Songs are touchstones of modern Afro American scholarship. They should be the base of any new studies on Afro American history, culture, psychology and social life. Du Bois was endeavoring to get down, to get all the way Down, to see from the very bottom of up under the

Veil. He says "between the other world and me" . . . he wants to see from all the way back, clear back, forward beyond ourselves. And help shape this hazardous road we've taken, help point us to a new and more humanly rewarding "there."

When *Reconstruction* appears thirty years later, Du Bois had been on quite a journey himself. *The Suppression of the African Slave Trade, The Philadelphia Negro, Darkwater, The Negro, The Atlanta Studies, Crisis* are all leading to this major work. Again and again in innumerable articles, essays, speeches, letters, he keeps moving toward this major work, this great work which should be and will be as impacting on the BLM as Lenin's *Imperialism: The Highest Stage of Capitalism* was and remains. Actually, the work it is most comparable to of the great teachers is Marx's *The Civil War in France.* That work also dealt with civil war and the role of different classes within the war, which led to the first "Dictatorship of the Proletariat"; though short lived, it was still the model Marx used to project what the fully constructed Dictatorship should look like. It is also a work analyzing the emergence of Imperialism, where the French bourgeoisie actually enlisted the Prussian (German) bourgeoisie for aid against the French working class! How perfect an analogy to the Civil War in the U.S., where the northern forces, after utilizing the 200,000 Black runaway slaves to defeat the Southern slavocrat secessionists, then enable and empower these same secessionists to impose a fascist dictatorship on Afro America (the Black South) and the whole of the Afro American people.

Black Reconstruction is such an immense and profound work, and still incompletely grasped by the Left, that its analysis and summation of the U.S. Civil War, the most central conflict in this country's history, has still not been put to clear and consistent USE. Most of us are still trying to rationalize, to put into understandable form, what we have learned from the work, the practical and revolutionary use, as a weapon of theory, as Cabral said, to help us lay waste to Black national oppression and U.S. and all imperialism forever.

First, Du Bois makes a masterful class analysis of the vital class forces of the South and the rest of the U.S., historically and in their interrelationship, particularly how these various classes impact on the Black struggle for democracy. Du Bois had read Marx by this time and Lenin and had visited the Soviet Union for an extended period, so that some of his earlier uncertainty about what the USSR meant to do, and in fact what the great socialist teachers were saying, had been laid to rest.

For instance, he had foreseen the updating that Lenin would have to do to the basic Marxist analysis of capitalism and the dictatorship of the proletariat. Indeed, Du Bois thought that Marx relied too heavily on the "productive forces" as ideological and political transporters of the working class to fully revolutionary positions. So that he welcomed the emphasis that Lenin makes on the formation of "a party of a new type," i.e., the proletarian headquarters the revolutionary party must be.

Du Bois still rejected entrance into the Communist Party USA at this time, because he thought the CP dismissed the leveling quality of Black national oppression by insisting that the class structure of the Afro American people was the same as the oppressor nation's. That is, the CP, except for the impact of Lenin's 1920s paper on *The National Question* and Marx's nineteenth-century analysis of the U.S. Civil War, has always tended to minimize the revolutionary function of the Black Liberation Movement, as a form of revolutionary democratic struggle against imperialism. This is a common failing of social democrats who make the struggle for socialism a single laser focus disconnected from (except for recruitment and too generalized propaganda) the spectrum of democratic struggles in the society.

This is the very opposite of what Lenin proposes in his works on the national question, certainly in *Two Tactics of Social-Democracy in the Democratic Revolution* and the essay "Our Tasks," among many other works, where he points out that the Vanguard party must be a leader in the democratic struggle, while all the time putting out the Communist program. In fact the party must develop a minimum line, which is its analysis and proposal for mass struggle for democracy, and a maximum or socialist line, which calls for the overthrow of capitalism and the building of socialism and the eventual emergence of Communism. Particularly when Du Bois, trying to grapple with the "twoness" of Afro Americans in the relationship to the U.S. as would-be citizens and an oppressed nation, begins to put forward more directly and openly his growing theories on the need for Self-Determination and the building of a broad political united front for Afro American democracy and economic and cultural cooperative organizations to begin to deal with the many problems Black people have which will not be solved by merely protesting. Because no matter how long and how strong we protest, the very protest itself is an act of self-determination. And this initial act must be followed by other such acts to raise the level of the struggle itself.

Some of the social democrats, and the Left, began to say that Du Bois was advocating segregation and nationalism. This was one of the sticking points in his struggle with White, Wilkins and their Black and white classmates, that protest, legal struggle, was not enough, that there had to be some substantive building of institutions and organizations even to further the struggle for democracy. At one point, some Negro said to Du Bois, when he was planning a celebration of the Emancipation Proclamation, that for Du Bois to raise the EP was racist!

But this is the essence of the deep class division between the revolutionary and bourgeois sectors of Black struggle. The struggle for Democracy is at root a struggle for self-determination, they are two sides of one coin. Even a minority — for instance, the Black masses outside the Black south, though they mostly live in twenty-seven cities where they are a substantial plurality or majority — has rights. No one lives anywhere at any time to be oppressed. Black people did not vote to be poor and exploited and uneducated; this is the result of the anti-democratic context historically of our lives, and even the struggle for democracy must be preceded by the act of and continuing struggle for self-determination. In other words, we must literally build the weapons we must use to defeat our national oppression. We cannot merely starve while demanding food, we cannot have our culture reduced to MTV and Def Jam and Death Row and Hollywood while we are demanding a democratic culture, we must create these things to the extent we can, even to intensify the demand for them.

Of course, the bourgeois sector of the democratic movement calls such thinking "separatist," just as they called Du Bois. But the whole scam that separates the movement for Equal Rights into one separatist wing and one integrationist wing is unproductive. Black people are struggling for national liberation, which is a democratic demand! We cannot struggle only through the institutions and traditional structures of the oppressor nation, "White America." The form and method and ideological essence of that struggle are acts of self-determination.

Where the bearers of the "abolitionist democracy" philosophy have too often been remiss is that in their struggle for democracy, they have put out only a program to gain equal access to U.S.

mainstream society (which we should definitely understand after the sixties) will be possible for only a small sector of the Black bourgeoisie and petit bourgeoisie. This was the truest criticism of Du Bois earlier, I feel, that in his focus on Democracy he did not completely correlate the function of Self-Determination, even to further that struggle. During the period in which people like Walter White, Ralph Bunche and A. Philip Randolph were calling him Nationalist, Du Bois advocated that we must begin to struggle for a stronger black unity politically and self-determination in education and a movement for economic and cultural cooperatives. For these would be the groundwork for a more informed and stable Afro American community, able then to intensify and raise the struggle for equal rights, by Self-Assertion, to new heights.

By the time he began to write *Black Reconstruction,* Du Bois had also been through the Garvey wars. He was being criticized by not only the Communist party and various social democratic nearbys, and by the Negro petit bourgeois, but by the nationalists like Garvey. I think this intense fire had some influence on Du Bois, and though he had made some precise criticism of Garvey and his movement, which proved absolutely correct (certainly about the shakiness of the Black Star Economic program and some of the con men who were high up in the UNIA, some of whom testified against him), both his and Garvey's criticism of each other sunk to demeaning bombast. Garvey was, at root, a kind of militant Booker T. Washington, with a catalyst of West Indian nationalism, directly connected to the land-based struggles that raged and still rage all over the Caribbean. Garvey felt the major class struggle was a form of racial contention (as Du Bois, to a certain milder extent, had felt earlier; see "The Conservation of the Races"). Plus, the historic role of the light-skinned Black or mulatto in Jamaica, Haiti, &c, is different in the sense that light-skinned Blacks have never been set up so completely "classed off," like they say, from the masses of the Afro Americans as in the Islands. In the U.S., since the whole of the Afro American people were a minority, the oppressor nation did not have to use them so clearly as surrogate rulers, a neo-colonialism of caste.

However, when Garvey began to change his line from Africa for the Africans and Black Self-Determination around 1919, and even began meeting with the Klan, Du Bois justifiably denounced him. Though in a summary later on, he tried to analyze Garvey's contribution on balance. But the influence of Garvey was in forcing

Du Bois to think more deeply about the question of what do we do till the "full manhood suffrage" comes, especially as Black people entered the Depression thirties. Now the teachings of Garvey about Black self-determination and self-reliance seemed more useful, and his belief in the leadership of what he called "The Talented Tenth" (the Black bourgeoisie and petit bourgeoisie) had been wasted by reality. So that he was also coming more clearly into recognition of the sharpening class struggle within the Afro American community, as he identified "a stunning kind of national selfishness" shaping the Black bourgeois classes that he did not understand would emerge naturally with the extension of democracy and capitalism within the Black community. His clashes with the NAACP Negroes and the "good whites" who were on the NAACP's board, no doubt, helped bring this class struggle to him with sharper definition.

Black Reconstruction begins with an epigram that sums up what it intends. Each chapter has a similar summation, which in themselves are concise analyses of the material to be handled. At the top of Chapter One, "The Black Worker," Du Bois says, "How black men, coming to America in the sixteenth, seventeenth, eighteenth and nineteenth centuries, became a central thread in the history of the United States, at once a challenge to its democracy and always an important part of its economic history and social development."

The first three chapters, "The Black Worker," "The White Worker" and "The Planter," present a general historic and precise socio-economic analysis of the main classes in action in the U.S. Civil War. As one reads these chapters, one is being loaded with the exact scientific and historic data, not only to understand the particularity of his further observations in "The General Strike" and "The Coming of the Lord," but also to be carried along from observation to observation, all tirelessly detailed and confirmed by any number of other observers, and lifted up into the revelational sweep of Du Bois's conclusions. For this work is not only a great work of science, of U.S. and Afro American history, but it is written as very few such works could ever be. For it is the soul of a poet that speaks to us, that points out and explains, that references and makes irony swim with gradual accretion of rationale for whatever he says. At times the poetry of the book is so stunning, it will make you pause to reread and savor, to read it aloud so that the other senses can dig it. The chapter called "The Coming of the Lord" actually made me stop and weep at such incredible power, that real life could be delivered to me silently, perfectly imaged by the facts it conveyed.

"The Black Worker" is a title of critical importance. Not The Black Slave, &c. Because Du Bois had understood, as some of us still do not, that The Black Slave was NOT a peasant. He was not a farmer. He was a **slave worker.** Such as Marx talks about in *Das Kapital* when he explains the corvée system as one basis of capitalism. In fact, Marx goes on to point out that North American Slavery is the anchor and base of capitalism generally. Saying that "without slavery" as its economic base, and the mode of primitive accumulation (of wealth to be turned into capital), Euro American civilization was impossible.

Du Bois makes it clear what is different about Black oppression, as he points out the similar exploitation and inhumane conditions that European workers and peasants and Asian peasants suffered, but he adds the stunning proviso, "But none of them was real estate"! This condition of the Afro American people remains at the bottom of our "twoness," this legacy has been a continuing division between the Black struggle in the U.S. and the rest of U.S. workers. Because, no matter that the U.S. Declaration of Independence and Constitution and Bill of Rights thundered a commitment to equal rights and democracy, African chattel slavery made those words hollow and created an actual society where "the conscience of the nation was uneasy and continually affronted its ideals." At base, the U.S. was rooted in the vicious seizure and attempted genocide of the native Akwesasne peoples and the African slave trade. It was also likewise based on the exploitation of European workers, but by the eighteenth century the U.S. rulers had seen that if the white indentured servants were not given a status somewhat different from the native peoples and the Black slaves they would continue to make alliances to overthrow their mutual servitude as the Servants' Rebellion (1663, Virginia) and Bacon's Rebellion (1802, Virginia) had shown, which led to the consolidation of a "racial slavery" (see "The Invention of Racial Slavery").

Du Bois shows the checkered history of equal rights for Black people anywhere in the U.S. where one year pre-nineteenth century you might be able to vote in Pennsylvania but not in New Jersey, maybe in Illinois, but not in Delaware, and then the next year it would change. That is, for the Blacks who had somehow gotten freed from chattel status, either by manumission for service in the Revolutionary War or having come up with the necessary monies, or at the bequest of some more kindly slave master.

In the North, and at first, in most of the South, Slavery was a domestic "house service," i.e., to make life easier for the mostly white owners. (A few Blacks and Native people had slaves as well.) But, as Du Bois expresses it with a hammering resonance, "Black labor became the foundation stone not only of the Southern social structure, but of Northern manufacture and commerce, of the English factory system, of European commerce, of buying and selling on a world-wide scale; new cities were built on the results of blacks' labor, and a new labor problem, involving all white labor, arose in both Europe and America."

This is so critical because it establishes both the centrality of the Afro American people to the rise of North America and Europe to world domination, but it also shows that with slavery, the separation of Black and white workers, as well as Black and white people, certainly in the U.S., was a fundamental characteristic of U.S. society. Chattel slavery was an actual contrasting material reality to what the rest of the American workers experienced. It was not just racism, i.e., persecution because of physical characteristics; it shaped an entirely separate perception of what America was from the outset.

Irony of ironies, the very cry of Democracy, accompanied as it has always been in the U.S. by slavery and Black national oppression, has allowed white workers to feel that somehow their destiny is separate from Black workers'. In fact, even today, many American workers refer to themselves as middle-class, unable to conceive of what a working class is. Plus, slavery, as an economic institution, created a competition with the so-called free white workers (who, in reality, were free only as far as their skin could eliminate wage slavery and the actual undemocratic nature of U.S. capitalist society).

Another striking point that Du Bois highlights is that for the white petit bourgeois and even large sectors of the working class, "The American Dream" not only seems achievable, but puts them in a psychological and philosophical mindset of not only believing this rich people's propaganda but of striving to be in all ways as much like their rulers as possible. Hence we still are plagued with television programs like *Escape With the Rich and Famous*. Freed from indenture, the white worker could envision that with a little luck one day he might strike it rich and become the rich and the famous. Until recently, with the advent of the Buppies, it is safe to say that such an illusion was not widespread among the Afro American people.

Du Bois says, "The true significance of slavery in the U.S. to the whole social development of America lay in the ultimate relation of slaves to democracy. What were to be the limits of democratic control in the United States? If all labor, black as well as white, became free — were given schools and the right to vote — what control could or should be set to the power and action of these laborers? Was the rule of the mass of Americans to be unlimited and the right to rule extended to all men regardless of race and color, or if not, what power of dictatorship and control; and how would property and privilege be protected?" The $300,000,000 American question.

Du Bois's class analysis digs deep into the reasons for the various classes of Americans to perceive and answer the question in their different ways. For the slaves, arriving in the U.S. as chattel took them outside the relevance of the question, as it was silently posed by the rulers and their sycophants and superficially traduced Americans. For Blacks the question, from the beginning, was freedom, the end of slavery. The entire spectrum of our history and culture is poised before this question. "The Gifts of Black Folks," "The Gift of Labor, of Song and Story, of Spirit" all are shaped, from Jump, by the material conditions of our chattel condition, however perceived through the ancient cultures we had come out of, as we adapted and changed but remained always another people's property. The U.S. is the society that asks the question, "Can property become a Citizen?"

By the nineteenth century most of the Black slaves were American born, and the folkways of Africa were continued and reinforced by the separation that slavery maintained. Stripped of the drum, all Black music is percussive anyway. Black Christianity is deeply African rooted, except when you get to Clarence Thomas's churches. The Africans were the great artists of the world and any unbiased look at this hemisphere, certainly in the U.S., will show that at the vortex and root of U.S. culture is the African and Afro American western hemispheric cultural continuum. Even the bizarre discussion of Ebonics points out the falsity of American assumption. I have a poem called "BullEating"; it says, "If white people/ Can play the Blues/ Black People can speak/ American." It means that just as the whole of U.S. and western hemispheric culture is a mestizo, a mix of Africa, Europe and Native Akwesasne, so is American speech. It is political power that determines what is correct or incorrect.

Slavery and National Oppression, with their segregation and discrimination, separate and unequal, have provided a continuity of Black national culture, that by this time, with the integration of full citizenship, would have provided a much more even distribution of its historic characteristics throughout the society. But even in chains, Black history, material life and culture have colored U.S. culture in a way that is profound and irreversible. So, too, the question of slavery and, past that, the Afro American National Question are at the center of any consideration of U.S. civilization. That is, there are very few aspects of historic U.S. life and culture that can be discussed, honestly, without reference to chattel slavery and the continuing national oppression of the Afro American people.

When Du Bois says The Black Worker, what he is asserting is that by the beginning of the nineteenth century, not only was it mostly Americans who were enslaved, but with the cotton gin and the extension of cotton production to an international market, what was feudal slavery became capitalist slavery. And those slaves were workers on an agricultural assembly line. The peasant is a small, middle or Big farmer, with a direct relationship to the land. The revolutionary potential of this class has been debated; the Trotsky-Lenin debate which led to Lenin's *Two Tactics*. *Two Tactics* states that not only can the small and middle peasants become a reserve of revolution, rather than a reactionary reserve of the bourgeoisie, but that their struggle for full control of the land (which Marx observed in his summation of peasant struggles, such as the peasant wars in Germany in the middle of the nineteenth century) should also be a force enlisted in the overall domestic force of revolution and even as a strategic ally in building the dictatorship of the proletariat.

But the slaves were not peasants, they were slave workers, except for the small groups of free Blacks and the overwhelming number of white farmers in the South. When chattel slavery was destroyed, the Black struggle also became a struggle for land, as the main democratic revolutions in Europe, Germany, Russia had been, so that the ex-slaves could become a class of small entrepreneurs, independent to some extent from the old chattel ties to the Planters. But with the betrayal of Reconstruction by the newly imperialist forces of northern corporate industrial power, the land (the vaunted forty acres and a mule) was seized by Wall Street (by 1873, eighty percent of southern lands were owned by northern capital), whose southern outpost was Atlanta.

The Mexican war of 1848, the ongoing pacification of the Native peoples, was followed by big capital allying itself temporarily with northern abolitionist democracy, as Du Bois called it, and the multinational southern working class, both Black and white, and once the two hundred thousand Black troops had completely destroyed the plantation owners as a class, the superficial move toward full democracy and land settlement, education, equal citizenship rights was tolerated until big capital secured full control of southern land and remaining institutions and then the white middle-class, the small businessmen, politicians, overseers, small farmers, professionals were transformed into a comprador for a rising Wall Street–based U.S. imperialism.

Add to this the fact that, aside from those white southern workers and farmers who had opposed the Planters historically and who quickly signed the declaration of loyalty to the U.S., the mass of poor whites often lived in ways comparable to slavery or worse. The historic existence of slavery, with its racial metaphysics, made the uniting of class forces against the rise of imperialism and its betrayal of Black democracy and workers' control of the south impossible. Plus, you knew it, there were Negroes involved with the betrayal, just as there are today. Telling us the war is over and if we are still exploited and oppressed it's just some more of that black stuff and we need to get more mature and quit being so self-pitying. Check the post–Civil War Negro politicians who went over to the insurgent democratic party, the party, they said, of the "poor white," which actually became the visible face of the ruthless reaction and counterrevolution that possessed the South once the Union military occupation had been removed, and the Black militia forces were disarmed.

What is so profound about Du Bois's analysis is that it shows that all the classes of modern capitalism had come to exist within Afro America *before* chattel slavery was dispatched. There were Black slave owners in New Orleans, Charleston, Richmond, pre–Civil War. There were a fairly significant group of freed Blacks who formed the basis of an expanding, land-owning petit bourgeoisie. And then, of course, the myriad house Negroes who usually became part of that class as well.

When chattel slavery ended, the mass of Blacks were then thrust into a feudal situation in contrast to the conditions of capitalist slavery, where they were in bitter contradiction to the planter ruling class, when the host of whites, based on the disease created by racial slavery, actually wanted to become planters, and despised the Black slaves because often they said the slaves lived better than the poor whites, whose condition Du Bois describes in chilling detail.

Sharecropping was a kind of feudal recidivism, where instead of becoming a small land-owning peasant class, Black people were now transformed into semi-proletarian agricultural workers, plagued now by The Black Codes (which Du Bois describes as the South looking backwards toward slavery and never ahead to the resolution of these conflicts). Andrew Johnson is analyzed at length in *Black Reconstruction* because of the grim irony which places this poor white southerner at the head of the nation by the end of the Civil War. And where he had heretofore been characterized as staunchly against the rich and the planter class particularly, in a few months, based on his "inability" (which he shared with many of the poor whites) to envision a South where Blacks and whites had equal rights. Du Bois implies that Secretary of State Seward, who was always less than supportive of Lincoln's decision to seek full suffrage for the ex-slaves, was an important influence on Johnson. But he also implies that the huge wealth the new northern imperialists were paying out had a little to do with Johnson's conversion to reaction.

It was Johnson who dismantled the Freedman's Bureau, which in its glorious futility had actually imposed a dictatorship of the working class and small farmers in the South, and had begun to distribute the forty acres and a mule that the two U.S. Senators who represented the Abolitionist Democratic philosophy, as Republican politicians, had put forth because they understood without some economic base, and with that, equal access to the ballot, education and a productive livelihood, the ex-slaves could not possibly become "citizens." It was Johnson, as well, again with Seward's urging, who immediately allowed the southern secessionists to re-enter the union, thus leaving the ex-slaves at the brutal hands of those who were looking backward, and those who sought to re-enslave Black people, which they did, as soon as possible. The book *The Economics of Barbarism* by J. Kucynski and M. Witt, points out that the Black Codes were Hitler's model for his Nazi racial laws.

The overthrow of the Reconstruction actually united fronts of workers and small farmers, heaved Afro America into fascism. There is no other term for it. The overthrow of democratically elected governments and the rule by direct terror, by the most reactionary sector of finance capital, as Dimitrov termed it. Carried out with murder, intimidation and robbery, by the first storm troopers, again the Hitlerian prototype, the Ku Klux Klan, directly financed by northern capital.

What the masses of racially twisted white southerners did not understand was that the overthrow of Reconstruction was necessary not just for pitching Black people into American fascism, but for the complete triumph of imperialism. Since the Plantation Owners, "The Planters," were the last force of *competitive capitalism* removed in order for imperialism to shoulder its way into power in the U.S. Du Bois says it was not until it was too late that the mass of working class and middle-class whites realized that the so-called "Redemption of the South" was actually the defeat of democracy for the entire South and the U.S. nation as well. By 1896, not only was Booker T. telling the U.S. rulers that "the wisest of my race understand the folly of struggling for equality" but the U.S. was poised for its entrance onto the stage of big-time imperialism announced by the Spanish-American War.

Lenin points out in his *Imperialism: The Highest Stage of Capitalism*, and also in *Critical Remarks on the National Question* that national chauvinism is the most finished form of opportunism, in which the rulers can get the workers of one nation to fight the workers of another. The South is obvious as an example of such deep and constantly justified opportunism, not just the crude racial chauvinism of the clearly ignorant, but the smooth b.s. of the various "educated" classes as well as the political forces.

This opportunism, manifest as national or racial chauvinism, has been historically widespread in the U.S. and is the single most damning weapon the bourgeoisie use to prevent broad class unity of a multinational working class. Du Bois points out that this chauvinism, this racism, is not left to spontaneity by the rulers. For sixty years, he says, after the Civil War, the media was filled with sick distortions and attacks on Black people (like today) to hide the heroic anti-slavery image that emerged as a result of Black struggle against slavery. Stepin Fetchit, Sleep and Eat, Birmingham and the various frightened, dishonest, funny negro foils were put forward to justify the U.S. determination not to grant equality to the ex-slaves, and to use these demeaning portraits as "proof" that Black people did not have the capacity for equality. Today we have the media in the same role, read the newspaper any day or look at the TV, count the anti-black stories, plus we even have some of the same bogus sham theories that dotted the nineteenth century proving Black "inferiority"; today we have *The Bell Curve* and Stanley Crouch.

Andrew Johnson's point position in overthrowing Reconstruction and imposing a racial fascism on Afro America and the Afro American people readied the whole of the U.S. nation for imperialist rule, which today has moved to complete control of the entire nation. The international network of finance capital has used its enormous power and wealth to dupe both the East and the West into a "cold war" and through this wrested billions and billions of dollars from nations, which all went into its coffers. Imperialism thus was able to bribe and finally overthrow the Soviet Union, but at the same time compromise the national or native bourgeoisie of most countries in the world, including the United States. By plundering all nations' treasuries, imperialism could then put itself in charge worldwide through such imperialist loan sharks as the International Monetary Fund and World Bank, thereby ruling the world by holding all the nations' purse strings. This is the reason for such a sharp upsurge of nationalism, especially on the extreme right because the social base of this nationalism is the national bourgeoisie and petit bourgeoisie, driven to outrage by their robbery and loss of status and democracy. Today the U.S. is governed by an imperialist ruling class, not even by its own national bourgeoisie. Notice, for instance, in the last election, the pitiful Perot could not even get to debate. It is the New World Order running the U.S., as it has moved to do openly since the Kennedy assassination, and a further sickening irony that both Kennedy and Lincoln were killed for obstructing the imperialist program for the Afro American people, and both were succeeded by Dudes from the South named Johnson. Obstruction to imperialist plans for Latin America must also be included in the assassination motive, Mexico and Central America generally for Lincoln, Cuba particularly was Kennedy's cause of death.

Imperialism was the triumph of opportunism, national oppression and Big capital of the northern banks and industrialists. The destruction of the Black democracy provided the necessary capital for international U.S. imperialist investment and annexation.

This was a period of the upsurge of Imperialism internationally. By 1888 the European powers met to divide up Africa, chattel slaves now replaced with Colonialism, the enslaving of the whole of Africa. The financial panic of 1873 was the economic ground for the 1876 Hayes-Tilden compromise, in which the ex-slaves and the whole South were officially returned to the fascist rule of the comprador southern middle classes. With the Black Codes, any white citizen could arrest, question, beat and even kill any Black person, like the recent Louisiana legislation that any citizen can shoot any person suspected of trying to steal his or her car.

The leadership of the Afro American people was a petit bourgeoisie not really interested in Self-Determination as much as "getting into the U.S.," focusing on their own narrow class interests more than the liberation of the whole people. The white leadership were sycophants of capitalism, whose mindset made them willing compradors, twisted gauleiters of a Wall Street "Neue Ordnung." The American Revolution had, in Marx's words, provided a leap up the social scale for the petit bourgeoisie, so the Civil War and end of chattel slavery provided a similar boost for the working class, but the destruction of Black democracy trashed all of that, with the ignorant collaboration of white workers and farmers "souped up" on white supremacy.

In 1879, the Paris Commune erupted, and like the ending of chattel slavery, the French working class should have continued the armed struggle . . . marched on Versailles, Marx says, just as the Afro American working class in strategic alliance with small and middle farmers and what democratic petit bourgeoisie existed, should have declared for Self-Determination and taken up arms again and fought for the Democratic Dictatorship of the working class, a People's democracy and a United Front government for Afro America, which is a multinational oppressed nation in the Black Belt South.

The proffering of U.S. citizenship, while legitimately intended by Lincoln and the abolitionist democracy he had come to represent, was suddenly an ugly lie. The Emancipation Proclamation has removed all relationship between the Afro American people and the secessionist South. Without the guarantee of democracy, made real by the gaining of political and economic self-determination and access to education, the re-enslaving of the Afro American people, the transformation of the Black South into an oppressed nation, was clear.

Du Bois spoke about "a nation within a nation"; he meant the self-determination of the Afro American people's revolutionary democratic struggle moving forward with national and anti-imperialist unity and the creation of economic and cultural cooperatives including education. Despite the bogus reentrance into the American union, the southern states still fly the confederate battle flags and U.S. apartheid did not end, de jure, until 1954; it has been equally clear that the South has never varied its backward-looking subjugation of Afro America, which has been permitted and joined in by the entire U.S. nation, where today, another Du Bois prediction, the entire U.S. is being "turned into a prototype of the South."

What the great Dr. Du Bois did was lay out the entire spectrum of the centralmost aspect of what characterizes the U.S. nation state, the most illuminating and concrete historical, class-conscious and scholarly study ever published in the U.S. The incredible pantheon of his writings, a bibliography that covers political journalism and social criticism, especially the articles in *The Crisis*, which he edited; scholarly and academic writings in sociology, social and political history, Pan African studies, education and literary and cultural studies. The major sociological studies, as well as six novels and a great deal of poetry, and even a historical pageant. The magazine articles alone measure some 10,000! *The Souls of Black Folk* (1903); *The Negro* (1915); *Black Reconstruction* (1935); *The World & Africa* (1947) and *The Autobiography of W.E.B. Du Bois* (1968) would be good places to begin to access this giant. His *The Philadelphia Negro* (1899) was the initial U.S. work and catalyst for urban sociology. His Harvard doctoral thesis, "The Suppression of the African Slave Trade (1896), is still in print!

Panels for Nathanael
Eli Gottlieb

1.

IN HIS COLLECTION OF EPIGRAMS *The Secret Heart of the Clock,*
Elias Canetti wrote: "At the edge of the abyss, we cling to pencils."
In Nathanael West's version, we jump. And we laugh as we fall —
a scalding, mocking laughter, the abyssal laughter of we-have-
nothing-left-to-lose. Not a typical satirist (from the Latin, *saturus,*
literally "filled or charged with a variety of things"), West belongs
to what we might term the Heroic-Caustic branch of the literary
pantheon. To wit: nothing in his books is built or upheld, nothing
grieved over; all is a falling-away, and the emotional tone of the
writing is one of spectacular, remorseless negation. As West himself said, "Not only is there nothing to root for in my work . . .
but what is worse, no rooters." Published in the reformist-minded
1930s, West's novels presented an evil-twin alternative portrait
of the America seen in the "proletarian" novels of coevals Steinbeck, Sinclair, Farrell and Dos Passos. In his books you will find
no set pieces on the hygiene of slaughterhouses, nor warmly written passages on the brotherhood of hobos; no soaring hymns to
the industrial might of America or "picturesque" depictions of the
marginal and alienated. West's America is brittle, deeply violent,
depthless, loud, scarifyingly unfair and as bright as a new toy. This
America traffics happily in images of bucolic splendor while
grinding people to bits in the urban clockworks. It drapes patriotic
banners over its most murderous acts and tactfully draws the
screen of "democracy" around its own proximity to mob rule. It
proposes as a final reward for long service the state (in both senses)
of "California," which turns out to be a jail of boredom, crammed
with latent violence and guarded by palm trees. Not unsurpris-
ingly, in this province of disappointed expectations, there is one
delusion that stands out above the rest: romantic love. Love, in
West's books, even more than religion, civic zeal or national pride,
constitutes the biggest, most ludicrous, most necessary sham of

all, and he lays bare its grandeurs like a med student pithing a dog.

2.

As novelist, he is intriguingly elusive, a shape-shifter, a protean wearer of authorial hats. Each of his books employs a new narrative template. His first novel, *The Dream Life of Balso Snell*, is a mediocre pottage of juvenile bathroom jokes leavened with highbrow allegorical references. His second book, *Miss Lonelyhearts*, is an astonishingly achieved novel, bearing as little resemblance to its antecedent as *Leaves of Grass* did to the wretched Whitmanian doggerel that preceded it. *A Cool Million*, his third, is a waste of his gifts, though it has a following among his contemporary devotees, and his fourth, *The Day of the Locust*, is shot through with brilliantly imagined scenes, which never entirely quite hang together as an ensemble.

A useful way to understand a body of work this variegated is through the Kafka paradigm. The Kafka paradigm suggests that the less obviously connected a Jewish writer is to Jewish themes or issues, the more deeply Jewish his writing is at bottom. Like many self-hating Jewish writers, West (born Weinstein) renounced all claims to the religion of his birth and seemed, for that, the more crucially, exactly Jewish. His apocalyptic, deadpan humor and ironic self-detachment, his Testamentary ferocity and his sense of writing as hurtling forward along a chain of collapsing expectations stamp him as an essential member of the ingathering of Isaac Babel, Harold Brodkey and Philip Roth — though he occupies a darker, more lexically fraught corner of it than they do. West was the writer Walter Benjamin would have been if he'd grown up and learned to hunt and fish in America.

The lone book out of all his work which represents the perfect fusion of his artistic means and his creative will is *Miss Lonelyhearts*. A fiery dance of literary binaries — academic and vernacular, tender and violent, sacred and profane, comic and pathetic — the novel is recounted in the spooling frames of a comic strip and moves with the inner logic of a fever dream. It tells of a few weeks in the life of a desolate advice columnist to the lovelorn who is detached from his faith, his girl, his job and finally his life in a kind of forced march to the verge of nonbeing. The beauty and the originality of the book reside in its supersaturated prose and the

Nathanael West. Courtesy New Directions Publishing Corporation.

architectonics of its spaces. It is built like a Bach fugue or a soaring tensegrity structure, with each sentence sharing equal load-bearing weight and a feeling of seamlessly phased recurrence of parts-of-the-whole. Harold Bloom, with good reason, calls the novel "the perfected instance of a negative vision in American prose fiction."

Brandishing his artistic credo ("A novelist can afford to be anything but dull"), West wrote *Miss Lonelyhearts* at the Flaubertian rate of a hundred words a day, each of them sounded out loud in the country air of a cabin in upstate New York. The result, aside from the drastic compression of the language, was a panoply of specialized effects similar to those of Expressionist film, in which a spotlight picks out a telling detail on an otherwise dark stage: lock or keyring. Arising out of the dense weave of the prose, these moments employ percussive metaphors to make West's larger point: that man is continually in danger of becoming a *thing*. The sky looks "as if it had been rubbed with a soiled eraser." A woman's arms are "round and smooth, like wood that has been turned by the sea." Miss Lonelyhearts' tongue is "a fat thumb," his heart is "a congealed lump of icy fat." A colleague at his paper has cheeks "like twin rolls of smooth pink toilet paper."

The only place where the seething, corrosive irony of the prose surface lets up is in West's descriptions of the natural world. An avid outdoorsman, West in later years kept a brace of bloodhounds as pets, the better to hunt with, and his caressing, sensual, yet oddly Cubist descriptions of plants and landscapes are clearly the product of affectionate observation: "There was no wind to disturb the pull of the earth. The new green leaves hung straight down and shone in the hot sun like an army of little metal shields. Somewhere in the woods a thrush was singing. Its sound was like that of a flute choked with saliva."

When Miss Lonelyhearts is dragged away to the country by his girlfriend, he has to admit, "even to himself, that the pale new leaves, shaped and colored like candle flames, were beautiful, and that the air smelt clean and alive."

It was part of West's genius in *Miss Lonelyhearts* to stretch a fine skin of caricature over the point-by-point presentation of his story and at the same time tune his ear for dialogue and emotional nuance to such a pitch as to produce real felt inhabited interaction between the characters. The sheerness of this interface, the slipperiness of this linkage, as it slides often within individual sentences from satire to laceration, comic sublimity to heartbreak, is without peer in American literature.

3.

Anyone reading West *en toto* knows that his descriptions of women are less than pleasant. In point of fact, they're brutal. Cast most often as shrews, temptresses, succubi and jades, the women of his novels are a distaff chorus of predatory energy, poised to strike. Though he was clearly a lover of the beauty and sensuality of women — again and again in his novels, women are described using striking tropes and phrases; some of his most ardent lyric sparkles are strewn at their feet — West seemed to fear their emotionality and power and rarely missed an opportunity to pour scorn on their intimacy with men: "She thanked him by offering herself in a series of formal, impersonal gestures. She was wearing a tight, shiny dress that was like glass-covered steel and there was something cleanly mechanical in her pantomime."

Sex, in his books, is always an agon — either primitive and animalistic or the product of a killing combat between men and women: "Her invitation wasn't to pleasure, but to struggle, hard and sharp, closer to murder than to love. If you threw yourself on her, it would be like throwing yourself from the parapet of a skyscraper. You would do it with a scream. You couldn't expect to rise again. Your teeth would be driven into your skull like nails into a pine board and your back would be broken. You wouldn't even have time to sweat or close your eyes."

In the following famous scene, West, who so often sketched women through the shorthand of an outstanding physical attribute, here achieves a reduction of woman to the pure immanence of the marine: "He smoked a cigarette standing in the dark and listening to her undress. She made sea sounds; something flapped like a sail; there was the creak of ropes; then he heard the wave-against-a-wharf smack of rubber on flesh. Her call for him to hurry was a sea-moan, and when he lay beside her, she heaved, tidal, moon-driven. . . . Some fifteen minutes later he crawled out of bed like an exhausted swimmer leaving the surf, and dropped down into a large armchair near the window."

4.

An overmothered child, West eventually developed a gentleman-farmer persona composed of equal parts Ronald Firbank and Buffalo Bill Cody. This calculated public front concealed a fierce ambition: he burned to be successful. He wanted very much to be a big-time novelist, a kind of *mitteleuropisch* John O'Hara. This being the case, the indifferent popular reaction to his books was a crushing disappointment. After *Miss Lonelyhearts*, he tried his hand at *A Cool Million*, a burlesque of the Horatio Alger myth, and the book, not to put too fine a point on it, was a hash. Told in mock-heroic style, its satire was deflected by the jarring period diction and its story slowed by a mass of picaresque improbabilities. West had written it quickly, to capitalize on the very positive critical reaction to *Miss Lonelyhearts* (fans of which included Edmund Wilson, Dorothy Parker and Thornton Wilder). Chastened by the scathing reviews of *A Cool Million*, he tried to write some glossy magazine stories to make money and reestablish himself. These were rejected. With F. Scott Fitzgerald's help, he applied for a Guggenheim, and was again rejected. Disgusted, he pulled up roots, moved to Hollywood and began working sporadically as a screenwriter, limning such classics of the genre as *Five Came Back, I Stole a Million* and *Spirit of Culver*. In the meantime, having long associated himself in a vague way with leftist causes, he continued to dabble in fellow-traveling. He published a Marxist poem in *Contempo*. He worked for the Loyalist cause in Spain. Gradually, he began the process of capillary absorption of the Hollywood milieu which would be parodied with such Westian verve in his next novel, *The Day of the Locust*.

Unlike *Miss Lonelyhearts*, *The Day of the Locust* is not a perfect book. A brilliantly acid portrait of 1930s Hollywood, it suffers from an ambivalence on the part of its author as to the extent of his own self-projection in its narrator, Todd Hackett. The character, a scene painter, remains too emotionally circumspect ever to come entirely alive. And though West's studies of the human fauna of Hollywood are superbly drawn, the cast of the book lacks the deeper motivational wellsprings of those in *Miss Lonelyhearts*. They flicker slightly, like country lightbulbs. Nonetheless, West manages scenes of astonishing power. His honest depiction of what William Carlos Williams called "the real, incredibly dead life of the people" is balanced, as usual, with a kind of gloating interest in the vanities and cupidities of human desire and with a morbid fascination and disgust with sex and bodily functions, the essential venality of American life and the human cost of the dream factory called Hollywood. His gallery of Tinseltown grotesques speaks with voices which, in the words of Edmund Wilson, have "been distilled with a sense of the flavorsome and the characteristic which makes John O'Hara seem precious."

The book, now considered a major American novel, was a flop at the time and, despite some good reviews, sold less than 1,500 copies. His publisher, Bennett Cerf, told West that *The Day of the Locust* was a failure for the simple reason that women readers — no doubt due to the violence with which they were depicted in the book — didn't like it.

In 1939, West wrote to F. Scott Fitzgerald: "Somehow or another I seem to have slipped in between all the 'schools.' My books meet no needs except my own, their circulation is practically private and I'm lucky to be published. And yet, I only have a desire to remedy all that *before* sitting down to write, once begun I do it my way. I forget the broad sweep, the big canvas, the shot-gun adjectives, the important people, the significant ideas, the lessons to be taught, the epic Thomas Wolfe, the realistic James Farrell — and go on making what one critic called 'private and unfunny jokes.'"

A little over a year later, while returning with his new wife from a hunting trip, West was killed in an automobile accident, leaving behind a single perfectly lit room in the house of American prose. He was thirty-seven.

Edgar Allan Poe. The Granger Collection, New York.

How to Tell a Lie, by Edgar Allan Poe

Joanna Scott

YOU WON'T BELIEVE IT! Remember those ladies who were massacred in an apartment in the Rue Morgue? Turns out they were killed by an orangutan! Yes, an orangutan, I swear, cross my heart! And speaking of hearts, that villain who murdered an innocent old man in his bed and buried him beneath the floorboards, he gave it all up because he thought he heard the muffled thumping of a beating heart drifting up through the planks! Which reminds me of the man who slaughtered his wife, walled up her corpse in the cellar and inadvertently sealed a live cat in with her! Wouldn't you know, the cat started yowling, shrieking, wailing in triumph, in horror, right when the police were searching the cellar for evidence!

The things people do! The strange history of our species!

"So you say he overacts?" asks Angela Carter in her story "The Cabinet of Edgar Allan Poe." "Very well; he overacts." But who can blame him, given the family tendency toward histrionics? Edgar's mother had "grease-paint in her bloodstream," Carter writes. His father "was a bad actor who only ever carried a spear." In Carter's version, the infant Edgar napped in prop baskets and nursed in the green room and before he could speak learned about the secret mechanics of theatrical illusion — an intriguing explanation for Poe's theatrical fiction.

But gee, he sure uses a lot of exclamation marks!

So what is the effect of Poe's histrionics? What happens when an extreme predicament is punctuated with hyperbole, as in these lines near the end of "The Pit and the Pendulum": "There was a discordant hum of human voices! There was a loud blast of many trumpets! There was a harsh grating as of a thousand thunders! The fiery walls rushed back!"

The more implausible the fictional claim the better, Poe seems to be proposing. His love of deception is apparent in the numerous accounts of visual disguise and verbal deceit that fill his fiction. But the most consequential deception in Poe's lifetime might be found not in his fiction but in a newspaper article he penned. His famous Balloon Hoax of April 1844 — a fraudulent account of a three-day balloon flight across the Atlantic Ocean — appeared anonymously in an extra edition of *The New York Sun*, and it was announced with a postscript filled with exclamations: "ASTOUNDING INTELLIGENCE BY PRIVATE EXPRESS FROM CHARLESTON VIA NORFOLK! — THE ATLANTIC OCEAN CROSSED IN THREE DAYS!! — ARRIVAL AT SULLIVAN'S ISLAND OF A STEERING BALLOON INVENTED BY MR. MONCK MASON!!"

Over 50,000 copies of the extra edition of *The Sun* were sold, thanks to Poe, who commented with obvious pleasure that the story caused an "intense sensation." Describing the excitement in the square outside the *Sun* building, he included a revealing remark: "Of course there was a great discrepancy of opinion as regards the authenticity of the story; but I observed that the more intelligent believed, while the rabble, for the most part, rejected the whole with disdain."

What I find so interesting here is not that Poe took pride in his deceit but that he so readily acknowledged the skepticism of "the rabble." And this makes me wonder about the disguises of his fiction: do the histrionics, the many exclamations, the swooning, the frequent shuddering, the implausible predicaments, invite skepticism? Must we suspend our suspension of disbelief? Are we really supposed to pant in sympathetic terror, or should we read with an eyebrow raised?

Poe seems to have found in theatrical melodrama, with its Jacobean plots and exaggerated behavior, a trove for his imagination. Melodramatic techniques could accommodate extremes of passion, while Victorian notions of verisimilitude demanded nuance and volumes of detail; melodrama could move beyond the border of the plausible; melodrama didn't turn up its nose at the exclamation mark. But in Poe's gothic tales, melodramatic passages tend to be fortified — and complicated — by his unique brand of verisimilitude. Shrieks and moans provoke richly ambivalent introspection; terror is given an elaborate physical and psychological context.

In one of the most allegorical of Poe's tales, "The Masque of the Red Death," he spends most of the narrative setting the scene. He describes the color of the walls in the chambers in Prince Prospero's secluded abbey. He describes the masks, the movements of the dancers and the expressions on the faces of the musicians.

Eventually, the detailed description becomes in itself a subject for inquiry.

> There was no light of any kind emanating from lamp or candle within the suite of chambers. But in the corridors that followed the suite, there stood, opposite to each window, a heavy tripod, bearing a brazier of fire that projected its rays through the tinted glass and so glaringly illumined the room. And thus were produced a multitude of gaudy and fantastic appearances.

Appearances lead and mislead the characters toward their fate. Narrative suspense is intensified not by events or actions but by the increasing instability of the imagery — images take on the status of hallucinations, and the festive dreaminess turns increasingly nightmarish.

Such visual uncertainty is often matched by psychological uncertainty — mysterious settings have their equivalents in secretive characters. In Roderick Usher's house, for example, the "general furniture was profuse, comfortless, antique, and tattered. Many books and musical instruments lay scattered about, but failed to give any vitality to the scene." Though the setting is motionless, the objects are "instable," the narrator tells us. Instability is signified by decay, which is mirrored in the cadaverous, mysterious Usher himself. But the narrator is the source of the most intriguing mystery. He describes his first impressions of the house as "superstitious" but admits that his self-consciousness only heightens the sensation of terror — "Such, I have long known, is the paradoxical law of all sentiments having terror as a basis."

One of Poe's recurrent mysteries, then, is the mystery of the *paradoxical law* behind terror. The material world of the fiction is dressed up in grotesque imagery, which provokes in the characters a sensation of horror infused with self-doubt. For Poe, heightened emotion — call it histrionics — is never a simple exaggeration; it is the expression of a complex ambivalence. Poe locks his narrators in terrifying situations and then puts them to work explaining the mysteries of the mind.

I'm reminded of Freud's distinction between reflection and self-observation. The reflective man "makes use of his critical faculties, with the result that he rejects some of the thoughts which rise into consciousness after he has become aware of them." The self-

91

observant man, on the other hand, "has but one task — that of suppressing criticism; if he succeeds in doing this, an unlimited number of thoughts enter his consciousness which would otherwise have eluded his grasp." Poe's narrators fall into both categories — some are selectively reflective, some are acutely observant — but the fiction always succeeds in revealing, directly or ironically, the critical thoughts. Even when a character attempts to dismiss his impressions as a dream or superstition, he won't be able to escape the implications of those impressions. The dream will be dreamt, the narrator will be swept up into it, and the fiction, filled with painstaking detail, invites us to sympathize, to recognize our own potential for extreme emotion, to feel overwhelmed, as Poe writes, "by a thousand conflicting sensations" and to understand the paradox of terror.

Poe's terrified characters become acutely aware of sensation, and often that intensified consciousness is thrown into confusion. The old man recounting his close encounter with death in "The Descent Into the Maelstrom" veers between vivid imagery and murky appearance. "The rays of the moon seemed to search the very bottom of the profound gulf," he says, "but still I could make out nothing distinctly," and in the description that follows he admits his confusion — he must have been delirious, he says. Yet in his delirium he attempted to calculate the velocity of the water as it rushed toward the foaming abyss. His language manages to be alternately precise and obscure, and the combination illuminates the complex force of consciousness as it struggles to control the predicament by making sense of it.

But the expression of confusion in Poe's tales often has another effect: confusion undermines authority. If a narrator admits confusion, his whole account becomes doubtful. Narrative confusion provokes skepticism. "I fancied a ringing in my ears," explains the narrator of "The Tell-Tale Heart." Fancied? This same narrator who asks "How, then, am I mad?" at the beginning of his tale demonstrates the answer as he boasts of his sanity. We don't believe him when he assures us that he isn't mad, and we're left to piece together some sort of truth from his questionable version. His narrative begs for an incredulous reader.

We can learn something about distrust from Poe's model reader, Monsieur C. Auguste Dupin, proto-detective and inductive genius. Dupin is so dry, so polished, so *skeptical*, and yet he's ready to believe anything, if necessary. He is the utterly rational, detached equivalent of Poe's terrified narrators. Like the characters on the verge of death, he lets in the thoughts that the reflective mind has been conditioned to suppress. In "The Murders of the Rue Morgue," he says of the investigating police that they have failed in their work because they are prepared only for an *ordinary* solution.

"They have fallen into the gross but common error of confounding the unusual with the abstruse. But it is by these deviations from the plane of the ordinary that reason feels its way, if at all, in its search for the true. In investigations such as we are now pursuing, it should not be so much asked 'what has occurred,' as 'what has occurred that has never occurred before.'"

The extreme predicaments dramatized by Poe are just this: situations that have never occurred before. And their effect is to give rise to thoughts that have never occurred before, to stir the mind of the character, and ideally of the reader — and extend the potential of self-consciousness. Skepticism is useful to Dupin, but it takes an unusual form — he is skeptical of ordinary possibilities and so he can imagine beyond the ordinary, beyond plausible situations, and he can stretch his consciousness to solve an irrational crime.

There's a passage in *The Narrative of Arthur Gordon Pym* that provides us with a blueprint for Poe's histrionics. Pym literally frightens someone to death. First he dresses up as the corpse of a dead sailor; he equips himself with a "false stomach" to mimic the swollen corpse; he puts on a pair of white woolen mittens and fills them with rags; he has another sailor rub his face with white chalk, then he pricks his finger and splotches his face with the blood. When he gazes at himself in the mirror, he is so impressed with his disguise that he is "seized with a violent tremor" and has to look away.

But verisimilitude isn't enough. What Pym needs, and gets, is a conjunction of circumstances, including a desperate group of mutineers, a storm and "an uncertain and wavering" cabin lantern. Without these details to enhance the disguise, Pym's audience would likely retain, as he tells us, the remnant of suspicion. "Usually," Pym reflects, "in cases of a similar nature, there is left in the mind of the spectator some glimmering of doubt as to the reality of the vision before his eyes; a degree of hope, however feeble, that he is the victim of chicanery, and that the apparition is not actually a visitant from the world of shadows."

When Pym appears in his disguise to the mutineers, they don't have the wherewithal to doubt what they see. The mate, in fact, takes one look at Pym and falls down dead. The others stare in "horror and utter despair." Pym succeeds in evoking terror in its purest form, a triumph that necessarily eludes his author. Except for instances of his newspaper hoaxes, Poe's deceptions fall one step short of Pym's. Fiction necessarily falls short. Fiction is a masquerade, a trick, an illusion, and the more it asserts itself as fact, the more obvious the lie becomes — which is just what happens in *The Narrative of Arthur Gordon Pym*. Poe casts Pym's narrative as a factual history in disguise — Pym explains in his preface that he fears himself too coarse to write his own story, so he tells it to "Mr. Poe," who writes and presents Pym's story as fiction. And at the end of the narrative Poe offers one final twist, interrupting the fiction at its peak of terror because that's where the unfortunate Pym supposedly left off his account.

Defoe, of course, casts *Robinson Crusoe* as fact, and in a review of the novel Poe acknowledges that he learned the "potent magic of verisimilitude" from Defoe. But Poe's frame in *The Narrative of Arthur Gordon Pym* hardly enhances the verisimilitude of the mighty strange tale Pym has to tell. Rather, it makes the inventor of the tale more prominent. Although all fiction writers are imposters, Poe surely must be ranked as one of literature's most outrageous liars. Critics have suggested that Poe had a low regard for popular taste and that with his melodrama he pandered to — and implicitly ridiculed — the audience he despised. But surely he could have chosen to give his fiction a Jamesian subtlety and replaced some of the *exclamations* with *emphases*. Or else, like Melville in *Moby Dick* or *The Confidence Man*, he could have made the histrionics more farcical, more chaotic.

Perhaps Poe's expressions of contempt for popular taste are themselves lies. Perhaps in the implausible and Jacobean scenes of terror, Poe makes room for those elusive thoughts that fictional verisimilitude as he knew it ordinarily suppressed. Perhaps Poe's fiction encourages readers to reach the point that Pym describes, when the awful vision exists in a state of profound uncertainty: does the disguise of fiction hide a truth, or is there nothing but illusion? Poe compels us to hesitate, and hesitation opens the gate to "a thousand conflicting sensations."

The "potent magic" of verisimilitude in Poe's theater of fiction is a performative magic — fiction is a wonderful deception, and an author is like a magician on a vaudeville stage, dressing up his words to make them *seem* to refer to a reality. The more extraordinary the trick, the more impressive the art. Poof, a mansion collapses! Poof, a gentleman meets his double! Poof, a cat starts to yowl behind a wall, an orangutan goes wild, a human figure shrouded in white floats across the water!

Poe invites us to believe not in the implausible outcomes of his tales but in their hallucinatory power and the verbal mechanics of illusion. See how a mind can fool itself, this magician shows us. So we pant in sympathetic terror and look on in disdain, for while the tricks themselves are thrilling, we know that they are tricks and that appearances can't be trusted, that we are the victims of chicanery, that fiction, especially Poe's fiction, is a performance of an unruly imagination.

Then what is true? What's behind the carnival mask? Who is waiting behind the next corner? Could a strange appearance be hiding something stranger? We hesitate, our imaginations fired up by Poe. And in that moment of hesitation, Poe cracks open the door to the observant mind, and the wild, unmanageable thoughts that deserve to be known come tumbling in.

Raymond Chandler. The Granger Collection, New York.

45 Calibrations of Raymond Chandler
Peter Straub

1. NOT LONG BEFORE HIS DEATH, he wrote, "I have lived my life on the edge of nothing."

2. Those who may speak honestly of the ambiguous but striking privileges granted by a life conducted on the edge of nothing tend to have in common that they have been faced early on with certain kinds of decisively formative experiences. Although it is never mentioned in considerations of his work, when he was six years old and living with his divorced mother in Nebraska, his alcoholic father, already more an absence than a presence, one day disappeared entirely. Also never mentioned is that in 1918 he was sent into trench warfare as a twenty-year-old sergeant in the Canadian Army and several times led his platoon into direct machine-gun fire. After that, he said later, "nothing is ever the same again."

3. He had no interest in either conventional mysteries or the people who read them.

4. He said: "My theory was that readers just *thought* that they cared about nothing but the action; that really although they didn't know it, they cared very little about the action. The thing they really cared about, and that I cared about, was the creation of emotion through dialogue and description."

5. His models were Dumas, Dickens, Flaubert, James and Conrad.

6. He once named a cop Hemingway for his habit of saying the same thing over and over again until you started to think that it had to be pretty good.

7. He could never understand why Americans were incapable of seeing the humor in his work.

8. Shortly after moving to a house outside Palm Springs, he wrote his publisher, Alfred Knopf, "This place bores me."

9. Raymond Chandler did not relish surprises.

10. He did not like looking at the ocean because it had too much water and too many drowned men in it.

11. In a sour moment, he wrote Knopf that he was going to write "one of those books where everyone goes for nice long walks."

12. Late at night, finished with work but unwilling to leave the typewriter, he wrote hundreds of extremely long letters, many of them to people he had never met.

13. Hollywood made him bilious, but he loved film.

14. In his notes for *The Blue Dahlia*, he said homicide detectives could "be very pleasant or very unpleasant almost without change of expression."

15. He was exasperated by people who told him they so admired his books that they wished he would write one without any murders in it.

16. He actually wrote his English publisher a letter containing the sentence "Don't think I worry about money, because I don't."

17. He was astonished to be informed that another mystery writer, one distinguished chiefly by his ingenuity, did not enjoy the act of writing. Instantly, it explained to him why he had never been able to read the man's books. Still reeling, he wrote a friend, "The actual writing is what you live for."

18. Throughout his life, he endured a spectacular, even brutal, loneliness.

19. Sometimes in restaurants he was so funny that the people at adjoining tables stopped talking to listen to what he was saying.

20. When J.B. Priestley, author of *Angel Pavement* and *Festival at*

Farbridge, came to California and held a dinner party in his honor, he failed to appear. It had never occurred to him that his presence might be any more crucial than anyone else's.

21. Upon discovering that it had been, he apologized but did not feel guilty or embarrassed.

22. Neither did he feel guilty or embarrassed when the news of his botched suicide attempt — the bullet did considerable damage to the bathroom but none to the drunken widower of two months holding the gun — appeared in newspapers all over the country. Some of the letters he received as a result of the publicity struck him as incredibly silly.

23. He understood that he was both romantic and sentimental.

24. After his first four books, he thought Philip Marlowe was romantic and sentimental, too, and decided that on the whole Marlowe was probably too good to be satisfied with working as a private detective.

25. He almost always knew what he was doing, even while making serious mistakes.

26. The year after his wife died, he was ejected from the Connaught Hotel for having a woman in his room, whereupon he moved to the Ritz.

27. He was unfailingly generous to young writers.

28. He wrote, "Plausibility is largely a matter of style." Later in the same essay, he added, "It takes an awful lot of technique to compensate for a dull style, although it has been done, especially in England."

29. He never won an award. He never networked or traded one favor for another. These things would have appalled him. Had he been offered the Nobel Prize, he would have turned it down because (1) acceptance would involve going to Sweden, dressing up in a tuxedo and giving a speech, and (2) the Nobel Prize had been given to so many second-rate writers that the effort involved in

Point One far exceeded its distinction.

30. While a guest in the Stephen Spender household, he imagined that he would soon marry his host's wife, Natasha Spender.

31. He was ripely endowed with the capacities for both love and scorn, sometimes for the same thing. One reason he liked Los Angeles was that he thought it had the personality of a paper cup.

32. Near the end of his life, he consented to become the president of the Mystery Writers of America, although instead of voting for himself he had thrown out his ballot.

33. He died alone at the Scripps Clinic in La Jolla, California. Seventeen people attended the funeral. They were made up of local acquaintances who had not known him well enough to be called friends, representatives of the local MWA chapter and a fanatical collector of mystery first editions named Ned Guymon.

34. He invented a first-person voice remarkable for its sharpness and accuracy of observation, its attention to musical cadence, purity of syntax and unobtrusive rightness of word order, a metaphorical richness often consciously self-parodic, its finely adjusted speed of movement, sureness of touch and its capacity to remain internally consistent and true to itself over a great emotional range. This voice proved to be unimaginably influential during his lifetime and continues to be so now. Real earned authority sometimes has that effect. (While drinking himself to death in the year of Chandler's own death, 1959, the tenor saxophonist Lester Young could look out of his window at the Alvin Hotel to observe the progress of his numerous clones down Broadway to Birdland, where, unlike him, they had gigs. Young said to a friend, "The other ladies, my imitators, are making the money!")

35. None of his imitators, not even the most accomplished, ever came close to surpassing or even matching him.

36. He wrote his English agent, Helga Green, that "to accept a mediocre form and make literature out of it is something of an accomplishment. . . . We are not always nice people, but essentially we have an ideal that transcends ourselves."

37. Chandler devoted his working life to the demonstration of a principle that should be obvious, that genre writing declares itself first as writing and only secondarily as generic. Because this principle was not always obvious even to himself, he felt defensive about being a mystery writer.

38. He wrote an English girlfriend that "my wife and I just seemed to melt into each other's hearts without the need of words."

39. "The things that last . . . come from deeper levels of a writer's being, and the particular form used to frame them has very little to do with their value," he wrote Helga Green.

40. He got better as he went along. Every writer presently alive wishes to do the same.

41. Okay. *Playback,* his last book, really was pretty bad. On the other hand, after it he began a book in which Palm Springs was renamed "Poodle Springs."

42. He once described his character as "an unbecoming mixture of outer diffidence and inward arrogance."

43. He wrote Helga Green's father, Maurice Guinness, that ". . . when a writer writes a book, he takes nothing from anyone. He adds to what exists. . . . There is never enough good writing to go around."

44. He never complained about his endless torment.

45. Writing to Lucky Luciano in preparation for an interview never published, he said, "I suppose we are both sinners in the sight of the Lord."

Ezra Pound. Circa 1909. Courtesy New Directions Publishing Corporation.

Ezra Pound:
A Seereeyus Precursor
Paul Metcalf

OVER THE LONG RANGE of Ezra Pound's productive years, his language and concerns evolved:

> And then went down to the ship,
> Set keel to breakers, forth on the godly sea, and
> We set up mast and sail on the swart ship . . .

From these Homeric opening lines of the *Cantos,* he carries us through the Confucian Odes and into the modern age:

> Disney against the metaphysicals

The language of Hart Crane — another Significant Precursor — is similarly filled with what we now call archaisms: "thee" and "thou," "doth" and "dost." Nevertheless, though similarly constrained in language, he broke an opening into the modern world:

> Dream cancels dream in this new world of fact
> From which we wake in the dream of act . . .

(In my first book, *Will West,* published in 1956, I used traditional English spellings: "centre," "theatre." In the new edition, in my *Collected Works* (1996), these have been brought up to date.)

As Pound's horizons expanded, it became apparent that in his conception of the poem, and subject only to the poem's own internal discipline, *anything* might be included. Anything. This is the most significant lesson that I learned from Ezra Pound — a lesson learned when I was young, struggling to find my way, a lesson I was unable to use for many years — but a lesson learned.

More and more as the *Cantos* progressed, Pound pulled apart the curtain of the "creative" and quoted directly from sources.

Paul Metcalf

> And 600 more dead at Quemoy —
> they call it political.

— and there were, of course, the diatribes against usury, Buddhists and Jews. How does one deal with these? In a late-life interview with Allen Ginsberg, Pound apologized. Leonardo da Vinci, a life-long atheist, is said to have accepted Christianity on his deathbed. To which set of words do we give credence? Those spoken in the fullness of maturity, or those that came near the end of life? This is a question that each individual must contemplate for him or herself.

In all of this Pound is refuting the notion that history is boring . . . the facts we had to learn in school . . . whereas fiction is the wonderful world of "the imagination." This is the Land-of-Oz illusion, and one forgets that the Wizard turned out to be a fraud, and all Dorothy wanted, throughout the book, was to get back to the grubby little farm in Kansas.

Still another lesson I picked up from Pound was his insistence on the specific, the particular. "Go in fear of abstractions," sez Ez.

*

At one point Pound referred to himself as "a seereeyus kerakter." He was, above all, a man of action. When he and William Carlos Williams were students at the University of Pennsylvania they took up fencing. Williams realized one day, this man is serious — he means to kill me!

From one of Pound's troubadour poems:

> I have no life save when the swords clash.

A philosopher named Horace Rackham wrote: ". . . the life of Action has no absolute value: it is not a part of, but only a means to, the End, which is the life of Thought." Pound read this and made a marginal comment: *"Nuts."*

In a letter to a friend: "Why the hell don't you have a bit of real fun before you get tucked under?"

I never entertained Pound's notion that by bringing ideas into the realm of politics, the course of history might be changed. I never, as Pound did, tried to get the ear of FDR. I never suffered, as Pound did, political failures. For me, going into action has meant cutting firewood. For Pound, it meant pounding the political typewriter: "I am held up, enraged by the delay needed to change the typing ribbon . . ."

His vision of misery:

> No more do my shaftes fly
> To slay. Nothing is now clean slayne
> But rotteth away.

*

For all that he engorged European and Asiatic cultures, he was quintessentially American:

> . . . for us, I mean
> Who bear the brunt of our America
> And try to wrench her impulse into art . . .

And always the pedant. His historical references are allusive, his intention being to drive the reader back to original sources. "If we never write anything save what is already understood, the field of under(s)tanding will never be expanded."

*

What would Pound and Melville have made of each other? (Their lives overlapped by a few years.) There is evidence that Pound thought Melville overblown. When Charles Olson published *Call Me Ishmael*, Pound, at Olson's instigation, wrote to Eliot suggesting that Faber & Faber bring out an English edition. "It's a labor-saving device. You don't have to read Melville."

To an extent, their lives followed similar courses, leading to late-life despair:

Pound: "Tho' my errors and wrecks lie about me."

Melville: "With wrecks in a garret I'm stranded . . ."

*

I share Pound's skepticism about formal religion. My wife and I lived for many years in the hills of western North Carolina, and to reach our house, in a somewhat remote area, we drove along Concord Road. A ramshackle country church, with outhouse, came into view at a bend in the road, and I often thought of Pound's line, from the *Cantos:*

105

Shit and religion stinking in concord.

*

At times old Ez could come off his perch, be wonderfully civilized:

It rests me to converse with beautiful women,
Even though we talk nothing but nonsense . . .

And civilized, too, in responding to his place in nature: ". . . the humane man has amity with the hills . . ." And the hills around Pisa were "the breasts of Helen."

Did he see these hills from the iron cage in which he was imprisoned?

*

William Carlos Williams on Ezra Pound:
"He doesn't know a damn thing about China . . . That's what makes him an expert. He knows nothing about music, being tone deaf. That's what makes him a musician . . . And he's batty in the head. That's what makes him a philosopher."
". . . not one person in a thousand likes him, and a great many people detest him . . ."
And yet . . . and yet:
"It's the best damned ear ever born to listen to this language."
Ah, it is that magnificent ear of his! When I read through the *Cantos*, when the content becomes dense and obscure, unintelligible, I read on, let the impeccable speech rhythms carry me through, until the light filters up — which it always does.
Pound:
"It is mainly for the sake of the melopoeia that one investigates troubadour poetry."

*

Late in life: "I will never learn discretion."
He is often linked with T.S. Eliot, but in some ways he makes more sense in company with Henry Ford and W.C. Fields.
Perhaps he's a cross between Dante Alighieri and Rush Limbaugh.
But I learned from him. I learned.

On Lillian Hellman
Ellen McLaughlin

I WAS FIFTEEN when I first read *Pentimento* and *An Unfinished Woman* and fell in love with the Lillian Hellman Lillian Hellman made up for us — that hard-bitten, no-nonsense, tough-talking dame, incandescent with anger and helpless candor. I was pleased to read the books, because, try though I did, I could never work up much enthusiasm for her plays, which still seem wooden, ideologically simplistic and, most importantly, not much fun to act, because the characters lack any psychological complexity. I suspected at the time that I'd end up being not just a writer but a playwright and there weren't many female playwrights to study when I was growing up. It boiled down to Hellman and Hansbury and, in a pinch, Shelagh Delaney. So I read the books with interest and relief. There is much to admire in the Hellman of the memoirs, her careless nobility and hectic bravery, her keen-eyed assessment of the whole rotten world. She is unsentimental about those she loves and charmingly self-denigrating to just the right degree — never veering too far toward either coyness or self-flagellation. At least I thought so then, back in the early seventies, when I was searching high and low for a female voice with pith and grit and passion.

Last week I got both books out of the library (I was shocked to realize that those books, which caused such a stir and were best-sellers in the 1970s, were out of print in the 1990s) and reread them for the first time since I was a teenager, but not before remembering and writing down the images that had stuck with me (a remarkably large number) since 1973.

One from *An Unfinished Woman* strikes me in particular: It is a description of Hellman sailing toward a dock, upon which stands Hammett, white haired, wearing a white shirt and white pants. She thinks: That's the handsomest sight I've ever seen. She drops the sheet and the sail billows. I remembered her description of him as being "like a knife thrown into the dock, glinting in the setting sun," and was so sure of that image as being Hellman's that, years later when something similar came up in my own work, I excised it, "remembering" the Hellman. Here's how the passage actually goes:

> I was returning from the mainland in a catboat filled with marketing and Hammett had come down to the dock to tie me up. He had been sick that summer — the first of the sicknesses — and he was even thinner than usual. The white hair, the white pants, the white shirt made a straight, flat surface in the late sun. I thought: Maybe that's the handsomest sight I ever saw, that line of a man, the knife for a nose, and the sheet went out of my hand and the wind went out of the sail. Hammett laughed as I struggled to get back the sail. I don't know why, but I yelled angrily, "So you're a Dostoevsky sinner-saint. So you are." The laughter stopped, and when I finally came in to the dock we didn't speak as we carried up the packages and didn't speak through dinner.
>
> Later that night, he said, "What did you say that for? What does it mean?"
>
> I said I didn't know why I had said it and I didn't know what it meant.
>
> Years later, when his life had changed, I did know what I had meant that day: I had seen the sinner — whatever is a sinner — and sensed the change before it came. When I told him that, Hammett said he didn't know what I was talking about, it was all too religious for him.

Well, I'm with Hammett about the Dostoevsky, but the description of the sight of him and how it causes her to drop the line is quite fine stuff, I still think. Most importantly, it has the feel of a true recollection, as the shouted reference to Dostoevsky and the implied hours of subsequent silence just do not. Perhaps she felt it was important to wrest the narrative away from the woozily romantic and remind us that, after all, this was a relationship between intellectual equals, writers, who might plausibly call references to Russian authors across the water to each other and spend an evening ruminating upon such things. But then of course my attitude toward the memoirs is different than it was when I was reading them as a teenager. Now it is safe to say that large portions of the memoirs, specifically and particularly the "Julia" section, are wholesale fabrications posing as fact. (The "Julia" section in *Pentimento* was Hellman's description of what is in retrospect a hilariously complicated money-smuggling gambit supposedly performed in 1937 for a beloved and suspiciously perfect friend —

Lillian Hellman. Circa 1941. The Granger Collection, New York.

played by Vanessa Redgrave in the subsequent movie.) The deeply unfortunate thing about the exposure of Hellman's lapses into fabrication is that it casts into doubt every sentence of the memoirs, or, to borrow Mary McCarthy's famous hyperbolic statement: "every word, including 'and' and 'the.'" And there are many fine passages in the books. Much of it is gloriously lean prose in which the voice is far more unforced and authentic than it is for any of the dialogue in her plays. The memoir voice might be said to be her finest creation — assured and vital and steeped in the barroom rigor and laconic irony of her day. But now you can't read any of it without smirking a bit, and that is a shame. I don't believe her anymore. And when a writer loses the trust of her readers, she is in a sorry state indeed, no matter how tough and taut she talks.

The other passage I remembered vividly from the memoirs was the memory about the spectacularly successful opening night for *The Children's Hour* on Broadway: Hammett is out in Hollywood and she calls him, very drunk, at some point during the night. A woman answers the phone and says that she is Mr. Hammett's secretary and can she take a message? Later, Hellman wakes up with a stupendous hangover, does the math on the phone call to Hollywood and realizes that she called at 3:00 A.M. California time and that the phone must have been answered by some chippie Hammett was seeing. Thereupon, Hellman hies herself out to the airport, takes a plane to L.A., goes to Hammett's house, smashes the soda fountain he is fond of in the basement of his house and, having seen no one, neither chippie nor Hammett, she immediately goes back to the airport and heads home to New York that very night. The memoir is remarkably similar to this in all important details. I suppose the reason I remembered this was that I was at an age when I was interested to know how a woman of spirit might handle jealousy and humiliation — emotions that I was right to assume were coming my way at about the speed of an oncoming freight train with every waking second of adolescence. The incident thrilled me as an example of a sublimely vengeful fantasy that, amazingly, didn't end the relationship with the extraordinary Hammett, who, one is led to believe, admired Hellman's spunk rather than eschewing her (and who could have blamed him?) as a seriously deranged harpy with too much time on her hands. Back in the days when looking for lies in the Hellman memoirs became a popular and tremendously rewarding sport among the literati, this story was also challenged, just on the basis of logic. Hellman asks us to believe that she flew all the way across the country, went to Hammett's house and, what? broke in? found a, what? sledgehammer? smashed the bar, brushed the glass from her dress, turned on her heel and, what? called a taxi? and went back to the airport to catch a, what? red-eye? (which didn't exist) back to New York? Uh huh. And why on earth would a woman answer Hammett's phone at 3:00 A.M. anyway, much less think that she could "cover" at that hour by pronouncing herself a secretary? The whole thing, like so much of the memoirs, falls to pieces if you think about it for two minutes, yet there was hardly a murmur of skepticism when it first appeared, which says much for the force of Hellman's prose.

But, you see, it's too bad. Because I rather liked that story. It was important to me, a somewhat timid girl who tended to keep her mouth shut about the wounding things done to her by men. I needed to hear about an unattractive writer who, nearly forty years earlier, had risked a relationship (and how) by punishing a desirable and powerful man for betraying her. And here I must admit that I really wish Lillian Hellman *had* smuggled money through Nazi lines to the Resistance in a big fur hat. Because if Lillian Hellman could do it, it gave me hope that someone as ordinary and flawed as I might be able to do such a thing, might have the courage to do something risky for people she would never meet, in the name of a principle and for the love of a friend.

I remember distinctly the frisson of shame I felt when the Julia story was uncovered as a lie. This had partly to do with the disorientation of having believed a fiction to be the truth, and certainly I was upset to learn about the dishonesty of a writer I had looked upon as a worthy role model. But there was more going on in the horror I felt than mere confusion and disappointment — what I felt was the awful guilt of recognition and relief when one thinks: that could have been me. I felt the shame of liars everywhere when one of our league is unmasked. Because I am a liar too. Oh, the stories I have told and retold about "my life" that have all the suspect smoothness and satisfying roundness of polished stones handled too many times to be trustworthy objects. For me, the worst of it was that she lied as only a woman would feel a need to lie — she kept putting herself in an effective and central position in relationship to events she was, in fact, powerless to be a real part of, precisely because she was a woman. For instance, she describes herself as being under bombardment in her fleeting visit to Spain during the civil war and heroically making her way through such fire to tape a radio broadcast one evening, when there is historical record of neither the bombardment she describes nor the broadcast. (Incidentally, her brave sojourn across town to the radio station provokes no less a personage than Hemingway himself to say to her, as he certainly did not, "So you have *cohones* after all.") It's embarrassing. But I'm not so different from Hellman in my desire for a nobler life story in which I play less of a supporting role and in which I've led a less equivocal and passive existence. Perhaps this is the nature of the writer's life, which is only possible because of a kind of quietude and stability which does not, in general, make for thrilling memoirs. Perhaps, too, there is a terrible secret here about what it is to be a certain kind of woman. The kinship I felt with Hellman when I first read her is all the more apparent to me now after her painfully compromised last years.

When I first read her work I could not have anticipated the ways in which our lives would differ and what we would ultimately have in common. I did end up becoming a playwright, though I am not nearly so famous as she was, nor am I likely to be. My politics have remained, like hers, distinctly leftist and, like hers, rather muddied by a lack of discipline of mind and an overly emotional and moralistic means of making sense of the world. We, both of us, tend to like clean edges, good guys and bad guys. For me, I believe this has to do with a fairly cool assessment of where my talents lie and a desire to use my reading time accordingly. For her, I suspect her political failings have more to do with an intolerance for nuance and mystery where morality is concerned. We have neither of us made the mark on the world that we would have liked, in our overwrought dreams of moral justice, to have made, although she was certainly more of an effectively political animal than I have ever been. Though *Scoundrel Time,* her dubious "memoir" of the McCarthy era, is marred by a scattershot viciousness, questionable chronology and her usual self-aggrandizement, the letter she wrote to the House Un-American Activities Committee on the eve of her hearing is her most widely quoted piece of work and probably the best writing she ever did. In it she managed to mine the rich vein of American political oratory, veering between the cannily colloquial "I do not wish to bring bad trouble onto other people" and the bluntly modest zinger "I will not cut my conscience to fit this year's fashion." She was lucky.

Her fame protected her as much as it provided a means for her voice to dominate the proceedings that afternoon. Others in that era risked more, lost more and had to back up their beliefs with jail time, but here was a singular instance in which Hellman's skills as a writer and her particular brand of stylized bravery were precisely what were needed and at last and for once there was a moment when she stood in the center of an event. I can't imagine that anything else, the great success of her plays and her books included, could have ever come close to the triumph of that moment in her professional life.

She and I are both childless women and perhaps it is because of that that we both have taken friendship seriously and have written about it as a central experience in our lives. The "Julia" story is, finally, a compelling and moving account of a woman she would like to have been and a woman she would like to have known and been loved by.

Much as I'd like to, I can't turn away from Lillian Hellman any more than I can turn away from the girl I was at fifteen and what I needed in a heroine. She served that purpose remarkably well and is still something of a spur to me now. I like her passion, her dedication to craft, her fierce independence and prickly nature. If she was only half as brave and difficult as she says she was, she was quite something, and she is still a force to be reckoned with. I will always like her for having responded to being called "one of America's foremost female playwrights" by saying, "I am a playwright. You wouldn't refer to Eugene O'Neill as one of America's foremost *male* playwrights." For all her dislike of most women, and her incessant use of "lady" as a pejorative term in her memoirs, she was a feminist of a sort and there were few enough in my childhood that she mattered deeply to me. Hellman is my colleague and my forebear. Her reasons for writing are not so different from my own, nor are the mistakes she makes as she puts her plays together. Her reasons for loving her friends and lovers are like my own and her reasons for lying are mine as well. I know her better than I would care to admit. And though she would certainly not have liked me, she would have recognized me. It is women and writers like us who will make the women writers who come after us cannier, wiser and stronger. They will look upon us and say, that is where I do not need to go again, that has been done, those mistakes, those triumphs are past. Let me seek a different ground.

113

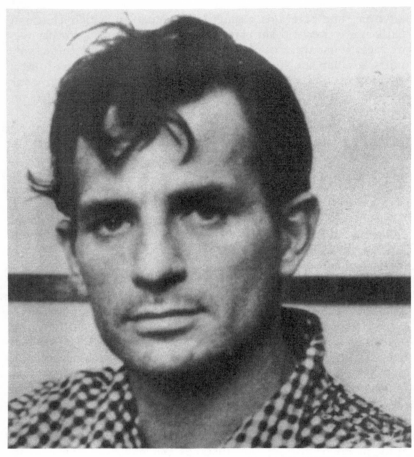

Jack Kerouac. Circa 1958. UPI/Corbiss-Bettman.

Language, Voice, Beat, Energy in the Poetry: Jack Kerouac

Anne *Waldman*

— *Dedicated to the memory of Allen Ginsberg*

WHAT SPOKE TO ME initially reading *Mexico City Blues* was passionate cry & heartbreak, sensitive, goofy, energetic lines popping open, antennae raw & in the wind, and the constantly shifting exchange of earth & sky. Down to earth, down to his own rhythm, then out with the spin of an infinite mind riff. And up, way up, to revelation like "The Victor is not Self" or "(ripping of paper indicates/ helplessness anyway)" or "We die with same/ unconcern we lie." Philosophical. And *stoned*. And details. And naming things. And naming people. And naming heroes, writers, musicians, Buddhist saints & Boddhisattvas & deities. So *everybody's included*. People's names are pure sound & sacred because they exist & are therefore holy. It's like the "sacred conversation" you see in Italian Paintings where all the saints are smiling beatifically and conversing in gentle tones on profound subjects. Nothing's excluded, and yet *Mexico City Blues* is a very discriminating sequential poem. It has an amazing clarity, honesty, aspiration. Nothing is unnecessary inside it. And friendly, too. A real experiment in original mind living in conditioned mind wanting to "blow" free. Pop through on other side which is sound, energy, shape on page of ear & eye. If you can't sustain the images, if you don't "get" his *logopoeia* right off, try staying with the sound and the persona and sheer energy. I also appreciate in here the idea of choruses. Reminiscent of Gertrude Stein's *Four Saints*. One thinks of angels & saints singing, choirs of kids in church, of resounding classical pieces singing out the sufferings of Christ or man. And in a particular vernacular mode. And the exhilaration too of salvation, redemption, life, life, life! It's always pounding like that. See, I'm *alive* I'm *thinking!* And everything around me has got life too. And these are sounds also made in heaven. *And I write because it's*

115

all fleeting & we're all going to die & my poetic duty is to make this experiment holy. This is certainly the sense you get when you hear Kerouac's voice reading aloud on the discs & tapes.

> Punk! says Iron Pot Lid
> Tup! says finger toilet
> Tuck! says dime on Ice
> Ferwutl says Beard Bird.

And improvising on a thought, a word, an increment of a word, a phone or phoneme and responding. So fast. A "perfect explication of mind" said the Tibetan meditation teacher Chogyam Trungpa after Allen Ginsberg read parts of the poem to him. Allen & I named a poetics school after Jack Kerouac at the Buddhist-inspired Naropa Institute in Colorado because he had the most spontaneously lucid sound. And he'd also realized the first Buddhist Noble Truth which is the Truth of Suffering. It wafts through all his work: deep pain & empathy. Sometimes it's as if he's just whistling in the dark in *Mexico City Blues.* And so *hip* for a quasi-white guy. And mixed-breed American being interesting ethnic Quebecois origin, and macho even, but a secret scaredy cat. But this funny Buddhist twist keeps coming around into everything. Because, I think, he was always thinking, following his mind, checking things out & reading sacred scripture (see his explicit massive journal/ poetics collage *Some of the Dharma,* Penguin 1997) which are subtle & spontaneous & illuminating insights into the very nature of mind. So what you have is the literal *practice* inherent in his mind-work. Each chorus is an examination & delight in language-mind.

> Starspangled Kingdoms bedecked
>   in dewy joint
> DON'T IGNORE OTHER PARTS
>   OF YOUR MIND, I think,
> And my clever brain sends
>   ripples of amusement
> Through my leg nerve halls
>
> And I remember the Zigzag
>   Original
>   Mind

of Babyhood
when you'd let the faces
crack & mock
& yak & change
& go mad utterly
in your night
firstmind
reveries
talking about the mind

The endless Not Invisible
Madness Rioting
Everywhere
— from "17th Chorus"

You've got here a "mental" sound as in

A bubble pop, a foam snit
Time on a Bat — growl of truck.

which also has terrific consonant mantra properties.

The glories of simultaneity explode all over the text. How can Lester Young in eternity, Cleopatra's knot, Rabelais, Marco Polo & his Venetian genitals, Charlie Chaplin, Joe McCarthy, Charlie Parker, various friends & family, and Buddha co-exist? *They do so in the mind of the poet.*

What I appreciated as a young teen girl growing up on MacDougal Street in Manhattan's West Village was this poem's particular accessibility. Its obvious relationship to jazz, to Dharma (I was seriously starting to read Buddhist texts at my Quaker high school Friends Seminary), to smoking pot (a hot experience & topic at the time). And how it was delineated by small notebook page. Perfect form/content marriage. I was writing shapely (goofy?) poems which had a look of e.e. cummings. But I wanted to be as romantic as Keats and Yeats with the cosmic consciousness of Whitman. These very tangible "Beat" literary poets were now walking my streets (Gregory Corso — quintessential *poète maudit* — lived just several blocks away on Bleecker Street), alive & in the world I too inhabited doing things I was doing. My friend Martin Hersey, son of the novelist John Hersey, was wandering around with a well-worn copy of *Naked Lunch* in his guitar case. I travelled to Greece & Egypt by the time I was 18, hitching around, sleeping on freighter-boats. 20 years old I caught a ride to the West Coast to the Berkeley Poetry Conference and then Lewis Warsh & I hitched to Mexico under false IDs (being underage) later that summer after founding our magazine *Angel Hair* at a Robert Duncan reading. One thinks of *influence*. The work? The life? I took a vow at Berkeley to dedicate my life to poetry & the sangha (spiritual community) of poets.

Kerouac was in stride poetically with many of the writers — the consociates — of his own time, not just his particular buddies. Certainly his companions were conducting some extremely outrageous experiments themselves. Burroughs's jump cuts, Ginsberg's cosmic adjectives — wanting to get all the details in — Gregory Corso's subtle autodidactic troubadour finesse, Gary Snyder's Buddhist thinking & content. And the idea of capturing the sound of the physical world (like Gertrude Stein wanting to get the rhythms of her dog lapping milk). Synesthesia. Kinesthesia. Mix of senses. A saw, a hammer — rip rap. But think, also, of Frank O'Hara's poetics statement "Personism," as a comparable poetics. The poem as a phone call. Think of endless rapping with Friends. How he wanted to get Neal Cassady's vocal rhythms down, Lucian Carr's etc. And also a jaunty persona as in Frank O'Hara poems, who also names his world. Places, people, things. Duncan & Olson's composition by field. Projective verse. Even Williams's "No ideas but in things." All this was in the air. And the example of Gertrude Stein (mentioned in *Mexico City Blues*) who also followed the *grammar of her own mind*.

Technically, aside from the phenomenal legacy of the prose, we have Poems as Poems — *San Francisco Blues, Mexico City Blues, Book of Haikus, Poems All Sizes*. The poems *as* poems. That look feel are defined as such. Pome: *If I don't use the cork/ I may spill the wine/ But if I do?* The insistent pitch of the blues poems.

> Mexico City Bop
> I got the huck bop
> I got the floogle mock
> I got the thiri chiribim
>   bitchy bitchy bitchy
>   batch batch
> Chippely bop
>   Noise like that
>   Like fallin off porches

Of Tenement Petersburg
Russia Chicago O Yay.

*

Mr Beggar & Mrs Davy —
Looney and CRUNEY,
I made a poem out of it,
Haven't smoked Luney
   & Cruney
In a Long Time.

Dem egges & dem dem
Dere bacons, baby,
If you only lay that
   down on a trumpet
   'Lay that down
     solid brother

'Bout all dem
   bacon & eggs
Ya gotta be able
   to lay it down
    solid —
All that luney
    & fruney

As an active reader of classic novels, I always identified with the (mostly male) protagonists. I've talked to other women writers of my generation about this. Yes, we went with the hero. We were classic "puer" types — wanting the picaresque freedom the youths had. A kind of artistic bisexuality? You could say something about Kerouac's stance as American male born 1922 in his life & in his novels & how that tugged on the particular heartstrings of understanding (maternal) women, the fruition of his generation's identity problems around being soldiers (warriors) & all the attendant strands of his karmic stream adding up to the solid man, poet, writer, battling the expectation of whatever that could be in some eyes. Heroic? Certainly. So that was a lure. And he looked like a movie star! Normal, athletic, well built, handsome, smart. And from such & such a family that he loved so deeply, loyally, the underdog class thing had sentimental appeal. His language was Quebecois & working Massachusetts, and all the types & personalities around him fed that sound. But don't forget he devoured literature,

119

he was a true intellectual, thinking, thinking. He was extremely well read as an early letter to Elbert Lenrow (see *Kerouac's Selected Letters, 1940–1956*, edited by Ann Charters, Penguin, 1995) indicates. Also the dominant *outrider* culture of the time: black jazz, scat singing. He was empathetic, symbiotic. But more than that Kerouac came through as a witness, a cosmic common denominator, one who would take the whole ride and then survive and tell you what it was like. And loving every minute of the telling. Propelled by an unnatural gift & original poetic idea to follow the grammar of his own mind & minds of others, a son of Gertrude Stein! Like the Tibetan "delog" who dies, travels & comes back to life to tell you what he or she "saw." The shaman's or poet's call & duty. Because he took a lot "on," Kerouac did.

He loved "scatting." With a nod toward black improvisational music, he made amateur recordings of himself scatting with Neal Cassady & John Clellon Holmes. Holmes had a record-making machine where you could record your voice directly onto vinyl. He wrote his improvisations down as "Blues." He read poems to Frank Sinatra crooning on the radio. He was drawn to this form for a number of reasons — he liked the spontaneous approach. He intended these blues poems to be heard, preferably with a jazz background, and made recordings for Verve & Hanover in 1958 & 1959. He performed with Zoot Sims & Al Cohn on one recording, with Steve Allen at piano on another. These now seem remarkable & unique auditory adventures. I could feel my own yearning toward performance (mixing poetry and music) back then. Composer/ musician David Amram who worked with Kerouac & Allen Ginsberg, others, became a close friend in 1962 (I was still in high school) & he'd take me around to some of the clubs. I met painter Larry Rivers at the Five Spot, another hipster linked to the poets. My former sister-in-law married Steve Lacy & I used to see Thelonious Monk at their loft. My mother was a nut for Mingus & Lacy. We listened to their music.

In "The Origins of Joy in Poetry" Kerouac conjures the new Zen-Lunacy. He speaks of the ORAL, of the exciting new poets like Lamantia and Whalen: They SING They SWING. "It is diametrically opposed to the Eliot shot, who so dismally advises his dreary negative rules like the objective correlative, etc. which is just a lot of constipation and ultimately emasculation of the pure masculine urge to freely sing."

He speaks of the "mental discipline typified by the haiku . . . , that is, the discipline of pointing things out directly, purely, concretely, no abstractions or explanations, wham wham the true blue song of man."

So his poetics so sensible in my own sensibility are clear and traceable in his letters, exchanges, explications, responses. You only have to read him aloud to get the brilliant oral torque & command. Although I never met the man he was everywhere in my immediate surroundings, and still haunts the premises, a holy ghost.

Edith Wharton. 1905. The Granger Collection, New York.

Edith Wharton:
A Mole in the House of the Modern
Lynne Tillman

EDITH WHARTON'S PASSION for architecture was foundational, evidenced by her very first book, *The Decoration of Houses*, a nonfiction. Wharton disdained the merely decorative in rooms and buildings, she disdained it in her fiction. Her writing is severe, deliberate in its attacks and restraints, and lives in every detail and in the structure. Wharton's novels and stories move from small moments to big ones (she manages to merge the two), from openness of opportunity and hope to inhibition and tragic limitation, from life's transitory pleasures and possibilities to its dull and sharp pains and immobilizations. Traps and entrapment, psychological and societal, life's dead ends become the anxious terminals for Wharton's literary search for freedom and pleasure. In her book, pleasure is freedom's affect.

The architect Wharton is always conscious of the larger structure, with her meaning central in each scene. She meticulously furnishes a room, so that all the pieces and lines in it function as emotional or psychological props, conditions or obstacles. Like cages or containers, her interiors keep characters in a place, often an internalized place. They enter rooms, meet, sit, talk, then Wharton lets them find the walls, the limits. She observes them in houses or on the street in chance meetings, and they fix each other — the gaze is her métier — to a moment in time, a truth (about the other or themselves), to a seat in the social theater. Everything that happens happens with effect, building her edifice.

Wharton selected her words with a scalpel, as if with or without them her patient would live, die; she was precise in her renderings, otherwise the construction might fall, and other such metaphors. Her writing isn't ever labored, though. Yet nothing's simple, or simply an object, and never just an ornament. The ornament is redolent and may even be causal.

Think of "The Bunner Sisters," the poor women whose fate hung on the repair of a timepiece. A twisted tale, but then Wharton is perverse, and sophisticated and surprising in her perverseness. Her version of the exchange of women among men might be "The Other Two." Mr. Waythorn meets, not by choice, his bride's two former husbands, men he didn't really know about but who are now in his life (have been in his wife), and whose existence confounds his sense of right, order, possession. At the story's end, Waythorn arrives home and finds the other two there. His wife, charming, composed, serves them tea. "She dropped into her low chair by the tea table, and the two visitors, as if drawn by her smile, advanced to receive the cups she held out. She glanced about for Waythorn, and he took the third cup with a laugh." End of story. She's in a lowly position, a vessel, the third cup, but he's the third cup too. If who he is is what he possesses, the joke's on him. He grasps that.

Wharton's stately, measured rhythms let the reader linger over a sentence, then move along, languidly. One may be stopped dead by some piece of psychological astuteness, a blunt idea, by brutal clarity, or staggered by an almost excessive, because perfect, image. Slowly, Wharton draws beautiful portraits, deceptive pictures. (I sometimes wonder if Wharton ever felt rushed by anything, then I remember Morton Fullerton and her love letters to him, that rush late in her life.) Beautiful language serves — like tea, an elegant service — ironic and difficult ends. It lures one into a network of sinister complications and, transformed, beauty leads to dreariness and viciousness. The reader will be torn by the loss of that plenitude, by failure, by hopelessness.

But Wharton is economical about elegance, stringent about lushness, display, every embellishment. Never extravagant. Maybe it's because she understood position and space, knew she didn't really have much room, no room for profligacy. She couldn't run from reality, even if she wanted to (and I think she did), so she had no room to waste, certainly no words to waste. The inessential might obscure the clarity she sought. She wouldn't let herself go, let her writing go. She understood the danger, she understood any form of complicity. Her often privileged protagonists fatally conspire with society against themselves, become common prey to its dictates, helpless to disown or resist what they despise in themselves and it. Wharton was profoundly aware that, seen by others, she was free to do what she pleased, a privileged woman dangling the world on a rich string. And wrote, perhaps explained, in *The House of Mirth*, "She was so evidently the victim of the civilization which had produced her, that the links of her bracelet seemed like manacles chaining her to her fate."

Architecture articulates space, the movement within walls and without them, delineates the relationships of the built to the unbuilt and surroundings. Wharton's prose makes its own space. Her ideas were modern — she wanted to clear the house of nineteenth-century vestiges, stuffed chairs and stuffed shirts, to question conventions of all sorts, numbing traditions, but she was not a card-carrying modernist. Wharton was skeptical about the new, not positive that progress was progress, not sanguine about the future or the joys of speed and flight, as the Futurists were. She took off and looked back over her shoulder at the past. (Maybe she was presciently postmodern.) She doesn't fit comfortably into the modernist canon.

It's one of those uncanny pieces of fate — less colloquially, historical overdetermination — that her reputation, her literary place, is inflected not just by her idiosyncratic relationship to modernism but also by three biographical facts: she was female, upper class and Henry James's younger friend. Not mentioning James in relation to her is not mentioning the naked emperor in the room which she did not design. Her critical reputation stands mostly in his large shadow. (Her primary biographer R.W.B. Lewis's first sentence in his introduction to *The House of Mirth* begins "Henry James . . .") Few U.S. writers who are women make it, as the song goes, to standing in the shadows of love, critical love. The ironist Wharton might have appreciated, in her perverse way, the secondary or minor position. (Perhaps in the way Deleuze and Guattari appreciate minor literature.) Ironically, undidactically, Wharton teaches that separate isn't equal; difference shouldn't be but usually is hierarchical, and change in any establishment or tradition is, like her sentences, slow.

William Faulkner. Photograph by Martin Dain. Center for the Study of Southern Culture, University of Mississippi.

The Sound of the Fury:
Faulkner's Aerial Surf
Paul West

I.

GLADLY MYTHIC FROM HIS early days, William Faulkner became my Palladium: a mustachioed equivalent of the five-foot Barbie doll of Pallas made by Athene and kept in the citadel at Troy. On this Temple Drake of a girl with her legs squeezed tight together, and equipped with spear and distaff, the safety and well-being of Troy depended. She personified both virginity and war or, say, the military impenetrability of Troy itself. So long as Troy held on to this statue, Troy could not be taken; but, once Odysseus and Diomede, as some tales have it, had found the underground path into the citadel and seized the Palladium, Troy could be had, even if only by treachery. And it was, plundered and destroyed. My own cranky version of this myth has to do with how minimalists and their ilk, through a not so underground way, have plundered Faulkner and all he stands for, thus suburbanizing the American fiction of our time.

Such is one way of recapturing Palladian Faulkner from the days when my image of America was one of Benny Goodman, king of swing, rolled into one with Count Basie and Woody Herman. I no sooner read those Chatto and Windus pocket Faulkners in their blue and gold uniform than I was hooked, and the face of America was his, no longer that of the kings of swing. I began, I think, with *Intruder in the Dust*, an odd overture, followed by *Wild Palms* and *Old Man* in one volume, alternating, and then *The Sound and the Fury*. I must have been eighteen because *Intruder* came out in 1948, and I now wonder what a little under-financed public library in an obscure coal-mining town bang in the middle of the Sitwell Derbyshire estate was doing with a hot-off-the-press Faulkner, who, from what I knew, was nowhere nearly as well established as Hemingway, although his stature increased like my physical one over the forties, even if not in France for he had always been revered in that educated country. The name of our exotic female librarian was Joyce Bramhall. Why was she accumulating Faulkner on his own shelf (by 1948 some ten volumes)? I see her now, leggy, with slightly swollen belly in a tweed skirt, her mouth a gash of scarlet, her glasses thick and opaque as if some tart secret infected the lenses. Her nails flashed scarlet too, her stiletto heels were huge, tottery and sleek. Was she La Belle Dame sans Something? A corncob woman? On I read, born addict who had at last found a drug more potent by far than swing. Only four years later I was reading *Requiem for a Nun* in New York City, a young Hamlet (my nickname then and there) at Columbia sent to roam Manhattan because I knew too much to be in William York Tindall's elementary graduate seminar, as he himself described it.

Thanks to Faulkner, to the very thought of him, between forty and fifty I began to feel unassailable in spite of everything. I wasn't, of course, but I felt that way, enough to get on with my writing and to mop up like high-calorie gravy such praise as came my way. If you fix one eye on Faulkner and the other on Melville, and you remember some of what Keats said about negative capability, you can just about manage to commit the delectable autonomy known as writing for its own sake — for the glory, the rebirth, the illusion of doing what nobody has ever done before. There's nothing more unassailable than that, even as things fall apart around you and you see the fruitflies ascending to power without composing so much as a paragraph. Vary the image a bit, amassing the bestiary of the foul, and you can add Zola's toad of disgust, which he said you have to swallow every morning before getting on with the work. Swallow it, note the hegemony of the fruitflies, and indeed the demise of yet another noble unicorn gone to roost in Paris or now plying trade on Wall Street, and you then become clear enough to write for the next few hours as if the world were waiting for your sun to rise and would do nothing serious without you. That's the feeling, the pumped-up, inspired elation that lofts you — me — from novel to novel even while the tweetie-pies of Stodge College, Oxbridge cough up some dark perilous matter and plaster it into their album of envious sorrow.

II.

You get to work, maybe shaky after a hump, aching to take a dump, but you don't, you force your keister onto that hard seat among the confetti of broken glass and the after-whiff of who knows what afflatus, and begin to tap, half suspecting this is one of the last things as your imagination cocks its leg and airs its wares, muttering take it from me, folks, yair, this is just about as candid as a belated Wagner gets, they are all watching, see how the next adj comes out, tooled to dovetail with the one already lolling there in quinquireme of Nineveh.

And WF is watching.

Another one at it, he dreams, in that riproaring sing-song of the affronted lyre, storming in upon phenomena with a head whose aim has to be sublime; just get the pandemonium down and pay your tax to Milton.

WF still watching from his post office counter. Yew got sumpen axplosive there, young greenhorn, you kin git awful wounded trading such, now you git offen your high horse and wraht rich. Taint your hoss nohow.

We have all heard him, hounding us or husbanding us, saying he is the father of the tradition, even a smuggler of rum once, writing as the night fireman of someone's estate, getting scalded by the hotwater pipe in his room at the Algonquin when in town to mingle with the nobs. His music is there before the words are. He is too melismatic to be reviewed. Bless him for being ornery, for winning *second* prize in some nationwide fiction contest.

My admission includes the fact that, apart from admiring his expertise at caricatural opera, I never took much interest in Yokna-patawpha, the fantastic name apart only slightly below Brobding-nag. They might have been pinball salesmen in Ethiopia for all I cared. What bowled me over was WF's noise, that humming and thrumming you heard in the distance even as you opened just about any novel of his except the first two. It was a deliberate obfuscation of meaning yet done with meanings, using meaning to obliterate some other meaning, and the message, if such, was something choral and echoic with in its intimate hinterland just about everything else of his you'd read. He wasn't creative-writing, he was doing solo recitative, singing to himself all the while, so that while you have Gavin Stevens in focus, one word of gab to eight hundred of deviant penumbral gesture, some of the sign-language a thousand years old animal to animal, there comes out of the distance this electric whirr like an old Chickasaw cooling fan gone wrong, making more noise than a door buzzer, and it the real diapason of sounds appropriate to being construed by them in

129

situ as have ears to see. On he goes, a-droning and a-gyrating, urging us to get the rhythm of all this, this the life-pulse of the banjo full of blood.

And then you come to earth, resavoring *Pylon* only to end up with the Editors' Note: ". . . his publisher made a great many changes in Faulkner's text — shortening sentences, adjusting paragraphs, and similar alterations — often without querying the author." You blink, note that he took care of all this later, restoring his text to its original form, and turn to the opening sentence of the novel proper:

> For a full minute Jiggs stood before the window in a light spatter of last night's confetti lying against the windowbase like spent dirty foam, lightpoised on the balls of his grease-stained tennis shoes, looking at the boots. Slantshimmered by the intervening plate they sat upon their wooden pedestal in unblemished and inviolate implication of horse and spur, of the posed countrylife photographs in the magazine advertisements, beside the easelwise cardboard placard with which the town had bloomed overnight. . . .

Who could resist it? Here, I thought when I first read this page, was a man unafraid of the language, unobliged to the comma, intoxicated with the compound adjective and fired with an impressionist's, pointilliste's, rendering of light as it sped past us. He goes on in an always nostalgic mutter for how things were only seconds ago, amassing clauses like courts of miracles, polysyllabically babbling his way home: "unblemished and inviolate implication"! Just hear it, like a scholarly rebuke to the Mickey Spillanes of the world. Here was a man with an organ in his head, and his main point, vastly important, was that the verbal impasto you make from phenomena not only adds itself to the original target, but briefly wipes it out in the interest of making the world verbal. Among twentieth-century writers, only Dylan Thomas, Wallace Stevens, Joyce, Proust (remember his romp with place names), Beckett and Nabokov do it. So you cheer up. That's quite a crew, but only WF has this enduring "light spatter" that preaches the interconnectedness of things, even their occasional fusion, but also warms you up for the arrival of slightly skewed sense-data. If Cézanne's doubt, according to that most readable of philosophers Maurice Merleau-Ponty, had to do with whether the world he drew was out there or only in his head, Faulkner wonders if it isn't a divine miracle that rapturous immersions in what's there go right through it and join it. To view the world is constantly to revise it, to make it molten before letting it set hard again in a different format. If this be sorcery, he lets us in, shows us how. The opening chapter I have just mentioned bears the title "Dedication of an Airport," but *Pylon* is the dedication of a language to aerial doings, the whole composed at white heat: "Faulkner began *Pylon* in October 1934, writing so rapidly that he sent chapters to his publisher in November and December, as he typed them." Was any prose less like typewriting? More like ectoplasm. I was only four then, long years away from discovering one of my favorite novels, and there he had been, pounding it out not long before.

So Faulkner is here to tell us he is a writer of voice, not of tone, much less than Henry James occupied with hyperfine finitudes of decipherable intonation, but more his own barker, not so much a voice-over as a chorus-over of his own endlessly speculative, insinuant noise multiplied by itself many times. He is proud of his wares, reluctant ever to let them go until voluptuously plumbed, and even then, when they have been emptied out over a long haul of seismic paragraphs, unwilling to leave them alone because they have become as sea-shells, culverts of his own clamor all over again. It is one of the most effective vocal tricks in literature, akin to but utterly different from Beckett's antic cavort and the one prevailing voice yapping about voices. Faulkner drains the tune out of all his people and refurbishes it for solo rant. Djuna Barnes in *Nightwood* and Gabriel García Márquez in *Autumn of the Patriarch* tried something similar, she assigning the incessant voice to one character who blooms vocally larger than the book, he melding the voices of a community into a presumptuous vox populi, both of them intent on how a voice can overpower not only listeners but also the mere sound of the world going about its business that Beckett called "aerial surf." The highly individuated characters in Waugh, say, and James and Nabokov never do this, so we might conclude that Faulkner makes an anthropological point in spite of his societal underpinnings. Faulkner works head-on with *élan vital*, intent on the ontological significance of the constant human shout amid which a narrator's characters vie for a hearing.

Astronomers speak continually not only of those who were truly great but also of blackbody radiation, the buzz left over from the big bang, still going on like a permanent cosmic hangover, more a hiss, perhaps, or even a sharp-edged sigh: an afterbirth with some disappointment in it. You can buy CDs of it or tune it in on a radio or a TV. Faulkner, I have felt, provides a similar obbligato in his prose, forever asking us to heed the fizz of things not immediately being written about. It is as if the vital presence of phenomena in the preceding sentence or paragraph leaks over into what follows it. So there is almost a simultaneity in the background, emphasizing that things, people, voices, matter not only in their own right but also for where they have come from. Inseparability of the context is a Faulkner fetish, but who is to gainsay him? Ground is his main figure because his view of humans is processive, which is to say he views them as subject to a process such as what's now called punctuated evolution going on in and through them even as they try to think about something else. He is an ace at this. It's why his novels feel so spacious — he needs the huge counterpoint for that stifling deep Southern ethos, smaller-seeming for being monotonous. He deals in the endless proliferation of connected characteristics, and this amounts to a vision of createdness reported by a crushingly observant man.

III.

In his way, Faulkner is as much part of an *entente cordiale* as that wonderful specimen of cosmopolitan grace and diplomatic ardor, the late Pamela Harriman. On the one hand, he just about qualifies under the old seven-years-before-the-mast rubric by having worked as deckhand on a shrimp trawler, house painter, carpenter, golf pro, postmaster and even amateur handyman fixing up his own house, Rowanoak. What could be more American? He comes right out of the American vein. On the other hand, in spite of all the aw-shucks and bubba-jabber of the Mississippi cycle, he has things in common with Gide, Bernanos and Malraux (not to mention Saint-Exupéry and Chateaubriand). Perhaps this transatlantic element drew me to him, I who began by whoring after Gallic gods instead of studying Sir Walter Scott and Sir Philip Sidney and other knights and now went after American ones. People used to ask me, when I was a novelty here, before I joined, what brought me here, and one of the answers was "Faulkner," who died as I arrived to stay. "Swing" would have been an earlier answer, of course, and a somewhat later one would have been "American classical composers," almost all of them. But, because I did not go to Paris, or Rio, I came here, and a jubilant, climactic year at Columbia in the fifties gave me a taste for American life in the round. It was Gallic Faulkner, though, who like me had served with the RAF, was plane-besotted, who egged me on at a distance, luring and filling my imagination, and my first novel was a well-received but disowned pastiche of Hemingway and him.

Inasmuch as this aims to be an essay not only about Faulkner but about my own response to him, I fear I have overshot, neglecting my childhood and early teens when, without knowing of Faulkner, I showed certain tendencies comparable to his: addiction to French, to French literature, intoxication with words, a preference for the *maudit* and the *conte noir*. In a way, between ten and eighteen, I set myself up as the ideal recipient of the European in him, who had read not only his household's Dickens but someone else's Baudelaire, Verlaine and Mallarmé. He had taught himself French in order to do it and it was no surprise that the enterprising, dangerous-living French should cleave to his work as, later, they cleaved to the *nouveau roman* (first welcomed by Americans). Faulkner ended up trying to get French results from American stuff, and I think he succeeded, certainly in *Sanctuary* (though at least one critic identified in it the holy grail of American myth criticism), *The Wild Palms* and *Requiem for a Nun*. If French fiction as well as being tart, curt and solemn is also sophistical, epistemological and atavistic, then Faulkner's is often French. Myself, I kept looking, all through my so-called education, for French results from English literature, and then I suddenly found them in English in Faulkner. Whatever it may be that Baudelaire, Verlaine, Mallarmé and Camus, Malraux and Proust have in common (these last, three of my own favorites), it must be something like voluptuous cliff-hanging, a certain pagan sensuality when dealing with the absurd.

When he was teaching at the University of Virginia, 1957–8, someone in one of his seminars asked if he deliberately patterned *As I Lay Dying* after *The Scarlet Letter*. Such a question must strike a sophisticated, educated reader as gratuitous, as if literary activity itself were a great big plot. Answering, Faulkner said

> No, a writer don't have to consciously parallel because he robs and steals from everything he ever wrote or read or saw. I was simply writing a *tour de force* and, as every writer does, I took whatever I needed wherever I could find

it, without compunction, and with no sense of violating any
ethics or hurting anyone's feelings because any writer feels
that anyone after him is perfectly welcome to take any trick
he has learned or any plot that he has used.*

Of course: there is a freemasonry attaching to such things, and the
best writers steal boldly and seize the best ideas. What matters is
not that Faulkner stole or didn't, or that he sometimes pinned
chapter-synopses on the walls around him where he wrote. His
writing was part of the main, especially shall we say the English
Channel and the waters off France's western coast. To him, more
than to almost any established American novelist, writing was
impetuous and involuntary, automatic even, and the element he
worked in was cosmopolitan. So, more than thinking he sometimes
appears to speak in tongues discovered in Dickens or someone
else, we have to concede that some of his cadences, his interpola-
tions, his initiations of a rhetorical unit owe something to the
manners of the French Symbolist poets, who go so far from everyday locutions into abstruse formality, Mallarmé most of all. This
is what gives Faulkner his often remote and sometimes obtuse
style, almost as if he got in his own way. Purifying the dialect of
the tribe, they honed it into an Ur-language of the future, whereas
Faulkner appears to be conducting, say, an octet whose players
do not create counterpoint so much as something perilously close
to stasis or deadlock, whose point always seems to be that narrative, "telling," auscultating, whatever we call this act of sugges-
tively overhearing, is earned within bitter constraints, not easily
yielded up by the world from everyday happenstance to unique
rendering. That the phrase "the sound and the fury" in *Macbeth*
spoke to and for him is no accident; what he managed to set down
came from amid a shocking pandemonium in his own head fueled
by regional storytellers such as Caroline Barr. His head was full of
the usual mess that aids and abets all novelists save the hardened
minimalist who makes a fetish of drawing on the sparsest materials and so makes a career garotting earthworms.

No, Faulkner is your irresponsible sponge who chants stuff to
himself and his typewriter, not so much getting it wrong as sen-
suously apocryphalizing it until it develops that peculiar doting

---

*Essentially the same view of art and artists as we find in Malraux's *The Voices
of Silence*.

crow of his, in which or amid which more things seem to be going on than are being narrated, simply because he cranks the language up to such a polyphonic pitch you are going to be hypnotized. This is what sets him aloft, a mumbo-jumbo of the anxious heart, looping and stunting around until the impasto is thick enough (almost after Joyce, who would not let Stuart Gilbert take a page away until it was obscure enough). Faulkner is not writing magazine fiction, not often, or for demure critics. The language sucks the improvisations out of him and those improvisations drive him even deeper into the arms of language. "What happened" counts, of course, but its bizarre and unique snail track through the tidy grid of print matters much more. You eventually become accustomed to the cranky reporter who moans around you with many voices, using almost a community throat, a fat orotundity, to weave his spell with, unable to plan or scheme because the lure of fiction writing lies in the vertiginous moment in which you will not discover (uncover) what you have to have unless you hang out at the cliff-edge, staring into silence and nothing, waiting for the "event" to form itself verbally in the teeth of never having existed. It was a game he adored to play, whether working as night stoker at the university power station or clerking in a Manhattan bookstore. Imagination, he reminds us, deals in what is not there, makes it seem real; it is not a camera, but it is savagely mercurial. It will sometimes let you down just because you are too tired to whip it into a sufficient frenzy, or, more common, because you have absorbed too much of the world. Inflating his see-through Yoknapatawpha balloon, Faulkner transcended his own limits even in the act of creating them.

Above all he reminds us, in this age of reverence for the natural and the organic, how important to us the artificial is. A character in Witold Gombrowicz's *Cosmos* recoils from the ravishing superabundance of nature because he feels it will smother and engulf him, as indeed one day it will; he prefers the man-made. And that of course includes language, style, symbol, to all of which Faulkner pays homage, brittle and arbitrary and merely ingenious as they are. Savants who preach biophilia remind us how nostalgia afflicts us, making us create gardens, opt for a view of the sea or the mountains, often spending most of our lives earning the ticket to a few months of guaranteed atavism. We do not hear anything like as much about the comfort of the artificial, the man-made, from window-pane to telephone, from language to mattress, and this is a pity, at worst unrepresentative of humankind, at best absent-minded — we take so much for granted, speaking across several thousand miles without even the distracting buzz of the old days, being hurled at several hundred miles an hour from exact point to exact point at thirty thousand feet. Our technology may beset us, but it saves us from dossing down on skins in caves. Faulkner, full of boundless primitive feeling as he is, recreates the world for us in a style that proclaims its artificiality. Nobody, even in the South, talks or narrates like that, with such a profusion of Latinate words moving as naturally from his mouth as elephants' teeth, worn-out, do from theirs. Yet, to his immense credit, while his style fits congruously into a world of toothbrushes, shoes, hearing aids, bulldog clips and sunglasses, it also develops a simulacrum of energy, seeming, no matter how artificial, to have an urge, an impetus, a crescendo akin to that of the planet itself — because his mind is always switched on, pounding, shoving (hardly ever the case with that mauve lyricist Hemingway). Hypothesis dogs *aperçu* in Faulkner, often rising to the level of what I would call internal combustion. He sweeps us along, omitting neither detail nor transcendent vision, until we almost undergo the illusion of being in the hands of a Creator who accurately mimics the habits of a bigger one, spewing the majestic around him in sheer exuberance. He is often at play in the fields of the deity, who owns them.

IV.

I have left to the end one other element, perhaps the key one in his writing: rhythm, by which I intend not merely the patterned interruption of a blank but also something improvisatory, shifting us from the familiar pleasures of iambic pentameter within a stanza, say, to an open-ended parabola made of words, lifting us beyond everyday discernment toward unpredictable recognitions made of iambs but incapable of exact decipherment — De Quincey's enigmatic *involute*, perhaps. From register to register you find yourself deliciously slung until you experience something ineffable but precise, far from the usual fodder of fiction, but not far from Bach or Hindemith, say, and sometimes felt in the work of Beckett, Joyce, Proust, Woolf and Barnes. It is not a matter of something divine's being vouchsafed, adumbrated, whatever the word might be; it's a matter of something exceptionally human, so vibrant and mysterious it seems to have come from a region not our own. We have to be careful about such artistic intervals, remembering how Aaron Copland's *Appalachian Spring,* almost seeming to have tapped the mind of God in a trance of exquisite rhapsody, was composed in a concrete blockhouse on a Hollywood studio lot. We must be careful not to delude ourselves; the miracle is that we are able to feel and respond to such things at all — ecstasy with the deity snipped off. This pagan divinity stalks all through Faulkner sustained by sometimes long sentences that seem to have come into being as rhythmic abstractions, imperious and final, into which some kinds of words have to be put. Which means, of course, that the vital thing here is the ongoingness of rhythm, its perpetual energy and the peculiar sense it evinces of dictating rhythms to come, several sentences away, which when they arrive feel like inevitable culminations, working on us like Gene Krupa in *Sing, Sing, Sing,* say, even as the words tell us what else is going on. In this sense, I suggest, Faulkner's best work is a model of the world: not a transcript or a photograph, but a working model of Creation, to be construed not as tract or fable but as expressive energy.

I am not enough of a philosopher to embark on theory of the model, certainly not in the wake of announcements that theoretical physicists, in their efforts to explain a huge burst of gamma rays at least two billion light years from Earth, came up with more than 140 different models. But I have had one experience, recounted fully in *Portable People,* bearing on it. Seated at a rather formal birthday party opposite a burly Germanic-looking gent with huge forehead and a crown of white hair, I found out that he was Hans Bethe, the man who figured out how the sun works and received a Nobel Prize in physics for his pains. He had actually worked the problem out while doodling on an envelope aboard a train from Princeton to Ithaca in the days when such trains ran. Someone had told him that one of my novels, *Gala,* was about a father and child who build a model of the Milky Way in their basement, and this tidbit of news entertained him, prompting him eventually, after some preliminary conversation, to ask me: "Was it a *working* model?" I have been told I see too much in his query; but I doubt it: buried somewhere in the vast erudition he brought to this bizarre social encounter with a non-scientist, there was a child's hypothetical longing to have that envelope of his come to life, be not just equations but the sun itself. You could see in his face a massive, proud naïveté that said he wanted all models to behave like their originals. Of course he was teasing me, but also himself. Even to understand is not to replicate. In his generous fashion he was enlisting me in the honorable and no doubt deluded company of model-makers, who wanted more than they could get and remained dissatisfied with their models.

And so back to Faulkner, whose models, while not working models of the sun or anything else, nonetheless give off the erratic, impersonal, daunting purr of a universe in motion, with God eloquent in the details, as Mies van der Rohe said. Something processive comes through, having nothing to do with plot, but much to do with style, obliging readers to perform feats, sometimes herculean, of decoding. Call the assembled works of WF the Faulkner manifold, or the Yoknapatawpha experiment; there leaks from them a clinical, epistemological hurdy-gurdy sound that recalls Nigel Balchin's psychiatry novel, *Mine Own Executioner*, in which the mind functions as a model of what it confronts and cannot dominate. Just as, for many novelists, art has become an obvious recourse to control and order in a frightening, chaotic world, so has the novel for Faulkner been the stage on which he sets the violence, the abyssal and helpless dynamism of the mind encountering a cosmos too vast to think about. There is nervous wreckage behind his sentences, nausea at the speed with which humans, nations, races, are consumed, with the result that the almost orderly procedures of fiction, muddled as they may seem, echo the assembled science pertaining to galaxies, clusters of them, and the beginning of the universe. Only Proust, who doted on science, provides a similar phobic context, not so much spelled out in technical terms as mimicked in a language almost out of control, beginning to falter and melt in the face of a physics that makes us want to think society is as much a given as nature itself, and more palatable.

Where memory upsets and steadies Proust, peering unnerves and beefs up Faulkner. They are both dealing with huger entities than dictionaries can master, both of them entrants in the stakes for ecstatic anthropology. When you come away from either, drenched in some ravishing destructive element epitomized in the ordeal of the prose, you have been subjected to an archetypal thrill in which the cave and the corncob/madeleine come together. Proust just happens to be more finesse-ridden than Faulkner, whose society is more primitive than his. Is this what Hardy was aiming for, this huge overview, or Balzac? They falter because they are not stylists enough, never taking chances, whereas Proust, forever amplifying and extending, Faulkner never quite managing to resist using the image not yet accepted, contrive to create an open-ended model, at least one that begins in the calm, temperate, obliging atmosphere that allows the enthralled human to say "This is a scale model of the Maia-Mercury seaplane combo," but takes you out, away from all your bearings into uncharted realms of memory and pre-history. They excel in what they do most intimately, insisting that the figure attract the ground and vice versa, and that decorous dichotomy no longer applies. The disastrous reading habit they both demand is the one that robs you of exquisite response and makes you consider the thing said as perhaps the most cogent way of acquainting you with the not-said. You are no longer allowed to concentrate. You have to take in everything that leaks into view from somewhere else. If this is total reading, then it has its precursors in painting and music; and literature, we might say, has only just begun to catch up. Joyce used connotation in much the same way, blurring exposition in the cause of woof. At bottom, all three participate in the same late-twentieth-century movement to rid literature of its arbitrary features, much as Robbe-Grillet tried to rid it of false dualisms. We will never lose the yearning to concentrate on something at the expense of everything else, nor will we ever lose that freebooter inclination to help ourselves to everything else as well. Tell looters to steal only alarm clocks and asbestos oven-gloves and see what happens.

In the long run, I suppose I prefer Faulkner's feeling for barbaric yawp to Proust's brothel argot and Joyce's molten lexicography, but it's an embarrassment of riches to choose from. Faulkner has also the narrative drive, the Gothic flagrancy, the others lack, something of the gross, brutal pounding in Shakespeare. There is much knocking at the gates in Yoknapatawpha, history red in tooth and claw, geography done to kinetic rhythms.

V.

One is glad that, so far as is known, Faulkner never went and sat ringside with Joe DiMaggio as Hemingway did. Faulkner's vicarious heroics would have taken him, rather, to reunions of the American pilots who formed the Eagle Squadron of the Royal Air Force (few survivors, alas). His true heroics, visible and audible on every page, depend on fecundity, on the constant chance of saying something original by way of oratory. It is safer to count on its happening than on its not, and if this gets him a Purple Heart, then so be it, so long as we understand by that term an added intensity, an irresistible chromatic sublimity, an impenitent yen to use the full orchestra of language, indeed to create an artifact so substantial it almost supplants the world it regards. He is the auto-pilot of crescendo, the artificer of sweep, the maestro of making things thicker, the architect of density and deviance. All through he tells a straight enough story, but the entire world's howling lingers in its margins, as if narrative were being faulted for neatness, selection, symbolism even. This guarantees him as a holist, an ever-present ancient mariner who not only gives us the full tale but augments it with what one has to call the act of agile stuffing. All along, he knows and imagines more than his completed *oeuvre* could ever contain, which is a monumental feat of knowledge, to be sure, but his salient contribution is not, I think, the fabricating of Snopeses, the fleshing out of that map in the back of *Absalom, Absalom!* and those appended chronologies and genealogies that read like belated challenges to himself rather than aide-memoires to the reader. Can these dry bones live?

They just have. Look where the east-west highway in almost Roman geometry intersects the north-south railroad and ringed spots like sperms with tails attacking an egg or the tadpole-like objects that astronomers call cometary knots tell us of sites: "WHERE OLD BAYARD SARTORIS DIED IN YOUNG BAYARD'S CAR," "MISS JOANNA BURDEN'S, WHERE CHRISTMAS KILLED MISS BURDEN, & WHERE LENA GROVE'S CHILD WAS BORN." It is the kind of map you need when recollecting emotion in tranquillity — not much use to you beforehand, of course, or even during. When he writes "WILLIAM FAULKNER, SOLE OWNER & PROPRIETOR," using two reversed Ns perhaps in fake redneckery, he is urinating on ground already written up and dominated. This was no thing to send in to Random House as part of a book proposal, but scent-marking by a literary tiger out on his own, beyond editors and Fadimans, creators of ingratiating short paragraphs and short sentences. Where Nabokov deals in almost scalding precision, a diagnostic triplet of definite or indefinite article, adjective and noun, Faulkner works himself up into an elephantiasis of augment, never quite sure how little to leave it at. As in this:

> He crossed that strange threshold, that irrevocable demar-
> cation, not led, not dragged, but driven and herded by that
> stern implacable presence, into that gaunt and barren house-

hold where his very silken remaining clothes, his delicate
shirt and stockings and shoes which still remained to remind him of what he had once been, vanished, fled from
arms and body and legs as if they had been woven of chi-
mæras or of smoke.

A prose puritan's version might run as follows:

He crossed the strange threshold, driven by that implacable
presence, into the household where his remaining clothes
reminded him of what he had once been.

Anyone can help the Third Reich, even the occasional half-wit,
and every incompetent can crank out a tale. What Faulkner manages to do here is convey the act of dressing and undressing in the
motions of the prose, the keenest of which is how the clothes
themselves undress *him*, themselves reject him and blow away,
an illusion that of course builds upon the *clad* quality of the narrative itself. It would have been a cliché to denude the sentences
themselves to proclaim the divestment of the last two lines, and
he goes nowhere near so obvious a trick. Then he resumes with an
affirmative, garbing the whole mental motion anew, filling in a
physique with an entire implied biography, the point of which—
nothing new—is that any given detail contains the whole story if
only you have the patience to draw it out and reveal it. It's a typical
patch of execution, doing several things at once, as he mostly does,
but it doesn't launch into the egregious kind of literate back-
stammer we get elsewhere in *Absalom, Absalom!* and which
makes it a visionary novel, a model of the impenitently pensive
work of art:

He was gone; I did not even know that either since there is
a metabolism of the spirit as well as of the entrails, in
which the stored accumulations of long time burn, generate,
create and break some maidenhead of the ravening meat;
ay, in a second's time—yes, lost all the shibboleth erupting
of cannot, will not, never will in one red instant's fierce
obliteration.

This is by no means the fiercest, most fluently asyntactical portion of the novel, but it does set him apart from thousands who toil

to accomplish a book without mistakes in grammar, their fervent hope that the grammatically flawless ipso facto becomes high art. Why, you could even cobble together a sentence, a pseudo-sentence, using his most portentous words merely to evince his linguistic interest in the unlinguistic doings of humans: *His metabolism had accumulated the meat of a maidenhead, at least until some shibboleth obliterated it.* Free the least redneck part of his idiom from the "Hit wont need no light, honey"s, and the big words, out in the open as it were, will form uncanny relationships with one another — the latent high-brow that over-animates the complete sentence or paragraph. It is as if the history of the language, there ever having been a developing language for there to be a history of, loomed up behind everything, minifying it in an erudite, fervent, unSouthern voice, all points of the compass speaking at once. That is how he works on you, doing within his pages what Proust put in the margins and in his tacked-on paper wings. The vision of the All haunts them both, at their most restricted and specific, alarming them with the discovery that the minutest particular has universal force, could you but let it loose. Every mouse a rogue elephant.

Less a phrasemaker than he was a texture-weaver, an apocalyptic compound voice of all the ages, Faulkner blazed the trail. Without him as forebear, some of us would never have been. He wrote in defiance, reserving the right to stylize until the "message" of his novels was that of their idiosyncratic twang. Sometimes, we are told, a surgeon works so fast, stitching, that his gloves catch fire. You sometimes sense this happens to Faulkner at his most incantatory. I am not sure his eminent performance helps me with plot or narrative line, with, for instance, what occupies me most these days: the image of the forsaken astronaut from another galaxy, perhaps a successor of Matthew Arnold's Forsaken Merman, who makes what he can of Earth, the planet he's been saddled with, thus becoming a new version of that old trope the alien observer only faintly aware of where he came from. But the furor and dionysian tenacity of WF's prose style empower me even as the fruitflies cabal and reject imagination. There's one big thing about Mr. Faulkner. He reminds you that, when the deep purple blooms, you are looking at a dimension, not a posy.

POSTSCRIPT

How much we expect of literature without wondering why. There
are two stages: one, we take it seriously (i.e., not trivially). Two: we
then expect too much of it. Looking for signs among the treasure-
trove of letters, we develop a habit we try to apply to the world
at large. We expect the ostensible microcosm to evince the macro-
cosm, and it never does, though we attach to our fiercest mental
longings a whole arsenal of allegory, symbolism, sign, epitome,
metaphor, simile, hint, personification, vignette and so on. The
truth is, we are always alone with literature; it never quite does
duty for the world, and our experience of it never quite matches
all that the world does to us, from neutrino to tumor. We nonetheless try to rehearse for life while reading, or to sum it up:
agenda or summa. There is the work of art and then everything
else, and all we can say is that the work enters the world, adds
itself to that, but only sketchily conveys it. I am wondering (and
pontificating) about the inadequacy of imagery, and this is what
Faulkner teaches us; that gathering, teacherly hum of his continually calls up the intractable ongoingness of the world outside the
artifact.

Oddly enough, in him as in Beckett and Joyce, the world becomes a symbol of itself. What art does not tell us, the world has
to, but only in a fragmented, dishevelled way. Having learned to
hunt for signs, we never get enough of them and so return to the
world unappeased, realizing there is no satisfactory symbol after
all. There is not even a suitable synecdoche. To cope with life, you
either have to accept an incomplete account of it, since you can
never soak up the All, or resign yourself to mere addition — one
damned thing after another.

The word *symbol* should haunt us, denoting as it does in Ancient
Greek things brought back together that were thrown apart. Let
us say the mind and all that is not mind. If this upset the Greeks,
by how much more must it upset us? We have many more phenomena to deal with than they did, and I am not even counting
the World Wide Web cluttered with the prattle of almost everybody. How arbitrary our sleuthing-out of the world is, how de-
cisive on feeble premises, how shallow on poor evidence. We live
and die without knowing much of the world, getting so much at
second-hand, and using only a measly fraction of our brains. The
best symbols, such as Beckett's Molloy "riding" his chainless bike

with the aid of crutches or Proust's imperious madeleine, first tempt us to construe them, then become the symbols of our own inability, our constantly stymied state. The world, including its symbols and microcosms, begins and ends as what I previously called an involute: De Quincey's idea of a compound experience incapable of being disentangled. Hence, literature or letters ends up as a cushion, an anodyne, a drug. Faulkner's great gift is that he shrouds all he does in the noise of mystery, cloaking significance in a texture of dubiety which, although verbal, happens to be more revealing on the level of agitated recitative than on that of explanation. He chants to us the nature of being, its overbearing abundance, its terminable gratuitousness. Ultimately, we do not ask the questions because we could not stand the answers.

Frank O'Hara:
Nothing Personal

Elaine Equi

I NEVER MET FRANK O'HARA, and in a way, it's a relief. Secretly, I've always suspected he wouldn't be terribly impressed with me. Where he's spontaneous, I'm calculated. Where he's gregarious, I'm not. And it can be so disappointing to admire someone intensely from afar, and then find out up close you've got nothing to say.

Besides, there are already so many versions of what-Frank-was-really-like in circulation, what could be gained from adding my two cents to the piggy bank of his mystique?

I did dream about him once, though, in 1988, right after I had moved to New York. In the dream, I was at a poetry reading. It was a drizzly night, and there were only a handful of us sitting on folding chairs in a dreary room. The poet was very young, a guy in jeans with longish hair and, in my opinion, nothing special as a writer. But when he finished, Frank O'Hara came up from the back of the room, where apparently he had been standing, and warmly congratulated him.

Frank was carrying a large shopping bag of towels or possibly sheets, and I overheard him say he had just come from checking out the largest new department store in Moscow. At the time, I considered the dream as I would any other recycled piece of Lower East Side folklore. It was sweet and in character to think of Frank as someone who still took time to encourage younger poets, even after his death. Only in writing this now do I allow myself to dwell on the rather disappointing fact that in my own dream, he didn't even say hi to me, one of his biggest fans.

It makes me wonder what purpose it might serve to construct this fantasy of being snubbed. Was I being shy or aggressive: "I don't deserve to be noticed" or "I don't need your endorsement"? But to be honest, I'm not terribly upset, as I wasn't in the dream, by his lack of attention. Because even if the ghost of Frank O'Hara does ignore me, his poems and mine have been carrying on the

most intimate of conversations for the past twenty years. Perhaps
this separation of poem and poet was at least in part what O'Hara
refers to when he says in "Personism": "It [his poetics] does not
have anything to do with personality or intimacy, far from it!"

Basically, I still read Frank O'Hara today for the same reason as
when I first read him in college: he makes me want to write. Not
all poets do. Some prefer you to simply admire their brilliance.
Some like to hide their tricks. Some pretend that they have none.

With Frank, there is always a feeling that he's encouraging you,
the reader — and that the poems were, in a very real way, written
to have you write back and respond. Kenneth Koch puts it this
way: "Sometimes he gave other people his own best ideas, but he
was quick and resourceful enough to use them himself as well. It
was almost as though he wanted to give his friends a head start
and was competitive partly to make up for this generosity." Koch
is, of course, referring to actual conversations he had with O'Hara,
yet the same generosity is inherent in Frank's poems whether you
knew him or not.

For anyone familiar with my work, O'Hara's influence is unmistakable. There's the use of humor and of pop culture, and on occasion, there's his rhythm. Something about that pace, maybe because
his poems are often walks or at least feel like walks, always reminded me of the way Joe Brainard described Frank O'Hara's walk.
"Light and sassy. With a slight bounce and a slight twist. It was a
beautiful walk. Confident. 'I don't care' and sometimes 'I know
you are looking.'"

Trying to approximate it was like practicing dance steps alone
in your room with the radio on or in front of the television, and
then feeling that you couldn't wait to try this out in public. In fact,
I guess it was Frank O'Hara who first made me understand the
intrinsically sociable and extroverted aspect to writing poetry —
no small realization, and one that continues to shape my poems
today. As does the O'Hara-esque idea of thinking of poetry as elevated talk, or as Allen Ginsberg once put it, "deep gossip" — eternal
banter between the living and the dead. One gets the impression
that talk was high on Frank's list of pleasures, possibly even
highest. In that respect, we're very much alike.

It's interesting, however, that even the most deliberate imitations of a poet's style will lead in a totally different direction. And
so, what's stuck with me most over the years is not so much a
specific this or that in terms of style, but rather the scope of Frank's

outlook, its largesse. That and the assurance his work gives that the poem is always there, always available, no matter how bleak, bored, confused or elated your mood. Thus one needn't be a visionary, nor suicidal to write well.

Oddly enough, what Frank's attitude toward writing most reminds me of is a Bible verse (Romans 10:6–8) — particularly if I substitute the word "poem" for "Christ." Having done so, it would read:

> Do not say to yourself, "Who can go up to heaven?" (that is to bring the poem down) or "Who can go down to the abyss?" (to bring the poem up from the dead). But what does it say? "The word is near you: it is upon your lips and in your heart."

To which Frank O'Hara, that most secular of poets, might reply without missing a beat: "My heart's in my pocket. It is poems by Pierre Reverdy."

MEDITATIONS ON AN EXCLAMATION POINT

The exclamation point (so like a hard-on) was one of Frank's favorite punctuation marks. Often he uses several in one line:

> full flowers! round eyes!
> rush upward! rapture! space

As a convention, they link his work to the unabashedly excessive declamatory style of Mayakovsky, Marinetti and the Futurists. But where Futurist poets often come off sounding bombastic and swaggeringly macho with their predilection for technology, speed and "the pure hygiene of war" (a position which by the 1950s was grimly laughable), O'Hara is sly enough to inject more than a note of parody into his celebration of "Kangaroos, sequins, chocolate sodas!/ You really are beautiful!" It's as if he's saying, if the Futurists were misguided in the placement of their enthusiasm, why make enthusiasm the villain?

It's also interesting that in borrowing from the Futurists what is essentially a mannerism designed for a public voice, O'Hara applies it to the personal and the private with startling results. Thus the most mundane acts are transformed into performances of a sort, and even a simple thing like a fallen leaf can become a melodrama of epic proportion.

Frank O'Hara. 1955. Photograph by Walter Silver. Courtesy Joe LeSueur.

Leaf! You are so big!
How can you change your
color, then just fall!

As if there were no
such thing as integrity!

All in all, the use of these multiple explosions (orgasms) through-out the poems (particularly his early ones) has a twofold effect. First, they give his work a giddiness and a buoyancy that has, in fact, become its trademark. But because the exclamation points are often used in humorous and incongruous places, and because they're overused, they also end up telegraphing a curious mix of the heartfelt and the insincere. Is he serious or putting us on?

The answer, of course, is always both. His poems ask to be read as genuine, even as they retreat into irony. It is a balancing act that Frank manages well, and one particularly suited to his times. For one can view the 1950s both as a moment when the autobio-graphical "I" was celebrated (by groups like the confessional poets) and also as one when the convention was beginning to unravel and become aware of its artifice.

For many of the more conservative critics of his era, the high degree of self-consciousness and irony in O'Hara's poems made it hard to take him seriously. For today's reader, however, perhaps the possibility that Frank is being sincere proves more of a prob-lem. Or as contemporary poet Jerome Sala once said when won-dering aloud why Frank O'Hara's reputation, if anything, seems to have faded a bit: "Maybe Frank O'Hara is too happy for people today to read?"

I know when I first began writing poetry in the seventies, it seemed a given that O'Hara would soon become a major poet of the stature of Williams and Stevens. So pervasive was his influ-ence, so in-the-air were his ideas, that it was almost not even nec-essary to actually read Frank O'Hara in order to pick up his style.

But from the perspective of the nineties, it's not simply a matter of asking why he hasn't received more critical attention. To a de-voted reader like me, it's a personal question full of bewilderment and surprise: why do Frank O'Hara's poems no longer speak to us the way they used to?

No doubt, part of the answer is that many poets turn to Frank O'Hara when they're young and just beginning to write. His enthusiasm and sense of hyperbole matches and fuels their own growing sense of self-importance and unlimited possibility. For similar reasons, Kerouac has always been popular with young people as well.

So yes, once we get older and more cautious, maybe even sober, it's inevitable that we'd find so much "happiness" — so many cocktail parties, such camaraderie between artists and intermingling of the arts — annoying. In a larger sense, though, it's important to remember that it's not only us who have changed.

Indeed, the whole social fabric is different, so that today we are almost diametrically opposed to the values of O'Hara's time. For example, the core of his work depends on the notion of scene and yes, even (artistic) community — while we find ourselves reading more and more articles about the lack thereof. People, and not just artists either, tend to be more serious, competitive and to have more specialized interests. Remarkably, even poets (who have so little financially to gain) have grown careerist and businesslike in their approach to writing. In such a climate it's hard not to feel a bit like the ant and the grasshopper when confronted by the casual, insouciant charm of much of O'Hara's poetry. Why's he having so much fun while we have to work?

But perhaps "annoyance" is not quite the right word to capture what it is about O'Hara's work that does not resonate or translate particularly well — that disturbs us in our present tenseness. Perhaps it is more a nostalgia for some lost idealism, a belief in the saving grace of art, that we have grown too cynical to accept.

Two examples of this gap come to mind. One is an old poem of mine, a parody of Frank's "Having a Coke With You," which I rewrote in the early eighties as "Having a Coke Alone." In contrast to Frank's effervescent desire to share everything he loves (the Frick, "The Polish Rider") is my rather wandering, melancholy account of spending an afternoon at the movies alone, which ends with the lines: "They have talking vending machines now/ but none that say anything the way you want it said."

One way to read my poem in relation to his is simply that we are at opposite ends of the same mood swing: he's in love and I'm not. But more than that, it's a poem in which I'm already beginning to struggle to explain — to Frank? myself? — some of the differences between his generation and mine.

Another more recent example is a piece by an experimental poet, Rod Smith, entitled "In Memory of My Theories." Written in the nineties, it cleverly takes O'Hara's masterpiece "In Memory of My Feelings" a step further down the poststructuralist road of depersonalization. It also underscores the shift from the "age of the artist" to the age of the cultural critic — and a rather somber culture it is at that. From Smith's book: ". . . for it is the experience of being powerless/ amidst people, not against nature, that/ generates the most desperate embitterment."

In death, as in life, a poet's reputation is not dependent simply on the quality of the work, but rather on its relevance to the historical moment. Thus, poets who once enjoyed enormous popularity, like Frost, may lapse into periods of polite neglect, while other poets relatively obscure in their lifetime, such as Zukofsky, are discovered by new and eager readerships.

Nevertheless, it's surprising that O'Hara isn't more influential. Especially because elements of his work seem to speak directly to some of our current preoccupations. At a time when identity and its various modes of construction have become not only an artistic but public and political issue, O'Hara's improvisatory approach to subjective style would seem to offer some revealing insights.

And besides, to be enthusiastic does not mean to be simple, nor does it mean you are happy all the time. Frank O'Hara's work has one of the most incredibly wide emotional ranges of any poet I can think of. Yet many would still classify him as being somehow frivolous. Sadly, in the reductivist mood of our times, when everyone oversimplifies for the sake of expediency, the exclamation point has come to be synonymous with the smiley face.

THE POETICS OF TEA

It's around 2 A.M. and I am doing something I can't imagine Frank O'Hara doing. Still I'm sure there were times he must have, though perhaps very discreetly. In other words, I am trying to write — with the emphasis on trying. And it is not going well.

Everything sounds flat. My particulars are not particularly interesting. In the past, I would smoke up to a pack of cigarettes at times like this as I'd consider one line, cross it out and start another. But now, in my forties, there's only a cup of Lipton tea on the table next to me. And even that seems wrong. Shouldn't it be oolong or jasmine? Passionflower? Chamomile or cinnamon? Or if I were a better writer to begin with maybe I wouldn't need to mask my desperation with these little touches of exoticism. Maybe

151

I could write about sitting and trying to write and the Lipton tea would work, would be enough.

I remember living in Chicago and reading Frank O'Hara and all the New York School poets and thinking that if I did what they did, it wouldn't work. And it wouldn't work precisely because I was in Chicago. So I didn't do exactly what they did. I didn't name-drop and talk about what street I lived on or what I ate for breakfast or who I had just gotten off the phone with. Instead I relied on a more generic brand of surrealism that I hoped would sound seductive. I did not think of the hierarchies involved in naming and being able to name, or the pleasures of articulating one's own taste. I did not know then that years later I too would live in New York and talk freely about the type of flowers on the table next to me — in this case, chrysanthemums the color of cold tea at 2 A.M.

Even with a writer you love, there are resistances and points of contention. At times like this, the myth of O'Hara's instantaneity seems especially oppressive. What, I wondered, would Frank O'Hara say if he were here now. He who supposedly wrote so effortlessly, who gave away poems (sometimes only copies) to friends.

I had done automatic writing before, but the results were always too anarchic and scrambled to mean much. This time, however, I simply thought of Frank, and the pen began to move easily across the page. It was almost like listening to a voice coming from inside myself and also just behind the chair. This is what it said:

> Untie your muse
> for an hour and stay with me.
>
> I come in pieces
> across a great test pattern
>
> or maybe it's what I used to call sky.
> The music is certainly blue enough
>
> but not without its own tenderness
> like an arrow shot I know not where.
>
> When will you see me as I am
> as industrious with grief as you are
>
> clever at hiding your tiredness.
> In poems we shine,

and though we say them with conviction,
the words are never really ours for keeps.

AGAINST BIOGRAPHY

"Now," said a friend of mine, licking his lips as if he were eyeing a juicy steak, "we'll have Frank O'Hara — *the man*." It was 1993, we were in a bookstore and what he was actually looking at was the new, thick (almost five-hundred-page) biography by Brad Gooch entitled *City Poet: The Life and Times of Frank O'Hara*.

Like my friend, I too was eager to find more about Frank O'Hara in print. Aside from Marjorie Perloff's *Poet Among Painters (1977)*, which is still arguably the best and most illuminating analysis of O'Hara's poetry, not much else had appeared. But perhaps as my friend's breathless anticipation implied, *the man* would prove ideal to fill the void. After all, Frank himself had been skeptical of critics ("the assassin of my orchards") as well as impatient with the ponderous rhetoric of much literary criticism. So maybe the best way to understand this apparently most blatant of autobiographical poets would be through the actual events of his life.

What I didn't have the heart to tell my friend at the time was that I had already read the book (having borrowed a review copy of the galleys) and that the events were not all that — well, juicy. Certainly O'Hara's love life seemed a complicated juggling act. And certainly every chapter is packed to overflowing with famous figures like Larry Rivers, Jasper Johns, Bill de Kooning and Franz Kline — Frank's own arty version of "the rat pack." But that was to be expected. What the book lacked were those truly lurid revelations, not necessarily sexual, but often simply bizarre, that provide the undercurrent of guilty pleasure to reading biographies.

In *City Poet*, Frank O'Hara does not shoot out the TV screen like Elvis, or eat dog food as Judy Garland is once reported to have done or even wear a bit of pale green face powder as one biographer claims T. S. Eliot did on occasion. What I did discover in the Brad Gooch biography is that Frank O'Hara drank rather more than I'd imagined, and that he had the potential to be quite nasty, as is often the case when people drink that way for years. In short, what I discovered was that Frank O'Hara was human.

To Brad Gooch's credit, he does indeed give us the man — not the legend. *City Poet* is a serious, respectful and impressively researched account of Frank O'Hara's life and development as an artist. And just as it does not exploit or sensationalize him as a more trashy bio might, neither does it idealize him. Given the provocative and charismatic nature of O'Hara's character, both impulses must have been hard to resist.

Still I'm not surprised that some people found Gooch's book disturbing. It seems inevitable that there could be no one definitive version of Frank's life to satisfy everyone. So while some found him too gay, since Gooch doesn't shy away from cataloging numerous sexual episodes, others found him not gay enough: "— sometimes sick, still in bed, often hung over."

What I found most troubling was the discussion of the poems: not so much interpretations as detailed tracings of the connection between names and images with the real-life people and events they refer to. Thus lines that I had given a more fanciful or imaginative reading suddenly seemed too grounded. Overall, rather than giving me a deeper appreciation of the poems, it made them seem more narrow. Or, as my writing students like to say about poems that use a lot of personal references, "We like it better when we don't know who the people in it are."

In all fairness, *City Poet* is a biography, not literary criticism, but what it helped me to realize is the problematic way in which the whole notion of biography (and not this one in particular) limits our reading of O'Hara's work.

More than any other poet I can think of, O'Hara's life is constantly equated with his poems in a very literal way, thereby giving the impression that there are no levels to his work. Serious critics who have never quite known what to make of O'Hara's writing, with its playful disregard for traditional ideas of what a poem could and could not be, have been content to look no further than the autobiographical surface. And in some of his comments, O'Hara himself is guilty of creating the impression that any in-depth explication of his poems is simply belaboring the obvious. Perhaps in the old-fashioned sense of conventional symbolism this is the case. But it strikes me as truly ironic that we could take a writer like O'Hara whose life and work are so much about levels of artistic mediation and somehow turn him into a realist.

Romantic, heroic, tragic — O'Hara is an ideal figure on which to project our fantasies about the life of the artist, though hopefully not at the expense of his work. Grudgingly, the literary establishment has included him in the canon, but I can't help feeling uneasy over the possibility that it's the man and not the poems they've canonized.

Perhaps another way to think of this is simply that Frank O'Hara hasn't been dead that long, and therefore his writing is still tied to his life and those that knew him, in a way that makes the work difficult to interpret freely. I'm not saying we should completely disregard the unique way O'Hara used his life and transformed it in his poems. But I do think that if O'Hara is to remain a vital influence, then his words must belong to everyone — and not just those who knew him best. Only then can new ways to interpret his work emerge, apart from even his own intentions for it.

There is something deeply satisfying about the myth of Frank O'Hara, as if it provided poetry with a face and a name for what previously were only philosophical ideas, a life that becomes a work of art and vice versa. And yet the two sides of the equation — his life and his poems — are not true equivalents. Given the choice, perhaps some would actually prefer the man. Not me. I have his poems. His poems are enough.

Langston Hughes. 1939. The Granger Collection, New York.

Langston Hughes:
"If You Can't Read, Run Anyhow!"
Kevin Young

THE CHALLENGE LANGSTON HUGHES PRESENTS is not that his work is obscure, his life operatic, or achievements invisible — rather Hughes as person and poet presents too much, is far too accessible. His personal history seems clearer than Dickinson, less tragic than Dunbar; like Whitman, his writing seems to need no explanation. Here, of course, lies the danger with Hughes, a writer who remains what I call "deceptively simple." Or, as a student of mine unwittingly, even intuitively reversed, Hughes is "simply deceptive." For all his clear language, precise diction and even his famous folk character Jesse B. Semple, Hughes is anything but.

This early life of the "Poet Laureate of the Negro Race" — a title Hughes wore with pride — speaks of the Great Migration of the early parts of the century. Born in Joplin, Missouri, he was up-rooted & lived with his grandmother in Lawrence & Topeka, Kansas. Most people don't think of black folks when they think Kansas; fewer would dream of poetry. However, as a fellow Tope-kan, I feel a special connection to Hughes & this early & by all accounts alienating portion of his life. Something in his poems' easygoing yet reserved tone feels forged from that Kansas background. Such pragmatic skepticism has been an open heartland secret to anyone who has lived there; is what over the years has kept Kansans going through drought & locusts & floods; and is what ultimately kept Bob Dole from winning the 1996 presidential election.

Kansans understand this skepticism verging on cynicism — and admit it to no one. We choose instead to export wheat & tornadoes &, oddly enough, black poets. Gwendolyn Brooks, the first African-American Pulitzer Prize winner, was born in Topeka though she lit out for the greener or at least taller pastures of Chicago by the time she was a few months old — this move to the big city also characterizes Kansans, including Hughes, who eventually settled & died in Harlem, U.S.A. Like Joyce's Ireland, or Baptist Heaven,

157

Kansas is a place defined by its absence, by distance. Not just the leagues that place contains, but the lengths from which we can see it well.

With this distance in mind, perhaps we can better understand Hughes's relation to his work & arguably his life — what I call his poetics of refusal. This painful Kansas past helps explain the "distance" sometimes found in his poems, as well as their underlying melancholy. In many ways, this ironic distance simply recasts a blues aesthetic — one in which "I don't got a gun, and I'm too blue to look for one." Du Bois's double consciousness becomes in Hughes's hands a double negative that for the blues author & audience adds up if not to a positive, then to a "dark" humor. *Laughing to Keep from Crying,* as Hughes named a collection of short stories; even more refusal is found in the title of his "novel" of the life of a boy in Kansas, *Not Without Laughter.* For Hughes & us "blues people," survival means the small distance between despair & laughter, between having & not, between buying a gun to off yourself & not being able to afford the bullets.

The difference between the blues figure & the hard-luck, absurdist stereotypes of minstrelsy so prominent in the early parts of the century is one of form — and audience. Both are things Hughes understood innately, and responded to — almost to a fault, in the case of audience, sometimes crossing the line he recognized between poetry & lighter verse. Of course, the innovations that Hughes achieved, in championing the folkways and form of the blues seem obvious or easy now, but when he published his *The Weary Blues* (1926) and even more importantly, *Fine Clothes to the Jew* (1927), he caught hell. The black bourgeoisie came down on Hughes the hardest, terming him the "Poet Low-rate of Harlem" for writing about common folk, what today's tastemakers might call "negative images": janitors, adulterers, juke jointers, bad men, loose women, real people people people. And what advice he gave them people! "Put on yo' red silk stockings,/ Black gal. Go out and let the white boys/ Look at yo' legs." Even today such images get read as "literal advice" and not, as Hughes called it, an "ironic poem."

"We know we are beautiful. And ugly too," Hughes wrote in his groundbreaking manifesto "The Negro Artist and the Racial Mountain" (1926), arguing against either whitewashing our images to make ourselves look better, or against (as he *signifies on* the unnamed "young poet," most likely Countee Cullen) wanting to be white. After climbing the mountain, Hughes dug in, breaking first ground, trying to dig his way back to the motherland by way of the Mississippi.

Interestingly enough, for such a landlocked childhood, Hughes's first famous poem was "The Negro Speaks of Rivers," a classic sounding, long-lined, Whitmanesque reverie. In many ways the poem foreshadows what some have called literary Garveyism, a returning to African roots — and in taking the "white man" out of Whitman, Hughes taps into a larger zeitgeist, taking us through the rivers Congo, Nile, the "Euphrates when dawns were young" and, ultimately, a river of the dead that unlike the mythical Lethe, refuses to forget. Or ignore his blackness — listen to the reason Hughes gives for writing the poem on a journey to see his expatriate father in Mexico: "All day on the train I had been thinking about my father and his strange dislike of his own people. I didn't understand it, because I was a Negro, and I liked Negroes very much." This long memory & literary acceptance of his own blackness, of the "motherland" as opposed to his "father's land" is part of his appeal, a defining quality of his long literary life.

But in describing his early life in his stunning autobiography *The Big Sea*, Hughes leaves out plenty. Arnold Rampersad, Hughes's biographer, literary executor and champion, sums this up this way: "In *The Big Sea*, deeper meaning is deliberately concealed within a seemingly disingenuous, apparently transparent, or even shallow narrative. In a genre defined in its modern mode by confession, Hughes appears to give virtually nothing away of a personal nature." Rampersad links this reticence, let's call it, to a sort of racial code, "a gamble" by Hughes to please white publishers while speaking to black readers who held a decoder ring. Particularly when dealing with issues of his white patron (whom he had a terrible break with) or his sexuality (conveniently left undefined or defined as "unattached" by most biographers), Hughes is less than forward — we learn little of his Eastern European female roommate or, more to the point, his days on board (& below deck) on a merchant marine vessel.

For me, Hughes's reserve is less the smiling face of the slave but rather an elaborate, elegant technique found in Hughes's poetry & in much great art. To read *The Big Sea* is to learn dissembling as an art form — not as pop escapism, but as a populist escape hatch — a refusal to give in, to give out and especially to give away anything.

To read the poetry or *The Big Sea* for traces of Hughes's life is to deny the dogged unautobiographical nature of his work. As he himself wrote about his second book of poems: "I felt it was a better book than my first, because it was more impersonal, more about other people than myself, and because it made use of the Negro folk-song forms, and included poems about work and the problems of finding work, that are always so pressing with the Negro people."

While certainly class dominates here, I want to highlight Hughes's first reason for *Fine Clothes'* success: "It was more impersonal." In our current confessional climate where the memoir meets the talk show—of which, if I had to, I would choose the latter—it may be hard to read the impersonal as desirable, or even achievable. But if we let go our preconceptions about poetry being "personal," we can see Hughes championing a poetry for all people that is not private—a verse that is truly "free," and open to the public. There is an anonymity to his poetry, or rather, a pseudo-nymity, that may startle us. "I have known rivers:/ Ancient, dusky rivers." Yet, if we look at his fellow modernists—the "extinguishing of personality" attempted by Eliot, or even Williams's lexicon of "thing-ness"—Hughes stands not alone but out, creating something new, vernacular, blues-based, as American as lynching & apple pie.

This merging of the American promise & its pratfalls—a fragmented violence in one hand, a homemade wholeness & even wholesomeness in the other—Hughes negotiates most of his life. Just as his grandmother's first husband who fought alongside John Brown for Bleeding Kansas, Hughes adds his voice to our many Americas. Examining his long career from the 1920s & the Harlem Renaissance to his death in 1967 during the Black Arts Movement, we discover many different Hugheses as well. Socialist, student, reporter, world traveler, novelist, sailor, dramatist, busboy, dishwasher, poet. The *Langston Hughes Reader* (1958) contains multitudes—poems, plays, blues, translations, autobiographies (plural), songs and, my favorite, "pageant." This short history of black people in the western world—straightforward, celebratory, funny, serious—takes in all the ways Hughes saw we are. Only Hughes of his modernist contemporaries—excepting perhaps Williams—would attempt such broad American history.

Odd then, or perhaps fitting, that Hughes would come under fire from the House Un-American Activities Committee in the

1950s. His more overt political poems, especially of the 1930s when he went to & wrote about the Spanish Civil War and Russia, came back to haunt him — in particular "Goodbye Christ," which raises Marxism & not the cross. For decades the religious right dogged Hughes, even though the poem had been published privately in the 1930s. And before the committee, Hughes recanted, and avoided the blacklist.

In contrast to Paul Robeson's stand-off with the HUAC & subsequent troubles, Hughes's giving in seemed like a betrayal. Hughes would go on to repress most of the work from this period, excising if not excusing it — to our great loss. Even if he was not blacklisted, black bars cover a great amount of what we think we know about Hughes. Hughes's poetics of refusal becomes a bit more understandable in this context — not just as the black tradition of *signifying*, whether talking trash or telling it slant, well described by Henry Louis Gates — but as the kind of talk Othello used to win Desdemona's father after he'd won her.

Such cagey talk did not serve him well in the straight-talking Black Arts Movement of the 1960s. We were impatient, sick of rhetoric — action was called for — as Amiri Baraka (né Jones) wrote, "We want 'poems that kill.'" This metaphoric murder, part of what the critic William Harris calls the "Jazz Aesthetic," involved offing the literary fathers, just as Baraka would say John Coltrane "murdered the popular song." Hughes took plenty of hits, yet few — even Baraka himself, who dissed Hughes in public (though later retracted) — had read deeply enough to know of Hughes's radical work.

But one wonders, even with the excised 1930s, what had they read? Hughes had been speaking in a black idiom from *The Weary Blues* to his book-length *Montage of a Dream Deferred* (1951), and even his last big work, 1964's *Ask Your Mama*. Somebody should have — she could have told 'em Hughes was getting down all along. Caught between the Devil & the deep blue sea, like Louis Armstrong, Hughes represented an earlier, seemingly bygone era — and though both artists responded to & even cleared space for radical changes such as be-bop, both did so in such a way as to make their virtuosity simple. Deceptive.

What gets lost in most critiques is the depth of emotion Hughes expresses, despite or precisely because of the "impersonal" quality he possesses. He paints a community, a "Lenox Avenue Mural," not a self-portrait. Even more why *The Big Sea*, a book which changed my life, looms large on the Hughes horizon. For, like any picaresque tale — and this is largely how he constructs his life — Hughes's autobiography reveals as much by its gaps, by its discrete molecular leaps, by what he refuses to say.

Take *The Big Sea*'s opening paragraph when Hughes throws his books in the sea, as dramatic an opening of a writing life as any:

> It was like throwing a million bricks out of my heart when I threw the books into the water. I leaned over the rail of the *S.S. Malone* and threw the books as far as I could out into the sea — all the books I had had at Columbia, and all the books I had lately bought to read.

By this Hughes achieves a sort of wry anti-ars poetica, a refusal of the "inkellectual." In refusing book learnin' he accepts something else: people. For

> ... it wasn't only the books that I wanted to throw away, but everything unpleasant and miserable out of my past: the memory of my father, the poverty and uncertainties of my mother's life, the stupidities of color-prejudice, black in a white world, the fear of not finding a job, the bewilderment of no one to talk to about things that trouble you, the feeling of always being controlled by others — by parents, by employers, by some outer necessity not your own. All those things I wanted to throw away. To be free of. To escape from. I wanted to be a man on my own, control my own life, and go my own way. I was twenty-one. So I threw the books in the sea.

Here we see Hughes's emotion, in a confession, or at least a protest. Black, Africa-bound and twenty-one, Hughes does not burn books that offend, but drowns books to defend. While participating in the African-American tradition of negation as affirmation ("Bad Is Good," one chapter is titled), more significantly — and to my mind, the reason such a powerful statement has gotten overlooked — his jettisoning the books flies into the headwind of current African-American criticism such as Gates's, which emphasizes literacy.

By this I certainly do not mean to say literacy has not factored into black lives, and naturally, books; or that Hughes, the prolific author, advocated any sort of *ill*iteracy. On the contrary, Hughes, in his poetry & in this and other symbolic acts in *The Big Sea* embodies & embraces what I call *aliteracy*. By *aliteracy* I mean a trickster-style technique that questions not just Western dichotomies (bad/good, black/white) but provides a system beyond which one can be defined, even by writing, or by literacy or ill-.

In other words, Hughes prefers the ability to read situations & power structures, over books — what Houston Baker describes, in speaking of Caliban in *The Tempest*, as "supraliteracy." For Hughes, *aliteracy* approaches more what we say when we say "she read him," as in figgered him for a fool. What Baker does not figure is the way in which Prospero's rejection of his books, thrown similarly into the sea, recognizes shifting societal orders and their relation to the word. Or that often literate & literary authors, whether Prospero as character or Hughes as writer, may abandon their words, in order to gain a new world. Or that, if we take Auden — who himself poeticized "impersonality," arguably for similar political/sexual reasons — & his "parable" of the poet existing in a dialogue between creative, beautiful Ariel and what Seamus Heaney calls "the countervailing presence of Prospero, whose covenant is with 'truth' rather than 'beauty,'" Hughes sides with Caliban, reserving the right to curse, to cannibalize, to talk out both sides of his neck. To leave such a truth/beauty dialogue altogether.

How significant, then, that Hughes, perched on a voyage back to Africa, old world, motherland, throws his books into the sea! In a reversal of the middle passage, Hughes creates a rite of passage, turning around the paradigm of the slave stolen from Africa & taught (or, more likely, forbidden) to read English. He also turns inside out the idea of the ignorant, illiterate black who don't know no better, massa — a figure which, despite their best intentions, African-American critics seem to reinscribe when they write of literacy & the history of (white) authentication of black authors. Hughes rejects it all, booklearnin' both black & white. Often I wish I could do the same.

I am tired of ideas. Tonight I prefer lives, especially lies. I am sick of confession, thought, analysis. Throw the books into the sea & let them swim for it like Shine, the mythic black porter who refused to stay on the sinking *Titanic*.

Dr. Seuss. Courtesy Random House.

Chemical Seuss
Ben Marcus

THE HARMING OF MEANING

I MEAN TO DISCUSS certain reveries of reading that occurred during the interment of childhood I served in my parents' home, reveries often centering around Seuss and his extreme attack on sense. Let's say that I was often read to, that books were made a gift to me, ones I could not understand or even read but that joined the detritus of objects meant to secure my character, my future capacity of knowing. The books were an investment in the person-shaping activities my parents had undertaken with respect to me. If enough books were piled into my room, perhaps I might emerge a person, someone ready to square off with the other challengers coming through the pipes of childhood. It was in my best interest to posture a knowledge of a book, even if that entailed exhibiting grave silence in response to the typical interrogative. Possibly I learned grave silence before I learned to speak — it is a useful way to deflect attention, project authority, become a reader. Thus I "read" Dickens and Melville before I could properly think, and a page from *Great Expectations* was solely a field to accommodate, sanction, my own dayhiding, rather than a source I was supposed to study for narrative images. Reading was a time for wayward falling, plunging inward (wherever) as far as possible until the book asserted its world again, disappointed me with its specificity. A "good" book was a book sufficiently absent to allow me to inhabit its space and dilate (grow, fall, miss, lose) in whatever manner seemed fluid, a book that wouldn't harass me overmuch with its own terms. Most of what I remember reading as a child is instead whatever I happened to be thinking while holding the book over my face, growing up behind the page, etc. Only later did I learn the obligation, the disaster, of following the words. Wasn't booked language the first sanction to let the mind form elsewhere? What a book is "about" is simply where you go when you read, where and how you move about in pursuit of yourself while the book is in action. It's not what the book is about at all, rather what and where the reader is about. Reading can be discussed as a physical posture, an attitude or position struck to enable certain kinds of thinking, to hell with the specific book, double to hell with "writers" and their visions. The book is just equipment for the daily hunt, a shield. If you hold up a book, the world will leave you alone.

There were therefore occasions of storytelling I slept through. I can admit that most of what was sent my way fell short. One learned to offer up the typical listening cues to the mother or father storyteller: smile during a break in the language, nod, toss and put an arm over the eyes. Mostly I slept as the language fell over me. There is no better way to sleep than when being read to, first because I do not like being watched when language is coming at me, I do not want to be seen waiting for language. Second because the sleeper loses his pace without an ordered effort, a syntax, to the pursuit — language gives shape to the sleep act, structures the body's drop, because to dream is to solicit pure grammar and thus perhaps discover something worth thinking, etc. One was often carried off to bed at this point, even when not sleeping, or awoken during the heave-ho, when it would be impolite to indicate I was awake. Childhood can be viewed as a set of strategies to secure carriage — in my case I was piggybacked, cradled, slung in a fireman's carry. I was tossed and held and passed along, but, most importantly, I was kept off the ground ("The sacred or tabooed personage must be carefully prevented from touching the ground; in electrical language he must be insulated, if he is not to be emptied of the precious substance or fluid with which he, as a vial, is filled to the brim" — James Frazer). One wanted to be in their arms, to be brought into other rooms, preferably dark ones upstairs with cold sheets and a wedge of bed for them to sit and touch my hair, kiss the face that represented me, then close in on my chest for the great blackout.

Yet this business ceased when Seuss entered the orbit of noises launched to my attention. A Seuss encounter harmed my private effort of world-building. When it occurred, I could not go elsewhere because there was no elsewhere, no such thing as location. There was only one word and it was the word I was hearing, nothing could be substituted, or substitute away and nothing changed, because the spine of the thing had grown. The Seuss architecture at once woke me and began its rabid scaffolding, asserting an inner syntax bone by bone that has given body to every subsequent language enacted before me, owned and marked all future texts with its deep skeleton. To my view, then, one does not read Dr. Seuss, one is built by him. He is a builder of persons. He cannot be slept through.

THE DEAFENING PROPERTIES OF EARLY ART

When I was five years old I suffered a period of deafness. Suffered might not be the right word, maybe engaged is better, because I regard the deaf period as one of the most fruitful in my regretful relationship with myself. Let's say I entered occasions of deafness that started with my mother, the chief soundmaker of my early time. Her voice produced a tightness in my head (a brightness too — sun, stars, the rest of it) and, to be frank, I rather enjoyed it, although a side "effect" was a sharp drop in what I could hear. This is my own diagnosis, you understand — maybe I was not deaf, was simply focusing on her, but it did seem that the world's acoustics had halted just short of my own body, which was acting as a baffle. The sound was falling at my feet and, as with most things, I saw its effect on others but could not feel it for myself. It is only now that I can consider that what she read to me, what she was reading to me that year, might have been the cause of my loss of hearing, that hearing the cadenced madness of Seuss was literally deafening, a force so exclusive it denied me other sounds, or echoed so resolutely that nothing new could approach, certainly a criteria for powerful literature, or powerful something, maybe just *power*. The completeness of her voice was enough to bind me in place, leaving no room for what else, the sound of our house breathing out our actions, the songs I made to remind myself I was alive. It is amazing to be denied even the noise of one's own hands, the ruffle of doing nothing. I was deaf for only so long, but long enough to become a vigilant watcher of the mouth, realizing that I had to get at the mouth to get what I wanted, the mouth being all. The Deaf are known for reading lips, not eyes, and they read lips because the lips produce a first language, regardless of sound, since sound proves to be incidental to language, only a technology of it. If I had to choose, I'd give up so-called landscapes, sunsets, flowers, sky, bodies, anything notoriously beautiful or hideous, for all of the completeness of watching a mouth, just the sight of a mouth

167

and what it does, given that the mouth renders other scenery ridiculous, swallows up the entire category of what can be seen. It is ultimately the only thing to see, and a mouth in the act of shaping out the Seuss lexicon is the premier vision. Stated another way, Seuss is brilliant because the mouth makes beautiful shapes to recite his work. That's as far as my literary criticism goes, my primary aesthetic criteria. In honor of Dr. Seuss, I will admit that I do not look people in the eye, that I don't regard the eye as the center of the "storm," but rather the mouth, or word hole, that carves language out of wind. The eyes cheat and hide; despite the lore, eyes have never "said" anything to me, they seem built chiefly of water, easily poured from the head and discarded. The only thing eyes are good for is to look at the mouth. Dr. Seuss is an artist of the mouth because a recitation of his work requires a first gymnastic of the face, a series of basic face codes as primal as, well, primal to me because it was my mother's face that undertook the gestures, or that was overtaken by them, a semaphore of the head that said everything and gave me not only a mother, but a world. My other senses, at the time, were irrelevant.

THE LITERATURE OF THE IMPOSSIBLE

My feeling is that the impossible must be made viable, and only through language, that language is not subject to laws of physics and therefore must not be restricted to conservative notions of "sense" or even "nonsense," but must pursue what appears impossible in order to discover the basic things: what to do, what for, how and just *what*.

We do not have language only to duplicate the mistakes our bodies make, or to try to represent the body in action. The body is heavy enough to represent itself; enough with the body, let it rot. Language so readily affirms the impossible that to deny this potential is to harm the future of what can be known or felt, which makes life impossible. Thus for life to be possible, language must pursue what is not. Seuss is a hero to me because he made manifest the rampant power of naming, proving that you can name a thing into being as well as name something right out of the world. Objects have no anchors, let's go after them all and send them into the ether, clear the world of what we already know. *If I Ran the Zoo* is not just a cute bestiary of impossible flesh, but proof that words are harder than things, that guttural announcements such as "the Bustard, who only eats custard with sauce made of mustard" are far more sublime and revealing than any book of crappy facts. "Oh, snow and rain are not enough! Oh, we must make some brand new stuff!" Hell yes! Has it ever been said any better? But Seuss makes new "stuff" because the language is built to amplify the catalog of things as long as we have artists able to laugh off the burden of boredom passed on by those "practitioners" who officially ruin the language each time they use it.

In this regard, Seuss is a doctor because he enacts a medicine of language that heals the scar left by reason, complacency, sense, predictability, a scar so complete it just looks like the world, and we often don't know any better, don't know we're living on a wound. He is a doctor of structure, able to liberate the head from its habit of easy, empty associations, allowing a delirious collision of objects to stand in for boredom and the disappointments of the eyes. The fool medicates the serious people, exposes the dullness of their gravity. "For almost two days you've run wild and insisted/ On chatting with persons who've never existed." But it's the fool who chatters at nothing who then allows for the nothingness to dilate, creating new rooms to be filled. Seuss plays the fool and enables the helium-knowledge of silliness, for to be silly is not only to lack sense but to be blessed, to levitate, transcend, stand above the earth (and not touch it). The medicine is triggered without contact. He does not need to touch us. We are healed into the future by his manipulations of the great brain of language, which must be massaged in order to grow, and shocked, and jarred, and kicked and injected. It is thus not untoward to consider that Seuss is a chemical. The vocabulary will always change for that inscrutable, necessary thing that creatures pursue. Why not simplify? In place of whatever is more basic than food, air, touch, water, without which we would not even have life enough to die, insert a word that stands for all of it: Seuss. It should forever stand for everything important. Water can only do so much.

Gertrude Stein. Southeastern France, September 1944 (with Alice B. Toklas and Basket). The Granger Collection, New York.

A Novel of Thank You
Carole Maso

— for Gertrude Stein

Begin in singing.

Chapter One
Rose.

A Longer Chapter
A word whispered. Called through green. In the years she was growing and lilting hills sung in the night and in the day and in every possible way over water rose the first word, the world. Was I loving you I was loving you even then.

One word. Rose

To Be Sung
Urgently, sweetly, with bliss, and sometimes with desperation

Chapter Bliss
Rose.

Chapter Wish
Rose. And Chapter hope . . .

And this is what bliss is this.

Rose to be sung against the sky and diamonds night.

Red Roses
A cool red rose and pink cut pink, a collapse and a solid hole, a little less hot

In direct sensuous relationship to the world.

Carole Maso

Chapter Early and Late Please
I found myself plunged into a vortex of words, burning words, cleansing words, liberating words, and the words were ours and it was enough that we held them in our hands.

Chapter
Sincerely Beverly Nichols Avery Hopwood Allan Michaels and Renee Felicity also how many apricots are there to a pound.

And this is what bliss this is bliss this is bliss.

They found themselves happier than anyone who was alive then.

Chapter Saint
Saint Two and Saint Ten
Saint Tribute
Saint Struggle
Chapter Grace
Chapter Faith
Chapter Example
Saint Admiration

Our Lady of Derision

Saint Deadline — not finished and not finishable. I like thinking of this.

How many saints are there in it? Saints we have seen so far:
Tributes are there in it? A Very Valentine — for Gertrude Stein.
Colors are there in it?
A Novel of Thank you. A Basket.

Saint Example and Saint Admiration
Thank you, how many, audacity religiosity beauty and purity your ease your inability to compromise ever thank you

very much.

Your freedoms Saint Derision, Chapter One

Do prepare to say
Portraits and Prayers, do prepare
to say that you have
prepared portraits and prayers and
that you prepare and that I prepare
    Yes you do.

A vortex of words very much.

For your irreverence and desire
extremity courage and good humorous
subversiveness
splendorous
    Yes you do.

For Your Beauteous
Language is a rose, a woman, constantly in the process of opening
thank you

your freedoms. Released at last from the prisons of syntax. Story.

For your —
Choose wonder.

Choose Wonder
Apples and figs burn.
They burn.

She had wished windows and she had wished.

A novel of thank you and not about it chapter one.

Rose, rose, rose.

Rose whispered, prayed over the child love love. Please please
sweet sweet sweet

Chapter
Susie Asado
Sweet sweet sweet sweet sweet tea
written for a particularly irresistible flamenco dancer

Please be please be get, please get wet, wet naturally, naturally in weather.

Chapter Alice

To not emerge already constructed, already decided, preordained. Thank you

The difference is spreading.

very much

The permission.

I like the feeling of words doing as they want to do and as they have to do.

I like the feeling.

very much.

The main intention of the novel was to say thank you.

A novel of thank you. In chapters and saints.

And it is easily understood that they have permission.

Without telling what happened . . . to make the play the essence of what happened.

A thing you all know is that in the three novels written in this generation that are important things written in this generation, there is, in none of them a story. There is none in Proust in The Making of Americans or in Ulysses.

Once upon a time they came every day and did we miss them we did. And did they once upon a time did they come every day. Once upon a time they did not come every day they never had they never did they did not come every day any day.

A novel of thank you and not about it.

A story of arrangements

When it is repeated or Bernadine's revenge. When it is repeated is another subject. How it is repeated is another subject. If it is repeated is another subject. If it is repeated or the revenge of Bernadine is another subject.

inner thought, silent fancies

There is one thing that is certain, and nobody realized it in the 1914–19 war, they talked about it but they did not realize it but now everybody knows it everybody that the one thing that everybody wants is to be free, to talk to eat to drink to walk to think, to please, to wish, and to do it now if now is what they want, and everybody knows it they know it anybody knows it . . . 1943

. . . not to be managed, threatened, directed, restrained, obliged, fearful, administered

multiplicity and freedom unfettered ecstatic

thank you

To begin to allow. To allow it.

I had to recapture the value of the individual word, find out what it meant and act within it.

Imagine a door.

To free oneself from convention again and again and again.
Thank you for suggesting once again. And again and again that story is elsewhere, that story must have been, been elsewhere. In every kind of other place. Thank you. Again and again. In every possible way.

Once upon a time they came every day and did we miss them we did. And did they once upon a time did they come every day. Once upon a time they did not come every day . . .

Chapters in the middle
So then out loud.
Everyone.
And so forth.
All and one and so forth.
By and one and so forth.

Grammar will. Grammar. Obliged.

Grammar is not grown.

Grammar means that it has to be prepared and cooked. Forget about grammar and think about potatoes.

Or gnocchi. We are touring Italy. Tuscany and Umbria a little.

Cypress cypress cypress cypress cypress pine.

Grammar is not grown.

Susan Howe, *My Emily Dickinson:*
To restore the original clarity of each word-skeleton both women (Gertrude Stein and Emily Dickinson) lifted the load of European literary custom. Adopting old strategies, they revived and reinvented them . . .
Emily Dickinson and Gertrude Stein also conducted a skillful and ironic investigation of patriarchal authority over literary history. Who polices questions of grammar, parts of speech, connection and connotation? Whose order is shut inside the structure of their sentence? What inner articulation releases the coils and complications of Saying's assertion? In very different ways the countermovement of these two women's work penetrates to the indefinite limits of written communication.

No one can know the difference between why I did and why I did not.

Not that kind of novel then.

And in my own very gradual real move toward a more abstract fiction who have been the models? Woolf, Woolf, Beckett, Beckett,

Woolf Woolf, Woolf, then Stein, Stein, now Stein. Stein now for some time very much. I've been loving you following you Chapter Gratitude. Yes for some time, time now so what about it say for example John Reed?

John Reed: She (Stein) lives and dies alone, a unique example of a strange art.

And where have you gotten your chronology from for your master narratives? And what has it cost you?

And what have you taken for legibility? And what has it cost finally?

Be nice. Try to be.

Thank you for the strangeness and the beauty. Reality is remote say it.

Imagine a door a room plenty of ice and snow also as often as they came in they went out.
And so forth . . .

They finally did not continue to interest themselves in description.

Chapter Derision just the other day one of The Famous Post-Modern Novelists says when asked about The Great American Writers: Oh not Gertrude Stein, no, no not Stein.

Joyce

Picasso on Joyce: He is an obscure writer all the world can understand.

Stein drains the text of psychological and mythical overtones thank you very much. She cannot be solved and thank you.

Leave me leave something to confusion.
And I thank you.
The central theme of the novel is that they were glad to see each other.

Carole Maso

Susan Howe: In the college library I use there are two writers whose work refuses to conform to the Anglo-American literary traditions these institutions perpetuate. Emily Dickinson and Gertrude Stein are clearly among the most innovative precursors of modernist poetry and prose, yet to this day canonical criticism from Harold Bloom to Hugh Kenner persists in dropping their names and ignoring their work. Why these two pathfinders were women, why American — are questions too often lost in the penchant for biographical detail that "lovingly" muffles their voices.

A novel of thank you and not about it.

It is a much more impressive thing to any one to any one standing, that is not in action than acting or doing anything doing anything being a successive thing but being something existing. That is then the difference between narrative as it has been and narrative as it is now. And this has come to be a natural thing in a perfectly natural way that the narrative of to-day is not a narrative of succession as all writing for a good many hundreds of years has been.

A space of time filled with moving.

To want everything at once. To write everything at once.

Susan Howe: Writing was the world of each woman. In a world of exaltation of *his* imagination, feminine inscription seems single and sudden.

Chapter Alice, Chapter Jane, Chapter Karen, Chapter Gina.

Chapters in the middle
Notes to myself: The plays conceived as painting. To be apprehended all at once. Meditations inviting dreaming, dalliance. Yet filled with internal movement. Living in itself. Intensity and calm. Mystery and joy. Surprise, delight. Robert Wilson's *Four Saints* last summer. Bliss. Joyous. Well fish.

A novel is a continual surprise.

Chapters as literary device rather than the natural division of novelistic time.

Listening to the Baltimore aunts telling the same stories over and over but each time a little differently.

Ricotta with a pear. This is a story of that in part. Don't forget the pecorino. In part.

A novel of thank you in chapters and saints. Children and fish. Thank you for desire. Reverence and Irreverence. Repeating.

Saints I have definitely seen so far.
Saint Catherine
Saint Francis
Saint Claire definitely

I am calling from Italy to say that there is smoke coming out of my computer and she says is there still a picture when you use the battery and and I say yes and she says don't worry it will all be OK wait until I get there. And I tell her I will meet her in the fortezza and I do, and it is.

The central theme of the novel is that they were glad to see each other.

A very valentine.

An arrangement of their being there and never having been more glad than before . . .

I will wait for you in the fortezza for as long as it takes.

Chapter written in the very hot sun while waiting.
Seeing Saint Catherine's Head. (Siena)

Loving repeating is one way of being. This is now a description of such being. Loving repeating is always in children. Loving repeating is in a way earth feeling. Some children have loving repeating for little things and story-telling, some have it as a more bottom being. Slowly this comes out in them in all their children being, in their eating, playing, crying and laughing. Loving repeating is then in a way earth feeling. This is very strong in many, in children and in old age being. This is very strong in many in all ways

of humorous being, this is very strong in some from their beginning to their ending.

Chapter Emily Rose and Katie Grosvenor

Again and again and again

A very valentine

How are the cats?

Thank you

Go red go red, laugh white.
Suppose a collapse in rubbed purr, in rubbed purr get.
Little sales ladies little sales ladies
Little saddles of mutton.
Little sales of leather and such
beautiful beautiful, beautiful beautiful.

Most tender buttons.

Trembling was all living, living was all loving, someone was then
the other one.

Please may I have a piece of your Pecorino di Pienza thank you
very much.

We have been planning a little trip to Italy in June.

Any time is the time to make a poem. The snow and sun below.

A short novel in cats
She loved her little black and white.
She loved her orange very much.
She loved her gray.
She loved her brown stripes.
But she loved her gray the most. Fauve.

It is because of this element of civilization that Paris has always been the home of all foreign artists, they are friendly the French, they surround you with a civilized atmosphere and they leave you inside of you completely to yourself.

An inner language

Merci beaucoup.

How many more than two are there. (I miss gossiping with you)

And I was once or twice in Vence and loving you very much. Chapter J and Z.

And on the rue de Fleurus.

The Germans were getting nearer and nearer Paris and the last day Gertrude Stein could not leave her room, she sat and mourned. She loved Paris, she thought neither of manuscripts nor of pictures, she thought only of Paris and she was desolate. I came up to her room, I called out, it is all right Paris is saved, the Germans are in retreat. She turned away and said, don't tell me these things. But it's true, I said, it is true. And then we wept together.

And then we wept.

How muffled the world suddenly — as if walking through snow

to the last village of Zenka, perched on a hill

where forever resides, and hasn't it been nice?

Having gone to London in the month of May and roses to say good-bye.

Already I miss you very much.

Chapter 5
And how to thank you.
It was very nearly carefully in plenty of time.

Carole Maso

Could if a light gray and heart rending be softer could it and light gray be paler could it and light gray be paler. Not the least resemblance between that and that.

Once more. Thank you very much. Once more. Once. Twice. Once more. I shall miss you. The things we used to do and say. And how we will not get to the Lago Giacomo Puccini this time.

The patience of a saint.
Not this time.

It takes a lot of time to be a genius, you have to sit around so much doing nothing, really doing nothing. If a bird or birds fly into the room is it good luck or bad luck we will say it is good luck.

A novel of thank you and a travel diary. With and without birds. Looking for an Agritourismo late at night. How many saints have we seen so far?

Saint Francis definitely all over the place, and Saint Claire and Saint Catherine from before.

And how many parts of saints?

Pray to the rib of the saint for strength. The leg of the saint.

It was not a mistake.

Allowed to watch composition. Witness creation. Thank you thank you.

Written in Vence on "honeymoon": A Sonatina. Pussy said that I should wake her in an hour and a half if it didn't rain. It is still raining what should I do.

Secrets, gossips, hopes, disappointments, household life, erotic life, artistic doubts, apologies, jokes, intimacies.

And if not the real story, then what the story was for me.
Chapter Ava.
Don't leave anything out.

To accomplish wishes one needs one's lover.
— for Helen P

Can we stay in Pienza one more day?

Don't leave anything out.

This must not be put in a book.
Why not.
Because it mustn't.
Yes sir.

Chapter
I know at least 4 or 5 Amys now.

To begin to allow. To allow it.

She was not to come again. She came and she asked and she was answered and she was not to come again not to come she was asked and she was answered and she was answered and she was asked and she was not to come again well she was not to come again. This is the first time she came she was not to come again.
To reason with Bertha and Josephine and Sarah and Susan and Adela and never Anns. What is the difference between chocolate and brown and sugar and blue and cream and yellow and eggs and white. What is the difference between addition and edges and adding and baskets and needing and pleasure. It was not a mistake.

When she was and help me when she was what was she to me.

. . . generosity depends upon what is and what is not held out and held up and held in that way.

Allow flowers.

A basket — for Gertrude Stein. And for Alice add flowers. And some eggs.

Explain looking. Explain looking again. Alice
explain looking again.

Carole Maso

The sound of thinking and the sound of thought. A piece of thinking. Don't forget to add flowers. First poppies and broom and then after awhile sunflowers come out. The yellow hovering.

Every color of saint.
Blue saints green saints yellow saints black saints and red angels.

A back and forth. A basket.

We need transference of letters and parcels and doubts and dates and easier.
A novel is useful in more ways than one.

Someday we will be rich. You'll see and then we will spend money and buy everything a dog a Ford letter paper, furs, a hat, kinds of purse.

For Helen, touring Italy. And we will buy a villa someday or a farm if that is what you really want I love you. A Florentine chandelier and a Venetian one. Two more Maine coons perhaps (another gray, another one with stripes) and time to write and all the time in the world to write. All the time in the world to write. Maybe another orange one.

What would you buy?
Time to write. Time to write. I would buy all the time in the world to write. I'd quit my job. Because it takes all the time.

One wish: 1) time to write.
              2) time to write.
And after that.
              time to write.

Stretches and stretches of happiness.

More time.

Left.
Left.
Pretty.
I

had
pretty
a
good
pretty.

I often think about another.

Who need never be mentioned.

Lifting belly high.
That is what I adore always more and more.

Some Amys in that way and some not.

A basket and so forth and what got lost.

Delirious and looking up from lip and clitoris and mound she sees the city of Paris lit up. Trembling was all living, living was all loving, someone was then the other one. The women walk the streets syntactic. Sing Paris Paris Paris Paris. A large white poodle dog and walking down the boulevard.

Chapter Pussycat
Touring through that part of Italy. Her meals: written in a note-book — penne with funghi, game hen with Norcia sauce, tiramisu.

She came to be happier than anyone else who was living then.

She came to be happier . . . In the gorgeous city of Paris. Poodle dog. Yellow flowered hat. Alice Babette.

10,000 paradises

Everyone dies. Say it enough times. Everyone dies everyone dies everyone even you everyone

with and without cats
with and without baskets

dies 10,000 kinds of thank you and paradise

First religion   She saw me and she said two
will stay and two will go away, two will go away and two
will stay and two will stay and two will go away. Can you
go away so soon.
First religion   First religion here.
Second religion   Second religion here.
Third religion   Third religion here.
Fourth religion   Fourth religion being here and having her and
she having been and she is perfection.
Third religion   Third religion being here or is
she perfection third religion is here and she is perfection.
Third religion or is she perfection.

We have left the cathedral behind us. Saints seen so far:

How many saints are there in it?

Beginning again and again is a natural thing . . . Beginning again
and again and again explaining composition and time is a natural
thing

A Little Novel
Any and everyone is an authority.
Welcome.
Does it make any difference who comes first.

What Does She See When She Shuts her Eyes, a novel
So the characters in this novel are the ones who walk in the fields
and lose their dog and the ones who do not walk in the fields
because they have no cows.

When she shuts her eyes she sees the green things among which
she has been working and then as she falls asleep she sees them a
little differently.

When she shuts her eyes . . . Everyone dies. I can't cope. A gun
would be nice. What's wrong with me? Please say it soon. Everyone dies.

You have cancer.
Why do you lie?

Everyone.

A Short Novel
I feel useless.

Is it in any particular corner?

What does she see when she shuts her eyes a novel.

Paradise. What does she see?

And how to thank you.
You changed my life.
And how to thank you.
It was nearly very carefully in plenty of time.

This is the time to do or say so.
Chapter

Not useless. Not a bird. Not a cherry. Not a third. Not useless.
Not at all. Not elite. Not small.

It's useless.

So the characters in this novel are looking out the window of a green Fiat touring Italy and one of them is thinking about Gertrude Stein and reading her out loud in between cypress cypress cypress and the map and the guidebook and I feel useless.

Zenka.

The month of June and Defiance due and The Bay of Angels excerpt due and The novel of thank you due for Martine. And that perfectly awful woman Mattie Garrett at the Tuscany Writing Workshop and the computer up in smoke.

Oh that perfectly awful Mattie Garrett, she thought turning toward the dark window, has spoiled all of our fun!

The fax this afternoon. Useless.

Blue birds on a black hat. And as it happens. Black birds on a blue hat. And as it happens. Blue birds on a blue hat. And not next to as it happens. Black bird and a black hat.

Chapters 84 and almost 85, but not quite

People die in and out of order
in easy and hard ways people die
people die out of —
The things we used to do
sweetness of the yellow broom.
even though you are 84
even though everyone must
everyone has got to

in or out of order
drinking vieux marc, a trip to the sea
as if love could send you back there again
swept up, side swept, wind
like magic as if love
your beloved Dylan Thomas and Eliot your friend,
he was always kind, he lent me money, not anti-Semitic, he lent
me money, nonsense, oh such nonsense.
And Gertrude Stein

People die in 5, 6, 7 and
7, 6, 5
in the day and the night.
Afraid and not.

Happy and sad times.
And that fall how I just thought if I could make a pot-au-feu I might survive — and you looked on sadly. And you took my hand after awhile. That fall you saved my life. For the first time. Thank you.

And if I could only help you now. Somehow. I want to very much.

Elissa and Annabelle and Anatole. Dale and Julie and Suzanne and Marilyn and Monica and the French Carole and Diana Chapmann she's called.

Judith.

Urgent. My darling Zenka passed away this morning. She was in the nursing home. Please call. Love, Judith

Letting love to have a mother. Letting love to have letting love to have a mother letting love to have.
In plenty of time.

Rose. The first word, the first world I know.
Thank you in every possible way.

Preparing a novel and paving the way.

Catherine, Caroline, Charlotte and Celestine.
In the place of no one not yet.

Miss miss miss miss miss and gossip

When they cannot stop it altogether when they cannot stop it altogether.

Come and kiss me when you want to because if you do you have more than done that which is a satisfaction to have been most awfully obliged to have as a delight and more than that.

Thank you.

Very much very much and as much and as much and then markets, markets are open in the morning and except on Monday.

Do you think we should follow the sign for Perugia?

very much

Chapters of magic near the beginning and end (interchangeable)

Puccini is striped like the campanile but it's all right.

Carole Maso

Sage grows.

Very content followed by five bells.
We are very well fish.

Sage grows so let it.
Children grow.
Let them.
Ideas.
Notions of the novel
So let them.
Wild capers grow everywhere.
A tribute to Gertrude Stein and a travel diary so let it.
Roses and rosemary everywhere

For my
beautiful mother
Rose
marie
Maso
the one word
of my world my father calling across the green
Rose

Chapter Always
These days thinking of you, always, always.

Chapter Alice
who named her Rose in hope, as the century turned 31

Grandma Alice very much

If they say and it is an established fact if they say that he has gone away is there anybody to ask about it. It is so very easy to change a novel a novel can be a novel and it can be a story of the departure of Dr. Johnston it can be the story of the discovery of how after they went away nobody was as much rested as they hoped to be.

Everything that will be said will have a connection with paper and amethysts with writing and silver with buttons and books.

I am a simple girl in some ways do not want the Isle of Capri the Lago Giacomo Puccini will do. If not this time then next. Looking all over Florence for the cross that got lost.

Consider whether they would be at all interested.

It can be easily seen that a novel of elegance leaves something to be desired.

Repeat. It can be easily seen that a novel of elegance leaves something to be desired. She knew in about the middle of it. Time to write.

Let me say it here. Everything I loved or wanted or feared.

Accuse me if you like one more time of overreaching. I miss you. Love you. Want.

And time to write.

This spa water is only for drinking. And the woman makes a breaststroke through the air, for swimming Bagno Vignoni, 30 kilometers away let's go.

In the green Fiat. Have to finish Gertrude Stein, have to finish Traveling Light — and the hills and the cypresses. Cypress, cypress, cypress, pine. Ava Klein turn over on your side.

There is never any altogether the easiest way is to leave out anything.

The whole chapter is thinking about the courage you afford and thinking out loud and the flowers and so not to be afraid. There is music in the head so sing continuously.

Chapter Rose
Who named you Carole Alice at mid-century. Thank you in every possible way.

Song of joy

And say what you need and like and want. Pleasure. A novel and you out loud. When she has been satisfied when she has been satisfied.

Begin again.

She may be coming in any moment darling.

Begin again.
Fanny irresistible.
Jenny recalled.
Henrietta as much as that.
Claribel by and by
Rose as plainly seen
Hilda for that time
Ida as not famous.
Katherine as it should have it in preference
Caroline and by this time
Maria by this arrangement Esther who can be thought of
Charlotte and finally.

She rolls the rosy aureole and pearl the world around and round. Sea pearl to pearl with her and lip she shudders honey gold and conjures — this must be Paradise — or maybe Paris. She came to be happier than anybody else who was alive then. Gorgeous lilting rosy pearl. She rides the women world syntactic. Sings Paris Paris Paris Paris. And they walk the poodle Basket.

Thank you.
The way it looks exactly like it.

The way you can get it to look exactly like you see and feel. Almost exactly. Thank you most of all for that.

Who in this world is luckier than I?

A very valentine — for Gertrude Stein.

Little by little and more and more I begin to understand you very much.

A novel and the future of the novel and the rest and the rest is diamonds.

Father calling to Mother, Rose across the world first word. Repeated again and again rose rose rose rose rose rose rose.

A novel of thank you and not about it.
It might be allowed

With thanks to Nicole Cooley, Keith Waldrop, John O'Brien.

Someone named Rose at mid-century named her.
In hope. 5 joyful 5 sorrowful mysteries.
Thank you in every possible way

Once more I thank you.

An arrangement of their being there and never having been more glad than before.

A list of addresses and who went to see them.

Bruschetta, crostoni, lentils with pasta, grilled lamb, tiramisu.

Spaghetti with clam sauce.

Come and kiss me when you want to.

We are very well fish
Lavishly well fish

And Alice Babette, petite crevette. On the rue Christine after the war. Adore. Picking flowers gentle. Rose is a rose is a rose eternal and I am I because my little dog knows me.
She wanders gorgeous key syntactic. Violet-breasted. Poodle Basket.

Third religion	Where.
Fourth religion	Where they grow vegetables so
plentifully.	
Fourth religion	If you courtesy.

Carole Maso

Second religion	If you hold a hat on your head.
Third religion	If they are not told.
Fourth religion	Across to me.
Fourth religion	She walked across to me.
Third religion	And what did she see.
Second religion	What did she say to me.
First religion	When she walked across to me.

I found myself plunged into a vortex of words, burning words, cleansing words, liberating words, and the words were all ours and it was enough that we held them in our hands . . .

I shall not speak for anybody. I shall do my duty, I shall establish that mile. I shall choose wonder. Be blest.

*

Footnotes

Our Walks
Often in the evening we would walk together; I greeted at the door of 5 rue Christine by Gertrude's staunch presence, pleasant touch of hand, well-rounded voice always ready to chuckle. Our talks and walks led us far from war paths. For generally having no axe to grind nor anyone to execute with it, we felt detached and free to wander in our own quarter where, while exercising her poodle, "Basket," we naturally fell into thought and step. Basket, unleashed, ran ahead, a white blur, the ghost of a dog in the moonlit side streets:

> Where ghosts and shadows mingle —
> As lovers, lost when single,

The night's enchantment made our conversation as light, iridescent and bouncing as soap bubbles, but as easily exploded when touched upon — so I'll touch on none of them for you, that a bubble may remain a bubble! And perhaps we never said *d'imperissables choses.*
— Nathalie Barney

Sweetnotes

Their Cakes
The discovery of cakes had always been a peace time pursuit of
Gertrude and Alice. Meeting them by chance at Aix-le-Bains, I en-
quired why they happened to be on the opposite bank of the Lac du
Bourget, and was informed of a new sort of cake created in one of
the villages on a mountain beyond. But first obliged to go on errands,
they descended from the lofty seat of their old Ford car — Alice be-
jeweled as an idol and Gertrude with the air of an Indian divinity.

She accepted her fame as a tribute, long on the way but due, and
enjoyed it thoroughly. Only once, in Paris — and indeed the last
time I saw her — did the recognition of a cameraman displease her,
for he waylaid her just as we were entering Rumpelmayer's patis-
serie. In order to satisfy the need for cake, and the photographer's
wish, she was photographed by him, through the plate-glass window, eating the chosen one.

Her meals — continued
Melon and prosciutto, artichoke risotto, grilled sausages, another
tiramisu. Ravioli with truffles, fish stew, panecotta and so forth.

Please another Piero della Francesca.

And so forth
I am not striving at all but only gradually growing and becoming
steadily more aware of the way things can be felt and known in
words, and perhaps if I feel them and know them myself in the
new ways it is enough, and if I know fully enough there will be a
note of sureness and confidence that will make others know too.
And when one has discovered and evolved a new form it is not the
form but the fact that *you are the form* that is important.

I find you young writers worrying about losing your integrity and
it is well you should, but a man who really loses his integrity does
not know that it is gone, and nobody can wrest it from you if you
really have it.

Hemingway you have a small income; you will not starve; you
can work without worry and you can grow and keep this thing

and it will grow with you. But he did not wish to grow that way, he wished to grow violently.

Everybody's life is full of stories; your life is full of stories; my life is full of stories. They are very occupying, but they are not very interesting. What is interesting is the way everyone tells their stories.

Thornton Wilder: The fundamental occupation of Miss Stein's life was not the work of art but the shaping of a theory of knowledge, a theory of time, and a theory of the passions . . . the formalization of a metaphysics.

Mina Loy: she swept the literary circus clear for future performances.

For a very long time everybody refuses and then almost without a pause almost everybody accepts. In the history of the refused in the arts and literature the rapidity of the change is always startling.

Wassily Kandinsky, 1910: The apt use of a word (in its poetical sense), its repetition, twice, three times, or even more frequently, according to the need of the poem, will not only tend to intensify the internal structure but also bring out unsuspected spiritual properties in the word itself. Further, frequent repetition of a word (a favorite game of children, forgotten in later life) deprives the word of its external reference. Similarly, the symbolic reference of a designated object tends to be forgotten and only the sound is retained. We hear the pure sound, unconsciously perhaps, in relation to the concrete or immaterial object. But in the latter case pure sound exercises a direct impression on the soul. The soul attains to an objectless vibration, even more complicated, I might say more transcendent, than the reverberations released by the sound of a bell, a stringed instrument or a fallen board. In this direction lie the great possibilities for literature of the future.

Martin Ryerson: If you realized that she worked insistently, every day, to be published the first time by a real publisher, publishing house after she was sixty. But I wonder who will do that, who will have the insistence, you understand the obsession, the surety the purity of insistence to do that. No concessions. She used to tell me, Don't you ever dare to make a concession. Then one walks down, down, down. There's no end of walking down.

Acts
Curtain
Characters
Characters
Curtain
Acts
There is no one and one
Nobody has met anyone.
>Curtain Can Come.
>(for Zenka Bartek 1912–1997)
>Curtain.

And this is
what bliss
is and
this and
this is
what
bliss is.

very much

White lights lead to red lights which indicate the exit.

Spaghetti arrabiata, spaghetti bolognese, polenta, grilled pork, escarole, spinach, ricotta, tiramisu . . .

Saint Francis hundreds of times, Saint Sebastian certainly, Saint Simon, Saint Claire is a big one, the head of Saint Catherine, Saint Francis is a very big one, Saint Peter and Saint John of course. Saint Bliss.

Preparing a novel prepared to stay.

And paving the way.

Thank you very much.

Carole Maso

Chapter Rose
Even then I was loving you

very much.

End in singing.

Who goes away tonight. They all do. And so they do.

Divining Stein
Lisa Shea

> There is no use in finding out what is in anybody's
> mind. There is no use in finding out what is in
> anybody's mind.
>
> — *How to Write*

FROM GERTRUDE STEIN I LEARNED that language is born in sense
and nonsense, in mystery and banality, in secrecy and subterfuge,
in dissonance and rhyme; that it can only ever be a beautiful, dan-
gerous, private offering; that it exists apart from its creator, un-
arbitrary and uncompromised, incapable of being duplicated and
therefore, in its way, divine.

I recall the photograph of Stein seated on the commodious sofa
in her famous Montparnasse salon, herself a monumental figure
whose near catatonic stare betrays nothing of her meticulous,
frank, sovereign, mischievous mind. She appears to be a still life
beneath the lively company of paintings by Matisse, Cezanne and
Picasso — including his appropriately outsized portrait of her —
whose friendships she cultivated and whose works she so sagely
promoted and acquired. And yet how her words on the page caper
and cavort, charm and conceal, comfort and confound in a cagey
effluence, not stopping until the whole enterprise of language itself has been put forth and put to rest, put forth and put to rest,
put forth and put to rest.

Reading, among other books, *The Autobiography of Alice B.
Toklas, The Making of Americans* and *Four Saints in Three Acts* —
savoring the serious, goofy brilliance of these works — was a literary liberation the likes of which I had never experienced. Stein's
"little sentences," as she called them, were revelatory. Especially
important for me was the marvelously colloidal *Tender Buttons*.
A series of disarming, aphoristic discourses on objects, food and
rooms, the work was seminal in my understanding of what was
meant by literary modernism.

Coming across exquisite, inscrutable lines like "Dining is west" and "A white hunter is nearly crazy" made me believe, as no other writer had — I was a senior in high school — in the supremacy of poetic language, the efficacy of its instruction and the stunning variety of its uses. I marvelled at how Stein's so-called automatic writing (she never called it that) concealed a powerful quality of deliberateness, of inevitability, how such earnest sounding prose contained an undeniable element of willful, high hilarity, how a single sentence could be made to tell an entire story. Stein had, somehow, got hold of the process of thought (her thought) itself and laid it down. Writing, Stein's heavily associative narratives seemed to proclaim, was a slipstream into and out of which flows this wondrous, unreliable entity called consciousness.

Stein had, in fact, studied psychology with William James at Radcliffe and medicine at Johns Hopkins University before taking off for Paris, about which she wrote, "America is my home but Paris is my home town." You can detect the science in Stein's writing — the doggedness, the specificity, the sobriety. It is nothing if not rigorous, the stuff of philosophical inquiry. And yet her work reads madly, obscurely, drunkenly. There is about it the quality of something rarefied, monastic; resistant to and defiant of being understood, learned from, made one's own. It is, in a word, difficult.

Stein's radical example, her conceptual and stylistic innovations, led me to the disparate, fiercely modern writings of Joyce and Beckett and Pound, and to such later cloistered yet adamantly catholic writers as Emily Dickinson, Wallace Stevens, Simone Weil, John Ashbery and Lydia Davis. I still find Stein's work wild and invigorating, pleasingly solecistic and not so much solipsistic as solitary, unto itself, by turns loquacious and taciturn, modest and good-naturedly vain, driven by wisdom, by wile.

I had first read Stein in the heady fever-dream of my own early creative writing efforts. The poetry (and poetic prose) I emulated and tried to imitate was "fancy," by which I mean highblown, willfully obscure and language-drunk. Inaccessibility was all. I worshipped Baudelaire, Ponge, Russell Edson, Rimbaud, Djuna Barnes, Ronald Firbank, Gerard Nerval, Henri Michaux. The works of these literary oddballs and experimenters, these writers of deranged sensibility (remember the wonderful story of Nerval walking his pet lobster on a pink ribbon through the Tuileries?) made the world seem, at last, desirable, strange, possible, new.

While Stein's writing was fancy, it also was plain. It read like poetry yet had the length and breadth and heft of prose. Reading Stein, I saw that it was possible to write something as real as a story — as opposed to the gorgeous fictiveness of poetry, so full of artifice, of art! — without losing poetic impulse and expression. Before Stein, I had loved the rapturous lines of Spenser and Chaucer and Donne, but not the more grounded paragraphs (I couldn't see the grandness!) of *a Tale of Two Cities* and *Silas Marner* and *The Red Badge of Courage.* How daunting were these substantial works of prose, how level compared to the lofty reaches of "The Mutabilitie Cantos," the bawdy excesses of *The Canterbury Tales.*

In Stein's work I found such freedom, an unfetteredness that I had thought only poetry, with its romance and luster, its mystery and abandon, could supply. It was Stein who gave me the nerve to start writing prose poems that slowly would lengthen into short stories and, years later, into a novel. Stein who made me seek out other fiction writers — George Eliot, Charlotte Brontë, Edith Wharton, Jane Austen, Virginia Woolf — whose biographies I had devoured but whose books I had never read. Stein who clearly proved to me that a writer could have, in addition to reputation, a life!

What has stayed with me about Gertrude Stein is that she was a genius. Like Wittgenstein — another passionate promoter of one's own "vocabulary of thinking" — Stein's work made me laugh. Better put, her writing (and his) tickled my mind at its absolute core. What a sense of delight and well-being I experienced reading Stein's splendid little sentences, crafted and canny like no others. The world of her words — stringent, moony, repetitive, humorous, surreal — still makes me long to linger in them, subsist on them, claim them as my own.

Henry James. Circa 1905. The Granger Collection, New York.

Henry James
Mona Simpson

IN HIS FINAL DELIRIUMS, when his fever was high, Henry James had wanted to write, Leon Edel tells us. He kept asking for paper and pencil. When he was given them, his hand would make the movements of writing.

The manual echo of what had consoled and steadied him so much of his life was what he turned to again, in the months and weeks before his death.

Like one of his own characters, Henry James had an American-scale ambition in his youth, though not towards the amassing of fortunes or the building of skyscrapers.

He wrote to his mother, "If I keep along here patiently I rather think I shall become a (sufficiently) great man."

He was devoted enough to the life of the artist and confident enough in his own gifts to describe an older sculptor's career as "a sort of beautiful sacrifice to a noble mistake."

He intended the nobility and the sacrifice. Not the mistake.

A portrait of the artist at twenty-eight: writing travel articles for *The Nation*, he claimed of Niagara Falls, "It beats Michelangelo."

"Youth," he wrote in his notebooks later, "was the most beautiful word in the language.

Once, at thirty, I bought a dress over the telephone. I'd tracked it down at Neiman Marcus, in Texas, because in a picture, it looked like the dress Isabel Archer wore her first evening in England, as she stepped out onto the Touchetts' lawn.

When it arrived, the dress proved unbecoming.

This was how I learned Isabel Archer, Albany girl that she was, stood at least five foot seven.

I didn't always love Henry James.

I only vaguely remember the tenor of my dissatisfaction. I felt, in an oblique way, he would find me — my class, my education, probably my wardrobe — wanting. I felt sure, in a word, that he wouldn't *like* me. I enclosed this secret insecurity with a certain "class anger," as we said at that time, in Berkeley. Of course, I'd not yet read "Brooksmith" or "In the Cage" or realized how, late in his life, Henry James worried about money.

"It got me out of Bakersfield," a boy in my freshman Introduction to Poetry Class at Berkeley said, in defense of *A Portrait of the Artist as a Young Man.*

I doubt that any novel or short story written by Henry James ever got any seventeen-year-old out of Bakersfield.

That is simply not what his work does.

In the same way people lead one to other people and the college freshman eventually moves past her dormitory companions to friendships of real urgency and meaning, books lead us to other books, to authors we need more and daily.

I already loved Proust; I'd seriously read my way through the Russians, the Latin Americans; I'd probably read *Middlemarch* seven times, but I think it was Virginia Woolf who finally led me to Henry James.

There are dalliances and sustenances in literature. In a daily way, I need James. Why do we love him so?

He helps us, the way an affectionate friend could, who also happened to be a born ironist, with his intelligence always available at his fingertips, lightly.

If Proust teaches us to give in to love while we're young and to save ourselves from dying over it, James gives us interiority, a longer, deeper process, if less tumultuous, less colored; he teaches how to furnish a square solitary room on a high floor and make it not only beautiful but comforting.

For me, Henry James has been a love in middle age, with exactly that temperature and depth.

James wrote of Dickens that life seemed "always to go on in the morning or in the very earliest hours of the afternoon at most" and that "Shelley, let us say . . . is a light, and Swinburne is a sound — Browning alone is a temperature."

Of course, James is famous for decrying Tolstoy's "large loose baggy monsters."

In Henry James, we dwell in a city apartment, although we might be in the country on a lawn, at dusk, visiting. If we are walking over that lawn it is nonetheless in city clothes, high heels piercing the thin membrane of webbed roots. The light is soft, that slowly graying dusk that takes an hour or more. We may be watching the sky from the back of a cab. But it is never a brazen season. We are never in the tropics, it is never noon. We are always among the thousand grays of home.

Fortunately (given the youthful vigor of his ambition), there was a time Henry James enjoyed success. As luck would have it, this was near the beginning of his career.

At thirty-five, he was and felt famous. "I have got a good deal of fame and hope some day to get a little money," he wrote to a friend.

Daisy Miller became a type, internationally famous herself, for whom dozens of young Americans claimed to be the model.

At this time, Henry James was prolific and impervious to criticism: "Never was a genius — if genius there is — more healthy, objective, and (I honestly believe) less susceptible of superficial irritations and reactionary impulses," he wrote to his parents, when they worried about criticism of one of his stories.

He was settled in England and retained some of the luxurious idolatry of his family one can have from an ocean away.

Of his mother, he wrote: "She was our life, she was the house."

She was the house. A novel in itself.

Even after meeting Turgenev, his revered mentor, in Paris, the Europeanized writer, at thirty-one, wrote his mother (*she was the house*) asking her to lay in "tomatoes, ice-cream, corn, melons, cranberries and other indigenous victuals" for his return home.

He asked his brother William to bring abroad some of his books, some American toothpaste and candy.

Though Henry James lived in Europe almost all of his working years, he retained dabs and cravings for Americanness.

"I wish I could tell you how characteristic everything strikes me as being," he wrote, returning, "everything from the vast white sky — to the stiff sparse individual blades of grass."

The plot of his younger brother's life is a story that might have appealed to Mark Twain. After fighting in the Civil War, Wilky James tried to run a plantation in Florida with paid black labor, failed, went west, lived a shiftless life as a railroad clerk and died at forty.

I would love to read what Henry James would *do* with such material. "The stiff sparse individual blades of grass" taunts us — he could sketch this landscape with the back of his hand.

But his eyes were turned the other direction, east. Back, he might have said.

So other voices, other heirs are left to write about Wilky's generation in the western expansion. Some of Alice Munro's recent stories have treated North American characters of James's (and Twain's) time, with a Jamesian sense of psychological precision and aesthetic intricacy.

An artist from Kentucky, a friend of Henry James, learned his craft by decorating altars in Catholic churches all the way to Canada, before going to Europe to study.

Some eight hundred ladies came to hear Henry James lecture (on "The Lesson of Balzac") in Los Angeles.

But these were simply not stories that attracted him.

"What does Oxford want of men from Nebraska and Canada?" he asked, incredulous, when told about the idea of the Rhodes scholarship.

I'd like to read what Alice Munro would do with that mythical altar-artist and those eight hundred ladies.

Henry James's heroes were George Eliot, Turgenev and Flaubert, all idols of his youth.

He had brilliant contemporaries too, Twain and Conrad, Kipling, Stevenson. In each case, he acknowledged their talent while not quite accepting that talent's completion.

Why is it almost impossible to accept the mastery of our contemporaries?

Probably because, as Henry James did, we meet them in person.

He befriended Turgenev in his youth, taking great pride in a dinner he gave in his honor on the occasion of the Russian's visit to London, and throughout his years in London, he was friends with the parents of Virginia Woolf, once staying for a fortnight at the scene of *To the Lighthouse.*

> I have hours of unspeakable reaction against my smallness of production; my wretched habits of work — or my un-work; my levity, my vagueness of mind, my perpetual failure to focus my attention, to absorb myself, to look things in the face, to invent, to produce, in a word. I shall be forty years old in April next: it's a horrible fact.

Henry James wrote this the year he published *Daisy Miller,* so we can assume his moods about his work were not entirely guided by external circumstances.

At forty, he wrote

> I believe however that I have learned how to work and that it is in moments of forced idleness, almost alone, that these melancholy reflections seize me. When I am really at work, I'm happy, I feel strong, I see many opportunities ahead. It is the only thing that makes life endurable. I must make some great efforts during the next few years, however, if I wish not to have been on the whole a great failure. I shall have been a failure unless I do something great!

This theme of greatness persisted for Henry James and perhaps the plot of his career was more fortunate for us than for him, because it forced him to question the nature and source of this aspired-to "greatness."

Of course, it's difficult to separate Henry James's feelings of insecurity from his older brother William, to whom he was close all his life and who was capable of great cruelty.

William harshly criticized Henry's work, often reading it with a crude and conventional ear. When William was elected to the Academy of Arts and Letters, he refused the honor in a letter with the addendum, "I am the more encouraged to this course by the fact that my younger and shallower and vainer brother is already in the Academy. . . ."

Yet Henry remained his "incoherent, admiring, affectionate brother" (this after an insulting letter about his work). At the time of Henry's death, he imagined William (who had predeceased him) to be in the house, though in another room.

Henry wrote to William, "I am always sorry when I hear of your reading anything of mine, and always hope you won't — you seem to me so constitutionally unable to 'enjoy it.'"

Twice, Henry James experienced great setbacks and both times after enormous efforts, direct bids, as it were, for money in the first case when he tried to become a playwright, and belated recognition, even posterity, in a final attempt, when he edited his New York Edition.

After his painful and public failure in the theater, he rebounded. "I take up my own old pen again — the pen of all my old unforgettable efforts and sacred struggles. To myself — today — I need say no more. Large and full and high the future still opens. It is now indeed that I may do the work of my life. And I will."

His renewed will resulted in a period of time when he was writing a story a week, while also sketching out *The Ambassadors*.

Still, Henry James never had the hit he so wanted.

After visiting his friend George du Maurier, whose *Trilby* was breaking records as a best-seller, he wrote, "I came back feeling an even worse failure than usual."

In London once, when John Singer Sargent took him to see Edwin Austin Abbey working on one of his large Shakespearean paintings, he "came away biting my thumb, of course, and with my ears burning with the sense of how it's not the age of my dim trade."

Henry James spent four years, from age sixty-three to age sixty-seven, preparing and editing his New York Edition, the collective edition of his novels and tales. He revised critical scenes in some of the novels, especially *The Portrait of a Lady* and *The American*, and worked closely with Alvin Langdon Coburn (a pioneer in photography), whom he'd selected to make the frontispieces.

It's hard not to be moved by the energy and devotion of James writing his prefaces, "fingering" and revising his stories and novels, squeezing things out to fit in the twenty-three volumes he'd decided on. He was preparing his work to pass on.

At the end, he would describe the Edition as "really a monument (like Ozymandias) which has never had the least intelligent critical justice done to it — or any sort of critical attention at all paid to it."

When the first royalty statement for his "monument" arrived, he was crushed. It was "a greater disappointment than I had been prepared for . . . a great, I confess, and bitter, grief."

"Is there anything for me at all?" he asks, sounding the eternal question of the artist at the end of his life, who has made his own deadlines, his own standards, perhaps his own beautiful sacrifice to a noble mistake.

This time, Henry James truly had a breakdown and was unable to write. He needed doctors and rest. He was in his mid-sixties. He spoke of his "black depression."

This time he could not work.

For someone who wrote beautifully, powerfully, *finally* about the danger of the missed life, the "beautiful sacrifice to a noble mistake" (for what else is "The Beast in the Jungle"), in his personal world, his other "real" life, Henry James seems to have *lived*. This is a great deal to say about someone who may have died a virgin.

Though he was decidedly heavy from middle age on, he'd always enjoyed the physical world — from his Roman horseback rides in the *campagna*, amidst imperial ruins, to his daily cycling around Rye.

And through the lace and web of his elaborate social universe, which seemed to swing from the magnificent to the annoying, he maintained exceedingly close relationships with friends and family.

At dinner parties, in Edith Wharton's Lenox house, when the guests were gone, James would draw his chair to the fire and say, "Now let us say what we really think."

His long friendship with her allowed him to forgive her for the mortifying discovery that she had fund-raised for his benefit in America.

The most significant tribute his work received was on the occasion of his seventieth birthday, when three hundred of his British friends collaborated in presenting him with a formal portrait by John Singer Sargent and a golden bowl.

At the beginning of his lifetime, as at the end, his greatest readers were his friends.

"We who knew him well know how great he would have been if he had never written a line," Edith Wharton wrote.

As he was dying, the person he seemed to favor was his young butler. His name was Burgess and he called him Burgess James.

His advice to his nieces and nephews was **"Be kind, be kind, be kind."**

Perhaps the books most written for friends are the ones that end up being read by strangers.

What James said of London could be said of his stories. They always end by "giving one absolutely everything one asks."

NOTE: All facts, such as they are, come directly from Leon Edel's five-volume biography of Henry James.

Bob Kaufman. Photograph by Chris Felver. Courtesy Coffee House Press.

Bob Kaufman: The Footnotes Exploded
Will Alexander

A VOYAGER ARRIVING in a darkened opal port, his verbal lenses honed by an ingrown aural preciseness, by an absence of buried mechanics. I think of the aboriginal Kaufman inwardly floating through explosive anonymities, never once singed by mundane repetition or sequel. His hearing is replete at the level of intuitive terminology, at the root of its most seminal spinning. His language, part aurora and lava, flowing from a central vitrescence. It partakes of the spell, being hypnotic and genetic in demeanor. I mean, there is insight into life which sustains itself by means of intrinsic purity, by means of necessitous obscurity, which can never be subject to rational decoding, to exoteric decipherment. Language then, is not a given, not a sum to be captured and examined under prevalent electron regalia. Verbal obstacle then leaps, the accessible as sense, the quotidian as assumption.

By his electrical presence Kaufman's language escapes the analytical, the moment by moment vacuum deemed climactic according to a precedent assumed by the rules of a rational exegesis. And such exegesis denies and destroys the spontaneous in favor of pattern. Again Kaufman, not a deleted fuchsia, but original respiration. A voice capable of traversing acres of fire, his mandibles torched by elemental tattoos, by various interior Grails. And what compels such attention is his superior analogical power aged by a fabulous turbulence. As if he had been cast into frictive waters at the center of a brimstone mountain. It is a poetic energy which continues to prevail, and by prevailing I mean sustained hypnosis as experienced by the reader.

When I first encountered the poem "To My Son Parker Asleep in the Next Room," an urgency, a vortex occurred within me, as if awakened to a new viridity. Such reaction is not an exaggeration for a nascent poet to experience, especially one instinctively seduced by subconscious dioramas. It is a writing seemingly soaked by a surreptitious light from a vacated sun. Then reading poems like "Sheila," "Unhistorical Events," "Blue Slanted Into Blueness"

211

became for me, like obscure motions spinning in a transfixed carbon house. I was magnetically engulfed.

As Kaufman poetically appeared with his broadsides he was already of seminal import, he was already the nizam, the rajah. According to the photographer Jerry Stoll, Kaufman was a "pioneer," a "functioning . . . critic of society," "much more social and political . . . than any of the other poets in North Beach . . ." He carried his own migrational light which led "people like Ginsberg" into a greater activists' capacity. In this regard, Kaufman was the proto-source, the engendered proto-Sphinx, who simply appeared without formal literary precedent, much in the manner of Lautréamont or Rimbaud. Of course, this is plain to us now, but in the atmosphere of the 1950s, with the case against the Rosenbergs still hissing, with the rasping carcinogens of McCarthy generally rife throughout the atmosphere, he showed unprecedented character. General threat corroded the foreground; metropolitan areas swarmed with informers, all enigmas were suspected. Noncondoned behavior was thought of as allergic, as partaking of treasonous errata. And Kaufman at this moment was the inscrutable lightning rod, possessed of courage and greenish defiance, who transmuted life into sound; into supernal ensembles of magic verbal liquid.

His "flaming water," his "Indian suicides," capable of conversing with a box of amoebas, capable of "shining" on "far historical peaks." Kaufman in this register remains eminently uncontainable. In this he literally embodies the surreal in that not a single line is operatically planned or thought out as regards publishable criteria. But upon reading his work, levels of intensity are not lacking, nor is a spectacular use of oral language convened to suicidally incinerate the printed page with aleatoric detachment. No, the language remains powerful in book form, fused in its leaps by antisedentary scorching. Yet Kaufman seemed to swelter with an inborn hostility to literature and its sustained identity in the reductive. Because of this, his verbal tremblings remain profuse with usurpation and voltage as he acknowledged "the demands of surrealist realization," as he challenged "Apollinaire to stagger drunk from his grave and write a poem about the Rosenbergs' last days" while smouldering in the "Death House." In the poem "Voyagers," he speaks of

Twice-maimed shrews, ailing
In elongated slots
Of public splendor.

or, in "Afterwards, They Shall Dance," he speaks of his face being "a living emotional relief map, forever wet."

Where do we find lines like Kaufman's in the present poetic American pantheon; lines stunning with irregular galvanic, with endogenous wingedness, with relentless surprise?

In the surge of Lamantia there are parallels, there are moments in Corso and Crane, in the visions of Daniel Moore, which synaptically lurk in the ricochets of his concussive charisma. He remains ulterior, clandestine, in the way his verbal cancellations deduct their actions in crossing subversive esplanades. And he poetically protracts this vapor across dialectical respiration being "eternally free in all things." He spoke of "Java," of "Melanesian mountain peaks," of Assyria's "earthen dens," of Camus as a "sand faced rebel from Olympus." So Kaufman continues to exist for me like a verdigris Phoenix, arising and re-arising from the poets' ill-begotten lot even as he smoulders "in a cell with a view of evil parallels."

The quintessential scion of chance linguistic praxis, Kaufman's poems continue moment by moment to irradiate electricity. Continue within the range of immaculate verbal searing, spun from green elliptical finery.

Saying this, do I place Kaufman on a pedestal just to celebrate him in death, to claim inspiration from the sum of an abstract mirage? I can answer without hesitation, no. During the late 1970s and the early 1980s I would travel to North Beach as towards some internal Mecca, wandering its labyrinths around sundown, just to catch sightings of the darting giant flitting in and out of enclaves. These illusive glimpses were like poetic talismans for me, sparks of gold in the labyrinth. I would always see him on angles from a distance, and near the end of one auric afternoon we stood face to face at oblique remove, and I called out his name, and at the evaporation of his name from my lips he literally vanished into one of the teeming dives in the vicinity of Vallejo. Which immediately brought to mind the parallel of Pessoa and his spontaneous disappearances during his walks across Lisbon.

During this period he lived adjacent to Philip Lamantia. And it was one morning after emerging from a dozen-hour dialogue with the latter, that we walked across Harwood Alley to Neeli Cherkovski's, who tended Kaufman during those days. It was about 8 A.M. one Monday morning, and Kaufman remained sequestered in the other room, as both of us peered at the original typewritten manuscript of *The Ancient Rain*. I mention this episode because both Kaufman and Lamantia have had instantaneous impact upon my poetic formation. Have made foray after foray into my hermetically sealed lingual athanor, and their verbal osmotics continue to seep into my imaginal ozone, letting me know moment after moment that imaginal radiance can prevail.

In discussing Kaufman, all academic insertion is passionately declined, is ravaged, with all its footnotes exploded. The contours blurred, the circumferences alchemically splayed by the beauty of mathematical absence. And I mean mathematics in its lower form, in its niggling banter concerning the petty matters of equated equidistance.

When poets sought shelter beneath an academic archway, Kaufman assaulted police, and was arrested more than thirty times in a single year. When poets sought for the proper form to ensconce their subject matter, Kaufman wrote of "Unholy Missions," of "Heather Bell," of the previously mentioned "Sheila" "cast out of rainclouds . . . on warped faded carousels." The verbal structures collapse and revisualize, not in terms of a furtive literary comment, nor as an ironic line sustained by the pressure of brilliantly acceptable wit. Kaufman's language condenses to aboriginal ubiquity, being that status of poet who heard his words as untranslated molten, like an abnormal eaglet deciphering his reptilian forerunners with intangible preciseness; the sound spun by "illusionary motion," by the liquor of exploded roses, blazing as quantum mass beyond the reasoned scope of antideracination.

A poet who followed his own endogenous helical road, roaming through "vacant theaters," erasing "taxable public sheets," Kaufman so derealized the archives that he negated all rational effort by sifting through auricular winds of dialectical transparency, thereby mining an inevitable verbal aurum. The three dimensions magnificently destabilized and fleetingly focused like "Tall strips of carrion moonlight sparing only stars." Thus he occupied a seditionary grammatical bastion, implying "a horror of trades." He knew like Rimbaud that "The hand that guides the pen is worth the hand that guides the plow." Thus, he threw routine and stasis into the quarrelsome antidotes of debris.

And even in death, Kaufman continues to magically advance across a blinding reticular sea, without the mercator's imprisoning symmetrics, electric with utopias, far outside the parochial reportage of mechanical matching burins, poised as they are against the pure "fluidity of desire."

Of course, Kaufman refuses to match, to sustain the subject of "conferences" à la Kerouac and Ginsberg, so crucially pointed out by Maria Damon. He continues to exist "beyond official Beat history," beyond its canon as inscribed by the Whitney Museum, beyond the delineated form of the countercultural figure within the scope of defined exotic boundary. No, there is a more sustained projection from his blood, which at present remove naturally leaps the specific mercury of a bygone era, transcending its once arresting intent, spiralling into an expanded counterrotation, which occupies the poets' true domain, which Parker Tyler on another occasion deemed the interior kingdom of "Elsewhere."

John Cheever. Ossining, New York, 1976. Photograph by Nancy Crampton.

John Cheever and Indirection
Rick Moody

I FIRST HEARD THE NAME at boarding school. What better place to learn of the bard of the suburbs, if that's who he really was. Creative writing at St. Paul's School — as at many of your private schools — was frowned upon. It wasn't considered a discipline. I enrolled two semesters anyhow, along with five or six other kids like me: marginal types who didn't write realistic fictions about their teenaged lives or their elegant hometowns. They wrote of their melancholies.

Mr. Burns, our instructor, read to us from Cheever's collection *The World of Apples,* and also from the novel called *Bullet Park.* The novel is noteworthy for the nomenclatural coincidences of its protagonists: Eliot Nailles and Paul Hammer. This conceit seemed too easy to me. In fact, since I was writing science fiction at the time — and not even the Philip K. Dick or J.G. Ballard kind of science fiction, the good kind — I didn't really understand Cheever at all.

For graduation, my dad gave me a trip to Europe — to Paris, London, Rome and Geneva. He also gave me a copy of *The Stories of John Cheever.* Foreign travel made me homesick, though, and I did nothing in London and Paris but read the Cheever stories. I lurked with my bulky red tome in the various parks near the hotel, in case Dad should permit me to fly home. In recognition of my afternoons spent reading, I decorated my hardcover copy of the *Stories* with a sticker (nontransferable) that allowed me to sit in a chair in Hyde Park. This luxury, back then, cost fifteen pence *per diem.*

I don't remember thinking much of the stories. I thought they were neither good nor bad. Fiction was narcotic, the way I saw it, and that was what I liked about this particular book, though I also remember admiring one piece, "Three Stories," in part narrated by a protagonist's stomach ("The subject today will be the metaphysics of obesity, and I am the belly of a man named Lawrence Farnsworth"), as well as a catalogue-story entitled "A Miscellany

217

of Characters That Will Not Appear."

Next came the punk rock years, during which I threw out most of my dinosaur records (Genesis, E.L.P.) and replaced them with totems of a new orthodoxy, the bands of CBGB's and of King's Row. As part of this dislocation, I began to bristle at aspects of my biography. I began, for example, to refer to St. Paul's as a *high school* — as if, like other people's alma maters, it was just down the road and had a prom night. I began to avoid certain garments (Oxfords with button-down collars, tartan boxer shorts, loafers, tweed jackets), and to ridicule writers or artists or musicians or anybody else who seemed to have anything to do with the upper middle class or station wagons or cocktail hour or golden retrievers or show tunes or tennis lessons or backgammon or the Episcopal Church or ambitions for success in the world of finance. I began to ridicule the very archipelago of suburbs that had spawned me. I ripped holes in my T-shirts and jeans. I had my ear pierced by a friend.

Cheever, along with Updike, I suddenly included on the list of enemies of my new state. Who was this khaki-clad, Scotch-drinking *New Yorker* writer scribbling his sentimental prose about ordinary life? My resentments became more acute during my first year at Brown University when my freshman creative writing instructor, a graduate student, brought in *The Stories of John Cheever* as a model of good form, going so far as to single out the celebrated last paragraph of its first piece, which runs in part:

> Oh, what can you do with a man like that? What can you do? How can you dissuade his eye in a crowd from seeking out the cheek with acne, the infirm hand; how can you teach him to respond to inestimable greatness of the race, that harsh surface beauty of life?

Well, I was the kind of student writer who looked eagerly for the dwarf or the burn victim or the heartbroken octogenarian, who scoured the newspapers for the tale of the pit bull who'd ravaged the schoolyard (three dead, scores injured), and I could hardly think of the close of "Goodbye, My Brother" as anything but propaganda for readers who wanted only affirmation of their conventions, an impression exacerbated by the PBS-style beauty of the last sentence, in which "the naked women came out of the sea." Nor did I care for the other, frequently anthologized Cheever stories my grad student instructor offered me: "The Enormous Radio," "The Sorrows of Gin," etc.

From freshman year forward, then, the mention of Cheever and any of his ilk was enough to provoke in me tirades about conformism and hypocrisy and oppression, about the schoolyard and country club cruelties I'd known back home. Ideally, youth is supposed to be flexible and open to ideas, full of reverence for the impromptu snowstorm or the poetry of kids crossing quadrangles with arms full of flowers and beer, overjoyed by certain loud guitars and amplifiers, altered once and for all in the thrall of great books, but above all disinclined to think prejudicially or to be contemptuous without investigation. Not in my case.

In the meantime, out of desperation and because of limited professional skills, I went to graduate school. There, in a literature class, I had yet again to confront those stories of Cheever. I'm powerless to describe exactly what changed in the five years between freshman year at Brown and spring semester of graduate school, what alchemy of bad jobs (recorded tour salesman, bibliographer), Upper West Side dusks and uncompleted romances did the trick, effected the transformation. I hadn't yet been through any real tragedies — not of the butchering sort into which one might suture a change of heart. Maybe I was just growing up. The Cheever stories, of course, had traversed the interval intact. Their language was the same.

But in spring of 1986 the stories suddenly had a richness that they hadn't displayed the last time I'd checked. They weren't about surfaces anymore, but rather about contradictions and ambiguities beneath the "harsh surface beauties of life." "The Fourth Alarm," e.g., struck me as unusually poignant this time, in which the narrator cannot, apparently, tell the story he needs to tell unless he indulges: "I sit in the sun drinking gin. It is ten in the morning. Sunday. Mrs. Uxbridge is off somewhere with the children. Mrs. Uxbridge is the housekeeper. She does the cooking and takes care of Peter and Louise." Then there was the justifiably celebrated "The Swimmer," in which a pastiche of idyllic suburban poolsides (and further gin and tonics) culminates not in the bland affirmations I associated with Cheever's early work but, rather, in a powerful and sudden desolation, as the swimmer approaches his home:

> The place was dark. Was it so late that they had all gone
> to bed? Had Lucinda stayed at the Westerhazys' for supper?

219

> Had the girls joined her there or gone someplace else? . . .
> The house was locked, and he thought that the stupid cook
> or the stupid maid must have locked the place up until he
> remembered that it had been some time since they had
> employed a maid or a cook. He shouted, pounded on the
> door, tried to force it with his shoulder, and then, looking
> in at the windows, saw that the place was empty.

There were oblique ambitions here that I had been too rigid to
notice earlier, and these ambitions were especially vivid in the
conjunction of Cheever's moral vision and the persistent inability
of his characters to measure up to this vision. The best example of
this later work awaited me, though, as I approached the last story
in the collection, "The Jewels of the Cabots." In recollection, it
seems that the only readers in my graduate school class who liked
the piece were the instructor and me. There was a persistent feeling, among my fellow apprentice writers, of mystification about
this final story. What was it about? Was it about anything at all?
Had Cheever perhaps gone so far with his rumored drinking that
he was capable only of a narrative so demented and fragmented?
"Jewels" had none of the crafted, understated grace of, say, "Goodbye, My Brother." It didn't seem to settle down and narrate. In its
events, it wasn't particularly credible. But for me it opened up a
new stretch of highway.

*

"The Jewels of the Cabots" begins conventionally enough: "Funeral
services for the murdered man were held in the Unitarian church
in the little village of St. Botolph's." Superficial impressions are
invited immediately. Cheever implies a conflict in the fact of
murder, with story to follow (that's the formula), and the landscape is evidently the kind of smalltown, suburban scenery that
we always associate with his work. In fact, St. Botolph's is a location used profitably by the author elsewhere, notably in the novels
The Wapshot Chronicle and *The Wapshot Scandal*. We're premedi-
tatedly in Cheever country.

Almost immediately, though, the story begins to attend to more
curious details: "The service was a random collection of Biblical
quotations closing with a verse." A random collection? The narrator muses upon the deceased, Amos Cabot, and Cabot's abortive
run at the governorship, as though this *were* the story, and so it

would seem, until this potentially straightforward second paragraph suddenly yields half its length to a parenthetical about the narrator himself, though he's neither a Cabot nor a significant actor in the lives of the Cabots. The substance of this preliminary digression is merely by way of introduction, in which this arguably fictional narrator encounters "a woman carrying a book of mine." A book with the narrator's photograph upon it. We are encouraged to take his aside either as "the truth" or at least as something quite near to it. This is either John Cheever's voice or a constructed version thereof, and John Cheever's remarks here constitute a violation of story space — one that's right at home in the fiction of the seventies, if not in the oeuvre of the writer of "a long-lost world when the city of New York was still filled with a river of light, when you heard the Benny Goodman quartets from a radio in the corner stationery store, and when almost everybody wore a hat."

Some conventional backstory follows. About the Cabots, about Mrs. Cabot's jewels, which she dries weekly upon a clothesline. But just as things are getting under way the narrator abandons the Cabots entirely, for a page or more, to tell us of a visit home to his own mother. She is, Cheever tells us, "terribly lonely," though that is not the substance of the encounter (one might argue, however, that it's so central as to avoid being mentioned) nor even is the following the reason for the digression: "I bring up, with powerful unwillingness, a fact that was told to me by her sister after Mother's death. It seems that at one time she applied for a position with the Boston Police Force."

No, Cheever digresses, apostrophizes, interrupts the story rather to illustrate the way the narrator and his mother communicate: after a venal display of anti-Semitism by his mom — "Your father said the only good Jew was a dead Jew although I did think Justice Brandeis charming" — after considerable friction on the subject, the narrator (whose wife, like Mary Cheever herself, is half-Jewish) can think of no way to address his mother's brutality further, but to change the subject.

> "I think it's going to rain," I said. It was one of our staple conversation switch-offs, used to express anger, hunger, love, and the fear of death. My wife joined us and Mother picked up the routine: "It's nearly cold enough for snow."

221

Here's the center of "The Jewels of the Cabots," as it begins to erupt in the framework of a more orthodox story: an acute longing for attachment, communication and affection that remains disguised, all but entirely thwarted, and addressed only laterally.

Formally speaking, the narrator then *changes the subject of the story itself*, which is to say that he abandons Mom to her antipathies, so that he may instead reminisce about the Cabot children. Two girls, Molly and Geneva, now grown up. A pair of paragraphs follow, traditionally nostalgic, about the narrator's love for Molly and about a bygone time: "It was so long ago that when you wanted to make a left turn you cranked down the car window and *pointed* in that direction [italics in original]." The purpose of this lateral construction (wasn't this supposed to be a story about Amos Cabot's murder? and when exactly are we going to learn about this murder?) is not, however, to speak of Molly or Geneva, but to introduce yet another tangentially related morsel: Once upon a time, in bringing home his beloved Molly from a date, the front door at the Cabots' house "was opened by a dwarf. He was exhaustively misshapen. The head was hydrocephalic, the features were swollen. The legs were thick and cruelly bowed. I thought of the circus. The lovely young woman began to cry."

A dwarf? The image should be familiar enough to readers of nineteenth-century novels. From *Jane Eyre*, etc. It's the madwoman-in-the-attic trope, used here with slight variation, to convey the mysteries beneath the surface of family, the things unspoken. Yet before we can learn any more about our dwarf (who never again steps into this limelight), the story embarks on another radical sideways movement, taking up instead the narrator's summer camp experiences, in particular a tender and platonic love affair with a fellow camper:

> We were together most of the time. We played marbles together, slept together, played together on the same back-field, and once together took a ten-day canoe trip during which we nearly drowned together.... It was the most gratifying and unself-conscious relationship I had known.

A romantic triangle muddies these unself-conscious waters, though, when the narrator's pal, DeVarennes, becomes jealous of his attentions toward a new camper called Wallace. Wallace, according to DeVarennes, in a moment of powerful vexation, is "Amos Cabot's bastard son." DeVarennes relents of his *jalousie,* however (after, literally, a heavy rainstorm), and his attachment to the narrator continues. Then why bring it up? Why the addition of Wallace? Is Wallace related to the dwarf? No, the dwarf is the progeny of an earlier Cabot marriage. What's the reason for the camp story then? Certainly, at a page and a half, it's a little long to be here simply for the sake of alerting us to "Amos Cabot's bastard son." Moreover, it violates, as does the earlier story about the narrator's mother, the standards of allowable narratorial intrusiveness. Yet, as with the earlier interruption, the melancholy and charm of Cheever's voice overcome our resistance, such that we begin to wonder, really, if the tale of the Cabots is the tale we want to hear at all.

At which juncture, perversely, the genuine plotting kicks in. Mrs. Cabot goes to dry her jewels on the clothesline, afterwards napping (while claiming not to nap), thereby moving the story along *and* giving us a diagram of the form of "The Jewels of the Cabots":

> She claimed that she had never taken a nap in her life, and the sounder she slept, the more vehement were her claims that she didn't sleep. This was not so much an eccentricity on her part as it was *a crabwise way of presenting the facts that was prevalent in that part of the world* [italics mine].

Mrs. Cabot's diamonds are then stolen by her daughter Geneva. Who absconds to the Mideast with the fortune, while sister Molly, much in lamentation, walks upon the beach with the narrator. "There had been a scene between her parents and her father had left. She described this to me. We were walking barefoot. She was crying. I would like to have forgotten the scene as soon as she finished her description." Predictably, the narrator elects *not* to give us the painful scene between the elder Cabots, but undertakes instead three entire pages (in a story of just over fourteen) of digression. And it was these very pages that first made clear to me, in 1986, how people really tell stories, how the well-made realistic story (including the sort of *New Yorker* sketch that Cheever himself once dazzlingly practiced) is composed mainly of *lies, lies, lies,* is incapable, with its repartee and banter, with its kooky characters and boundless sympathies, with its trailer parks and high-rises, of getting through its stylized and artificial frame to the genuine vacillations and peregrinations of the heart. Thus the narrator:

> Children drown, beautiful women are mangled in auto-mobile accidents, cruise ships founder, and men die linger-ing deaths in mines and submarines, but you will find none of this in my accounts. In the last chapter, the ship comes home to port, the children are saved, the miners will be rescued. Is this an infirmity of the genteel or a conviction that there are discernible moral truths? Mr. X defecated in his wife's top drawer. This is a fact, but I claim that it is not truth.

That's just for starters, in a disclaimer that is evidently an elabo-rate catalogue of the very things disclaimed. Later, e.g., in this three-page flourish, we find a lengthy portrait of "a male prostitute who worked as a supervisor in the factory during the day and hustled the bar at night, exploiting the extraordinary moral lassi-tude of the place" (Doris is the name of this unfortunate, and s/he is accorded an entire paragraph in "Jewels," though he has little to do with the tale), who in turn produces in the narrator, catalytically, further reminiscence of the past, of the stifling suppressions and repressions of home, during which, after he excavates some ugly exchanges between his own parents, this story-within-story finds the narrator's mother again changing the subject: "She would sigh once more and put her hand to her heart. Surely this was her last breath. Then, studying the air above the table, she would say, 'Feel that refreshing breeze.' There was, of course, seldom a breeze."

The anguish of these digressive pages comes from the fact (as in "A Miscellany of Characters That Will Not Appear") that the impressions that most aggrieve Cheever are both invoked and banished — so that what is suppressed becomes a vital source of energy and poetry, so that the thing feared within is projected without. This tendency is to me moving and genuine. By the end of the digression (which is still not complete with his mother's flourish), Cheever is cataloguing instances of intrafamilial cruel-ties far and wide (in his own home, in the American world around him and, for some reason, in Rome), desperately, compulsively and lovingly,

> Then one hears across the courtyard the voice of an American woman. She is screaming, "You're a God-damned fucked-up no-good insane piece of shit. You can't make a nickel, you don't have a friend in the world and in bed you stink . . ." Why would I sooner describe church bells and flocks of swallows? Is this puerile, a sort of greeting-card mentality, a whimsical and effeminate refusal to look at the facts? On and on she goes but I will follow her no longer.

The denial that closes the paragraph seems particularly forlorn to me, and thus intensely wise. Not long after it, the digression at last sputters to a close, again with its own exhausted attempt at evasion: "Feel that refreshing breeze."

Cheever, of course, is *not* describing church bells and flocks of swallows in "Jewels," not so often as he is erupting with the alarming but thoroughly verifiable truths that pass between people outside of the frame of realistic short fictions. This is a narration at once fierce, dignified and deeply neurotic, and it's a whole lot like the way the people I know talk and think. "My recollections of the Cabots," he thus finally admits, "are only a footnote to my principal work," but not before telling us, at last, of the awful confrontation between Amos and Mrs. Cabot, delayed by his splendid evasions. "The scene that I would like to overlook or forget took place the night after Geneva had stolen the diamonds. It involves plumbing."

Because of Mrs. Cabot's reign over the household, Amos is forbidden use of the one and only bathroom on the second floor, and therefore "obliged to use a chamber pot." He is thus engaged when Mrs. Cabot comes to the door of his room:

> "Will you close the door? Do I have to listen to that horrible noise for the rest of my life?" They would both be in nightgowns, her snow-white hair in braids. She picked up the chamber pot and threw its contents at him.

After which, Mrs. Cabot poisons her husband. "The Jewels of the Cabots" then concludes with a short scene, two paragraphs only, during which the narrator visits Geneva Cabot in Cairo. She has become a "fat woman" and married a relative of the king. "On the last day I swam in the Nile — overhand — and they drove me to the airport, where I kissed Geneva — and the Cabots — goodbye."

This last collected short story in the Cheever canon (I have in my possession a couple of uncollected later examples, and they are equally fascinating) occupies for me the place that "The Dead" has in Joyce's *Dubliners*. It is a *summa* for what has come before, a farewell that announces its farewell, a commentary upon the confining formula of the early stories and a discovery — while working both within and without this formula — of a tremendous liberty to delight and to move. And it is all these things while positing a sober and enlightened idea of human emotions and relationships. Here, in the twilight of the Cheever oeuvre, yearning and disgrace, generosity and cruelty, love and contempt are all equally near.

*

The term I appropriated for the beguiling strategy of "The Jewels of the Cabots," when I was trying to understand what was special about it and why I liked it so much, was *indirection*. Through which we speak very little of what needs to be said. Through which we find other figures and tropes for these central issues. Through which we evade and equivocate and pay for it later. This strategy had, I thought, as its reliable techniques, digression and lateralness (the "crabwise motion" of Mrs. Cabot's discourse), fragmentation and denial, and the more you looked for it, the more you found it in some surprising places. Salinger, for example, wrote one of the great indirect stories: "Seymour: An Introduction." Or there's Sterne or Proust. Or Beckett's *Watt*. Or just about anything by Thomas Bernhard. What makes all this work intelligible is not event or character, but voice. In "Jewels," the characters are relevant — Molly Cabot and poor murdered Amos are rendered with a genuine sympathy — but it's the psychology of the narrator that has the central role in the text. It's the narrator who offers the broadest palette with which to render the heavy weather of human emotions.

How does Cheever come by this strategy? What, in his case, makes it so organic? An acquaintance with his biography suggests that indirection had a far more important role in who he was — and how he thought and felt — than we can intuit from merely reading the stories and novels. It's possible to see, from a later vantage point, that the tropes of indirection were part of a larger struggle throughout the process of his work.

Which is to say that just as I was racing through the Cheever canon (after graduate school), *Home Before Dark*, Susan Cheever's memoir of her father, was beginning to have its impact on his reputation. I'd seen an excerpt from its pages, but at last I sat down to read it entirely, and to take in its difficult lessons. In it, there is of course John Cheever's progressive and overwhelming alcoholism to contend with (it's the reason I don't much like *Bullet Park:* the novel feels marred by the nearsightedness of drink), and his premature death from renal cancer, and these sorrows alone would color an interpretation of his voice and make it even more poignant than it already is — especially in the case of alcoholism, where ethical paradoxes always flourish. Strikingly, *Home Before Dark* also presented the first excerpts from Cheever's journals, and these painted an indelible and harrowing portrait: of a writer fighting hard to avoid drinking in the morning and then giving in, of a writer wandering Boston, flask in hand, of a writer struggling to work and so forth.

Alcoholism would be enough to make indirection and its techniques compelling, but there is yet another biographical theme that needs addressing in light of Cheever's later style. Initially, one of the most surprising revelations of *Home Before Dark* was the fact of John Cheever's bisexuality. However, for me, and perhaps for many readers, this revelation was like that refreshing breeze (of "The Jewels of the Cabots") blowing through a constrictive environment. Here was the personal dimension inexplicably missing from the Cheever legend as he was rendered by publicists and magazines and awards committees; here was a convolution (as distinct from a flaw, though Cheever himself may have felt his bisexuality to be a flaw); here was a revelation. John Cheever was a person, at last, not merely an upstanding citizen (if indeed there are any upstanding citizens); John Cheever was a troubled but resolute adventurer in the trenches of self.

The fascination with this "other" sexuality apparently started early, if indeed it was not coeval with Cheever himself, and grew more and more to be a part of him, as I understand it, until, as an older man, he accepted it thoroughly. In the work, we know well of this ambiguity, once we are attuned to it, as an opportunity for some powerful indirection. From "A Miscellany of Characters That Will Not Appear," e.g.:

> 6. And while we are about it, out go all those homosexuals

227

Rick Moody

who have taken such a dominating position in recent fiction. Isn't it time that we embraced the indiscretion and inconstancy of the flesh and moved on?

Or this passage from *The Wapshot Chronicle:*

And now we come to the unsavory or homosexual part of our tale and any disinterested reader is encouraged to skip.

Or there is Doris the male prostitute in "The Jewels of the Cabots," or the summer camp affair or countless other allusions, until, by the publication of *Falconer,* with its prison locale and prison language and prison sexuality, homosexual experience is quite close to the surface of the work.

In due course, first in *The New Yorker,* and then between hardcovers, we had a larger sampling of Cheever's journals with which to contextualize his stories, and with which to attempt in more detail the questions of Cheever's sexuality, his drinking and his melancholy. I read the journals hungrily in *The New Yorker,* when they first appeared, and many of my contemporaries did as well. They were an event. Everyone seemed to be quoting from these installments in the late eighties, from their descriptions of weather, from their synonyms for sadness, from their poignant declarations of love. They were so overpowering, these meditations, so different from the emotional reticence of the short stories, so full of great romantic longing, so swollen with complex and affecting perceptions of Cheever's wife and family. Where the stories take pride in their thriftiness toward revelation, the journals intoxicate themselves with it: "Assuming that there is some sort of absolution in recording the most tedious and mistaken conduct, I will set down that the following took place." Or: "My routine has been to write a page or so . . . no more — and mix a drink at ten. This means, since I cannot write and drink, that my working day is very brief." Or: "I want to come clean on the matter of homosexuality and I think I can." Or: "It is my wife's body that I most wish to gentle, it is into her that I most wish to pour myself, but when she is away I seem to have no scruple about spilling it elsewhere. I first see X at the edge of the swimming pool. He is sunbathing, naked, his middle covered by a towel." Or: "I was sprung from the alcoholic-rehabilitation clinic yesterday. To go from continuous drunkenness to total sobriety is a violent wrench."

228

The truth is a powerful thing, especially a posthumous truth. Benjamin Cheever, the author's son, in his introduction to *The Journals of John Cheever* tells us that Cheever, late in life, asked him to peruse a volume of the journals in front of him, and that father wept as son read: "At one point I looked up, and I could see that he was crying. He was not sobbing, but tears were running down his cheeks. I didn't say anything. I went back to reading. When I looked up again, he seemed composed." To John Cheever, this candor, this illumination of literature in the deadbolted attic of dwarves and madmen and women, the attic of repressions and desperations, must have felt both liberating and terrifying. I can't imagine that he thought seriously about not publishing these pages.

Does the candor of the journals invalidate indirection as a strategy? Does it give the lie to the formal feints and dodges of "The Jewels of the Cabots" and its colleagues? In 1997, up at Yaddo, where I'm writing this, in Cheever's old haunt (the wood-panelled bedroom where he often slept not fifty yards from here), I suspect that Cheever's *Journals* have now become — as Richard Howard has suggested — his most lasting work. One finds a more violent and indelible evocation of the seesawing of psychology here, though the stories are still magnificent. In the journals, it's as if the narrator of "The Jewels of the Cabots" finally had the luxury, once and for all, to excise the Cabots from the tale (they are, after all, only a footnote), to let go of St. Botolph's and call it, say, Ossining, and to begin the arduous adventure of telling the truth. For me, this process up to and through the glow of self-consciousness, from the excellent but icy storytelling of the early stories through the tricky and shape-shifting forms of the novels and the late stories, to the profound investigations of self that mark the posthumous journals, is one of the great literary journeys of this century. It has instructed me.

You will notice, however, that some ambiguities are never resolved ("I open Nabokov and am charmed by this spectrum of ambiguities, this marvellous atmosphere of untruth," Cheever says in his journals) — ambiguities in the matter of sexuality, ambiguities elsewhere. Always another rock with its subterranean communities to overturn and consider. Always the lie that tells a deeper truth. Always a cache so secreted away as to be invisible. The writer under forty who thinks he knows himself is arrogant indeed. It's in this climate of individuation that we find the opportunity for the psychic density of indirection, in which our foibles,

229

seeded in the mulch of youth, begin to express themselves in correlatives, as we are driven to get them down, until we have said what we're here to say and are left instead with quiet and the stir of time past: "Now I'm undressing to go to bed, and my fatigue is so overwhelming that I am undressing with the haste of a lover."

Phrenological Whitman
Nathaniel Mackey

REGARDED AS A PSEUDOSCIENCE nowadays and subject to parody and caricature, phrenology was "the science of mind" in the United States during the nineteenth century. It was taken seriously by a great number of people and Walt Whitman was one of those people; Fowler & Wells was a phrenological business whose Phrenological Cabinet he visited frequently in New York. In the 1855 preface to *Leaves of Grass*, Whitman includes the phrenologist among those he describes as "the lawgivers of poets": "The sailor and traveler . . the anatomist chemist astronomer geologist phrenologist spiritualist mathematician historian and lexicographer are not poets, but they are the lawgivers of poets and their construction underlies the structure of every perfect poem." He reiterates this in "Song of the Answerer": "The builder, geometer, chemist, anatomist, phrenologist, artist, all these underlie the maker of poems." In "By Blue Ontario's Shore," he asks:

> Who are you indeed who would talk or sing to America?
> Have you studied out the land, its idioms and men?
> Have you learn'd the physiology, phrenology, politics,
>   geography, pride, freedom, friendship of the land?
>   its substratums and objects?

Earlier in the poem, he praises mechanics and farmers, particularly "the freshness and candor of their physiognomy, the copiousness and decision of their phrenology." Phrenological terms, terms such as "Amativeness," "Adhesiveness" and "Combativeness" that were used to describe the phrenological faculties, are scattered throughout this and other poems.

Phrenology portrayed the brain as divided into different faculties that controlled the various aspects of personality. "Adhesiveness" was its name for the propensity for friendship and camaraderie, "Amativeness" its name for romantic, sexual love, "Philoprogenitiveness" its name for the love of offspring, and so on. There was

231

disagreement among the different versions of phrenology as to how many faculties there were, the number ranging from thirty-five to ninety-six, but phrenological nomenclature pertaining to the faculties contributed significantly to the vocabulary of Whitman's poems. In "Mediums," regarding future Americans, truly fulfilled Americans, he proclaims: "They shall be alimentive, amative, perceptive, / They shall be complete women and men." "Adhesiveness" became Whitman's favorite phrenological term. In "Song of the Open Road," he writes: "Here is adhesiveness." And in "So Long!": "I announce adhesiveness, I say it shall be limitless unloosen'd." "A Song of Joys" doesn't explicitly name the phrenological faculties, but the joys that it catalogs are each related to a specific phrenological "organ" and, taken together, constitute a model of phrenological well-being. The poem was inspired by one of Orson and Lorenzo Fowler's phrenological manuals, *The New Illustrated Self-Instructor in Phrenology and Physiology*.

The documentation of Whitman's interest in phrenology dates back to 1846. An article on phrenology that he clipped from an issue of *American Review* that year has been found among his papers. In November of that year, while he was editor of the Brooklyn *Daily Eagle*, he wrote a review of several phrenological manuals, a review in which he announced: "Breasting the waves of detraction, as a ship dashes sea-waves, Phrenology, it must now be confessed by all men who have open eyes, has at last gained a position, and a firm one, among the sciences." Four months later, in March 1847, he wrote an article called "Something about Physiology and Phrenology" in which he praised the leading proselytizers of phrenology in the United States, Orson and Lorenzo Fowler and Samuel Wells: "Among the most persevering workers in phrenology in this country, must certainly be reckoned the two Fowlers and Mr. Wells." Whitman was not alone in his interest in phrenology. It was an interest he shared with most if not all of the writers and thinkers of his day, including Edgar Allan Poe, Horace Mann and Ralph Waldo Emerson, as phrenology played an important role in various movements for self-improvement and social reform. Its basic precept was appealingly simple: the faculties within the brain display their degree of development by protrusions on the cranium, bumps on the head. Hence the other name it was known by, "Bumpology." Phrenologists would read, as they put it, the bumps on a client's head, particular bumps corresponding to particular faculties. The head was thought to offer a map of the client's mind and personality. Whitman had his bumps read by Lorenzo Fowler in July 1849.

Orson and Lorenzo Fowler, who were to become publishers of the second edition of *Leaves of Grass* in August 1856, transformed phrenology into a business enterprise during the 1830s. Orson Fowler became interested in phrenology early in the decade while he was a student at Amherst. In Vermont in 1834 he gave his first lecture on phrenology and during the next few years, with his brother Lorenzo, he made a number of lecture tours around the country. In 1838 he set up an office in Philadelphia called the Phrenological Museum (also called the Phrenological Cabinet and the Phrenological Depot) and began to publish the *American Phrenological Journal and Miscellany,* which would eventually publish some of Whitman's own reviews of *Leaves of Grass.* This was a year after his brother had set up the New York Phrenological Rooms on Broadway in Manhattan. In 1842 the two of them joined forces when Orson moved from Philadelphia to New York; there they established, with their brother-in-law Samuel Wells, who was married to their sister Charlotte, the Phrenological Cabinet that Whitman grew fond of visiting. Speaking of his return from New Orleans in 1848, Whitman wrote in one of his reminiscences: "One of the choice places of New York to me then was the 'Phrenological Cabinet' of Fowler & Wells, Nassau Street near Beekman." It was there that he had his bumps read by Lorenzo Fowler and he kept the chart all his life. It was published five times: in the Brooklyn *Daily Times* in September 1855, in the first, second and third editions of *Leaves of Grass,* and posthumously by his literary executors, to whom Whitman had given it during the last year of his life, in a book called *Regarding Walt Whitman.*

Whitman published and republished his chart to credential himself; it was, according to phrenological opinion on the subject, a poet's chart. Wells and the Fowlers were interested, as were others, in the poetic personality and the making of the poet, and in the *American Phrenological Journal* they featured articles on the phrenological characteristics of poets. These articles stressed the balanced, well-rounded character of the poet, the equitable development of the poet's faculties and the manifestation of this equitability on the poet's head. The expression "well-rounded" had to do with the phrenological belief that the best head is a round head, a head whose bumps are equally developed and distributed. Whitman's chart describes his head as "large and rounded in every

233

direction" and he offered it as evidence of his poetic qualifications. He makes his own case for the poet's well-roundedness in the 1855 preface when he writes: "The poet is the equable man." This, by then, was a phrenological commonplace. An article published in *The Phrenological Journal and Magazine of Moral Science* in 1846, for example, argued:

> Good Taste consists in the appropriate manifestation of each and all of the faculties in their proper season and degree; and this can only take place from persons in whom they are so balanced that there is no tendency for any one of them unduly to assume the mastery. When such a mind is prompted by some high theme to its fullest action, each organ contributes to the emotion of the moment and words are uttered in such condensed meaning, that a single sentence will touch every fibre of the heart, or, what is the same thing, arouse every faculty of the hearer. The power is known as Inspiration, and the medium in which it is conveyed is called Poetry.

The power of poetry resides in an equitable development of the faculties; the mind should be a democratic ensemble in which no single faculty dominates. This idea is central to Whitman's sense of himself as poet and to his sense of the American poet's democratic vocation.

Phrenology's attention to cranial manifestation of mind, its postulation of a tangible, tactile availability of mental attributes, epitomized a physiological accent which had obvious impact on Whitman's work. In one of the Fowler & Wells publications we find the following: "Poets require the highest order of both temperament and development. Poetry depends more on the physiology than the phrenology. It consists in a spiritual ecstasy which can be better felt than described. Not one in many thousands of those who write verses has the first inspiration of true poetry." Whitman's long song of bodily exuberance and appetitive touch tends at times, in ways that this formulation would have ratified, toward a hypersensitivity of a convulsive sort, bordering on ecstatic susceptibility: "You villain touch! what are you doing? . . . my breath is tight in its throat; / Unclench your floodgates! you are too much for me." Likewise, his emphasis on bodily health and development was in keeping with the practical phrenology of such as Wells and the Fowlers, who were in the forefront of influential

Walt Whitman. 1867. The Granger Collection, New York.

movements for social and individual reform. They not only advocated change in such areas as education and criminology but were proponents of vegetarianism, water cures and the like. They conducted a campaign against tight clothing and rigid posture whose influence can be seen in the famous photograph of Whitman published in the early editions of *Leaves of Grass.* This too was a self-credentialing move; his relaxed pose and his unbuttoned shirt show him to be phrenologically correct.

A significantly commercial undertaking, practical phrenology marketed the idea that a person could change his or her character; bumps, like muscles, could be made bigger or smaller through more or less exercise. A belief in the changeability or, even, perfectability of personality was crucial to phrenology's program of self-improvement and social reform, a program whose commercial as well as ideological aspects we find Whitman very much in the thick of. Fowler & Wells sold and distributed the first edition of *Leaves of Grass,* which Whitman published himself, and then published the second edition the following year. Whitman had had an earlier connection with them; he worked as a bookseller in 1850 and 1851, and very prominent on his shelves were books published by Fowler & Wells. He reviewed *Leaves of Grass* anonymously, as previously mentioned, in their *American Phrenological Journal,* and for several months in 1855 and 1856 he wrote a series of articles called "New York Dissected" for another publication of theirs, *Life Illustrated.* His call, in *Leaves of Grass,* for a reformation of poetry and for poetry as a means of reformation partook of and took its place within a reformist atmosphere in which phrenology played a central part.

Before it could sponsor reform in the United States phrenology itself had to undergo a reform of sorts, revision, in its migration from its place of origin, Europe. Under the name cranioscopy, phrenology was developed by the German physician Franz Joseph Gall, who began experimenting with it in the late 1700s and lecturing in the early 1800s; his book *On the Functions of the Brain and Each of Its Parts* was published in French in 1825 and in English in 1835. He advanced four basic principles: 1) the moral and intellectual dispositions are innate; 2) their manifestation depends on organization; 3) the brain is exclusively the organ of mind; 4) the brain is composed of as many particular and independent organs as there are fundamental powers of the mind. Gall raised, as a kind of corollary, a question: "How far [does] the inspection of the form of the head, or cranium, present a means of ascertaining the existence or absence, and the degree of development, of certain cerebral parts; and consequently the presence or absence, the weakness or energy of certain functions?" This question occupied a peripheral position in Gall's original formulations but it was seized upon by later phrenologists and vigorously promoted in a series of revisions that popularized phrenology and brought it to the United States. No longer a question but a central tenet, an assertion, it became known as the doctrine of the skull.

It was Gall's assistant, Johann Caspar Spurzheim, who began to popularize cranioscopy, changing its name to phrenology and coining the phrase "phrenology, the science of mind." He formulated four basic tenets as well, though they're significantly different from Gall's, especially in their incorporation of the doctrine of the skull as a central principle: 1) the brain is the organ of the mind; 2) the mind is a plurality of faculties, each springing from a distinct brain organ; 3) in the same person, larger organs show more energy, smaller organs show less; 4) the size and form of the skull are determined by the brain. The doctrine of the skull, thanks to Spurzheim, became canonical wisdom for phrenologists and their followers. John Davies, in *Phrenology: Fad and Science,* characterizes the difference in outlook between Gall and Spurzheim, a difference which makes it clear why Spurzheim's revision of Gall lent itself to the democratic ethic phrenology became bound up with in the United States:

> Gall accepted the existence of evil in the world, and particularly of evil propensities in mankind, even labeling one region of the brain "Murder." The great majority of men, he thought, were composed of mediocrities, and he emphasized the creative role of genius and its destined function to command; his science would be the instrument by which the elite could govern effectively and rationally the mass of mankind. In keeping with the aristocratic clientele with which he had been associated, his was neither a democratic nor a liberal creed.
>
> Spurzheim, on the other hand, deliberately omitted from his categories all faculties which were inherently evil; on the contrary, all were intrinsically good and only from the abuse of them could evil result. Mankind was created potentially good, and in contrast to Gall's cynical pessimism, Spurzheim looked forward to the perfection of the race by the aid of phrenology.

Spurzheim brought a sense of mission to phrenology. He learned English in six months in order to make a lecture tour of Great Britain in 1814. He published a book on his and Gall's findings, *The Physiognomical System of Drs. Gall and Spurzheim, Founded on an Anatomical and Physiological Examination of the Nervous System in General, and of the Brain in Particular,* which was harshly critiqued by the *Edinburgh Review,* occasioning a trip to Edinburgh to answer his critics. It was in Edinburgh, where he stayed for seven months, that one of the later proselytizers of phrenology heard him speak. Spurzheim eventually visited the United States, embarking on a lengthy lecture tour in August 1832, in the course of which, three months later, he died. He was given an elaborate funeral at Harvard and was buried in Boston, his death contributing considerably to the popularization of phrenology in the U.S.

George Combe was a Scotsman who heard Spurzheim speak in Edinburgh and became a vigorous crusader for phrenology. (In his novel *The War of the End of the World,* Mario Vargas Llosa merges Combe with Gall; one of the characters, a Scottish phrenologist named Gall, goes to South America and inspires peasant revolts.) Combe was looking for a way out of Calvinism and later said that "phrenology conferred on me the first internal peace of mind that I experienced." He and his brother formed a phrenological society and began publishing the *Phrenological Journal* in 1823. In 1828 he published a book that became very influential, *The Constitution of Man Considered in Relation to External Objects,* a book that Emerson called "the best sermon I've read for some time." Combe toured and lectured in the United States from 1838 to 1840, further increasing phrenology's popularity. Thomas and Grace Leahey comment in *Psychology's Occult Doubles:* "To Gall's physiology Spurzheim wedded philosophy and Combe wedded reform. It only remained for Americans to wed this *ménage à trois* to business." Practical phrenologists like Wells and the Fowlers took up and marketed Spurzheim and Combe's idea that phrenology was the key to reform and self-improvement. It was a somewhat self-reflexive idea; phrenology itself had been the object of reform, "improved" by Spurzheim's revision of Gall.

Phrenology in the United States, in Whitman's text as well as outside it, became entwined with nationalist feelings and millenarian hopes. The Fowlers wrote in their *American Phrenological Journal* in 1849: "Our present desire is this — to PHRENOLOGIZE

OUR NATION, for thereby it will REFORM THE WORLD. No evil exists in society but it sternly yet calmly rebukes, and points out a more excellent way. No reform, no proposed good, but it strenuously enforces. It is the very 'Head and Front' of that new and happy order of things now so rapidly superseding the old misery-inflicting institutions of society." Their optimism rested on an analogy between mental development and muscular development that they resorted to again and again. Like muscles, bumps put the degree of development of particular faculties on display; they also, again like muscles, make it possible to increase development through exercise. Phrenology thereby offered a way both to know oneself and to change oneself. "The organs," Orson Fowler wrote, "can be enlarged or diminished . . . even in adults. The exercise of particular mental faculties, causes the exercise, and consequent enlargement, of corresponding portions of the brain. Man is not compelled to carry all his faults, excesses, and defects to the grave."

Phrenology's mind/muscle analogy contributes, in Whitman's work, to an athleticization of mind, brain as brawn, and the trope of a gymnastic text. Thus, in "So Long!": "To young men my problems offering — no dallier I — I the muscle of their brains trying." In prose as well as verse he advances the figure of mind as muscle, calling for writing which would make reading a kind of calisthenic. In "Democratic Vistas" we read:

> In fact, a new theory of literary composition for imaginative works of the very first class, and especially for highest poems, is the sole course open to these States. Books are to be call'd for, and supplied, on the assumption that the process of reading is not a half-sleep, but, in highest sense, an exercise, a gymnast's struggle; that the reader is to do something for himself, must be on the alert, must himself or herself construct indeed the poem, argument, history, metaphysical essay — the text furnishing the hints, the clue, the start or frame-work. Not the book needs so much to be the complete thing, but the reader of the book does. That were to make a nation of supple and athletic minds, well train'd, intuitive, used to depend on themselves, and not on a few coteries of writers.

He returns to this idea in the essay "Poetry To-day in America — Shakspere — The Future." The participatory-democratic ethic or ideal is obvious, but one of the more interesting things about Whitman proposing this role for the reader is that it's not a role that seems to apply to his own work. Whitman would appear to be a writer who does it all for the reader ("what I assume you shall assume"), offering an explicit, self-evident text of a prodigiously declarative, transparent sort. Is this a symptom of the ideological nature of Whitman's stance, the false consciousness doctrinal exuberance can't help but be compromised by? The idea of the reader actively contributing to the construction of the text has become something of a commonplace by now, advocated by a range of twentieth-century experimental movements that includes the French New Novel, the Fiction Collective and the Language Poets, to name a few. The writing advanced by this idea is characteristically opaque, oblique, convoluted, often refractory — hardly "reader-friendly," however much it invites the reader's participation (or, more to the point, *because* it invites the reader's participation). The sort of work Whitman's advocacy of a gymnastic text might lead us to expect — recondite, elliptical work that catches us up in extended puzzlement and indeterminate exegesis, work we hermeneutically wrestle with, the sort of work offered in his own century, for example, by Emily Dickinson — is not what we get. Whitman teases the brain with paradox and contradiction on occasion, but his most characteristic manner is aggressively straightforward and accessible, requiring little of the reader beyond turning the page.

The demand is actually elsewhere — or directs the reader elsewhere. Whitman doesn't invite the reader to dwell on the text at great length. Rather, he cautions against exactly that, turning the reader away from the text. At the end of "Whoever You Are Holding Me Now in Hand" he admonishes:

> For it is not for what I have put into it that I have written
>   this book,
> Nor is it by reading it you will acquire it, . . .
> For all is useless without that which you may guess at
>   many times and not hit, that which I hinted at;
> Therefore release me and depart on your way.

Such admonition borders on abolishing the text. Whitman imagined world reform of such magnitude as to do away with the need for poetry. In "Thou Mother with Thy Equal Brood":

240

Brain of the New World, what a task is thine,
To formulate the Modern — out of the peerless grandeur of
the modern,
Out of thyself, comprising science, to recast poems,
churches, art,
(Recast, may-be discard them, end them — may-be their
work is done, who knows?)

The work to be done goes beyond the page but takes up its image, for the gymnastic text is not the text as such but a turning toward the world as text. The athleticism resides in that turn, a conversion to the work of reform which is willing to envision poetry's abolition, poetry as literary text replaced by poetry as concrete action.

Whitman and phrenology shared a reliance on tropes of textuality, figurations of human character and action as forms of writing or printing. Phrenological prognosis was viewed and referred to in such terms; one had one's bumps *read*. A contemporary account of an afternoon at the Phrenological Cabinet contains the following: ". . . you hear some one reading rapidly. Looking up, you find that it is from a page of Nature's imprint, and that . . . the reader does it by the sense of touch. Standing beside a young girl, with his hands upon her head, forthwith that head under his deft manipulation turns tell-tale . . . betraying her idiosyncrasies." This was consistent with the motto under which Fowler & Wells published the *Phrenological Almanac:* "Nature's Printing Press is Man, her types are Signs, her books are Actions." The presumed legibility of human beings was crucial to the promises of individual and social reform with which both Whitman and phrenology were involved. Democracy itself was believed to hinge on it. Democratic community, the argument went, depended on the ability of human beings to know one another; the democratic imperative was not only to know oneself but to know one's fellow citizens as well. We find the *American Phrenological Journal* insisting that nature aids this project of knowing by making people legible to one another, imprinting signs upon human surfaces:

> To this requisition — *imperious demand* — for knowing our
> fellow men, Nature has kindly adapted the *expression* of
> those mental qualities on the one hand, and our recognition
> of them on the other. Nature has ordained that we do not
> hide the light of our souls under the bushels of impenetra-

241

> bility but that we should set them on the hill of conspicu-
> osity, so that all that are with insight may observe them.
> She even *compels* such expression. She has rendered the
> suppression of our mentality *absolutely impossible.* She
> has rendered such expression *spontaneous and irresistible,*
> by having instituted the NATURAL LANGUAGE of emo-
> tion and character . . . which compels us to tell each other
> all about ourselves. . . . It is desirable for us to know *all . . .*
> *all* the existing emotions of mankind *are legible. They*
> *come to the surface.*

Haunting such insistence is an anxiety over the limits of know-
ability, the specter of an opaque latency resistant to full disclosure.
Phrenology's assurances of providential imprint sought to dispel
that specter. According to Henry Ward Beecher, a friend at Amherst who introduced Orson Fowler to phrenology: "Men are like
open books, if looked at properly."

Whitman's famous "Camerado, this is no book, / Who touches
this touches a man" is the converse of Beecher's formulation and
bespeaks a two-way, phrenologically informed translation between
body and book, person and poem. His assurance and exhortation
in the 1855 preface that "your very flesh shall be a great poem"
agrees with a statement made by Lydia Fowler, wife of Lorenzo
Fowler and one of the first female medical students in the United
States: "every bone and muscle is an unwritten poem of beauty."
Castings of body as text and of text as body recur with notorious
insistence throughout *Leaves of Grass:* "the expression of a well-
made man" that "conveys as much as the best poem" in "I Sing the
Body Electric," the phallic "poem drooping shy and unseen that I
always carry, and that all men carry" in "Spontaneous Me," the
assertion that "Human bodies are words, myriads of words" and
that "In the best poems re-appears the body, man's or woman's" in
"A Song of the Rolling Earth," and so on. There is, though, more to
this than there might seem, as phrenology's accent on textuality
and self-improvement moves away, in Whitman's work, from
simple surface cheer and celebration of health toward evocations
of death and disappearance. The translatability of body and book
subsists on writing as sublimation, compensation, the two-way
traffic between text and flesh on a sense of the text as an alternate
body, mind masquerading as body, flesh's death or sublimation
as text.

There is a great deal in Whitman's work that suggests that writing is a kind of dying, a disappearance into (in order to live on in) the book, that the alternate body afforded by the book is an improved, augmented body, the page a place of alternate growth (grave plot and a compensative going forth: "leaves of grass"). In the same poem in which he writes, "I the muscle of their brains trying" and "Who touches this touches a man," a poem tellingly entitled "So Long!," he writes: "I spring from the pages into your arms — decease calls me forth." And at the end: "I depart from materials, / I am as one disembodied, triumphant, dead." A poem whose final version was completed in 1881 and included in a section of the 1891–92 *Leaves of Grass* called "Songs of Parting," it can, of course, be read as Whitman, having entered his sixties, referring to an approaching and quite literal death. But the first version was completed twenty-one years earlier, in 1860, a fact suggesting that "decease" is also a figurative death afforded by writing, that writing was valedictory all along, a long rehearsal for death, also that death equates with words as nondeeds, not-doing. One of the notable things about Whitman's phrenological chart is that he was rated very high in "Cautiousness"; Lorenzo Fowler, evaluating the faculties on a scale that ran from 1 to 7, gave him a 6. Several critics and commentators on Whitman's relationship to phrenology find this surprising, given the audacity of *Leaves of Grass*, but they miss the fact that in his written assessment Fowler says to Whitman, "You are more careful about what you *do* than you are about what you *say*." Fowler may have, phrenology notwithstanding, happened upon an accurate characterization, for all the questions and doubts that have been raised as to what Whitman actually did rather than said he did or wrote about as though he'd done — questions and doubts about an affair in New Orleans, about the children he claimed to have fathered, about whether he was sexually active at all, etc. — suggest a relationship of compensation between words and deeds in his life and work. Words compensate for the not-done, improving on deeds hemmed in by caution and convention. In "Ventures, on an Old Theme," Whitman argues that poetic audacity, a disregard for social propriety of the sort found in *Leaves of Grass*, serves a necessary function:

> One reason [for not respecting the rule of society in my poems], and to me a profound one, is that the soul of a man or woman demands, enjoys compensation in the highest

directions for this very restraint of himself or herself, level'd to the average, or rather mean, low, however eternally practical, requirements of society's intercourse. To balance this indispensable abnegation, the free minds of poets relieve themselves, and strengthen and enrich mankind with free flights in all the directions not tolerated by ordinary society.

Borges is right: "There are two Whitmans: the 'friendly and eloquent savage' of *Leaves of Grass* and the poor writer who invented him. . . . The mere happy vagabond proposed by the verses of *Leaves of Grass* would have been incapable of writing them." The idea of poetry as compensation explains, in part, Whitman's turning the reader away from the text and his willingness to envision poetry's extinction. If poetry subsists on lack and not-doing, the reader, if there is to be substantive fulfillment and realization, mustn't be encouraged to linger with it.

Writing, self-improvement and death form a matrix in Whitman's work that echoes phrenology's advocacy of writing—specifically, epitaph writing—as an aid to self-improvement. Lorenzo Fowler counseled his audiences, "Write your own epitaphs in legible characters on a slip of paper; make them as flattering and eulogistic as possible. Then spend the remainder of your lives, endeavoring not only to reach the standard . . . you have raised, but to go far beyond it." Self-eulogy abounds in *Leaves of Grass*. A sense of the book as an epitaph is evident throughout, nowhere more explicitly than in the 1881 poem "As at Thy Portals Also Death": "I grave a monumental line, before I go, amid these songs, / And set a tombstone here." Whitman's investment in a compensatory sense of writing closes off the possibility of living up to and even beyond, as Fowler would have it, the standard such writing sets, but the specter it raises of textualization as a shortcut to self-improvement, a means to fraudulent self-improvement, applies to phrenology as well. Practitioners such as the Fowlers, who were, after all, running a business, appear to have sweetened their readings to make them appeal to their clients. A person who had undergone a reading wrote in 1835: "The faculties the phrenologist made mention that I possessed were in almost all cases very true so far as I can judge of my own mind. I am rather inclined to think he neglects to tell the evil passion as in my case and many others none were noticed which I am confident we possessed. Perhaps self-interest prompts him." The reading itself was an act of improvement.

The Fowlers, responding in the *American Phrenological Journal* to questions regarding the accuracy and integrity of their readings, admitted that "if we must err, we prefer to err upon the side of charity."

Phrenology's sweetened readings remind us that both the advantage and the danger of textualization is the ability to erase and to revise. This sheds some light on Whitman's decades-long revision of *Leaves of Grass,* a process which included a revision of the phrenological chart which he published with the first three editions, a revision in which he took a cue from the Fowlers. Finding his scores in some faculties not high enough, he changed them (not an altogether surprising move for someone "6 to 7" in "Self-Esteem"). After the first edition he edited Lorenzo Fowler's

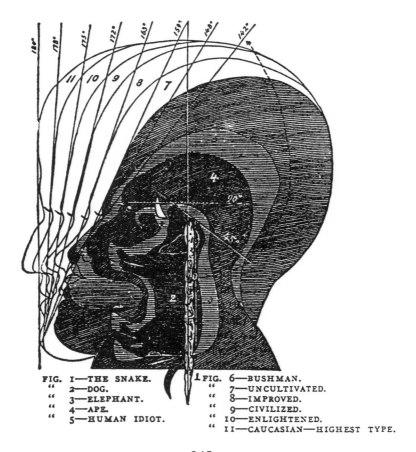

FIG. 1—THE SNAKE.
" 2—DOG.
" 3—ELEPHANT.
" 4—APE.
" 5—HUMAN IDIOT.

FIG. 6—BUSHMAN.
" 7—UNCULTIVATED.
" 8—IMPROVED.
" 9—CIVILIZED.
" 10—ENLIGHTENED.
" 11—CAUCASIAN—HIGHEST TYPE.

comments; among the phrases he excised was one describing him as "too unmindful probably of the conviction of others," a trait inconsistent with the democratic outlook he advertised. Reduced to textual manipulation, the project of self-improvement borders on self-parody, as does the frequently hollow ring of Whitman's exclamations in *Leaves of Grass*, but not without saying something real about nineteenth-century U.S. aspirations. "Self-made or never made," one of the Fowlers' most famous mottos, says more than they intended perhaps in its implication of an urgency (a desperation even) willing to risk vanity, self-aggrandizement, mere self-service.

Phrenological revision, both the revision of Gall's founding precepts and practical phrenology's willingness "to err on the side of charity," served an American optimism beginning to make a move on world ascendancy. It offered a hopeful hermeneutic, banishing the threat of dark recesses with an assurance that everything could be brought to light, everything seen, everything brought to the surface. The *American Phrenological Journal* in 1846 claimed that phrenology offered *"tangible, certain, absolute*, KNOWLEDGE," going on to exclaim: "Behold, then, the true SCIENCE OF MIND! Behold the study of this godlike department of our nature reduced to DEMONSTRABLE CERTAINTY!" Uncertainty, doubt, was the serpent in the Garden the New World was taken to be (Whitman refers to "doubt nauseous undulating like a snake" in "Rise O Days from Your Fathomless Deeps"); phrenology said no to that serpent. One of the critics of phrenology, Dr. Thomas Sewall, warned that "nature does not reveal her secrets by external forms." Likewise, several major writers assumed a much more skeptical stance toward phrenology than did Whitman. Poe, though he favorably reviewed phrenological journals early on and used phrenological categories in some of the characterizations in his fiction, went on to write parodies of it. Twain dealt skeptically with it as well. Melville, in *Moby Dick*, has Ishmael attempt to phrenologize the whale only to conclude that it can't be done; a work having so largely to do with inscrutability would of course find phrenology's hopeful hermeneutic suspect.

If, as Allen F. Roberts observes in an essay on the epistemology of the Tabwa people of Zaire, black is "a looking inward at what is not apparent but is nonetheless the essence of being," "an artfully indirect suggestion or insinuation — the gnawing suspicion that an act or event has meaning beyond what one sees," phrenology was a white way of knowing. It valorized obtrusion, surface, apparency, warding off the obscurities and indeterminacies of recess, crevice, fold. It was also white in another sense, serving other senses of whiteness. While its advocates preached self-improvement and social reform, the emphasis was by and large individualistic, seeking to better society through individual cultivation of the virtues of self-help—thrift, hard work, purity, perseverance. Its advocacy of social reform, while populist in many respects, failed to offer its beneficence and promise of improvement to those who were not white; its will to reform didn't extend to reforming notions of racial determinism or the social relations upheld by such notions. Phrenology in fact shared with these notions an assumption that human surfaces offer incontestable evidence of the qualities, capacities and traits not only of individuals but of groups. Its attention to cranial bumps is consistent with and occupies a place within a mode of reading human prowess which also attends to skin color, hair texture and other phenotypic and physiognomic features. As the frontispiece to his *Phrenology: Fad and Science,* John Davies reproduces a phrenological diagram which compares, along an evolutionistic scale of development, the cranial shape and the forehead slope of eleven creatures. It shows four animals and seven humans; the animals, in order of development, are a snake, a dog, an elephant and an ape; the human figures, in order of development, are designated "Human Idiot," "Bushman," "Uncultivated," "Improved," "Civilized," "Enlightened" and "Caucasian— Highest Type."

Racist evolutionism textualized earth surfaces as well, ascribing a providential imprint to bodies of land. Representative John A. Harper in 1812 employed a trope which was to be repeatedly taken up in the rhetoric of manifest destiny, arguing that "the Author of Nature has marked our limits in the south, by the Gulf of Mexico; and on the north by the regions of eternal frost." The decimation of indigenous populations and the wresting away of their lands was an act of erasure and revision, a providentially mandated improvement in which a superior race vanquished and evicted an inferior one. Whitman, as he was with phrenology, was on intimate, speaking terms with such notions. He was an admirer of John L. O'Sullivan, whose *Democratic Review* he frequently wrote for and who, in support of annexing Texas in 1845, invoked "our manifest destiny to overspread the continent allotted by Providence for the free development of our yearly multiplying millions."

In March 1846 Whitman wrote in favor of acquiring Oregon, saying that "the name of 'American' must, in a few years, pale the old brightness and majesty of 'Roman'"; in the same year, when Yucatan seceded from Mexico, he wrote an editorial, "More Stars for the Spangled Banner," arguing that "she won't need a long coaxing to join the United States"; he supported the war against Mexico from its beginning in May of that year.

Like phrenology and along with phrenology, manifest destiny provided a hopeful hermeneutic, offering assurances of legibility, providentially mandated certainty, self-evident truth. Phrenology presented a version of manifest destiny at the individual level, mapping the head and making it readable, imprinted with a legible future, the individual's destiny manifest in the very bumps on his or her head. Whitman was greatly attracted to such externalist, self-evidentiary ways of knowing, the valorization of a certain articulacy and eloquence to be found in the available, on the surface, in the overt. His drive, power and originality as a poet derive in large measure from that attraction; the majority and most characteristic features of his work are given over to it. Still, he acknowledges the brain's "occult convolutions" in "Song of Myself" and promises "untold latencies" in "Shut Not Your Doors." This makes for a certain tension. One of the things I find most interesting in Whitman's work is that tension, the unarrestable play between latent and manifest that brings an otherwise hopeful hermeneutic to grief.

It brings it to grief and into an order of non-self-evident import. This is most notably the case in "Drum-Taps," the poems written in response to the Civil War, whose outbreak was traumatic for Whitman, amplifying and setting in motion many an inner ambivalence and contradiction. It was a conflict in which the nation's most fundamental contradiction came to the surface and exacted its toll, a contradiction which, as he did other features of the nationality he said the poet should incarnate, he himself embodied in various ways. For one, he refused to accept that the war was about slavery and the status of black Americans, even though he had, over a span of more than a decade before the war's outbreak, taken stands against slavery and the spread of slavery. In 1846 he supported the Wilmot Proviso, which prohibited slavery in any territory acquired from Mexico, and lost the editorship of the Brooklyn *Daily Eagle* for doing so; in 1854 he wrote "A Boston Ballad," a poem protesting the arrest of the fugitive slave Anthony

Burns in Boston by federal marshalls complying with the Fugitive
Slave Law of 1850, a law he spoke out against again in 1856 in "The
Eighteenth Presidency!"; he wrote an article exposing and con-
demning the illegal slave trade in New York for *Life Illustrated* in
1856. However, he was not, by his own admission, a "red-hot"
abolitionist and his record was uneven, especially when the issue
was not the status of the institution of slavery but the status of
African Americans. While editor of the *Daily Eagle*, he let the
voting down of black suffrage in Brooklyn in 1846 go without
comment or condemnation; after the war, he was against universal
suffrage, falling out with his longtime friend and admirer William
Douglas O'Connor over this issue in 1872. In the 1850s he argued
that blacks could never be assimilated into American life, invok-
ing the familiar trope of providential imprint: "Nature has set an
impassable seal against it." For Whitman, the war that George
Lamming calls the Slave War was fought not against the degrada-
tion of black Americans but against "devilish disunion." He refers
to it always as the Secession War and writes to O'Connor during
the conflict: "In comparison with this slaughter, I don't care for
the niggers."

Repressed acknowledgement of the manifest cause of the war,
the enslavement of African Americans, creates curious perturba-
tions. In "Song of Myself," first published before the war, Whitman
portrays himself aiding a runaway slave in section 10, professes
love for a black coachman whose "polish'd and perfect limbs" he
praises in section 13, then identifies with "the hounded slave" in
section 33. In "I Sing the Body Electric," also first published before
the war, he insists in section 7 on the pricelessness and humanity
of a slave on the auction block: "In this head the all-baffling brain, /
In it and below it the makings of heroes." However, in a post-war
poem, "Ethiopia Saluting the Colors," included in "Drum-Taps"
and first published in 1871, the inchoate and contrary sway of
emotions and ambivalences tapped by the war has him wondering
why a black woman salutes the flag, referring to her as "so ancient
hardly human" and repeating it, "so blear, hardly human," but regarding her nonetheless as a "fateful woman," wondering, "Are the
things so strange and marvelous you see or have seen?" More
curious yet is the moment in "Song of the Banner at Daybreak"
when, expressing love for the flag, he sees in it the undulant, ser-
pentine quality attributed in "Rise O Days from Your Fathomless
Deeps" to doubt:

O you up there! O pennant! where you undulate like a
    snake hissing so curious,
Out of reach, an idea only, yet furiously fought for, risking
    bloody death, loved by me,
So loved — O you banner leading the day with stars brought
    from the night!

Albeit not altogether unvisited by sweetening, something moves
here more than surface conviction. Whitman's optimism, under
duress, wants to rebound, darkened by what the nation has been
through. Unhinged hope and the recovery it seeks move into an
embrace of captious flutter, a liminal epiphany coded in wavelike
hiss (earlier in the poem: "hissing wave") and snakelike undulacy.

    Cloth is cover, capricious cover, as fitful turning out as in. The
flag's flutter and flap attest to agitant intangibles. Robert Farris
Thompson, in *Face of the Gods*, discusses the Kongo derivation of
the flag altars maintained by the Saamaka of Suriname, descendants
of eighteenth-century maroons:

> The Kongo contribution to the flag altar, the *nsungwa*, held
> by a processioneer at a funeral, is a towering staff onto
> which a narrow strip or strips of cloth are tied at the very
> top. To honor the dead, processioneers shake and elevate
> *nsungwa* in the air. The cloth strips atop these staffs encode
> *mambu* (words, matters, problems) that the living seek to
> communicate to the dead; one activates the attention of
> the other world by "waving the words" (*minika mambu*), a
> basic Kongo metaphor for spiritually activated admonitions.
> This ritual act "vibrates" (*dikítisa*) cloth-coded prayer, so
> that the ancestors cannot fail to comprehend. . . . Finally,
> for Kongo, motion imparted by wind to flags directly dem-
> onstrated ancestral presence. *Banganga* (ritual experts)
> phrased this belief in the following way: "The wind on the
> flag is a vibration shared by the two communities, the living
> and the dead."

Earlier, the poem, in its dialogue between Child and Father (speaking parts are also given to Poet, Pennant and Banner), recalls section 6 of "Song of Myself," where the child's question "What is the
grass?" is answered, "I guess it must be the flag of my disposition,
out of hopeful green stuff woven." The flags in "Song of the Banner
at Daybreak" are woven of different stuff, threatening to woo the

Child away from acquisitive progress and material pursuit, "valuable houses, standing fast, full of comfort, built with money," what would eventually be called the American way of life. The Child says of the flag:

> O father it is alive — it is full of people — it has children,
> O now it seems to me it is talking to its children,
> I hear it — it talks to me — O it is wonderful!
> O it stretches — it spreads and runs so fast — O my father,
> It is so broad it covers the whole sky.

The Father tells him, "Cease, cease, my foolish babe," tells him to look at "the well-prepared pavements" and "the solid-wall'd houses" instead. Then Banner and Pennant instruct the Poet:

> Speak to the child O bard out of Manhattan,
> To our children all, or north or south of Manhattan,
> Point this day, leaving all the rest, to us over all — and yet
>   we know not why,
> For what are we, mere strips of cloth profiting nothing,
> Only flapping in the wind?

Spiritually activated admonitions, the flags' flap and flutter disburse reminders of manifold latency, maroon intangibles ever bettering manifest capture. How striking that an African way of knowing should assert itself where the knowingness of Africans was anything but held to be self-evident.

Elizabeth Bishop. Brazil, 1954. Photograph by J. L. Castel. Courtesy Special
Collections, Vassar College Libraries, Poughkeepsie, New York.

Elizabeth Bishop's Prose: Atmospheres of Identity

Sven Birkerts

THE WRITING OF A MASTER always makes us reflect, again, on the mystery of writing—how it happens, what it *is*. For a master reminds us with her every sentence that while prose can be, in some cases, improved, there are no directions or guides for "rightness," that quality that strikes us as an embodiment beyond all analysis, as a form of being that has surpassed its orchestration of moving parts. Here we include—but do not confine ourselves to—verbal texture, rhythmic movement and modulation, diction, the selection and placement of detail, the presentation of situation and the decision about digression versus elision that is renewed at every pen-stroke.

The best prose, masterly prose, is a window onto the self of the writer—not the self enslaved by the contingencies of the moment, but the self more essential: the self that looks out artlessly from the photographs of the child, or that feels like a thing gathered and hoarded behind the concertedly thoughtful poses of the adult. How is it that one self writes one way and another completely differently? The sentences of different writers move—even breathe—differently. Nouns have different weight depending on what sort of medium they are suspended in. A certain sensibility will always insert the qualifying phrase, the discriminating twist, as if to say that with enough pressure, enough care, the words can map the least iridescence on the shifting scales of the world. Another will approach to pounce, or grip by main force, then suddenly round on himself, breathing in essences and exhaling them as a kind of cloud formation.

I think of Orwell, or Hazlitt, or Hoagland, or M. F. K. Fisher, or any number of other writers whose worlds I happily inhabit and who are entirely exclusive of one another. How completely, I wonder, does a given reflection or episode take its character from the mode of narration? And how much of what we regard as narration is just a more or less oblique transposition to the page of the mysterious formations of the self? In other words, is there really any world to be encountered in a writer's prose, or do we go to that prose to feel how the complex projections — manifestations — of the author's sensibility merge with or ricochet off our reading selves? Could these engagements with books really be the occasion for the subtlest linguistic intimacies, with subject matter merely serving as a legitimizing pretext? And what if it were so?

I have had these inklings and questions in mind recently because I have been reading the prose of Elizabeth Bishop. Reading it to discover what it says, yes, but also in order to study the deeper manifestations of the *how* of the saying. I first opened *The Collected Prose* because I wanted her particular impressions of things — her childhood, Brazil and so on — but I soon found myself more occupied with the atmospheres of identity that seem to hover everywhere around the matters presented. Something about Bishop's writing made me feel as if I were in contact with the self behind the sentences, almost as if the reverie induced by my reading were not merely adjacent to but contiguous with her own language impulses.

Bishop, it should be said, is a great poet, alive across a generous spectrum; as a prose writer she is brilliant, but only in the narrowest way. In her various memoir essays and stories she brings forward, over and over, the soul of the child she was — either directly, in writing about childhood memories, or indirectly, by filtering some other subject (travel in Brazil, her friendship with Marianne Moore) through the scrim of an innocent's sensibility. This, as will be seen, is operative even on — *especially* on — a syntactical level.

I will not report here on the stuff of Bishop's prose, except to affirm that much of it retails impressions from her girlhood years, especially the period when she lived with her grandparents in a village in Nova Scotia. The other pieces — her witty memoir of working at a correspondence school for would-be writers, her introduction to the diary of Helena Morley, etc. — finished as they are, lack the special intensity that derives from her efforts to write her way back into the earlier epochs of her life.

Interestingly — and tellingly — a selective tissue-sample approach to the writing does not do violence to some larger integrity, not much anyway. Bishop's prose does not, as does the prose of so many other writers, ride on accretion. Her unique ability, which is directly bound up with her limitations in the genre, is to render the world as if seen through the eyes of a preternaturally watchful child. There is a powerful — and fruitful — tension on the page between the highly receptive senses and the countering force, the fear, that would keep the world at a manageable distance.

Here is a passage from her autobiographical essay, "The Country Mouse":

> Grandpa once asked me to get his eyeglasses from his bedroom, which I had never been in. It was mostly white and gold, surprisingly feminine for him. The carpet was gold-colored, the bed was fanciful, brass and white, and the furniture was gold and white too. There was a high chest of drawers, a white bedspread, muslin curtains, a set of black leatherbound books near the bed, photographs of Grandma and my aunts and uncles at various ages, and two large black bottles (of whiskey, I realized years later). There were also medicine bottles and the "machines." There were two of them in black boxes, with electrical batteries attached to things like stethoscopes — some sort of vibrator or massager perhaps. What he did with them I could not imagine. The boxes were open and looked dangerous. I reached gingerly over one to get his eyeglasses, and saw myself in the long mirror: my ugly serge dress, my too long hair, my gloomy and frightened expression.

I offer this paragraph in order to make a few observations. First, that it, like most of the other paragraphs in the essay, is excerptible. We don't require background information: the prose does not refer backward, nor does it ride on the surge of anticipation. A portion of the world is registered, described, almost as if a camera eye had lopped off one full portion of the past and would soon be taking the next.

But this is no mere surface oddity. The writing embodies the perceptual movement, and this verges — here and elsewhere — on dissociation. We feel almost no sense of cumulation or causal connectedness. Rather: one thing, another, another. The Humean world, the child's world. Intense, not yet grounded in the explanation-making impulse.

Reading, we are affected by the calm tone — uninflected, utterly unemphatic — as well as by the simplicity of the expression. Colors are white, gold and black. The chest of drawers is merely "high," the black bottles "large." Nor are the presumably mysterious machines regarded in any way that reflects a child's deeper curiosity;

only the surfaces are grazed. Moreover, the sentence constructions are passive, the syntax parsimonious in its means ("The boxes were open . . ." "There were also medicine bottles . . .").

But how could it not be so? The little girl is terrified — by life, by loss. She is living with her grandparents because her mother has been institutionalized — she is reflexively compelled to hold the looming particulars of the adult world at a distance, even if the natural movement of a child's sensibility would be to get in close, devouring each protruding bit of matter. How differently Nabokov would have written it! But then he, as a child, was lord of the dacha. From Bishop's presentation we glean intuitively, without having to be nudged, that these are the observations of a child who is stepping hesitantly into a foreign space; she will not linger to investigate because she is deeply cowed. Her only actual brush with the surface of things comes late, when she reaches "gingerly" to get the eyeglasses.

Bishop's technique here is in some ways similar to that used by Hemingway in his fiction, though his adaptation of primer constructions was more stylized. Hemingway deployed his repetitions and pruned back observations to suggest the badly damaged nerves and depleted responsiveness of his characters. Bishop, by contrast, transmits an almost arrested innocence — a self struggling to stave off further news of the adult world. The black bottles are not, just then, understood to contain whiskey, though Bishop sees fit to tell us that she realized this later; the possible purposes of the machines remain unplumbed.

It is natural, of course, that a writer seeking to recreate the childhood scape from the inside would use the stylistic devices at her disposal. But what we discover as we read on is that Bishop has, perhaps unconsciously, adapted these very same options for her other purposes as well, in the process producing a prose that could be called "faux naive": not primitive — Bishop is too enamored of the natural surface for that, but syntactically restricted in a way that keeps the surface simpler than her mastery of diverse means might otherwise allow.

In 1967, Bishop wrote an essay, "A Trip to Vigia," in which she narrated a visit she had undertaken with a shy Brazilian poet to a town some hundred kilometers distant from where she was then living. Here we see a different sort of convergence of matter and method. This is a travelogue, and what is a travelogue but a sequential showcasing of the world as it offers itself to the senses?

The best ones — and Bishop's is delightful in every way — give evidence that new sights and experiences have broken the crust of habit. The renewal of perceptual clarity is seen, invariably, as a return to a state of prior innocence.

Here is Bishop entering a small backcountry store during a stop:

> The store had been raided, sacked. Oh, that was its normal state. It was quite large, no color inside or cloud-color perhaps, with holes in the floors, holes in the walls, holes in the roof. A barrel of kerosene stood in a dark stain. There were a coil of blue cotton rope, a few mattock heads, and a bundle of yellow-white handles, fresh cut from hard *ipé* wood. Lined up on the shelves were many, many bottles of *cachaça*, all alike: Esperança, Hope, Hope, Hope. There was a counter where you could drink, if you wanted. A bunch of red-striped wicks hung beside a bunch of rusty frying pans. A glass case offered brown toffees leaking through their papers, and old, old, old sweet buns. Some very large ants were making hay there while the sun shone. Our eyes negotiated the advertisements for Orange Crush and Guarana on the cloud-colored walls, and we had seen everything. That was all.

As with the earlier passage, we get a sense of the eye moving deliberately from thing to thing, only here — and perhaps this is an indication of maturity, or greater self-confidence in the presented "I" — discriminations supplant what were formerly approximations. The handles are "yellow-white," and the toffees are seen "leaking through their papers." The eye lingers now, engages more with the grain of things. But the enumeration also feels — as it can in Bishop's numinously charged poetry as well — like a way of holding other aspects, or awarenesses, at bay.

This description also violates many of the standard precepts for lively writing — almost, we feel, deliberately. "It was quite large . . ." "A barrel of kerosene stood . . ." "There were a coil . . ." And on and on. Yet the perceptions themselves — the barrel standing in the stain, the odd invocation of "cloud-color" — flex against the bonds of the rudimentary sentence structure. We finish the paragraph with the feeling that we have been and have seen, even if the impression itself is humble and in some primary way gravity-bound.

A prose style *is* a metaphysics, and the fact that we do not just now pay much attention to writers' styles only means that we are letting our relation to things — the things which are the case — get muddled. In Bishop's work — and this is one of the reasons she is so prized by readers — there is no such confusion. We come away from whatever we read, poetry or prose, with a sense that the world has been seen steadily, indeed with the kind of heightened (or restricted) focus that we feel we may possess in our finest moments. The writing confers an impression of control, of elusive materials caught into place; of specific things known because observed with great care.

But by the same token we rarely feel that the "I" of these pieces ever acts upon the world, or in any way even ruffles the surface of things. This sensibility would never presume; its reticence is Prufrockian. To act, to interfere, to get caught up in any sort of business with other people — this would be almost hubristic. It would presuppose a volitional self, and Bishop's is not. Recall her famous poem "In the Waiting Room," wherein she reports her experience — she is almost seven — of realizing "you are an *I,/* you are an *Elizabeth,/* you are one of *them.*" Reading her prose I often think that it was all she could do to hold that precious awareness intact through her life, that there was scarcely enough surplus to use for living. Bishop's great achievement was to turn what would be in a less grounded person a serious psychological deficit into the cornerstone of her art. In her work self-effacement is somehow transmuted into what feels like an extraordinary humility before life — not just things and beings, but the underlying — or in-dwelling — force that makes them possible. "I'm just looking," she seems to be saying, but as we look with her we feel the world recharging itself for us.

*

The final piece in the book, "In the Village" — called a story, but by Bishop's own admission a scarcely modified work of autobiography — is the narrative of life in a Nova Scotian village as seen through the eyes of a little girl. It is, more particularly, the account of a mother's return from a stay in an institution — before the collapse that would return her there for good. "Unaccustomed to having her back," writes Bishop, "the child stood now in the doorway, watching." The mother is being fitted for a dress; she wants to come out of mourning for her husband. But suddenly the dress

258

seems all wrong and she screams. The daughter is transfixed; in her imagination the scream hangs over that village "forever, a slight stain in those pure blue skies." And if we look, following the risky path of the explanatory conceit, for some way of understanding that limpid, detached, slightly stunned quality in Bishop's writing — where it comes from — we might linger meditatively on the image of that little girl standing in that doorway, observing as the dressmaker "was crawling around and around on her knees eating pins as Nebuchadnezzar had crawled eating grass."

Anaïs Nin. Photograph by Soichi Sunmi. Department of Special Collections, University Research Library, UCLA.

Anaïs Nin
All the Rest Is Origami
Ana Castillo

— for Monsterrat and for Ronnie

I WAS NINETEEN YEARS OLD and an avid reader of Anaïs Nin when she finally won the success and fame that she had dreamed of all her life. Born in 1903, Nin had worked in the midst of male writers who had achieved renown long before she did. In her fiction and journals she faithfully wrote her observations and experiences from her feminine, if not feminist, perspective. Nin had loved passionately; in everything she did, she remained devoted to her art and lived to tell all about it.

Far away from the white feminist movement on the West Coast that had discovered an appetite for her diaries, I was living in Chicago with Mexican parents who said, you cannot leave this house until you're married. You must work and help out in the household. Lofty goals like college, art, writing were useless to my factory-employed mother and father. But I, like many women, simply as a stepping stone to freedom, married — the inimitable actress Maria Felix comes to mind. My young husband was no Hugo Guilar. Although he was nice enough, and, as I look back, sincerely adored me, he was mostly unemployed and unambitious, and I couldn't get divorced fast enough. In the seventies, living my new independent life free of parents and husband, I was surrounded by mostly male artists, the writers of my own Latino community. I continued to read everything that was published by and about Anaïs Nin. Her conversations with Lawrence Durrell and Henry Miller rang true for me in my own search for literary meaning. I must say, however, that mine were never quite as interesting or held as much depth as those of Nin and her male intellectual acquaintances — Antonin Artaud, Gore Vidal, her therapists Otto Rank and René Allendy, to name a few. I was hungry for similar discussion and in her works I felt a little less alone. I was hungry too, like many women, for validation of my right to write. Since

261

there were no established U.S. Latina writers twenty years ago, I chose to read books by women from various cultures and countries who told their stories in a world that hadn't yet heard them, and had not wanted to hear them. Other women who kept me company by the time I was twenty-four years old — burned out from community organizing, looking for a paying job, disillusioned with my Latina activism — were the wondrous *Woman Warrior* Maxine Hong Kingston, who warned me that it would take twenty years to be heard, and Toni Morrison, who said that African-Americans, like Mexicans in the United States, believed in ghosts too. I even strained a potent line from *The Female Eunuch* by which to make a plan for myself. Germaine Greer let me know that the most important thing I had to attain as a woman was happiness. It's a lot harder to come by than you might think — if you are determined to rock the testosterone-filled boat of the new world order.

But it was Anaïs Nin to whom I kept returning over the years, not because I identified so much with her life. I didn't. And maybe partly *because* I didn't. Like the romance-novel junkie, after I did laundry, tended to the beans on the stove and put the baby down for his nap, I would return to Nin's writing — whatever was available; I couldn't get enough of that woman's fanciful life.

I didn't even *like* her experimental fiction writing style — although I read everything. But through Nin's lush use of language, she indulged, indulged, indulged her relentless exploration of her inner life. Her external life too, was ardently portrayed, rich with fascinating characters, surroundings, travels — Paris in the thirties, post–World War II New York, Fez, Mexico — and always, her tenacious commitment to writing as art.

Recently, an extensive biography by Deirdre Bair was published that seemed to fill in the blanks for many of us who had wondered about certain details regarding Nin's life. Who paid, for example, for Nin to have that magical lifestyle she led all her adult life? Who was the father of the stillbirth in her diary account of "birth story"? How did she resolve her issues with her father's abandonment for which she underwent psychoanalysis for years? To say that Bair was less than sympathetic in her treatment of these questions is an understatement. The paradigm she seemed to fix on with regards to Anaïs Nin, the "major minor writer," as she refers to Nin in the introduction, was that of woman centered vs. self-centered. But as I see it, although the blanks were filled in, Bair may have made some prejudiced assumptions. As in all stories, as listeners we must keep in mind that it is not only important what is being told to us but what is being left out and why. Certainly Anaïs Nin knew this very well. She rewrote incidents and apparently enraged more than one person portrayed in her diaries. She, of course, omitted a lot. So, too, did her biographer with her determination, I feel, to *judge* Anaïs Nin's life. She referred to Nin's first abortion, for example, as monstrous, when Nin not only did not want to have children, she wasn't even sure who had gotten her pregnant. In fact, there was a strong possibility that the man involved was not Nin's husband, maybe not even the cad Henry Miller, and just possibly it might have been her own father, as they were having an affair at the time.

"After you've f----- your father, all the rest is origami," a writer friend of mine told me recently when I asked her about Anaïs Nin. My friend knew Nin during her last decade.

Very soon after the white feminists of her day embraced Anaïs Nin for her woman's perspective as an artist, she came under suspicion. How could a true feminist, for example, be financially dependent on a man all her life, they queried, not to mention her ongoing emotional dependence on men — including her father. So maybe Anaïs Nin did not go out and get a job — a lie she told her second husband when she got money from the first to contribute to her second household. (Nin, as it turns out, was also a bigamist.)

But half a century ago she believed she could stand her ground intellectually with men. Long before feminists were discovering the joys of the orgasm through the *Hite Report* and Masters and Johnson, Nin was entrenched in her own personal research. Despite the fact that abortion is legal at the end of the twentieth century in this young country, many women who label themselves feminists find the subject morally troubling. Yet six decades ago Anaïs Nin took control of her body and determined that she would not become a mother, did not have to, not for her husband's sake and not for society's sake. She thought of herself as beautiful and sensual and surrounded herself with beauty and sensuality. And though some may judge her now as a simple narcissist, I admire her because unlike so many women — especially those who consider themselves above superficial social consciousness, unfettered by pressures of fashion — she considered herself downright lovely!

Unlike the work of other women writers who taught me *how* to write, I must say that Nin's creative writing efforts did not influence me much. But her determination to claim the right to her own body, her soul and mind — at a time when there was no movement to support her — did. Even now, nearly a century after her birth, women — at least those from the Catholic culture she and I share — can't do that without paying a hefty price.

"The problem with Anaïs," my friend who knew her said, "is that she lived too long." The feminist community had found Nin outdated — what a critic today might feel an impulse to call a *border-feminist*. Someone else might say that perhaps she had been born too soon. Nin herself told a new audience that she had wanted to live the dream. For her, that meant finding true erotic and psychic fulfillment as a woman. Because she chose to document her journey and her quest, other women were also able to believe in such a possibility — a woman like myself — who at forty-three years of age is still pursuing the dream. Ever without guilt.

Gatsby's Glasses
Siri Hustvedt

I FIRST READ *The Great Gatsby* when I was sixteen years old, a high school student in Northfield, Minnesota. I read it again when I was twenty-three and living in New York City, and now again at the advanced age of forty-two. I have carried the book's magic around with me ever since that first reading, and its memory is distinct in my mind because unlike many books that return to me chiefly as a series of images, *The Great Gatsby* has also left its trace in my ear — as enchanted music, whispering, laughter and as the voice of storytelling itself.

The book begins with the narrator's memory of something his father told him years before: "Whenever you feel like criticizing anyone, remember that all the people in this world haven't had the advantages that you've had." As an adage for life, the quotation is anticlimactic — restrained words I imagine being uttered by a re-strained man, perhaps over the top of his newspaper, and yet without this watered-down American version of *noblesse oblige* there could be no story of Gatsby. The father's words are the story's seed, its origin. The man we come to know as Nick Carraway tells us that his father "meant a great deal more" than what the words denote, and I believe him. Hidden in the comment is a way of living and an entire moral world. Its resonance is double: first, we know that the narrator's words are bound to his father's words, that he comes from somewhere he can identify and that he has not severed that connection, and second, that these paternal words have shaped him into who he is: a man "inclined to reserve all judgements" — in short, the ideal narrator, a man who doesn't leap into the action but stays on the sidelines. Nick is not an actor but a voyeur, and in every art, including the art of fiction, there's always somebody watching.

Taking little more than his father's advice, the young man goes east. The American story has changed directions: the frontier is flip-flopped from the West to the East, but the urge to leave home and seek your fortune is as old as fairy tales. Fitzgerald's Middle

265

West was not the same as mine. I did not come from the stolid advantages of Summit Avenue in St. Paul. I remember the large, beautiful houses on that street as beacons of wealth and privilege to which I had no access. I grew up in the open spaces of southern Minnesota in one of the "lost Swede towns" Fitzgerald mentions late in the book, only we were mostly Norwegians, not Swedes. It was to my hometown that Fitzgerald sent Jay Gatsby to college for two weeks. The unnamed town is Northfield. The named college is St. Olaf, where my father taught for thirty years and where I was a student for four. Gatsby's ghost may have haunted me; even in high school, I knew that promise lay in the East, particularly in New York City, and ever so vaguely, I began to dream of what I had never seen and where I had never been.

Nick Carraway hops a train and finds himself in the bond trade and living next door to Gatsby's huge mansion: a house built of wishes. All wishes, however wrong-headed, however great or noble or ephemeral, must have an object, and that object is usually more ideal than real. The nature of Gatsby's wish is fully articulated in the book. Gatsby is *great* because his dream is all-consuming and every bit of his strength and breath are in it. He is a creature of will, and the beauty of his will overreaches the tawdriness of his real object: Daisy. But the secret of the story is that there is no *great Gatsby* without Nick Carraway, only Gatsby, because Nick is the only one who is able to see the greatness of his wish.

Reading the book again, I was struck by the strangeness of a single sentence that seemed to glitter like a golden key to the story. It occurs when a dazed Gatsby finds his wish granted, and he is showing Daisy around the West Egg mansion. Nick is, as always, the third wheel. "I tried to go then," he says, "but they wouldn't hear of it; perhaps my presence made them feel more satisfactorily alone." The question is: in what way are two people more *satisfactorily* alone when somebody else is present? What on earth does this mean? I have always felt that there is a triangular quality to every love affair. There are two lovers and a third element — the idea of being in love itself. I wonder if it is possible to fall in love without this third presence, an imaginary witness to love as a thing of wonder, cast in the glow of our deepest stories about ourselves. It is as if Nick's eyes satisfy this third element, as if he embodies for the lovers the essential self-consciousness of love — a third-person account. When I read Charles Scribner III's introduction to my paperback edition, I was not at all surprised that an early draft of the novel was written by Fitzgerald in the third person. Lowering the narration into the voice of a character inside the story allows the writer to inhabit more fully the interstices of narrative itself.

The role of the onlooker is given quasi-supernatural status in the form of the bespectacled eyes of T. J. Eckleburg, and it is to this faded billboard of an oculist in Queens that the grieving Wilson addresses his prayer: "You can't hide from God." When his friend tells him, "That's an advertisement," Wilson doesn't answer. He needs an omniscient third person, and he finds it in Eckleburg, with his huge staring eyes. Nick is not present for this conversation, and yet the quality of the narration does not change. It is *as if* he is present. Nick's stand-in is Michaelis, a neighbor of Wilson's, who has presumably reported the scene to the narrator. Together Michaelis and Nick Carraway form a complementary narration that finds transcendence in the image of Eckleburg's all-seeing, all-knowing eyes, an element very like the third-person narrator of nineteenth-century novels, who looks down on his creatures and their follies.

There is only one other pair of noticeable spectacles in the novel, those worn by "the owl-eyed man." One of Gatsby's hundreds of anonymous guests, he is first seen in the "Gothic library," a drunken fellow muttering excitedly that the books "are absolutely real." He had expected cardboard, he tells Nick and Jordan, and cannot get over his astonishment at the *reality* of these volumes. The owl-eyed man returns near the end of the book as Gatsby's only mourner besides the dead man's father and Nick. Like the image of Eckleburg, the owl-eyed man is both thoroughly mysterious and thoroughly banal. He tells Nick and Jordan that he's been drunk for a week and that he thought the books might help "sober" him up. Nameless, the man is associated exclusively with the library and his large glasses. Nick does not ask the owl-eyed man to attend the funeral. He has kept the day and place a secret to avoid gawkers and the press, but out of nowhere, the man makes his appearance in the rain, and during that time he removes his glasses twice. The second time, he wipes them, "outside and in." I can see him doing it. For me the gesture is intimate, and although it is not mentioned, I see a white handkerchief, too, moving over the rain-spattered lenses. The cleaning of the glasses is ordinary and magical. The strange man is a second, specifically literary incarnation of Eckleburg, a witness to the problem of what's real and what isn't, a problem that is turned inside out by the idea of seeing through *special glasses* — the glasses of fiction.

The Great Gatsby is an oddly immaterial novel. In it there are only two characters with bodies that mean anything, bodies of vigor and appetite: Tom Buchanan and his mistress, Myrtle Wilson, whose alliance causes the book's tragedy. The rest of them — Gatsby, the hordes of guests, Jordan and, above all, Daisy — seem to be curiously unanchored to the ground. They are pastel beings, beings of light and sound — creatures of the imagination. At Gatsby's parties "men and girls" come and go "like moths," accompanied by an orchestra as if they were characters in a play or a movie. When Nick first sees Daisy and Jordan in East Egg, they are reclining on a huge sofa. "They were both in white, and their dresses were rippling and fluttering as if they had just been blown back in after a short flight around the room." They are as weightless as dollar bills, or maybe hundred-dollar bills, blown up in a wind before they settle again to the ground, and whether or not Fitzgerald intended this lightness as another image of money in his novel, money is the source of the charm that envelopes the ethereal creatures. Daisy's music is her own "thrilling" voice, and it sounds, as Gatsby says, "like money." But Nick is the one who elaborates on its timbre. In it he hears the jingle of coins and the rain of gold in fairy tales.

It may be that New York and its environs is the best place in the world to feel this particular bewitchment, which all the pieties about honest poverty cannot disperse. Fitzgerald is right. Money in the Midwest may be respectable and it may even be considerable, but it is nothing like New York money. There was no money where I grew up, no "real" money, that is. The turkey farmers did well, and the dentists in town had a certain affluent shine to them, but on the whole, status was measured in increments, a new *economy* car, unused skates, an automatic garage-door opener, and there was a feeling that it was wrong to have much more money than anybody else, and downright sinful to flaunt it if you had it. When I arrived in New York, the money I saw flabbergasted me. It sashayed on Fifth Avenue and giggled in galleries and generally showed itself off with such unabashed glee that it was impossible not to admire it or envy it, at least a little. And what I saw during my journeys through the city in the early eighties was no different from what Nick saw. Money casts a glow over things, a glow all the more powerful to people who haven't got it. No matter how

F. Scott Fitzgerald. Late 1920s. The Granger Collection, New York.

clean or morally upright, poverty has cracks of ugliness that nothing but money can close, and I remember the sense of relief and
pleasure that would come over me when I sat in a good restaurant
with white tablecloths and shining silver and flowers, and I knew
that my date was a person who could afford to pay. And it happened during my lonely, impoverished student days that a man
would lean across the table and invite me to an island or to another
country or to a seaside resort, to an East Egg or a West Egg, and the
truth was that the smell of money would waft over me, its scent
like a torpor-inducing drug, and had there been no Middle West,
no Northfield, Minnesota, no home with its strident Lutheran
sanctions, no invisible parental eyes always watching me; in short:
had I been somebody else, I might have been blown off to an Egg in
a gust of wind and have floated across the beach and out into the
sound to the strains of some foolish but melodic accompaniment.

Gravity is personal history. That is why Nick tells the reader
about his family right away. The Carraways have been "prominent
well-to-do people for three generations," three generations founded
on the rock of a *hardware* business, a business that trades in real
things. In the East, Nick trades not in things as his father does but
in paper, bonds that will generate more paper. Money that makes
money. And money has built Gatsby's castle, a place as unreal as
a theater set erected from bills or bonds or "cardboard," as the owl-
eyed man suggests. It is a blur of excess and anonymity as vague
as Gatsby's rumored past — a past we learn in bits and pieces but
which is never whole — for he is a man interrupted, a man who
has broken from his old life and his parents to become not somebody else so much as "Nobody" — a brilliant cipher. "Mr. Nobody
from Nowhere" is Tom Buchanan's contemptuous expression.
Gatsby's connections to others are tenuous or fabricated. When he
first meets Daisy in Louisville, he misrepresents himself to her by
implying that he comes from her world. Again the image of wind
appears in Fitzgerald's prose. "As a matter of fact, he had no comfortable family standing behind him, and he was liable at the
whim of an impersonal government to be blown anywhere about
the world."

Still, in this ephemeral weightlessness of Gatsby's there is
beauty, real beauty, and on this the whole story turns. The man's
monstrous accumulation of *things* is nothing if not vulgar, a grotesque display as pitiful as it is absurd. But what Nick under-
stands, as nobody else does, is that this mountain of things is the

vehicle of a man's passion, and as objects they are nearly drained of material reality. The afternoon when Gatsby takes Daisy through his house, we are told that he "stares at his possessions in a dazed way, as though in her actual and astounding presence, none of it was any longer real." His nerves running high, the owner of the property begins pulling shirts from his closet, one gauzy, gorgeous article after another, "in coral and apple-green and lavender and faint orange, with monograms of Indian blue," piling them high before Nick and his beloved. Then Daisy bends her lovely head and weeps into the shirts. "It makes me sad because I've never seen such — such beautiful shirts before." I marveled again at the power of this passage. At once tender and ridiculous, Fitzgerald lets neither feeling get the upper hand. Daisy pours out the grief of her young love for Gatsby into a heap of his splendid shirts without understanding her own feelings. But she recovers quickly. Some time later the same afternoon, she stares out the window at pink clouds in a western sky and says to Gatsby, "I'd just like to get one of those pink clouds and put you in it and push you around." The shirts, the clouds, the dream are colored like a fading rainbow. Gatsby stands at the edge of his lawn and watches the green light from Daisy's house across the water. The last suit Nick sees him wearing is pink. If your feet are rooted to the ground, you can't be blown willy nilly, but you can't fly up to those rosy clouds either. It's as simple as that.

Things and nothings. Bodies and nobodies. The ground and the air. The tangible and the intangible. The novel moves restlessly between these dichotomies. Surely Fitzgerald was right when he said that *The Great Gatsby* was "a new thinking out of the idea of illusion." Illusion is generally coupled with its opposite, reality, but where is the real? Is reality found in the tangible and illusion in the intangible? Besides the nuts and bolts of hardware out west, there is *ground* in the novel, the soil of ashes in West Egg, the ground that Eckleburg unblinkingly surveys, but it is here that Fitzgerald lavishes a prose that could have been taken straight from Dickens, a prose of fantasy, not realism.

> This is the valley of ashes — a fantastic farm where ashes grow like wheat into ridges and hills and grotesque gardens; where ashes take the forms of houses and chimneys and rising smoke, and finally, with a transcendent effort, of men who move dimly and already crumbling through the powdery air.

271

With its crumbling men, the valley of ashes plainly evokes that other biblical valley of death, and this miserable stretch of land borders the road where Myrtle Wilson will die under the wheels of the car driven by Daisy. But like the pink clouds, the land lacks solidity and dissolves. The difference between the vision of Gatsby's mansion and that of this earth is that money does not disguise mortality here. The gaping cracks of poverty are fully visible.

Nevertheless, among the residents of this ashen valley is Myrtle Wilson, the only person in the novel to whom Fitzgerald assigns "vitality." The word is used three times in reference to Mrs. Wilson, Tom Buchanan's working-class mistress. "There was an immediately perceptible *vitality* about her as if the nerves of her body were continually smoldering." As Nick passes Wilson's gas station in a car, he sees Myrtle "at the garage pump with panting *vitality* as we went by." And in death: "The mouth was wide open and ripped at the corners, as though she had choked a little in giving up the tremendous *vitality* she had stored so long" (all emphasis mine). It is this vivid life, not her character, that makes Myrtle Wilson's death tragic. A silly and coarse woman, she is nevertheless more sympathetic than her lover, Tom, who is worse: stupid and violent. Between them, however, there exists a real sexual energy that isn't found elsewhere in the novel. The narrator's attraction to Jordan is tepid at best, and Gatsby's fantasies about Daisy seem curiously unerotic. The slender girl has no body to speak of. She seems to be made of her beautiful clothes and her beautiful voice. It is hard to imagine Gatsby actually having sex with Daisy. It's like trying to imagine a man taking a butterfly. And although her marriage to Tom has produced a daughter, as a mother Daisy communicates detachment. She coos endearments at the child, Pammy, and then dismisses her. Only once in the novel is the reader reminded of Daisy as a creature of flesh and blood, and significantly, it is through a finger her husband has bruised. Daisy looks down at the little finger "with an awed expression." "You didn't mean to," she says to Tom, "but you *did* do it." The passage is not only a premonition of Tom's brutality, which erupts horribly in New York when he breaks Myrtle's nose, or of Myrtle's bruised and opened body on the road. Daisy's awe expresses her remote relation to her own body and to mortality itself, which her money will successfully hide — not forever, of course, but for now.

What Tom and Myrtle have that Jay and Daisy don't is a *personal* relation with its attendant physicality and mess. That is why, after admitting to Nick that Daisy may have once loved Tom "for a minute," Gatsby comforts himself by saying, "In any case, it was only personal." What Gatsby has been chasing all these years is neither *personal* nor *physical*. Its transcendence may have been lodged in the person of Daisy, but it is not limited to her. Her very shallowness makes Gatsby's dream possible. But Myrtle Wilson is not a simple incarnation of the flesh and its weaknesses. She harbors dreams as well. As it does for Gatsby, her intangible wish finds form in an object. In her drawer at home, wrapped in tissue paper, Mr. Wilson finds the expensive dog leash Tom once bought for her to go with the dog he also bought. The dog didn't come home. The useless, beautiful thing is a sign of absence, a string of absences, in fact—the dog, the lover and the emptiness of desire itself. Just as the green light shining from Daisy's house may be counted among Gatsby's "enchanted objects," one he loses when Daisy actually enters his life again, the dog leash possesses the same magic. It is the tissue paper that makes me want to cry, that sends this frivolous possession into another register altogether, that imbues the silver-and-leather dog leash with the quality of true pathos.

The tangible and the intangible collide to cast a spell. But can a person or thing ever be stripped naked? Can we ever discover reality hiding under the meanings we give to people and things? I don't think so. And I don't think Fitzgerald thought so either. His book meditates on the necessity of fiction, not only as lies but as truths. The play between the material and the immaterial in *The Great Gatsby* is riddled, not simple. The fairy tale contains the valley of ashes as well as the castle by the sea, the heavy weight of the corpse and the pretty bodies blown in the wind. And which one is more real than the other? Is death more true than life? Are not dreams as much a part of living as waking life is? The book goes to the heart of the problem of fiction itself by insisting that fiction is necessary to life—not only as books but as dreams, dreams that frame the world and give it meaning. Nick imagines Gatsby at the pool just before Wilson kills him. The man has understood that there will be no message from Daisy, that the great idea is dead.

> He must have looked up at an unfamiliar sky through frightening leaves and shivered as he found what a grotesque

thing a rose is and how raw the sunlight was upon the
scarcely created grass. A new world, material without being
real, where poor ghosts, breathing dreams like air, drifted
fortuitously about . . . like that ashen, fantastic figure gliding toward him through the amorphous trees.

This passage tells of dramatic change, but it is not a change from
illusion to reality, from enchanted nature to real nature. This
world may be new, but there are ghosts here, and they are fantastic.
It is now a world made of matter, but that matter is no more real
than the magic lights and music of the summer parties that went
before it.

One can argue that nearly every word of dialogue uttered in the
novel, every exchange and every event is ordinary. Tom Buchanan
and the poor Wilsons are glaringly limited and unattractive.
Gatsby's business partner, Wolfsheim, is clever and dishonest
without the grandeur of being satanic. Daisy's charm is not revealed in anything she says. Gatsby converses in a stiff and clichéd
manner that sets Nick back on his heels. Jordan is a cheat. These
characters do not elevate themselves above the crowd. They are
not remarkable people, and yet to read this novel is to feel as if
you have taken a walk in a fairy wood, as if while you are reading,
you glimpse the sublime.

The magic is in the book's narration, in its shades of sunlight
and darkness, its allusions to fairy tales, to music, to songs, to
dusty dance slippers and bright voices. Better than any other
writer I know, Fitzgerald captures the tipsy aura of parties, that
slight glazing of the mind that dawns after two glasses of cham-
pagne. The ordinary world trembles with *adjectival* enchantment
here — Fitzgerald's prose is dense with surprising adjectives. Although some of his characters are glib, the narrator is not. The
sorcery that infuses the book cannot be explained as the golden
effect of money, although that is part of it, or even by youth. They
are mostly very young, these people, and life still holds an un-
wrapped newness for them. Nick Carraway's voice carries a deeper
understanding of enchantment, which at once grounds and ele-
vates the narration. It returns us to the beginning. The father's
words render up a world in which every human being, no matter
how flawed, is granted an essential dignity. Remember, every
person is a product of his own history, one that is not necessarily
like yours. He or she has come out of a particular story and to

judge that man or woman is not fair unless you know the story. The advice is a call to empathy, the ultimate act of the imagination, and the true ground of all fiction. All characters are born of this effort to be another person. And its success is rooted in the grounded self. The "carelessness" of Tom and Daisy manifests itself in flightiness. Unballasted, they flit from one place to another, and their wealth only facilitates their disconnectedness. Yet we trust Nick, this man who speaks to us, and we believe him when he says, "I am one of the few honest people that I have ever known." And we trust his *imaginings*, because the imaginary is crucial to his tale. He did not witness Gatsby's murder. He cannot be Gatsby, but he says, "He must have . . ." Nick Carraway's voice bears the conviction of his empathy.

Fitzgerald did not give part of Nick's story to Michaelis because it was convenient. By seamlessly transferring Nick's vision into Wilson's Greek neighbor, Fitzgerald lifts the narration out of the "merely personal." Nick sees beyond himself, and this second sight is reinforced by the eyes of Eckleburg and the owl eyes of the man in the library. Nick sees vicariously what Michaelis and another man actually witness: Myrtle's dead body, the body Daisy will not see and cannot face. It is more than enough. The men undo Mrs. Wilson's shirt "still wet with perspiration" and see "that her left breast was hanging loose like a flap, and there was no need to listen to the heart below." Later Nick tells Gatsby, "She was ripped open." He did not have to be there to see. For a moment, with Nick, the reader literally stares into the heart of being, and it has stopped. I see what I did not see. I experience that which is outside my own experience. This is the magic of reading novels. This is the working out of the problem of illusion. I take a book off the shelf. I open it up and begin to read, and what I discover in its pages is real.

Ralph Ellison. New York City, 1973. Photograph by Nancy Crampton.

The Visible Man: Ralph Ellison
Quincy Troupe

I WAS IN HIGH SCHOOL when I first read Ralph Ellison's *Invisible Man*. I was about fifteen or sixteen and had just finished reading Richard Wright's seminal novel, *Native Son*. I loved Wright's book, was really knocked out by it and totally identified with Bigger Thomas and his situation. His was my experience, his dreams mine, his anger and frustration what I felt and knew. I could also identify with the young man for whom the "Invisible Man" was named because I was going through the same thing attending an almost all-white high school of three thousand kids — there were seven black kids, including me — who hardly paid attention to me except when I was out on the basketball court. I loved *Invisible Man*, but the novel was dreamlike, close to being a fantasy, all the scenes so unfamiliar to me. That is, I could identify with what the invisible man was going through but I couldn't seem to get a grip on the settings he was in; I just hadn't experienced any of those settings yet, though all of that would change soon after when I went to college.

I attended Grambling, a then all-black college in Louisiana, and the president of the school, Dr. Ralph Jones — who also doubled as my baseball coach — reminded me eerily of the president of the black college in Ellison's novel, although he was nowhere close to being as evil and manipulative. The vesper services at Grambling also reminded me of the one in *Invisible Man*. Somehow the novel was becoming clearer to me in college, and after I read it again there, my respect for Ellison grew by leaps and bounds. Over the years, after college, when I decided to become a writer, Ralph Ellison became one of my genuine literary heroes, someone I definitely wanted to meet. After coming to New York City to teach at the College of Staten Island in the early 1970s, I met the late Larry Neal and Albert Murray, who knew Ellison well, socialized with him on a regular basis, so I thought it would be through one of these men that I would meet Ellison. But I was wrong; I would meet him through an altogether different source.

277

The first time I encountered Ellison was in 1974, at a reception given by the Academy of American Arts and Letters held at the old Museum of Indian History on Broadway and 155th Streets in Harlem. The guest of my longtime friend Ishmael Reed (who had received an Academy Citation at an awards ceremony preceding the reception), I remember seeing Ellison and being shocked when he didn't applaud when Ishmael's name was called. Later, at the reception, Ellison came up to us with a drink in his hand and began arguing with Reed about something. Then he called Reed a "gangster and a con artist." We were shocked. I looked at Ishmael to see if he was going to respond. He just kind of shrugged as Ellison's wife, Fanny, appearing a little nervous, dragged him away. I remember Ellison's eyes being on fire that day, red, really angry. Why was he so angry? We hadn't said anything to him. I don't know but I think it had something to do with his thinking that Ishmael might be being groomed to replace him — an absurd notion — within the New York literary establishment. I don't know. I mean, what a way to meet one of your literary heroes!

In 1977, I participated in an interview that Ishmael Reed and Steve Cannon conducted with Ellison. On this occasion Ellison revealed himself to be a witty, charming, absolutely brilliant raconteur, as well as an irascible, cantankerous and tenacious defender of his beliefs. We all got into arguments with him but I remember that he and Reed got into some very heated discussions about literature. Reed asked Ellison why he was always putting our generation of writers down when he had read only a few and didn't know any of the poets. But Ellison never backed down, although he did seem a little disturbed by our line of questioning. Still, he laughed and joked and reprimanded us throughout the interview.

On the other hand, I remember Mr. Ellison being meek as a lamb during a telephone conversation with the great American poet Sterling Brown (who died in 1989 at the age of eighty-eight). Sterling was staying at my Harlem apartment on one of his periodic visits to New York City from his home in Washingon, D.C., around 1982. He asked about Ellison, if I knew him, had his number. I told him that I knew him, that I did have his number. So he asked if I could call him, that he'd like to speak to him because he hadn't for some time. So I called Ellison and when Fanny answered I told her that Sterling Brown wanted to speak with Ralph, was that possible? She said she was sure it was, then she left and Ralph came on almost immediately, happy to talk with Sterling. After exchanging a few pleasantries I handed the phone to Sterling, who almost immediately — after less than a minute had passed — inquired about the state of Ellison's long overdue second novel. Now, I don't know exactly what Ellison was saying to Sterling at his end of the phone but I do remember Brown telling Ralph in no uncertain terms, "Oh, Ralph, just finish the goddamn book and stop all this hand-wringing bullshit. Just finish the goddamn thing, son! Just do it." I could tell by the tone of the conversation that Ellison wasn't putting up a fight, that he was indeed being lectured to by the older man. Maybe that's why Ralph didn't say anything because Sterling *was* his elder and Ellison respected him. I never forgot that conversation and every time I saw Ellison after that he would look at me curiously, as if I had set him up.

The only time I was invited to his home was in 1977. I remember his eighth-floor apartment on upper Riverside Avenue in Harlem being full of light, with a fabulous view of the Hudson River and across to New Jersey. Books were everywhere, as were record albums, sculpture pieces, African and otherwise, the walls graced with great paintings by his friend Romare Bearden and other artists of his generation. It was a large, elegant apartment, the kind you imagined a great writer, intellectual or artist would live in. It wasn't a cold place but had a lived-in, comfortable feeling about it. I recall thinking at the time that it showed taste, was a reflection of a refined sensibility and I remember promising myself that I would one day strive to live like this.

Ralph Ellison was an enigma for many writers of my generation, born as we were a couple of decades after him. We were the so-called "World War II babies" (Ishmael Reed, Haki Madhubuti, the late Toni Cade Bambara, John Edgar Wideman, Al Young, Alice Walker, Nikki Giovanni, Sherley Anne Williams, myself and others) and our view of the world was decidedly more political — almost radical, if you will — than was his. We all thought Ellison a great, seminal twentieth-century American writer, who had exerted a powerful influence on our own writing. We learned from his mastery, held him in very high esteem. And yet our relationship remained strangely vertical. He was "up there" and we were "down here." We never understood why he insisted upon identifying himself with the term "Negro" — we could appreciate that it was *his* prerogative to call himself whatever he liked, but he called us *Negro*, too. *We* didn't want to be identified with that term, and that was *our* prerogative. Yet he insisted upon calling us that any-way and heated arguments ensued when and if we protested. For the most part, Ellison was a conservative man, a product of the "Negro" old school who thought blacks should wage a more rear-guard, less confrontational approach toward the American White power structure than my generation was advocating. So he didn't trust many of us, especially those of us who were still involved in and sympathetic toward the political and cultural ideas that spawned the upheavals of the 1960s. In person he was always un-pretentious, unassuming, a charming man, engaging, with a keen, even self-deprecating sense of humor. Still, we sensed an air of aloofness about him, a distance, a sense of always being above the fray, while seemingly swimming around in it. A great conversa-tionalist, he seemed to know a little bit about everything. In other words, his was a formidable personality.

Like Ellison the man, Ellison the writer is complex. Very. A magnificent prose stylist, one of the greatest of this century, in my opinion, his grandeur and his lyrical, powerful poetic gifts evoke and sing the language. This is especially evident in his one published novel. This gift for language, structure and style is also present in snatches of his unfinished, yet unpublished second novel, in a few very good short stories and in many great essays like "The Little Man at Chehaw Station," "The Shadow and the Act," "The Myth of the Flawed White Southerner," "Going to the Territory," "Twentieth Century Fiction and the Black Mask of Humanity" and others. His essays were gathered in *The Collected Essays of Ralph Ellison.* However, it is for his great achievement in *Invisible Man* that Ralph Ellison's fully deserved reputation finally rests.

When Ellison's *Invisible Man,* published in 1952, won that year's National Book Award for Fiction, he was the first African-American writer (Ellison would prefer that I call him a "Negro" writer here) to win this prestigious award. The award changed Ellison's life forever. He went from being a respected writer to becoming a famous and venerated one, in a very short period of time. *Invisible Man* became both a best-seller and an instant classic of American literature. The novel, a picaresque, coming-of-age story of a young African-American unnamed male, explores with astonishing in-sight the concept of invisibility as experienced by black people in the United States. Besides his page-turning story-telling ability, the lyrical way he uses language throughout to tell the story and the loose twelve-bar blues–based structure of the novel, Ellison also dishes up a rich host of memorable, compelling characters: Trueblood, the man who impregnates his own daughter, and who is treated "fine by the white folks . . ." but "the niggers up at the school don't like" him; Dr. Herbert Bledsoe, the powerful president of the Negro College, who suspends the Invisible Man from school and sends him to New York with sealed letters that say, "Keep this nigger boy running"; blind Reverend Homer Barbee and Mr. Norton, the powerful, rich white northern financier and trustee of the college who stands in awe of Trueblood's incestuous act because he, too, loves his own daughter. Then there's the Invisible Man's grandfather; there's Tadlock, Halley, Supercargo, Sylvester, Doc Burnside and a whole host of other crazy characters from the Golden Day Saloon. There's Lucius Brockway, the irascible old black man in the bottom of the Liberty Paint Factory; Tod ("death" in German) Clifton, the disillusioned revolutionary led astray by one-eyed white Brother Jack, leader of the brotherhood party. There's Brother Tarp, who presents the Invisible Man with "a slave's leg chain . . . a link to his past and his future," Mary and Ellison's great trickster figure, and master of disguise, Rinehart, who is a preacher, briber, lover, gambler, runner and master confidence man. There's Ras the Destroyer, the almost mythical black nationalist leader based on the character of Marcus Garvey and a whole panoply of others.

Invisible Man is a novel full of great scenes, set pieces that serve as metaphoric rites of passage. Take, for example, the "battle royal" between the Invisible Man and Jackson. At a smoker, a blond, buck naked, voluptuous young white woman with an American flag tattooed on her stomach dances seductively in front of the Invisible Man and Jackson as drunken white men hoot, jeer and threaten them before throwing heaps of coins on an electrified rug that shocks the blindfolded young men as they are forced to retrieve the money; Mr. Norton's encounter with Trueblood and his — and the Invisible Man's — experience at the Golden Day Saloon; the explosion in the Liberty Paint Factory, whose company slogan is "Keep America Pure With Liberty Paints," with the most celebrated product being a paint called "Optic White," whose secret is "ten drops of black paint stirred into the white solution"; Lucius Brockway, an old black man, is the keeper of this solution; the Invisible Man's subsequent symbolic lobotomy, or if you prefer, transformation; the riot scene; encounters with Rinehart and Ras the Destroyer; the 1,369 light bulbs screwed into the Invisible Man's ceiling, which are kept on all the time so that he can see himself; the Invisible Man almost cutting to death a white man who runs into him on a dark New York City street and then won't apologize because he refuses to acknowledge his presence; Tod Clifton on a Harlem Street selling Black Sambo dolls, who dance when Clifton pulls their strings; the dolls are effigies of himself; and finally, the Invisible Man's taking on the role of Rinehart and his confrontations with Bledsoe and Brother Jack. Each of these scenes is a different metaphor for the experience of African-Americans — and indeed *all* Americans — in the United States. Each scene is a rite of passage that leads ultimately to the Invisible Man's understanding of his destiny and place within the American society. These metaphors — and so many others in this book — are instructive on so many different levels.

Invisible Man is a polemical, anti-Stalinist, anti-Black Nationalist novel, very American in that it is pro-integrationist in its political, social and cultural outlook. (The irony of this is that it was the very same thing he accused my generation of being — overly polemical and political; although he misread us, thought all of us were dyed-in-the-wool Marxists or Black Nationalists. Some of us were but the majority weren't.) With the exception of Mary — whose role is still small — there are no major female characters in this book. Women are almost invisible throughout this novel; men, black and white, are everywhere. I'm not accusing Ellison of being a male chauvinist — which he probably was — but I *am* saying that he and the novel were products of their time, a time when men were always out front and center, dominating, with women pushed to the margins to play minor roles. Still, with these flaws, *Invisible Man* is a major achievement, one of the great novels of this century, a book I return to time and again.

If I had to pick a character from Ellison's novel to compare him to, it would be Rinehart the trickster, the master of disguises. Ellison probably saw himself as a Dr. Bledsoe–type figure vis-à-vis the New York literary establishment, and, maybe he was in his lived life. But in his writing, at least for me, he was closer to being a Rinehart figure — sly, unpredictable, slippery, hard to pin down, brilliant and political; in his writing, Ellison was no Uncle Tom but the real thing, whether you agreed with him or not. He was also an astute listener and critic of music, at least of the music produced during his generation. He loved Duke Ellington, Count

Basie, Louis Armstrong and the blues. He was also an avid collector of African art, could speak eloquently about Romare Bearden, Jacob Lawrence, Hale Woodruff, Charles Alston, Norman Lewis and other black painters of his generation. It goes without saying that he was a penetrating reader of American and world literature produced during his generation. His readings and insights into Dostoevsky (whose *Notes From Underground* had a profound influence on *Invisible Man*), Thomas Mann, Hemingway, Faulkner, Mark Twain, Henry James, Saul Bellow, James Joyce, Herman Melville, Hawthorne, Stephen Crane and others were absolutely stunning, right on the mark.

At the time of his death on April 16, 1994, at the age of eighty, Ralph Ellison was rumored to be close to completing his long-awaited second novel begun in 1958, tentatively entitled *Cadillac Flambé*, a 368-page draft of which — Ellison's only copy — was lost in a fire that destroyed his Plainsfield, Massachusetts, summer home in 1967. Ellison was devasted by the loss and refused on many occasions to discuss the book. Over the years he painstakingly went about reconstructing the novel but was never fully satisfied with its total structure, according to James Alan McPherson, a close friend of Ellison's and himself a Pulitzer Prize–winning short story writer. I have read sections of the novel — at least eight sections were published. I love the surreality, the wackiness, the beautiful writing.

Ralph Ellison wrote with the sense and timing of a fine jazz or blues musician (which he was; he once played the trumpet). Consider this passage from *Invisible Man* where Tod Clifton, rapping a street-corner vendor's pitch, tries to sell his Black Sambo dolls on a Harlem street corner:

> Shake it up! Shake it up!
> He's Sambo, the dancing doll, ladies and gentlemen,
> Shake him, stretch him by the neck and set him down,
> — He'll do the rest. Yes!
>
> He'll make you laugh, he'll make you sigh, si-gh.
> He'll make you want to dance, and dance —
> Here you are, ladies and gentlemen, Sambo,
> The dancing doll.
>
> Buy one for your baby. Take him to your girlfriend and she'll love you, loove you!

He'll keep you entertained. He'll make you weep sweet —
Tears from laughing.
Shake him, shake him, you cannot break him
For he's Sambo, the dancing, Sambo, the prancing,
Sambo, the entrancing, Sambo Boogie Woogie paper doll.
And all for twenty-five cents, the quarter part of a dollar . . .
Ladies and Gentlemen, he'll bring you joy, step up and
     meet him,
Sambo the . . .

What makes him happy, what makes him dance,
This Sambo, this jumbo, this high-stepping joy boy?
He's more than a toy, ladies and gentlemen, he's Sambo,
     the dancing doll, the twentieth-century miracle.
Look at that rumba, that suzy-q, he's Sambo-Boogie,
Sambo-Woogie, you don't have to feed him, he sleeps
     collapsed, he'll kill your depression
And your dispossession, he lives upon the sunshine of
     your lordly smile

And only twenty-five cents, the brotherly two bits of a
     dollar because he wants me to eat.
It gives him pleasure to see me eat.
You simply take him and shake him . . . and he does the rest.

Pure music, poetry, very symbolic of the struggle of black people.
Goes right to the core. In the following passage the Invisible Man
has come upon an old black man and his wife after they've been
thrown out of their Harlem apartment. They have been rendered
worthless, totally invisible by a system that has never seen or
recognized them one single day in all their long lives. In this scene,
the Invisible Man talks to the old couple, to people in the crowd
that has gathered and gives a speech:

"And look at that old couple . . ."
"Yeah, what about Sister and Brother Provo?" he said. "It's
an ungodly shame!"
"And look at their possessions all strewn there on the
sidewalk. Just look at their possessions in the snow. How
old are you, sir?" I yelled.
"I'm eighty-seven," the old man said, his voice low and
bewildered.
"How's that? Yell so our slow-to-anger brethren can hear
you."

"I'm *eighty-seven years old!*"

"Did you hear him? He's eighty-seven. Eighty-seven and look at all he's accumulated in eighty-seven years, strewn in the snow like chicken guts, and we're a law-abiding, slow-to-anger bunch of folks turning the other cheek every day in the week. What are we going to do? What would you, what would I, what would he have done? *What is to be done?* I propose we do the wise thing, the law-abiding thing. Just look at this junk! Should two old folks live in such junk, cooped up in a filthy room? It's a great danger, a fire hazard! Old cracked dishes and broken-down chairs. Yes, yes, yes! Look at that old woman, somebody's mother, somebody's grandmother, maybe. We call them 'Big Mama' and they spoil us and — *you* know, *you* remember . . . Look at her quilts and broken-down shoes. I know she's somebody's mother because I saw an old breast pump fall into the snow, and she's somebody's grandmother, because I saw a card that read 'Dear Grandma' . . . But we're law-abiding . . . I looked into a basket and I saw some bones, not neckbones, but rib bones, knocking bones . . . This old couple used to dance . . . I saw — What kind of work do you do, Father?" I called.

"I'm a day laborer . . ."

". . . A day laborer, you heard him, but look at his stuff strewn like chitterlings in the snow . . . Where has all his labor gone? Is he lying?"

"Hell, no, he ain't lying."

"Naw, suh!"

"Then where did his labor go? Look at his old blues records and her pots of plants, they're down-home folks, and everything tossed out like junk whirled eighty-seven years in a cyclone. Eighty-seven years and *poof!* like a snort in a wind storm. Look at them, they look like my mama and my papa and my grandma and grandpa, and I look like you and you look like me. Look at them but remember that we're a wise, law-abiding group of people. And remember it when you look up there in the doorway at that law standing there with his forty-five. Look at him, standing with his blue steel pistol and his blue serge suit. Look at him! You don't see just one man dressed in one blue serge suit, or one forty-five, you see ten for every one of us, ten guns and ten warm suits and ten fat bellies and ten million laws. *Laws,* that's what we call them down South! Laws! And we're wise, and law-abiding. And look at this old woman with her

285

dog-eared Bible. What's she trying to bring off here? She's let her religion go to her head, but we all know that religion is for the heart, not for the head. 'Blessed are the pure in heart,' it says. Nothing about the poor in head. What's she trying to do? What about the clear of head? And the clear of eye, the ice-water-visioned who see too clear to miss a lie? Look out there at her cabinet with its gaping drawers. Eighty-seven years to fill them, and full of brick and brack, a bricabrac, and she wants to break the law . . . What happened to them? They're our people, your people and mine, your parents and mine. What's happened to 'em?"

"I'll tell you!" a heavyweight yelled, pushing out of the crowd, his face angry. "Hell, they been dispossessed, you crazy sonofabitch, get out the way!"

"Dispossessed?" I cried, holding up my hand and allowing the word to whistle from my throat. "That's a good word, 'Dispossessed! Dispossessed,' eighty-seven years and dispossessed of what? They ain't *got* nothing, they caint *get* nothing, they never *had* nothing. So who was dispossessed? Can it be us? These old ones are out in the snow, but we're here with them. Look at their stuff, not a pit to hiss in, nor a window to shout the news and us right with them. Look at them, not a shack to pray in or an alley to sing the blues! They're facing a gun and we're facing it with them. They don't want the world, but only Jesus. They only want Jesus, just fifteen minutes of Jesus on the rug-bare floor . . . How about it, Mr. Law? Do we get our fifteen minutes worth of Jesus? You got the world, can we have our Jesus?"

I used to read this passage over and over because like the Invisible Man, I recognized the reality of *many* human lives in this scene. It has such detail, the evocative power of a great minister or orator's voice. The language is astonishing, American, so right, the repetition (the couple's "eighty-seven years" and all their broken-up possessions) repeated until it becomes a refrain in a blues song, or a jazz riff or a mantra. This device builds the text to a point of explosion. This climactic scene charts class and racial fault lines of twentieth-century America, and describes the plight of "dispossessed" people (regardless of race or class) everywhere. Because they, like the black people in *Invisible Man*, are invisible, too. *Invisible Man* accomplishes what great literature is supposed to: it illuminates, evokes, provokes, challenges, provides insight, lifts the reader to a higher level of humanity. *Invisible Man* accomplishes all of the above, is a thought-provoking work of profound clarity and beauty, one that introduces us to an original American literary voice. In the future when literary historians look back at the twentieth-century and assess its literary production, *Invisible Man* will occupy an honored, central place in that literature, one of the key works if one is to have a better understanding of racial and human relations in America.

Shirley Jackson. Photograph by Lawrence J. Hyman. Courtesy Bantam Books.

Shirley Jackson:
"My Mother's Grave Is Yellow"
Dale Peck

I FIRST DISCOVERED Shirley Jackson's *We Have Always Lived in the Castle* in my high school library. "Discovered" seems a grand word for the experience: the library in Buhler High School was hardly a place where one "discovered" anything. It was a single, brightly lit, drop-ceilinged room lined with walnut-stained particle-board shelves scaled down to the size of pre-growth-spurt freshman arms. Devoid of mystery or charm or whatever it is that people who work with children like to call "wonder," the B.H.S. library was little more than a room with books in it, in stark opposition to the grand libraries that haunted the books on its shelves, the dark dusty magical rooms found in the novels of C. S. Lewis or J. R. R. Tolkien (or, often, Shirley Jackson), but it was, nonetheless, what I had to work with, and I like to imagine I ferreted out what few secrets it actually possessed. I looked for books the way my stepmother shopped for vegetables: by picking them up one at a time and checking them for desirability. I went wall by wall, shelf by shelf, book by book, my search conducted under the watchful eyes of the high school librarian, a tall, thin young woman whose name I can't quite remember — Sybil? Sybert? Seibert? — who could see virtually every book from her post at the checkout counter. The books were, of course, indexed by the Dewey Decimal System, but, in a gesture that both acknowledged and reinforced the mundanity of my school's low standards, handwritten translations had been added to the labels, viz., *900-999: reference.*

Buhler High School was itself a simplification of a more complex code: Buhler, Kansas, was a tiny town of conservative Mennonites — 888 as of the 1980 census and shrinking all the time — located a dozen or so miles northeast of the small city of Hutchinson, where most of its students actually lived. The only reason a high school had been built in Buhler at all was so that Hutch's more affluent residents, who lived on the northern and eastern sides of town, could bus their sons and daughters to a school free of the poorer—read: nonwhite—element which made up a large part of Hutch High. Only two black students actually enrolled during my time at B.H.S., although there was a brief appearance by a Chilean exchange student who, after three or four solitary weeks, disappeared from our hallways. I remember being aware of this gerrymandering even then, and I suppose I was so conscious of it because I had moved to Kansas from Long Island when I was seven; most of my peers regarded our school's virtual whiteness as a naturally occurring circumstance, but to me it always seemed odd, especially given the number of blacks and Latinos who were visible just ten miles to the south. Not surprisingly, the school board that produced such a segregated institution was solidly religious and conservative, and, also not surprisingly, this school board banned books as a matter of course. I don't remember being able to find *The Color Purple* when the movie came out, nor was *The Catcher in the Rye* available in our library; every year, I remember, the protests of that year's rebellious student (I was 1984's) led to a short-lived debate on whether the novels of Kurt Vonnegut were appropriate reading material for teenagers, and every year the conclusion was that some of them were and some of them were not, but just to be on the safe side all of them were banned.

I doubt that Shirley Jackson was ever the subject of such debate simply because, by 1981, when I entered high school, she had been almost completely forgotten. Jackson published her first novel, *The Road Through the Well,* and her most successful short story, "The Lottery," in 1948, and she remained a well-known, well-read writer until her death in 1965, at the age of forty-six. During her brief professional life she produced dozens of short stories, six novels and two works of nonfiction—sly satires on family life that must have gone right over the heads of the *Leave It to Beaver* crowd—but since her death her reputation has steadily declined. That decline continues: a recent collection of short stories was received respectfully but without enthusiasm; her novels are either out of print or languish in the young adult sections of public libraries—which is why I was able to find it. I stumbled across the single copy of *We Have Always Lived in the Castle* our library possessed in, as they say, my tender, formative years. I'm now convinced the experience scarred me for life.

*

Of course, there was "The Lottery." Everyone in America reads "The Lottery"; everyone, I should say, *must* read "The Lottery," just as everyone must read *To Kill a Mockingbird* and *Huckleberry Finn* and at least an abridged version of Anne Frank's *Diary of a Young Girl,* and as a result the story inhabits the invisible realm of overscrutinized objects, shoelaces and toothbrushes and librarians, objects whose enormous effect on our lives is never quite acknowledged; I first read the story in eighth grade, and of that original reading I only remember gleefully noting that the surname of the woman who wins the lottery was Hutchinson.

Briefly, for those who somehow escaped the story, "The Lottery" is a sketch of an unnamed "village" whose citizens say "Dellacroy" rather than "Delacroix," "m'dishes" instead of "my dishes." The villagers are simple folk who grow crops and clean house and, each June 27, hold a lottery whose winner is stoned to death. This lottery is performed with a kind of mesmeric simplicity by rural stereotypes who, at story's end, kill their friend with the same automatic gestures with which they might till a field or cook a meal. On the one hand, their mindlessness is what makes the story so horrifying, but it's also, I think, what renders "The Lottery" nothing *more* than a horror story: characters identifiable only as types are dismissable for the same reason. Though the story might, on first read, be shocking, it's not haunting — or, at any rate, it didn't haunt me. I was a native New Yorker living among the stereotypes Jackson was describing. Kansans said "pop," "scoot," "put it up" where I was inclined to say "soda," "move," "put it away," but that didn't mean I ducked every time someone picked up a rock. Violence is relatively rare in the Midwest, although when it does come it's explosive. I remember a fellow third-grader having his leg broken when he was thrown across a table during the course of a classroom argument; the boy who sat cattycorner from me in ecology my junior year used a shotgun to blow the heads off his girlfriend and the twins she was baby-sitting because he thought she was cheating on him; the only reason the lynch mob didn't get the black date of a classmate during our five-year high school reunion was that its members were too drunk to find her hotel. Shirley Jackson was perceptive enough to realize that the balding farmer of Grant Wood's *American Gothic* might very well stab his daughter with the pitchfork he held, and it was this possibility that she explored and expanded upon in "The Lottery"; but even in the eighth grade I recognized the more mundane truth, which is that Wood's farmer would probably go out to the barn and bale hay like he was supposed to, and maybe — *maybe* — sneak a nip from a flask hidden in the hayloft.

We Have Always Lived in the Castle is, in one sense, another version of "The Lottery" — in, say, the same sense that a *mousse au chocolat* is another version of Jell-O chocolate pudding. It tells the story of an eighteen-year-old orphan, Mary Katherine Blackwood, who lives with her older sister Constance and invalid uncle Julian in their family's ancestral home. The novel, like "The Lottery," is set in a rural backwoods; a contemporary setting is signaled by the presence of automobiles and telephones, but Jackson is deliberately vague in her descriptions of these and other modern machines, and as a result the novel could take place any time after 1925 or '30. This temporal reticence is crucial to the story's theme: despite the fact that the novel is set in contemporary America, the characters behave as though they live in the middle of the last century, much like the characters of "The Lottery." But where the story's setting is essentially its subject, in the novel the setting is merely the ominous backdrop for a turgid family drama, which is why the novel succeeds where the story falters — and also, I think, why it was so particularly powerful to me. My father had moved us to Kansas because his third marriage in as many years had ended, and if the bleak landscape and odd customs of my new home filled me with confusion and not a little fear, it was nothing compared to the strangeness of what went on in my house.

The Blackwoods are not proletarians like the cast of "The Lottery," but wealthy landowners living just outside their own unnamed "village," whose poorer residents, Mary Katherine declares in the opening pages of the novel, "have always hated us." Why that is so is never made clear; the assumption, of course, is that the typical antipathy between the rich and poor is at play here, but gradually it emerges that the situation is more complex. The Blackwoods are, well, they're weird, to put it plainly; not just Mary Katherine's parents but also her brother and Uncle Julian's wife are dead, all killed by arsenic put into the sugar bowl one evening at dinner. Constance, the family cook, was acquitted of the murders, but the villagers are convinced of her guilt; in fact, Mary Katherine was the culprit. Twelve years old at the time, she had been sent to bed without supper. In retaliation, she put the poison in the sugar bowl, knowing that her beloved sister Constance never touched sweet things (Uncle Julian's survival was nothing more than dumb luck: he didn't eat enough poison to die, merely to destroy his gastrointestinal tract and, as well, to upset a brain that seems to have been already addled). But the novel is hardly a mystery: Mary Katherine's emotions and observations are so peculiar that it's hard *not* to suspect her of something. On her twice-weekly walk through the village for household supplies, she is lost in a reverie of "catching scarlet fish in the rivers on the moon" — remember, this is an eighteen-year-old — when she

> saw that the Harris boys were in their front yard, clamoring and quarrelling with half a dozen other boys. I had not been able to see them until I came past the corner by the town hall, and I could still have turned back and gone the other way, up the main highway to the creek, and then across the creek and home along the other half of the path to our house, but it was late, and I had the groceries and the creek was nasty to wade in our mother's brown shoes, and I thought, I am living on the moon, and I walked quickly. They saw me at once, and I thought of them rotting away and curling in pain and crying out loud; I wanted them doubled up and crying in front of me.

Note the detail with which the alternate path is described: Mary Katherine knows each step she will take long before she takes it. The magic of passages like this is that even as Mary Katherine — Merricat, as Constance calls her — fantasizes about the violent, painful deaths of nearly everyone she comes into contact with, she also communicates an awestruck, childlike view of the world, so that when her guilt is finally revealed it still comes as a shock — not the shock of the unexpected, but the shock of recognition, of a long-denied truth. The moral triumph of the novel is that, by the time Merricat mentions her crime aloud, we have already justified it in our minds; she never needs to, and, indeed, if she did, she would be much less likely to win our sympathy.

All of this is, as it were, merely compelling back story, developed in tandem with the main narrative. As the novel opens, the murders are six years in the past, and Mary Katherine and Constance and Uncle Julian have settled into their Never-Never Land existence, with tomboy Mary Katherine cast in the role of Peter Pan, fair-haired Constance as Wendy and wheelchair-bound, rambling Uncle Julian as a kind of grotesque Lost Boy. Into this perfect world, of course, comes Captain Hook: Cousin Charles, an apparition so horrible that Merricat "could not see him clearly, perhaps because he was a ghost, perhaps because he was so very big." Merricat stresses Charles's resemblance to her dead father, and, in her eyes, he is more than the "intruder" she calls him: he is an unknown element in a world so fetishistically ordered that the simple patterns of housekeeping, bathing and eating are imbued with magical force, an adult come to drag her from her childhood paradise, and Merricat deals with him accordingly.

> Eliminating Charles from everything he had touched was almost impossible, but it seemed to me that if I altered our father's room, and perhaps later the kitchen and the drawing room and the study, and even finally the garden, Charles would be lost, shut off from what he recognized, and would have to concede that this was not the house he had come to visit and so would go away.

"Altering" in this case means destroying; Merricat first does simple things like smash his watch and foul his bedding, but when that doesn't work she resorts to drastic measures: she sweeps his smoldering pipe into an open wastebasket full of paper (although Freudian interpretations are often overused, I think they're appropriate here). In Merricat's mind the room Charles inhabits — her dead father's room — is distinct from the house she lives in, but, of course, the whole building catches fire. Charles goes for help — the Blackwoods have no phone — and returns with the villagers. Some of them work to put out the fire but most watch the house burn; for his part, Charles tries to steal the safe which contains whatever's left of the Blackwood fortune, but it's too heavy to move. But the drama isn't quenched when the fire's extinguished. Like vampires, the villagers are empowered by their official invitation into the Blackwood home, and, like vampires, they put their power to ill use: what the fire hasn't destroyed the villagers do, in an orgy of Dionysian passion, and while they work, adults and children both chant a local nursery rhyme:

> Merricat, said Constance, would you like a cup of tea?
> Oh, no, said Merricat, you'll poison me.
> Merricat, said Constance, would you like to go to sleep?
> Down in the boneyard ten feet deep.

*

I made up my own nursery rhyme when I was a child, when I was five or six, much younger than I was when I first read Jackson's novel. The "rhyme" was only one line long—"My Mother's Grave Is Yellow"—and I recited it sometimes in bed, more often when I crawled beneath the coffee table in our living room. The table's wooden underside had been branded with the letters MMGIY, and for a few years, for the two or three years after my mother's death and before I was too big to hide under the table, I cast about for the hidden message in those initials, finally alighting on that one line: "My Mother's Grave Is Yellow." In fact I didn't know what color my mother's grave was. I'd never been allowed to see it, just as I'd never been allowed to see my mother when she was dying in the hospital, just as I'd never been allowed to see my father's mother because they didn't speak, or see my mother's mother because she didn't want to have anything to do with her children or their lives, or see dozens of my other relatives because they were dead or missing or simply too far away. There were more secrets in my family than revelations, but what was hidden was nevertheless known, the hatred or violence or simple fear that produced and informed my family's silences could be felt if not named, and if it took me years to recognize this force as the operating principle of *We Have Always Lived in the Castle,* I nevertheless sensed it: the novel spooked me so badly that I returned it to the library and resolved to never read it, or Shirley Jackson, again; with the exception of the inescapable "Lottery," which I must have encountered at least a half dozen times in subsequent years, I kept that promise for fifteen years.

Jackson structures her novel so that its climax comes just after Merricat confesses her role in her family's death. The juxtaposition of the two events is what drives home the novel's true point: that the difference between ruler and ruled is one of means, not temperament (my father terrorized me because he was bigger than me, but if I'd been bigger than him . . . !). In some sense, "The Lottery" can be dismissed as a sophisticate's paranoia about the proletariat — Jackson and her husband, the critic Stanley Edgar Hyman, were both intellectuals based in rural North Bennington, Vermont, where Hyman taught at the college—but *We Have Always Lived in the Castle* presents a world view that is both more personal and more complex than that of "The Lottery." Just as the villagers' poverty is the justification, conscious or unconscious, for their ignorance, Merricat's hoarded wealth allows her to build her own shell of ritualized unknowing. Not surprisingly, after the villagers have trashed the Blackwood house, life resumes its former pattern. Charles, stymied, leaves; the villagers, spent, abandon all overt contact with the Blackwoods, but each night a basket of food is deposited on their porch in atonement; Mary Katherine, clothed in an old tablecloth and drinking from the last unbroken cup, speaks the novel's final words without a trace of irony: "'Oh, Constance,' I said, 'we are so happy.'"

The link between this book and another subversive fairy tale, Orwell's *Animal Farm*, might not be apparent, but in fact Orwell's is simply a politicized treatment of the theme Jackson confronts on a social level: ignorance is bliss. But it's rarely accidental. In an ironic gesture of fate that I'm sure she would appreciate if not exactly welcome, Jackson's relegation to high schools and rural libraries has left the intellectual audience she wrote for ignorant of her words, whereas the rural clodhoppers she wrote about have access to her books but pass by them unknowingly. Only their children read them, and, I imagine, learn from Merricat's example: if the life you see is ugly, shut your eyes and dream of a better one. My mother's grave is yellow, would you like a cup of tea? The poison in this cup is the dark side of the imagination, the unconscious, but it's also the bitter antidote to a more quotidian but no less certain death, of conservatism, or provinciality, or just plain old-fashioned boredom.

Frank Stanford
Of the Mulberry Family:
An Arkansas Epilogue
C. D. *Wright*

ONE DOES NOT APPROACH who one is by going back down there. One approaches who one is by going down. Down is not where. When what one needed, what one thought one most had to have was love. Wild and radiant. Only love. It did not matter where one was. There. Down was where it had to be gotten. At any cost. Not that anyone suspected it would cost more than one could afford. Not that anyone suspected it would cost more than what was offered. Not that it has ever been otherwise. Further down. There. Where: a tendency lingers among country people to say *suspicioned* instead of *suspected.*

It was not regional it was systemic. It was hell. There. Then. Down. No. It was sweet. It was nearly poetry, which in its pure state exudes a sweetness keener even than pain. If not Southern then gothic: grotesque, mysterious, desolate. Sepulchral, yes. It takes all. Then it takes off. Explanations don't help. Excuses don't count.

Mockingbird, you tell it differently every year:

She was never going to leave. There. Down. She had no intention of leaving. The hills. The crooked green rivers. The rutted brown roads. Smoke sleeving out of farmhouse chimneys. Collapsing barns. The mineral-streaked bluffs streaming with maidenhair. Railroad bridges in fog. Redbud, dogwood, wild plum and service-berry in spring. Pronounced *sahrvussberry.* Horse apple by itself in a field. Pond by itself in a pasture. Alive. To love. To be loveable. To be loved. The geotropic life. Lived. Perceived. For the venation of one's own leaf.

C. D. Wright

If you take root you will grow. She had been told. He told her. The full-blown poet. The land surveyor. He had a calling. He had a living. Her roots had yet to outgrow a coffee can: student, poet-in-waiting, barmaid.

*

Some of you already know these books: *The Singing Knives, Shade, Ladies from Hell, Field Talk, Arkansas Bench Stone, Constant Stranger, Crib Death, You, The Battlefield Where the Moon Says I Love You, Conditions Uncertain and Likely to Pass Away, The Light the Dead See.* If not, do you believe me when I say you don't know what you're missing. If you're not young and crazy it may be too late. Maybe you were never that young, that nuts. Believe me when I say you are better off. *Better to stroke the best than to hit it/ and forfeit the eleven stars of your youth.*

*

Kicked back: in the transitory heaven of Pharoah Sanders records and blue ribbon beer. Talking carnally at a trestle table under a locust tree. The honey locust shedding freely. Driving around. Driving around in the truck. Poking around in the woods.

The surveyor and his catspaw. The poet and his follower. Poking around in the woods with a transit. He shot the lines. She held the plumb bob. Squatted in a stand of cedar to pee. Watch yourself: copperhead country. The sweet sachet of cedar and urine.

Mockingbird calling attention to one's vulnerable position.

On top of Markham Hill. Dug a little pit with the heel of his workboot and the prong of a church key. *Church key,* the ubiquitous ersatz for *bottle opener.* They were under the ample branches of the horse apple. Emptied his wool herringbone trousers of coins. Covered them up. There, he said. If you ever need money. This will get you in a double feature. *Double feature,* that's history.

She loved how he smelled, *osage orange.* But when he had not washed, he conceded that *the goat got him.* It could give you an instant headache.

Twin desks made from unstained doors on sawhorses. She smoked unfiltered brown cigarettes. She had to drive to the mall to get the special cigarettes. He bought records. Books. She bought cigarettes. Books. He but lay his hand on the book and inhaled the contents. She underlined everything and retained next-to-nothing. She liked to go somewhere with a book, make herself small and smoke.

She and the dance teacher smoked, Sylvia of the Balanchine extensions and candy-only diet. Bone-cold-cancer reamed Sylvia. If smoke were not permitted, she and Sylvia didn't bother going in. He tolerated secondhand smoke. He didn't give a scintilla for a crowd.

Maclura pomifera: Occurs as a single tree in more or less open situations in mountainous regions . . .

*

He read the living and the dead. She read the dead. He read the French, the Italian, the Americans. She read the French, the Russians, the Americans. They were in the South, so to speak. The Upper South. When you think about it, his beautiful sepulchral language was her first living poetry: *Because none of you know what you want follow me/ because I'm not going anywhere/ I'll just bleed so the stars can have something dark to shine in . . .* The poet wrote. Small wonder. First blasted, living, everloving poetry. *Horses fuck inside me and a river makes a bend in my shoulder.* No goddamned wonder.

*

Educated by the Benedictines of Paris (Arkansas) and the levee hands of Snow Lake (Arkansas). Earned no academic degrees, taught at no college. Nor did he give public readings. In the main, he avoided cities. Published with obscure presses. Started an obscure press, Lost Roads.

Save for placing fourth in 1958, in a contest sponsored by the Ninth District Tennessee Federation of Women's Clubs, he went unhonored.

*

Frank Stanford. Photograph by Meredith Boswell. Estate of Frank Stanford.
Courtesy C. D. Wright.

When the sun shone quote unquote regular again, he hung the herringbones up by their suspenders and donned light khaki; leathered up the same workboots year round. A big head of girly curls, a long torso and short legs. The intimation of a satyr.

She adopted war fatigues and unflattering flannel shirts. Public-health glasses. A lash of tawny, horsey hair. She was split-rail thin but for the breasts, cream beaten with wine. Nails chewed beyond repair. The intimation of a maenad.

Nobody cooked.

Foreign films screened in the student union. Every Sunday night. They feasted: *Children of Paradise, Weekend, The Discreet Charm of the Bourgeoisie, The Romantic Englishwoman, The Gospel According to St. Matthew, Lucia, Brief Vacation, Rashomon, The Conformist, The Apu Trilogy, The Battle of Algiers, Shadows of Forgotten Ancestors, Shame*. It was heavy fare.

*

Fruit globular, two to five inches in diameter, greenish yellow or yellow, somewhat resembling a large, rough orange, fragrant . . .

She took classes: mime, saxophone, poetry, ballet. Doing *pliés* she was visited by the residual scent of their constant screwing.

Sap like that of rest of tree, milky and sticky . . .

She and her coruscating redheaded friend practiced the beautiful figure series in the old gymnasium. The studies Etienne Decroux created for Jean-Louis Barrault: *Children of Paradise*.

She waited tables. All the young women waited on the young men. Down. There. But she was perfectly sorry at it. Sullen. Slow. Forgetful. Untipped. Every other night she janitored in the student union while her co-worker talked to her inaudibly, without stopping, over the institutional vacuum cleaners.

He called it *bodark*, from *bois d'arc*, *wood of the arches*. When the trees rained arrows on the French searching for the Vermilion Sea.

301

Imagined running a bait shop. She liked to be on the river, and one could foresee reading there with few interruptions. In a bait shop. Lulled by riverwater. Maybe she would write something. By and by.

Imagined being caretaker for the Civil War cemetery. Crosses not tended by living kin, crosses whose numbers would not increase.

The Civil War cemetery was in the black neighborhood. It was different from the college, different from the mall and different from her hometown. Her white-on-white hometown. The jukebox was better in the black bar than the college bar, and she liked to sit in the highbacked wooden booths shamelessly looking at faces and listening in. The talk by itself inebriated. Maybe she *could* write something. By and by.

*

There are poems in his published collections dating from 1957 when Frank was preposterously nine years old. The work is that continuous. See *YOU:* "The Wolves" and "The Burial Ship."

*

Couldn't be a surveyor. Like him. Couldn't fathom the math. Couldn't go where snakes slept, slithered and multiplied.

Shut up, mockingbird.

*

More commonly known as the *Osage-orange* or *mock orange . . .*

Branching erect on young trees; vigorous branches bear a straight stout thorn about one inch long at each node . . .

Why it takes so Christly and beastly long to learn to walk upright. The hands, the distances, the tools, the eyes one wears out scrabbling through the archeology of one's shifting layers before the book one wanted to read, the very book that would set one on one's two flat feet pushes to the surface. Branching erect . . .

The book that could set one's life in inexorable, joyful motion. Headed in the right direction. As Miss Toklas was wont to say of

Miss Stein's driving—she goes forward admirably, she does not go backward successfully—that seemed the way to go. Straight and stout . . .

Going down. Always entails going. Down. There. To the woeful *telos* of that love. The love for, face it, the already-spoken-for, the now seventeen-years-amouldering poet.

It was a long time ago. It would take a very long time to fell.

Wood heavy (forty-eight pounds per cubic foot), exceedingly hard, strong, tough . . .

Everyone who met him stirred to his vision.

I guess you couldn't help but like him, her father's taciturn ruling. How the entire mess must have pained them. The lenient, upright parents. Watching her be whelmed. For love only love. Radiant, wild and terminal. Knowing he was spoken for. Not interfering. Not expecting anything good to come of it. Not foreseeing the worst.

Imagined the poet astraddle a cane-bottom chair staring at the unvarnished planes of floor. An ensemble of women performing the shadow dance at his back.

The hide is clean with me, the poet's guarantee. Huh?

The centrifugal field of lies ever-expanding. A veritable seiche of lies. In a few forevers they would all be gnawing the roots of dandelions, but in this one he alone would be dead, and there would be no actual cauldron to scour the hide.

Nor would this ever be actually over.

Nor would she ever be the only soul, afterwards, to experience frequent sightings of the now seventeen-years-amouldering.

To dream sightings. Arriving late, impossibly, to her nonexistent sixteenth birthday party, dressed for surveying. But not getting out of the cab of his truck, slumped instead over the wheel. Not stirring. Living. Loving. The radio in the cab moaning "Wild Horses."

Nor the sole survivor to fondle the few things the poet touched that she had kept. Who learned to part with them, the fondled things, as they wore out, by force of will.

Not the only one to remove the human figures whose forms disrupted the view. To make of her foes, ciphers. And of those ciphers, foes. Forcibly.

Nor to paper over the errors, the failures, the sins which no brace of doves, no blood of the lamb could ever remit. To all but wear the beloved's foreskin as wedding ring. To let another existential being be her whole actual world. And so on and so forth. Her kind. Down. There. Then. We were expert at acts of self-delusion and distortion.

The mockingbird has a million licks. At least one poor yodeler doesn't have to re-learn the same-old saw every sad-ass spring.

*

Yet he acquired a sizable, devoted readership in his lifetime. It would be unwarranted to think his reputation profited by his premature death. On the contrary, the work suffered and to some degree remains tainted on this account because death was his subject. He has rightly been called one of its great voices.

*

It was there. Then. Down. Where this very instant a domestic artifact of little consequence insists on poking out, on being lit up:

The bed belonged to her grandmother. It was funky. A crudely scrolled two-tone veneered headboard. A set of springs not even boxed. A bathetic mattress. How many times had she wet her grandmother's cotton gown sleeping alongside her grandmother's passive body.

When sleeping with the grandmother, even in the most hateful of winters, the window was propped up with a yardstick. The hammer nested in its own cold light under the pillow. The grandmother would pray, Now honey, don't make a lake. And she would peep, See you in the morning, grandma. To which the grandmother would pray, Lord willing and the crick don't rise. And in the

304

THE NINTH DISTRICT

TENNESSEE FEDERATION OF WOMEN'S CLUBS

presents this

Certificate of Award

to

~Frankie Stanford~

whose outstanding poem was awarded

THE *fourth* PRIZE

in the

POETRY CONTEST

sponsored by the Ninth District

for school students in the Memphis and Shelby County Schools.

President, Ninth District

April 14, 1958

Poetry Contest Chairman

Frank Stanford's Ninth District Fourth Place Prize. Courtesy C. D. Wright.

morning, the grandmother would ruefully bear witness to her soaking side, the risen crick.

How many times would she ladle her poet's gorgeous body in the cavity of their hand-me-down bed.

The other grandmother called it *rabbit hedge*, had a small one in her yard but considered it a nuisance, too much trouble to fell, the wood so hard.

She herself knew it as *horse apple*. She often heard it called that. But she didn't think horses ate them. But what did she know about horses. One by the name of Duke lived on Markham Hill.

*

The bed with the white candlewick spread. . . . She remembered the candlewick bedspread. The one that would later be used to rake the leaves into, wrap around the borrowed mover, shroud the cat.

The last male cat, Bowtie, hit-and-run-down in her absence. When she returned she opened the top of the refrigerator to its cadaver. He explained that he thought she would want to see him before he buried him. Later he told her he took care of it. Next she discovered the thawing remains of Bowtie in the garbage can in a paper sack. She went back in the house for the bedspread. Thinking no further than death wanted a winding cloth.

For once she did not bother to confront him. She should have buried her own star-crossed pet.

*

Flowers of two kinds borne of different trees . . . male in an elongated cluster, female in a round ball

When the South was the South and not the same. Not the same as up here or out there or *yonder*. When: she was learning who she was. Loveable. Unloveable. Loved. Unloved. Loving. Beginning to walk upright. Loving it.

*

Going back in the summer is preferred to winter. When it's all leafed out. Grown over. Winter is bald. The hawks are seen as easily as they see us. We see the new houses on the denuded hills. The hawks see the denuded hills beyond the houses, where the newer ones will be. The hawks see the future too clearly. They are nowhere in it.

durable wood prized for longbows; known by hunters as bow wood

Going back is not the same as not going back. Going back is not the same as not going off to begin with. We leave to be who we will become. We go back to see who we are. We are no less than our struggle or that of our foes, even those we would make ciphers.

Who died there. Who is dying. Who forfeited a once-perfect breast. Whose once-lovely daughter fell asleep with a desolate cigarette. Whose body wears a bag to pee in. Who is a hundred percent queer now. Who knew it all along. Whose youngest son drowned in their stupid bean-shaped pool. Who got born again. Who made a pile of money gypping people out of their savings. Who was a party switcher. Who came home from the city to help his widower father fend. Who is left. Who left.

Whose heartwood yields a dye comparable to fustic.

*

Who shot himself to death in her paternal grandmother's bed. With a target pistol. Who ran in the room to straddle the body, pump the dead poet's chest. Who ran out the door. Who called the police.

Who opened their doors to the mourners. Who was wedded to whom the same afternoon on Petit Jean Mountain.

Who photographed the last blaze rose in the rented yard.

She remembers. She misremembers. She disremembers. Like everyone.

She goes back. She doesn't go down. There. Anymore. It is not poetry. It smells of mortality. Sepulchral.

And here is the peeling rent house by the ravine. This is the ravine where she threw the telephone receiver to make herself stop calling and calling when one was there and the other was not.

This is where everyone who heard, who knew or thought they knew, or felt as if they had known entered a separate landscape of pain and loneliness. Everyone came and stood apart like a boat in a field. Then came the young men in uniforms. One young woman in uniform. And the poet was covered, rather he was bagged, tagged and taken away. Very little blood. Only powder burns. No more sound.

And everyone who came to hear, gradually, they came too and sat on the stoop or stood in the garden more or less motionless. Photographs were taken of the last blaze rose. People who didn't like each other, who had never liked each other, felt a burning love. Backs were patted and the lady cat was stroked. Old stories got told. Everyone drank until they went to sleep wherever they folded over. And on the weekend came the musicians, out of the Delta and over the mountains in the beat-up bus.

The memory of it is very hard. It goes down. There. Geotropic. It would take a long time to fell. It is not poetry. It is a scratched, repetitive record of loving. Unloving. Losing. Leaving.

Maclura pomifera: The largest specimen on record was a sixty footer. Over. In Hickory Plains, Prairie County. The soil wouldn't raise one that tall. In the Ozarks.

*

Over here is the periphery. From whence you came. Can you describe it. In detail. What you remember is moving. Backward. You do not see the beginning. Words scumble the view.

Here is the center of your enterprise. Your life. Almost miraculously, without a sound, it grew up around you protective and full. You abide in it. Volatile yet alive. Living. Loving. Loved. For the venation of one's own leaf. Into its plenary.

Back there. Down. When. Is the ruinous forever. Yearning for perfection.

C. D. Wright

*

YOU

Sometimes in our sleep we touch
The body of another woman
And we wake up
And we know the first nights
With summer visitors
In the three storied house of our childhood.
Whatever we remember,
The darkest hair being brushed
In front of the darkest mirror
In the darkest room.

— Frank Stanford
(August 1, 1948–June 3, 1978)

Loren Eiseley. University of Nebraska-Lincoln Archives/Special Collections, UNL Libraries.

The Strange Case of Dr. Eiseley
Phillip Lopate

LOREN EISELEY DIED IN 1977, just over twenty years ago. At the time he had a solid reputation, based on titles such as *The Immense Journey, The Night Country* and *The Unexpected Universe,* as a scientist who could write, though name recognition was beginning to fade, going the way of Joseph Wood Krutch and the other worthy, dusty science and nature writers who had served their purpose, laying the groundwork for the contemporary school of Stephen Jay Gould, Lewis Thomas, Edward Hoagland, Gretel Ehrlich, Barry Lopez, Bill McKibbon, Scott Russell Sanders, etc. etc. I myself was happy to ignore him, being somewhat biased against science/nature writing in general.

Why the bias? Several reasons: 1) as an ignoramus about science and the mechanics of the natural world, I do not enjoy being lectured on matters I will never grasp; 2) I abominate the tone of wonderment and abstract mystic awe which afflicts the "alone with the universe" genre; 3) I miss the human tension, the drama of individual behavior in relationships and the ensuing guilt which informs the literature I like best; 4) I mistrust the persona of the nature writer, the too-often pious, self-righteous goody-goody who considers himself the last noninterfering witness of a wilderness about to be overrun by dunderheads.

All this by way of saying that, before reaching the conclusion that Loren Eiseley was a major American writer, I had to overcome considerable resistance.

It did not happen at one stroke. When I was reading materials for my anthology, *The Art of the Personal Essay,* I kept being urged to check out Loren Eiseley. I read *The Night Country,* which convinced me that he was master of the sentence and of a classically meandering essay construction. But I was still put off by his posture of lofty isolation, which seemed to lack humor. (I find it very difficult to appreciate any literature which is not somewhere humorous.) Then a friend sent me "The Star Thrower," his signature essay, a most peculiar meditation touching on seacoasts,

311

evolution, death, Goethe, Eiseley's deaf mother, mental illness and the struggle to commit to life. I was struck by its go-for-broke air of at times inconsolable bitterness. Singular it was, and dark—almost too harsh for my taste. I didn't know what to make of the rawness of pain underneath the immense knowledge and Emersonian epigram. In the end I realized I didn't understand the essay enough to include it, and put Eiseley aside, much as one might pull back from a brilliant acquaintance who is simply too neurotic for easy companionship.

But something about Loren Eiseley kept nagging at me. I felt I had failed him as a reader, not he me as a writer. Then, in a used bookstore, I came upon his autobiography, *All the Strange Hours*, published two years before his death. On the back cover was a photograph of this gaunt man with a haunted expression and gray pompadour, very much the male literary ideal of an earlier, more existentialist era, wearing a raincoat, a brother of Philip Marlowe. The jacket carried a quote from W. H. Auden, saying "I have eagerly read anything of his I could lay my hands on." (Interestingly, Auden also had a liking for Raymond Chandler.) I bought it, let a year go by, then picked it up. Aha! I saw immediately that here was the key—for me at least—to all of Eiseley's works, which would allow me to return to the earlier books with keener understanding. I have rarely received as much satisfaction or enlightenment from a memoir. That this out-of-print masterpiece, surely the greatest American autobiography that *is* out of print, fell into my hands at precisely the moment when the memoir has come to dominate the literary scene, was irony enough; but even more delicious was the way its concentrated intelligence, its restraint, its disenchanted obligations to wisdom and maturity acted as a reproach to the victimized darlings of the season.

*

All the Strange Hours is fittingly subtitled "The Excavation of a Life." Eiseley's scientific training was in archaeology and anthropology, which gave him a long, long perspective into the shiftings of time, his philosophical obsession. In the twilight of his life—though still shy of seventy—he approached himself as a ruin: "A biography is always constructed from ruins but, as any archaeologist will tell you, there is never the means to unearth all the rooms, or follow the buried roads, or dig into every cistern for treasure. You try to see what the ruin meant to whoever inhabited it and, if you are lucky, you see a little way backward into time."

Eiseley uses two devices to structure his criss-crossed ventures into the past. The first, and most important, is the "strange hours" promised by the title, a reexamination of moments when he came face-to-face with the uncanny, whose continuing resonance within him he seemed to find much more indicative of what counts in a life than any straight narration of external events.

The memories evoked in *All the Strange Hours* frequently revolve around cruelty and shame. Auden, whom he came to befriend, asked him what public event he remembered from his childhood, and he muttered something about a prison break. But later, another memory surfaced. As a boy he was playing with some chums, trying to escape the overprotective care of his deaf, hysterical mother: "She pursued us to a nearby pasture and in the rasping voice of deafness ordered me home. My comrades of the fields stood watching. I was ten years old by then. I sensed my status in this gang was at stake. I refused to come. I had refused a parental order that was arbitrary and uncalled for and, in addition, I was humiliated. My mother was behaving in the manner of a witch. She could not hear, she was violently gesticulating without dignity, and her dress was somehow appropriate to the occasion. . . . Even today, as though in a far-off crystal, I can see my running, gesticulating mother and her distorted features cursing us. And they laughed, you see, my companions. Perhaps I, in anxiety to belong, did also. That is what I could not tell Auden. Only an unutterable savagery, my savagery at myself, scrawls it once and once only on this page."

In *All the Strange Hours*, many confessions are flung out "once and once only" in this lacerating manner by Eiseley, who seems to be purposely violating his privacy — the encapsulated, solitary silence of a son raised by a deaf mother — only to return to it, spasmodically, the next moment. Rarely has a memoir exhibited such an odd mixture of the bared and the withheld. Mabel Langdon, Eiseley's wife and lifelong support, is mentioned only three times — and then, only in passing. We do not learn in the book, for instance, that she was his high school English teacher, a woman seven years his senior, who devoted her life to him. The biographer Gale E. Christianson reproduces a letter from Mabel, stating that Eiseley was only following her stated wish that he protect the privacy of their marriage by not writing about it, though one might also wonder if long conjugal descriptions would have marred the picture he was trying to create of himself as a solitary. In any event, his reticence on this key relationship, like many other omissions, creates an intriguing space of freedom in the reader. Since he is so honest and forthcoming on other matters, you do not begrudge him his secrets.

It was Auden, in an essay-review of an Eiseley collection published in the *New Yorker,* who noted: "Dr. Eiseley's autobiographical passages are, most of them, descriptions of numinous encounters — some joyful, some terrifying. After reading them, I get the impression of a wanderer who is often in danger of being shipwrecked on the shores of dejection. . . . I suspect Dr. Eiseley of being a melancholic." Eiseley, a devotee of old English writers, would have relished this lineage with Robert Burton, author of *The Anatomy of Melancholy.* His fellow Nebraskan and good friend Wright Morris nicknamed him "Schmerzie," short for *weltschmerz,* or world-pain. Certainly he comes across in his autobiography as a connoisseur of painful memories: his dying father, listless around him, perks up when his older brother Leo enters the hospital room; contracting tuberculosis himself, he is bluntly told by doctors that he has no chance to live; becoming a drifter in the Depression, he is almost pushed to his death by a railroad worker, and a fellow hobo gives him the lowdown: "Just get this straight. It's all there is and after a while you'll see it for yourself. . . . The capitalists beat men into line. Okay? The communists beat men into line. Right again? . . . Men beat men, that's all." Later on, a full professor and provost of a distinguished university, Penn, he is sickened by academic politics and remembers this saying: Men beat men. Eiseley makes all his periods and personae coexist on the page, so that you still see the anxious ten-year-old running from his mother, or the drifter hanging onto the boxcar for dear life, when he is acting the part of university dignitary.

And beyond that, you still see the animal lurking in the man, a Darwinian ghost. The second device by which Eiseley structures his memoir is to superimpose on the narrator various fellow creatures — a rat, a dog, a cat, a worm, a wolf — whom he encounters along the way. Both as an evolutionist and as a loner, more comfortable, it would seem, with any other animals than humans, Eiseley takes the position, as he wrote in *The Immense Journey:* "In many a fin and reptile foot I have seen myself passing by — some part of myself, that is, some part that lies unrealized in the momentary shape I inhabit." He is never far from glimpsing what he calls "the frightening diversity of the living," or the instability of organic forms, over the long haul, which gives him an almost schizophrenically empathic vision of pullulating creation, such as one finds in Virginia Woolf's *Mrs. Dalloway*—though Eiseley is calmer about it.

Among the most poignant episodes of creature identifications is the one in which he accompanies a medical researcher to the animal house to fetch a dog for purposes of dissection. "We entered. My colleague was humane. He carried a hypodermic, but whatever dog he selected would be dead in an hour. Now dogs kept penned together, I rapidly began to see, were like men in a concentration camp, who one after another see that something unspeakable is going to happen to them. As we entered this place of doleful barks and howlings, a brisk-footed, intelligent-looking mongrel of big terrier affinities began to trot rapidly about. I stood white-gowned in the background trying to be professional, while my stomach twisted.

"My medical friend (and he was and is my friend and is infinitely kind to patients) cornered the dog. The dog, judging from his rest-less reactions, had seen all this happen before. Perhaps because I stood in the background, perhaps because in some intuitive way, perhaps—oh, who knows what goes on among the miserable of the world?—he started to approach me. At that moment my associate seized him. The hypodermic shot home. . . . He did not struggle, he did not bite, even when seized. Man was a god. It had been bred into this creature's bones never to harm the god. They were immortal and when they touched one kindly it was an ecstasy. . . . But he had looked at me with that unutterable expression. 'I do not know why I am here. Save me. I have seen other dogs fall and be carried away. Why do you do this? Why?'"

Eiseley reports his failure to "protect, save, or help" thousands of threatened animals in his lifetime. He concludes: "Men, too, it seems, have a bit of common dog in their natures. But in the shelter by the stones the dogs slept and thought I would be coming back. They have an enormous, unquenchable, betrayed trust in man."

The placement of that one word "betrayed" is priceless. I have said that I don't like writing which has no humor; and, while there *are* funny passages in Eiseley's memoir, much of it is grim. Then why do I like it? Because his humility, his finely honed irony, his

315

elegant precision of language and his unflinching eye function in the same way as humor. They produce the same *frisson*.

Eiseley is a supremely self-conscious stylist. A bibliophile who dug through used bookstores as methodically as he excavated archeological sites, he was, for all his scientific training, as much a literary man as a scientist. In *All the Strange Hours* he makes the point outright that his favorite form is the personal essay: "I had long realized an attachment for the personal essay, but the personal essay was out of fashion except perhaps for humor." He cites as his models Montaigne, Emerson, De Quincey, Coleridge, Sir Thomas Browne, Sir William Temple, Chesterton, Hardy. (Eiseley also wrote several volumes of poetry, where he showed himself more under the influence of Robinson Jeffers.) *All the Strange Hours* is, in effect, a memoir in the form of a string of personal essays. This is what gives the book its circling, interconnected quality. What gives the book its dignity and power is something else, something much more unique: Eiseley's determination to go to the bottom of his experience, and cleanly distinguish between that part which he understood and that part which remained unknown, perhaps unknowable.

When his mother died, he reports: "I was an unnatural son. I did not weep. I outdid the reserve of a professional undertaker. There was nothing in me." Standing over her grave, he thinks: "We, she and I, were close to being one now, lying like the skeletons of last year's leaves in a fence corner. And it was all nothing. Nothing, do you understand? All the pain, all the anguish. Nothing. We were, both of us, merely the debris life always leaves in its passing. . . ." On the other hand, he argues (when a Mexican driver takes the mountain curves too tightly while trying to frighten him with a speech about life not mattering) that *"La vida,* she *does* matter" and is *"muy importante."* His resolve in his mature years is to live with uncertainty, to embrace ignorance and overthrow youthful certitude. As he puts it in "The Star Thrower": "I would walk with the knowledge of the discontinuities of the unexpected universe."

That a writer who died only twenty years ago, who was my contemporary for a time, should so willingly address on the page such large questions about life and the universe, and do it, moreover, with such fullness of intellect, technical knowledge and reflective depth, may help explain Loren Eiseley's appeal. Thanks in part to his generous sharing of sufferings and chagrin, he has actually brought me around to *like* nature and science writing.

316

Henry Miller:
Exhibitionist of the Soul
Steve Erickson

OF COURSE HENRY MILLER remains the forbidden writer of American fiction. Where once he was forbidden for the right reasons, he is now forbidden for the wrong, where once he was forbidden by conservatives and moralists he is now forbidden by liberals and the culturally correct — though what originally made him forbidden hasn't really changed at all. He is forbidden because he speaks from the dark heart of some place beyond ideology or the refinements of civilization, he is not progressive or regressive but the literary inhabitant of a place in the psyche where human experience recognizes no forward or backward, where the shadows of the soul know no time.

I'm not here to make excuses for him now. I'm certainly not here to make excuses for myself or for the way, as when I heard Ray Charles for the first time, Henry Miller rearranged the furniture in my head, where the sofa of "aesthetics" had been placed just so, against the window, and the reclining chair of "taste" had been moved ever so carefully before the fireplace, and everything was where I and all my teachers and all the other writers I had read assumed they were supposed to be. Miller swept through and left everything in shambles and in the process said, to paraphrase the notorious opening declaration of *Tropic of Cancer*, here is a gob of spit in the face of excuses. So I won't make excuses for him; he would hate it and I would hate myself. Clearly much of what he wrote about women is infantile when it isn't appalling, as further demonstrated, for whomever needs the demonstration, by the evidence of his own biography, ever younger women populating an ever aging life, until all you could do was be embarrassed for him. That he was first and foremost a romantic cannot excuse some of these attitudes, since a romantic can be as destructive to women as the stalker hiding around the corner at midnight; in his own mind, of course, the stalker is a romantic himself. It was Miller's own emotional limitations that prevented him from transcending the botched and bleeding love affair he had with his second wife, that made him unable to really write about her at all until it was too late, at which point love had ebbed away leaving only wounds. That he could not change the way he loved left him a man who, for periods of his life, apparently could not love at all in any way that could fulfill himself, let alone a woman.

It excuses nothing to point out that all of his gorgeous spleen is part and parcel of an assault on the artifices of human dignity as democratic as it is gleeful. One sometimes wishes of course that he had confined this assaultive gusto to those who could afford it most, such as the powerful and the social elite, and spared those who could afford it least, particularly in the thirties when scape-goating would be raised first to political art, then to governmental institution, ultimately to millennial nightmare. The truth was that Miller's feelings about Jews, for instance, were nearly as complicated as those about women, anchored as they were by his deepest disgust of all, which was for the Aryan, which is to say himself, since Miller openly hated everything about his German heritage and strove to reinvent himself free of it, perpetuating the self-image of a carefree bohemian living in happy and willful squalor when it has been duly recorded he was the most teutonic of housekeepers, the tidiest of domestic managers, the most compulsive and anal antithesis of the joyful anarchist in *Tropic of Cancer* who watches the lice leap to and fro on the bed mattress with great amusement and jauntily chucks extra francs and centimes out the taxi window just because they get in the way of his lower finances.

This may be where I come in. I am not German but I am half Scandinavian, which is altogether close enough to being German, sharing that pathological German orderliness and, as Miller did, so detesting it that once, years ago, I begged an old girlfriend to go into my apartment and completely disorganize all my books and records beyond recognition, while I waited outside. Naturally, as soon as she finished I cried out in anguish, "My God, what have I done?" and rushed back into the apartment and frantically put everything back in its place. So for me the heroism of Henry Miller is the way that he — or, to be more precise, his literary incarnation — disrupted the order of my head beyond repair; after I read *Tropic of Cancer* as an aspiring young novelist of twenty-one there was no putting everything back where it was. Art was not about rules or formalism or structure or "dramatic unity" or what

Henry Miller. Photograph by George S. Barrows, Jr. Courtesy New Directions Publishing Corporation.

the literature teacher could diagram on the blackboard, it was about passion and imagination and courage, and when it wasn't about those things in at least some measure, there was no point to it at all and it was just a waste of everyone's time. And for all the many things that Miller was wrong about in his work, he was right about that; one of his best books, called *The Books of My Life,* so renews its reader with the exhilaration of reading that by the time the reader has finished, it has become one of the books of his or her life.

He wrote only one truly great novel, his first published and still his most famous. *Black Spring, Tropic of Capricorn* and *The Cosmological Eye* fill out the story and almost constitute the Miller bible that Lawrence Durrell encouraged his mentor to write; but *Tropic of Cancer* remains the great hurled gauntlet of early twentieth-century fiction, a book that more persuasively and passionately than any other says to art and history and all their mavens: *I truly do not give a fuck.* On one level this is pure nihilism; beneath that is the level of pure outrage; but beneath that there is the brave Moment in which, when everything else seems shallow and fleeting, all of us sooner or later aspire to live, and end up wondering why we cannot. The narrator of *Tropic of Cancer* is another literary American henry pushed through the glass darkly, the Henry James who lived in America but was haunted by Europe now returned to the heart of Europe only to be haunted by America, and in the process returning with a voice and heart stripped of all continental sensibilities, an American voice stripped of every reassurance but Whitman's electric song and the Ginsberg howl to come, in rapacious pursuit of one sensual interest above everything else. That interest, of course, is eating. There is a misconception, largely among those who have never read *Tropic of Cancer,* that the book is about sex. In fact Miller's interest in sex in *Tropic of Cancer* is only intermittent, which was the truly shocking thing about the book when it first appeared, that it talks about sex not heatedly but casually, and no differently than it talks about survival in general. What Miller really cares about in *Cancer* is scoring a good meal. He constantly puts his genius to the matter of getting fed with a determination he only rarely applies to getting laid, devising an elaborate plan that finally commits seven different friends to each inviting him to dinner one night a week.

Though it is the book I have read more often than any other — I suppose a half dozen times, but out of respect to Miller's anarchy

I've tried not to keep track—I would certainly not want a whole literature of *Tropic of Cancers*. A literature of *Tropic of Cancers* just becomes cranky and self-indulgent in an obvious and cheap way; it is one of the very greatest American novels, but only in the context of an American literature that also includes *The Adventures of Huckleberry Finn* and *Light in August* and *Invisible Man* and *Appointment in Samarra* and *The Member of the Wedding* and *The Long Goodbye* and *Moby Dick* and *Native Son* and *The Sheltering Sky* and *Tender Is the Night* and *A Lost Lady* and *Red Harvest* and *Cane* and *The Deer Park* and *The Postman Always Rings Twice* and *The Violent Bear It Away* and *Go Tell it on the Mountain* and *The Killer Inside Me* and *The Names* and *Blood Meridian* and *Gravity's Rainbow* and *The Transmigration of Timothy Archer* and *Ozma of Oz*. You can't always live among overturned furniture. Whether the reclining chair is before the fireplace or not, sooner or later you want to sit on it. But though you might not approve of it, though you might reproach the book, remove *Tropic of Cancer* from the above canon and, if you're honest, you will acknowledge that everything about fiction in the twentieth century changes, and it changes for the worse. Everything about twentieth-century fiction becomes less vital, less alive and of course less free; it is startling to note how recently and publicly Miller has been dismissed by writers whose very right to sensational provocation was won in the battles Miller fought for them. That's all right, though, because Miller's true importance is not as a pioneer of free expression but as an exhibitionist of the soul, and lies in the triumph of one man over chaos that is achieved in an ironic collusion with chaos. The great passion of Henry Miller and *Tropic of Cancer* is nothing less than life-sized, or maybe even cosmos-sized, the relentless raging juxtaposition of the gutter with the heavens, of the beastly with the transcendent, never judging one above the other, loving not the harmony of it all but the disharmony, delirious at the prospect of the great pending Crack-Up of mankind. This is a writer beyond the reach of your reproach, because he has so completely obliterated the value of that reproach; his is the long love-riddled guffaw of failure that is too mad to be fearful and too sane to survive unscarred.

Ambrose Bierce. The Granger Collection, New York.

Bierce

Mac Wellman

TALES TOO TERRIFYING, too real to be told in polite circles; epigrams too dark for easy appreciation. A body of work too real for realism. Ambrose Bierce may be the most unjustly (and unwisely) neglected of great American writers.

Multiple viewpoints, withheld information, inquests that establish nothing and reports from beyond the grave all support a linguistic architecture as complex, as impressive as any in our literature. And yet, and yet.

Birth: the first and direst of all disasters; a definition of the sort that damns Bierce as a cynic, a limited writer. Contrariwise, Samuel Beckett's very similar observation certifies him a genius.

But Bierce is so much more than the jaundiced hack-author of a dozen or so memorably scary stories. The implicit moral profusion of his work seems to involve every atom of it, perceptible or not. Indeed, strange absences are almost common in his work; positive, aggressive absences that tear the unlucky, or unwary, out of the fabric not only of life, but of being itself. "The Difficulty of Crossing a Field," for instance, or in his definition of the word "kill": to create a vacancy without nominating a successor. In a wholly other context, the ancient Greeks named this *anangke,* and it is one of the primal motors of tragedy, a kind of positive, and therefore paradoxical, negation.

I see him as a drastic moralist; like Nathanael West, Ezra Pound and Katherine Anne Porter. Absolutists all, absolutists of moral intuition. Bierce's craft is impeccable, uncompromised and of a classical elegance that is as uncanny as his vision itself.

The drastic moralist functions as the scourge of sentimentalism; and in our American context, this sentimentalism may be defined as a nostalgia for what never existed (another bizarre absence). This force is as strong, perhaps, as anything in the culture, and Bierce certainly knew what his odds were in the struggle against it. On a more mundane level, he fought as a convicted abolitionist in the Civil War most of the better class of yankee writers avoided;

and, later, against the San Francisco real estate and railroad tycoons in a truly epic war of words. Yet, who today can be bothered to consider the importance of such unfashionable struggles?

Sentimental America still hates Bierce, as well it should. He and his writing stands for everything we have not become.

Frederick Prokosch
Lawrence Osborne

THE FATE OF FREDERICK PROKOSCH'S REPUTATION is a hard lesson in the laws of vagary. In 1935, the twenty-nine-year-old won international acclaim with one of the century's most eccentric and iridescent novels, *The Asiatics*, a work hailed as a masterpiece by the likes of Thomas Mann, Albert Camus and André Gide. To this day, *The Asiatics* is among the most read American novels in France, where Prokosch has always been adored, and French translations of his books were omnipresent in the Latin America of the fifties and sixties, demonstrations of lyrical hyperreality which the magical realists took to heart.

Yet Prokosch's fame in the land of his birth is all but extinct. Although Warner Brothers made his wartime novel *The Conspirators* into a 1944 Hedy Lamarr movie complete with a superspy hero named The Flying Dutchman, Prokosch's aristocratically aloof and resolutely internationalist fiction failed to mesh with the growing parochialism and bloated realism of postwar American culture. In a literary mall now gone mad with gut-wrenching confessions, family incest and TV overspill, he is more exotic than ever.

In fact, America has little time for its own exiles now, and even less for landscapes which are not its own, unless they can be decked out with winsome "third world" political credentials determined by a connection with ethnicities or ideologies largely present in its own interior. The psychological voyage *out* into the exterior world of an "undeveloped" existence must now drip with sanctimonious excuses and pseudo-political reportage. The lonely, austere odyssey of a Paul or Jane Bowles or a Frederick Prokosch — Americans trying deliberately to expand or sabotage their inherited cultural wiring in places which have no relevance whatsoever either to American guilt or to geopolitical self-interest — is now only vaguely irritating and confusing. Recently, it took the efforts of an indignant Spanish schoolgirl to have Jane Bowles's remains disinterred from under a planned parking lot in Malaga. Perhaps the greatest American woman writer of the twentieth century doesn't even have a grave largely because she had the whimsical impertinence to die abroad. It would be like Colette being buried under a Grand Union in Poughkeepsie and no one in the French-speaking world caring less.

Of course, the cruel roulette of Fame has its necessarily unfortunate turns. Not every deserver gets a winning number. Is Prokosch silenced because he turned his back on the gigantic hugger-mugger of American suburbia which has given other post-war writers their chloroformed but instantly recognizable field of dreams? One cannot say. Perhaps the gentle and the aloof simply get pushed aside, unprotesting, and resign themselves to their grim transparence in a cultural landscape dominated mainly by airports.

In a long and affectionate essay on Prokosch for the *New York Times Book Review* fifteen years ago, Gore Vidal, considering the propensity for Amnesia (America) to forget yesterday's dinner, describes a hilarious evening long ago in the sixties when the already forgotten Prokosch visited Vidal in the Hudson Valley. The two attend a party of "hacks and hoods" from the local grove of Academe, who snub Prokosch mercilessly. "They knew he had once been famous in Amnesia but they had forgotten why." Prokosch listens politely to the absurd literary chit-chat, in the course of which a tenured radical declares the classics of Western civilization to be irrelevant and oppressive. Prokosch then quietly begins to recite in Latin a passage from Virgil. The room grows "very cold and still." "It's Dante," one of the professors murmurs to his wife. "Those words," Prokosch says when he has finished, "are carved in marble in the gardens of the Villa Borghese in Rome. I used to look at them every day and think, that is what poetry is, something that can be carved in marble, something that can still be beautiful to read after so many centuries." Stunned silence.

So Prokosch has entered the sinister twilight zone of nonfame, or postfame, a state so terrifying and colder-than-death to Americans that they cancel out all trace of such catastrophic possibilities, whatever the glory of the allotted fifteen minutes. Yet with canons tumbling and rising again, and general insurgence setting off corks in all directions, it is now a good time to become eccentric and maraudingly revisionist readers. Prokosch speaks to us with his lightning-flash peacock-dandy prose, his gorgeously lithographic travel writing, his luminous and brush-quick descriptions, his thirties aerodynamism and lyrical sleekness. He wanders

Frederick Prokosch. Provence, France, 1986. Photograph by Nancy Crampton.

homeless through imaginary landscapes shaped like continents that seem to be geographically real until we realize that Prokosch never travelled in any of them. Prokosch wrote most obsessively about Asia, not in the old spirit of *ex oriente lux*, but as a way of enacting a purely internal voyage which had to have some outward form. In fact, his books always wander through worlds that are thoroughly hybrid and unreal, populated with characters as extravagantly miscegenated as those of *Star Wars* or *Alice in Wonderland.*

I first came across *The Asiatics* in a bookstore in Marrakesh many years ago when I was a student spending a summer at Ouazazarte in the Sahara. It was the ideal book for a solitary odyssey into the desert at the far side of the Atlas and I remember reading it in the bouncing back of a bus hauling its way over the gloomily Gothic peaks of Tizi-n-Tichka, the highest mountain in Africa. At once I found myself with the very opening images of the book: a night watchman singing to himself in a street in Beirut, an air filled with mosquitoes, shabby Ford cars, silent prostitutes standing on the far side of the street and an old man in whom "loneliness had sharpened [the] instincts." The swift cinema scenes unconnected by logical narrative swept me along roads almost exactly like the ones passing below my own window. The road to Damascus with its beautiful Syrian boys, its tin-roofed slums and villages slumped among giant cactus, caves filled with outcast families and then the sad apricot trees of Damascus and deserts rustling with locusts, "a pathetic sort of antiquity . . . cheap with age."

The novel is not a novel, of course, but a hallucination, its scenes bursting as lurid flashes of light and feeling. It had the fluid linear form and endless embellishments of an alien expression, like Arab lute music itself. It seemed to me that he had entered into the deep, subterranean flow of landscape, an intuitional complicity which operates upon us as an electrical force field disturbing in some as yet unexplained way the "internal" senses. Hence his light-flashes are not really descriptions. In all of Prokosch's books, these moments of illumination appear as surges in a mysterious flow of intuitive impression which is never stable or solid.

In *Storm and Echo*, for example, we find this glimpse of an alien territory: "On and on. The light of the moon seemed to penetrate the waste, to grind it into something shrill and homicidal. It wasn't land we were crossing, it was some awful spiritual concoction, an embodiment of bitterness and pain, a scene of pure melancholia."

Well, I took *The Asiatics* with me to Ouazazarte and on to the oasis village of Tinerhir, a surreal eighth-century village made of thousand-year-old mud where I read it walking up and down through a spectral Atlas landscape on my way to the nearby Gorges du Todra. It seemed to me that I was in a purely Prokoschian place. The same crazy outcasts sleeping in dried oueds, the same oases and plantations, the same disorientated Westerners and fluid, rapierlike interactions between strangers wandering along decrepit roads. In fact, I think of *The Asiatics* as the first road movie, and by far the most interesting. "Nothing is as beautiful as a road," George Sand once said, and I think of it as Prokosch's motto. He is a sly late Sufi wandering alone along roads where he might find fiery miracles, visions, sudden encounters, mystical friendships and perhaps even the severed head of the venerable Shams so ecstatically imagined by Rumi.

Both *The Asiatics* and the later memoir, *Voices,* are built around sudden encounters with strangers, meetings as epiphanies that arise, reach a quick crescendo of intimacy and illumination, then melt away into a formless flow which the writer disdains to turn into anything cumulative. The result is something curiously archaic, like Buddhist fables or the eighteenth-century *conte philosophique.* It has also earned Prokosch a certain amount of rebuke, with a predictable string of accusations: "precious," "self-glorifying," "contrived," etc. No doubt there are moments when the process fails. The meetings in *Voices* with a galaxy of the great, worthy and wise do seem a little fable-like and precious at times, as if the habit of writing down every conversation in progress, as a bemused André Gide points out to his young interviewer, had become a peculiar, voyeuristic tic.

But the center of gravity in Prokosch is his solipcism, which dispenses with any pretenses to writerly "relevance" to historical realities. Here, it is the quest of the writer that matters, nothing else. Thus, every vibrant encounter with other "voyagers" has a self-evident profundity. As Prokosch looks back to his childhood, we see Thomas Mann's leonine head through his eyes, framed by misty hockey fields as he visits the Prokosch home (Prokosch's father was a famous professor of Indo-European linguistics). We see, too, the young Frederick creeping up behind James Joyce at Sylvia Beach's bookstore in Paris, noticing the grubby elegance and the mode of handling a teacup. Auden in a Turkish bath in

New York looking like "a naked sea beast" with his "embarrassed-looking genitals," Lady Cunard and Hemingway dueling it out in Paris to the thunder of Hemingway insights such as "There's a pro and a con to Russia, as with all these fucking countries." "There are three different kinds of happiness," intones Peggy Guggenheim in one chapter, and proceeds to tell us what they are, though without much effect. In an excruciating interview with Virginia Woolf, the young American poet is made to feel flylike as he sits in a lugubrious room facing what must have been a withering and aloof stare, which nevertheless does not obscure her "exquisite beauty." It is all part of a deliberately Twainlike peregrination overflowing with canny naïveté and acid detail.

Some of the most enjoyable episodes are those that deal with his hushed encounters with cultural high priests like F. R. Leavis and fellow lepidopterists like Nabokov. "Eliot?" snaps Leavis at high tea in Cambridge. "He is gratuitously and fortuitously obscure. Obscurity has been known to conceal an inner vacuity." Nabokov we see in a darkened and gloomy Swiss hotel sitting mysteriously in a large armchair. "I felt a dark suspense, as though confronted by an oracle." Nabokov tells him that he has tried to see the world through the eyes of an insect; they discuss the *Agrias* butterflies of the Amazon, the exile's voice "stained by a harrowed anonymity," and Prokosch tells of how he climbed a mountain in Corsica mentioned in a Nabokov book in order to pursue Europe's rarest butterfly, the *Papilio hospiton,* the Corsican Swallowtail. The beast's color, he observes quietly, is *not* quite that described by the brilliant stylist of *Glory.*

In this same passage, Nabokov tells Prokosch that "America is in a continual state of trance. Even the mountains and the forests have an air of the hallucinatory." And that the artist is inevitably an exile, whether externally or internally being largely a matter of the complexion of each individual. "And the exiles end by despising the land of their exile." For Prokosch too, perhaps above all, nostalgia, roaming quest, immersion in the hallucinatory pervade the writer's inner air. As Nabokov settles in Lucerne, Prokosch gets a little house for himself in Grasse in southern France. "How glorious," he writes, "to grow old!" Exile, oblivion and contentment consonant with an overwhelming recognition of the endlessness of all roads. A spirit of mystical spontaneity could demand nothing less.

In his preface to his early novel *The Seven Who Fled,* Prokosch tells how he came to imagine seven Western fugitives on the high-roads of Asia, shadows who imprint their meanings "on the deserts of Asia like shapes on a film." Coming out of "a marvellous dream" filled with burning mountains one night in 1935 in Mallorca, he looks down at the Bay of Alcudia "black as the fur of a yak" to see seven fishing boats with seven torches burning on the horizon. Some meaning, "a flaw in a twilit crystal," sets his reverie in motion and he begins to walk along seven roads "in a fit of love." The result is a typical Prokosch book: a fantasy of escape edged with the hardness of an eye which tirelessly hardens its otherworld with glass-bright imagery and sulphurous fear.

Do these peregrinations acted out with the pen and not the feet have the power to compete with those of Marco Polo or Bernal Diaz? We will not really know. It is clear only that Prokosch was himself one of those who fled, who sought "a mysterious and revelatory depth" on roads that can only be invented and who became as he went one of the rarest and most agile butterflies of an Amnesia which no longer collects.

Emily Dickinson. Daguerreotype, circa 1847. The Granger Collection, New York.

To Dickinson
Diane Williams

SERIOUSLY AND POLITELY I tell the story to persons of the loss
of you.

It was good to see you.   It was really good to see you. Oh,
you are lucky.

If the pleasant world contains, as we hope it does, anything of
lasting value, which was once mine, I believe you have it.

In anger, therefore, in anger, I send documents in the midst of
this ritual as I tell the story of the loss of you. This is the delayed
discovery of you somewhere mysterious here in New York City,
then the disappearance of you again and again! — is it that you do
not approve of me? That's what I think.

I will not say anything bad about your rebellion. Your unceasing
progress, your reforms, your improvements of every kind, in every
way — you may be the best person who has ever lived.

Robert Duncan. Photograph by Jonathan Williams. Courtesy Robert Kelly.

Robert Duncan & The Right Time
Robert Kelly

1.

I AM LOOKING at a picture. It is a large color photograph of Robert Duncan, and it came at just the right time. The *right time* is the deepest, most pervasive and (to me) the most salvific keynote of Duncan's poetics. And Duncan's instrumentality in the world.

2.

The right time. I had been asked to contribute to this assembly of memorials and témoignages, and three poets at once stood forth in my mind (like the past Masters of music who beautifully and eerily address Palestrina in Pfitzner's great opera, at last to be done this very summer in New York).

Charles Olson. Robert Duncan. Paul Blackburn.

I thought and thought; to those three men I owe so much — stance and sense of work — both because of the fresh new way, *dolce stil nuovo*, they developed that renewed American poetry in the 1950s, and also because of life experiences in which they engaged me. They were masters for me, and very generous men. As it happened, I had just written a brief memorial of Blackburn for another journal, and wanted to rest with that a while, before writing a study of one of his early poems that stays in mind. I have long wanted to deal with Olson's later poetry, talk about the way it connected with the man I knew, the talk I heard, the early work it fulfilled — I wanted to talk about the Olson of Volume III, but didn't yet feel ready. But I felt it was the right time to talk about Robert Duncan; he stood clearest in my mind, and I wanted to thank him out loud.

3.

I am looking at a picture. It is a color photograph and shows Robert Duncan at the side of the picture, holding, not without a certain amusing awkwardness, a large painting. Duncan seems to be restraining himself from smiling, or his face seems in that mode half clairvoyant half giggling that anyone who knew him must remember as his — the face of Mrs. Maybe, maybe, or the playful spirit medium.

4.

The painting he holds is not shown completely, cut off by the photo's iron rectangular habits. What we do see is plenty, though. It is Jess's portrait of Robert's mind — though that seems too pompous a way of describing this delicious registration of Items in the House: a portrait of Robert himself, younger, and looking more serious (youth is a serious business indeed), paintings, a bookcase, a candlestick in flame (shades of Arnolfini's wedding — for this also is a portrait of the painter's mind, the house, life, work he shared for so many years with Duncan, his life companion, and hence a portrait of their marriage, where the shy bride is present as the flesh of the painting itself — and no one has ever used impasto with such intimate, domestic sensuality as Jess has). A hanging Tiffany lampshade before a fragmentary window. A bowl of flowers on top of a bookcase, and some books arrayed: *Pistis Sophia*, the five volumes of *The Zohar*, two spines of the three volumes of *Thrice Greatest Hermes*.

5.

Pictures of pictures. And me looking at a photo of it. It or them? Jess has played, as ever, with the representation of representation. He who has made the greatest collages (in my guess) of our century, or sharing that grandeur only with Max Ernst, is delighted in his own paintings to play the same elaborate ludus — never condescending to *trompe l'oeil* — of image and representation, the one wrapped within the other, level upon level. His paintings, like Duncan's poems (but just to breathe this, not to carry on about it), delight in embedding texts and references, the bibelots and hand-me-downs of a well-stocked mind. Redeeming the sparks of the Glory. G. R. S. Mead's *Thrice Greatest Hermes* stands on the bookcase, the great turn of the century (that century) chrestomathy of the original Hermetic writings, translated and popularized by Mead, the celebrated Theosophist. It is ardent aspiration towards redemption of (or sometimes redemption through) the material world that animates such texts, and that will again and again occur in Duncan's writings, from *Mediaeval Scenes* to the last measures of "The Regulators."

6.

The right time. Forty years ago I was a young man persuaded of myself and my powers, and knew I could do wonders in poetry. At the time, I was caught up in all the last-gasp formalisms of the 1950s — pallid imitations of Hopkins, Eddic measures, Welsh meters, Auden, blank verse monologues. I felt a certain perverse pleasure in those things, but could smell as well as the next person the mouse-droppings on them, and see the dry pale moth take flight. Some vital spark was missing in the poets I liked and imitated, yet in the other contemporary work I got to see of an anti-formalist inclination, while I found some vigor, it was all yawp and coarse, scarcely deep-funded in the lore of poetry. For I wanted all things — the measure and the immoderate, the archaic trove of all high poetry but also the vivid "language of flesh and blood" — itself a phrase as old as Wordsworth. We keep repeating the same experiment, century after century. It's clear we all and always need what I needed then — the archaic and the instantaneous, the moment no less than Merlin.

I began to do what I could, to work away from the habits I had learned, and see whether I could find some music in other ways. For all my reading I was terribly illiterate in what was actually happening. Then one day, at the right time, my friend Hugh Smith (himself a poet of the determinedly regular, anglophile, exalté) put into my hands a copy of a book by Jonathan Williams. The very title punned its way through my defenses: *The Empire Finals at Verona*. This was his Catullus, englished, updated, coarsened, lightened, but also refined, alert, vivid. It was the first book I had seen that suggested to me there was life in an American verse, an American language way. It was the right time.

And then I found — at that little drugstore on Sheridan Square — the small square book that came as close to being a best-seller as anything Duncan ever published: the City Lights edition of Robert Duncan's *Selected Poems*. Then on David Ossman's radio program "The Sullen Art," I heard Duncan reading his "Poem Beginning With a Line by Pindar." It struck me then and strikes me now as the richest enactment of poetry I had ever heard with my ears. By ear you could hear new measures of poetry discovering themselves, falling back into traditional metrics, rising into exaltations of formal Shelleyan, Shakespearean language, leveling out into broad powerful music of the sacred ordinary speech of living folk. You could actually hear verse stammer and give way to prose, hear

337

prose in all its difference struggle back towards the towers of verse. It seemed a trove of antique power and a school for sense. Not just the luscious musics of the man, but a music that supported, revealed, exalted the operations of mind.

7.

For I had come to realize that the only gift the poet surely has is to disclose to a patient, quiet, often indifferent audience (the shape God takes in our time) the delicate, complex, total operations of the poet's mind — and that articulation of knowing is the only music worth attending to. This is what Duncan seemed to be about, and why the "narcissism" and "self-involvement" (that I found people were always quick to blame him for as person and poet) were in fact mere negative labels for an absolutely essential concentration, by the poet, on the only universe the poet truly has to study, observe, report from and come back singing.

8.

What else does the poet have? The world the poet shares with the audience is expressly words. And only by studying the "tones given off by the heart" can the poet have anything worth reporting, worth taking our time. And that is where Robert Duncan and Charles Olson, so utterly different, yet always for me an "ordered pair," represent the immense possibilities that their masters — Stein, Pound, Lawrence, Williams — had so variously opened.

9.

So there was this Duncan, suddenly, and I realized that (it sounds so dumb to say it, so true, the experience we all have if we are lucky) I was not alone. This man, so unlike me in all his social gesture, his sexual orientation, his sense of order, his poise, his grace — this man was the closest to what I always knew it was possible to become: a poet for whom the old great tradition was still alive, but who still knew the rainy light of Hollywood and the smell of buses, the pervasive, inescapable twist of the beloved through all the day's conduct, all the chambers of the visual. Who did not busy himself forging fake antiques but allowed the vigor of the old music to hold sway in his mind until he could hear himself think. Who was founding — or was it finding — (who can really ever tell them apart, bird or oboe, tree leaves or rushing water?) our colloquial eloquence.

10.

The right time. I sat down this morning to start writing this homage to my dear friend Robert Duncan. I read the news, and the news told me that the princely Thurn-und-Taxis family was selling their castle at Duino on the Adriatic coast, the castle where Rilke wrote the Elegies. How shocked I was! Not that the family is selling it, but that the castle is actually there, actually surviving. That a castle of the mind is also an object of Italian real estate. That the world exists at all is always the strangest news. That there is, or seems to be, something there when I finally get around to opening my lazy eyes.

11.

I sat down to write about Duncan and stared at the picture. A few days ago, Jonathan Williams (whom I got to know years after *The Empire Finals*) and Tom Meyer, whose creative union has been a wonder of the commonwealth for thirty years, and whose friendship has been my delight, paid me a visit. They were carrying a red cat from Carolina to Vermont — fit employment for poets in any age. I told them that I had been invited to write this piece, and asked them what they thought. A blessing, I guess I wanted, some kind of go-ahead. I always seem to be asking for permission. Here was I, persistently heterosexual, trying to write a decent homage to the greatest poet I had known, a poet who insisted on being identified as a homosexual, and on locating in his elaborate and excited sexuality the wellsprings of his work. I suppose I was asking them for an idea. Like Mary Baker Eddy, I believe that the real angels are good ideas. Ideas that teach us to go on. To go new.

12.

Jonathan said: I have a picture for you. And handed me a print of his color photograph of Robert Duncan holding a painting of Robert Duncan.

The five volumes of *The Zohar* are, of course, the Soncino Press edition, translated into English by a team of rabbis including Paul Levertoff, father of the poet Duncan admired so much and felt so warmly towards, Denise Levertov. The translators left out the more arcane tractates of operational magic as unsuitable for the enlightened modern audience to which they brought the classic of Qabbalah — those treatises are the strange meat of MacGregor Mathers's *Kabbalah Unveiled* — a book not shown on Duncan's shelves, though important to the Golden Dawn, and thus to Yeats, of whom Duncan was a singular inheritor.

The books are in the foreground. The work is always in the foreground. The work is what matters. I'm reading Nathalie Blondel's new *Life of Mary Butts* — a writer Duncan spoke of highly, and frequently urged upon his readers and friends. It was Duncan who made me first, and most, aware of Butts, and from him directly or through Ken Irby came the earliest precious tattered xeroxes of her remarkable work now at last coming back into print. Today in the Blondel biography I find Stella Bowen saying, as she reminisces about Mary Butts: "I should have known that the way to enjoy any artist is to attend to his work and not allow one's self to be confused by that lesser thing, his character."

13.
Mary Butts. Gertrude Stein. Hilda Doolittle. Duncan gave us these writers, or restored them to us. His serious *Stein Imitations* understood Stein not as an influence but a School in which a poet might study and learn the craft. The craft of speaking, of letting writing go on. Stein was a mere celebrity, H. D. a vanished imagist or faded luminary, Butts not even a name, according to the accepted wisdom of the 1950s. Duncan did more than his share in restoring Stein to her rightful, mother-of-us-all status, the Queen of Language, by which all telling is made possible. Duncan aimed us firmly at these women's work, by whom writing and its various registers and genres could be restored. Robert Duncan was more than generous. He gave us not only himself, he gave us others as well — and that is a rare generosity in a poet. The one time I heard Dylan Thomas read, in the flesh as we so rightly say, he spent the first half of his program reading late Yeats — I had never known "The Circus Animals' Desertion" till I heard him read it — and only then his own work. An amazing arrogance, an amazing humility conjoined — and to this day I am grateful to Thomas for himself and for opening another door on Yeats. As we are grateful to Duncan not only for his huge symphonies and demanding chamber music, but for his clear bardic eye that caught, sensed and restored the writers who came before him.

14.
The poet's worst enemy is bitterness. Envy and jealousy of other poets are the sickening, blighting hazards of a calling with few

obvious rewards. And often those who have, from Muse or Society, won true rewards, rewards like sweetness of life or life companions, do not recognize their own good fortune, do not grasp that they have been rewarded by the same principles to which their work gave voice. Duncan always saw his good fortune, grants or no grants, even though most of his life and most of his work was spent with the smallest presses, the most exiguous — and exigent — audiences. Knowing his good fortune, he had the grace of kindness. While he could be catty, or venomous as a surukuku, when the mood took him, his generosity towards the living and the dead was phenomenal. More a generosity of spirit (like a fan letter he wrote to James Dickey about a poem he'd read and respected — unanswered, *tu sais*) than of deed, it allowed him to praise, welcome, take delight (and therefore creative energy) from the good work of others. If energy is a product of delight, then all the pleasure we take from the good work of others will surely feed our own.

15.

Once when Duncan was staying in my house for a few days, I found him one morning gazing at my stacks of paperback mystery stories arrayed in a great copper-lined cavity meant for firewood. He walked over to the kitchen table and began talking about our affinity, the only time he ever spoke of any such thing, an affinity grounded in the joy of reading. He felt at home in my house, he said, with these piles of thrillers, of sacred trash, since he too read and took pleasure from such things. We discussed them a little while, noting the way certain pieces of our work had been subtly affected by this thriller or that — Ngaio Marsh, Dorothy Sayers, Michael Innes. Then he went on to say how sad he found it to meet so many younger poets, or would-be poets, who took no pleasure in reading, no pleasure in books. How can you write if you don't read? How can you create a powerful new work if the power of such actual works is closed to you? We read, he said, we like to read. We take pleasure, we know how to take pleasure from reading. We learn how to give pleasure through writing. The important thing is the energetic act of reading, of pleasure welcomed through the engagement with the text.

16.

I thought of Duncan's drawing of the Ideal Reader — he'd drawn it I think for that limited edition of *Letters*. It showed what seems

341

to be a woman of middle years, comfy of disposition, seated in her garden, a great sunhat shielding her features, her whole posture "bent to her book." That picture is one of the most shocking avant-garde proclamations of its day. A book is to read.

This was 1963. I was starting to understand the way writing spilled out of reading. But that sounds bookish and mandarin — not the worst things in the world, but I wanted more. In Duncan I grasped the balance, a balance I tried to specify in a book title of my own a few years later: *flesh, dream, book* — all the sources of our poetry: experience, vision and reverie, and reading. How could we ever write a poem if we did not know that there was such a thing to be written? And yet we always, always look for it, the poem that presupposes no previous poetry. That seems the aim of every manifesto, every new school. A child without a mother. A poem that is an absolute. Perhaps a hunger for such a poem pre-disposes humans to imagine a moment of creation ex nihilo, a word spoken out of nowhere.

17.

The right time. Duncan knew what it was. Punning on the French word *bonheur*, he called happiness the *good hour*. And what made it good? It was the hour that called us to work, the hour that issued through the instrumentality of the poet an articulation of all that was going on in the world. In the mind. A scientist of the Whole, is what I'd called the poet, back in some ravings in the sixties. Duncan explained the exact instrumentality of that science — the poet writing is itself speaking to itself, while we listen. So of course (he was clear) there could be no traffic in greatness, in call-ing so-and-so a Great Poet — there was only one great poet, the poet of whom we are all variously, crazily, fingerprint individually, metabolically, literally, tunefully instrumentalities. So our good-ness lay not in *what*, but in the fact *that* we were able to declaim. And that sweet doctrina rescued poetry, for me, from the clashing teeth of the confessional and the propagandaic, the two molochs of the time I was growing up, when Duncan was the sudden clear voice of poetry I heard speaking in our idiom.

18.

The right time. In the Pindar poem, after telling of Psyche's hard tasks, and all the creatures that had come to help her out, Duncan turns to himself, the deed or task it is to write a poem, this very poem, a word the hour calls out to be written:

> . . . So, a line from a hymn came in a novel I was reading to
> help me. Psyche, poised to leap — and Pindar too, the editors
> write, goes too far, topples over — listend to a tower that
> said *Listen to me!*

So Jonathan Williams wrote a book that fell into my hands, and
jabbed a little chink in my armor, and I began to take notice. Forty
years later he comes by, when I need a push, and slips me this
photograph he took of Robert Duncan holding the painting of
Robert Duncan by Jess.

The photo was taken probably in 1968 or 1969, which is about
when I visited Duncan and Jess for the first time at their house in
San Francisco. I saw the painting then, and studied it, and my
memories of it then aid my seeing of it now. I saw the whole of it,
but memory has ruined the picture even more than the cropping
of it by the photograph. I am left with what I feel. And a little bit
by what I see. So I am looking at Duncan — he wears a striped shirt,
clean and neat over a white T-shirt. His sideburns are full, even
bushy, and his almost-smiling face is a little plumper than I remember it, content seeming, well-fed, but with some haunting
under the eyes. His arm comes up and crosses over his head to
support and balance the top edge of the painting. In doing so, it
happens that the hand shields his eyes. The painting reveals a
world of art and artifact elaborately indoors (John Muir said to
Emerson, Mr. Emerson, yours is an indoor philosophy), but the
photo is otherwise — from the weathered gray wood behind Duncan and his painting, we see we're in the back yard, not yet a
garden, of the house on Twentieth Street.

He needs to shade his eyes from the California sun. His damaged
eyes, the great eagle wandering eyes of him, so disconcerting, so
penetrating. Is it the left one, is it the right one, that is the wanderer? I look at the photograph, and can't tell — because the second
thing one notices when you look at the photo is that it has been
printed backwards: the titles of the books are mirror-style, left is
right and Duncan's slightly unfamiliar plumpness is the inversion
of nature, the "accidental" *contra naturam* that is so close to the
essence of art. And no doubt my own memories have polarized,
magnetized, trivialized, kellyized, many fine specifics of what I
see. Of what I saw.

343

19.

Right time? 1919 when he was born, a year after the war. 1988 when
he died, at sixty-nine. In the days when he was blocking out *Groundwork* as the summa of his life work, he had planned out, with some
explicitness, the work of his seventies, the work of his eighties —
the work of my senility, he said, planned already. Perhaps planning
such things is enough. How can one plan for an hour that has not
come, when what our best work is really is the voice, tone, tell, tale,
told of that hour? It was his jest, a bold jest, with time. It pleased
him to plan ahead, as it pleased him to conduct his own performances of his latest poems, using a strange cheironomy, his hand
waving like Leonard Bernstein's conducting his own music, but by
no means indicating beat or evident rhythm. Instead the hands were
more Picasso's hands, inscribing the moment of the poem's out
loud onto the visual air. When Duncan was teaching at Bard College
in 1982 and 1983, I watched as he read aloud, over several evenings,
perhaps twelve hours of his late work — always the hand moved, a
bird beside the text, a shadow sometimes taking on solidity.

20.

Elsewhere I have written, but that is my story and not his, how
twice, in the most literal manner, Duncan saved my life. Save me
he did, from wanhope and foolish hauteur and dumb desperation,
when I too was "poised to leap." He was the tower who spoke, and
like the tower in Apuleius's story, there is no life in the question
of whether or not the tower "liked" Psyche. I have no idea if Duncan liked me — he said more than once that my constant harping
in those days on women, on making love, was tiresome — but
maybe that was just a playful gay way of telling me he didn't like
my work, while generously giving me a way of enduring that
displeasure without too much pain. What I do know is that his
generosity of work and presence enriched that whole generation
of poets who wanted to do the hard thing, the salmon-folk of
language, who wanted, like Arnaut Daniel our master (Dante's,
Pound's, Duncan's, Wieners', Rattray's, Lansing's, Stein's, Irby's
master) always to swim against the stream, to leap upstream
against the falling water so as to release their own starry influence
up there, where we come from. Duncan's pressure still moves in
the language poets, in the new romantics, in the neoformalists, in
the many contradictory squabbling heirs of his mind and his song.
I feel a gratitude to him I can hardly yet begin to speak.

Encounters with an Americano Poet: William Carlos Williams

Victor Hernández Cruz

MY FIRST POETIC EFFORTS in the English language were to try to compose *coplas* and *décimas,* metric structures from my first language, Spanish. It was very difficult to continuously come up with rhymes in English. Not that it's impossible — look how Keats swings the sound — but my bilingual head was never solidly in the English; communication and perception for me are always a pendulum between the Latin and Germanic foundations of the two languages which the forces of history have bestowed upon me.

As I grew and read and heard the sounds of English I began to appropriate its tempo. When I read the English translation of Lorca's "Poet in New York" and, even more important and penetrating, the poetry of William Carlos Williams, I began to feel how I could bring the rhythms of my language up to an immediate and urban speed. To make things shine in the present moment of our senses, in the language that circulated within the air of the city. I felt the pulse of Free Verse or, more accurately, Open Verse. Free Verse might imply a randomness or an aspect of chance and gamble in the writing, whatever comes up; there are many inner laws and concerns involved, such as cadence and the harmony and blending of words; things must fit within the language of the poem.

The poetry of WCW was like a gentle opening, things came at you, in the order that they were found, no effort to undo them, as to undo the world with concepts. The conceptual seemingly came at the end within a resonance of the words. The natural order of things in motion — almost like a practical poetics. As if it were a rush for air after being submerged within water to the point of drowning. A poetry of the Emergency Room, a grasp for time — WCW was a doctor and had little leisure time throughout most of his life, so he got glimpses in motion, flashes between labor pains. The black ink of his words flowing down the page like a spring breeze.

The way you feel streets when you are young, bubbling and

345

constantly changing, coming at you, full of surprises and chances, apparitions which the ordering of the poem orchestrates: a voice comes from a window — music is heard from another — a forest of bricks — blue walls inside — a flower on a table — a pretty girl passes dividing the nocturnal air in half — a scream — sirens — a police car — sudden thirst and hunger — a bodega — coconut soda — plaintain chips — while in the grocery store an old lady comes in dressed in black — she and the grocer hook into a conversation — the contents of which are from a previous encounter — it is more like an ongoing process.

— Well Soraida wrote to me and she says they've thrown a road up into the mountain where she lives, out there in nowhere, in the inferno — imagine what progress.

— Everything is like that there now, can't be in peace, not even in Barranquitas by a river — now phones are ringing inside coconuts — Cafe and the olive oil — she says — while I stand with coconut soda, his brown hands find a brown bag to put the items in one at a time.

Now through the English comes the sound of Spanish as if a spirit was cooking in the beans — not in the vocabulary which is Saxon but in the march — the dance of uneven steps broken sound — the splash of almost right or left diction. Leaving the bodega as the door opens the chime of a bell, glancing up I notice San Miguel slaying a dragon, the old lady dressed in black moves towards the street as the fragrance of Florida water. Into the breeze walking with all the lights — the fires of candles that are now the image of a tropical river.

That's how WCW poems were jumping in my head:

> Starting to come down by a new path
> I at once found myself surrounded
> by gypsy women
> — from "Asphodel, That Greeny Flower"

Williams then sees the Passaic River — reality is just a meltdown linguistically — the metropolis turns into a desert — look at things — up close — like slow motion — amplification — from a philosophic mountain down to a broken bottle strung on a street — from a passing car a woman's breast inspires — the picture burns the windshield. A new land peeling through the windows of the words; his poetry brought me right to where I was standing with the dictionary inside my sneakers.

William Carlos Williams. Photograph by Charles Sheeler. Courtesy New Directions Publishing Corporation.

Victor Hernández Cruz

William Carlos Williams was born in 1883 in Rutherford, New Jersey, to a Puerto Rican woman and a British father — both moms and pops were foreigners, immigrants to a new land. Williams's father was from the English-speaking Caribbean:

> He grew up by the sea
> on a hot island . . .
> like an Englishman
> to emulate his Spanish friend
> and idol — the weather.
> — from "Adam"

Raquel Helene Rose Hoheb was a woman of many ancestral weavings as are all Caribbean people. Williams says that she was half French (out of the French island of Martinique); her mother was Basque. Other writings mention that she had Dutch blood and in other places it is hinted that she had some Jewish in her. She was a hodge-podge from the Caribbean mercantile middle or upper classes. She grew up in a big house in the city of Mayaguez on the western side of the island. Her family either had slaves or servants — she grew up around Afro-Puerto Ricans, hearing the songs and the stories.

The decision to move north to the states made by her and her husband, William Senior, was apparently devastating to her warm spirit, according to Eric Williams in a forward to WCW's account of his mother, *Yes, Mrs. Williams:*

> . . . this multinational mongrel gentlewoman transplanted
> to a north temperate zone suburb of a major metropolis
> that was infested with WASP entrepreneurs who cared not
> a centimo for her religious, social, or cultural background.

Williams felt this struggle of his mother to survive in a strange cold land, he felt her foreignness and otherness and he felt his own odd drama. In so many open and hidden instances he explored this theme in his poetry. Julio Marzan, a Puerto Rican poet and scholar, has written an extensive study of this link of WCW with the Latino world, *The Spanish-American Roots of William Carlos Williams.* There are also at least two books which explore the intriguing relationship between mother and poet. She had a great influence on her son's path to poetry, to art. She herself studied painting for three years in Paris in her youth and worked on a couple of translations with her son of Spanish novels. Despite the fact that she was a señora of the upper classes, turn-of-the-century Puerto Rico — she was full of the habits, customs and refrains of the popular peoples of the island. The wonderful thing about this book is that the poet just allows his mother to talk — and it is her voice which takes over most of the book — here is where you truly feel a Latino-Caribbean mental structure. You feel her wit and toughness, even her harsh verbal hurricane. It is full of her ghost stories and her medium spiritist wonderings, her splashes into tongues. Her English was always broken and spiced with Spanish and French words. All of these things sailed into Williams's poetic lines. He was among the first to use Spanglish as a literary device as in the little experimental book of spontaneous prose, *Kora in Hell*, and throughout his work there is this bilingual spirit.

I don't know to what extent he accepted, reached for or even understood this Latino element or if he even cared about it at all — but it was just there by nature. He lived in an age when this ethnic insistence would not have been popular and had friends such as T. S. Eliot and Ezra Pound who were full of phobias and racism. Pound discouraged Williams's pursuit of his mother's world: ". . . William Williams, and may we say his Mediterranean equipment, have an importance in relation to his temporal intellectual circumstance." Notice how here Pound leaves out Williams's middle name, Carlos.

When I first started reading Williams in the midsixties I had no idea that he was part Puerto Rican. The information might have taken ten years to get to me. I read him because of the way he sat on an image, the momentum of his pictures, a sure and pure unrestrained language. Williams was like a literary hydrogen bomb — he wrote over forty books and worked all the forms and the new ones he was inventing as he went along, working as a doctor delivering poems and babies. There is much to learn in Williams's books and much energy which can give us strength to continue stretching out the language to fit all of our Americano needs. Thank you, Dr. Williams. And to his mother, Helena, *merci-gracias.*

Sylvia Plath. 1959. Photograph by Rollie McKenna.

Sylvia's Honey
Catherine Bowman

THE YEAR I FIRST TASTED Sylvia's honey. Dipped my fingers deep into the page, into what was raw and unfiltered. *Queer alchemy, zoo yowl, heel-hung pigs, nerve curlers, smashed blue hills, exploding seas, bald-eyed Apollos, freakish Atlantic, midget's coffin.* That year and forever after. *Honey feast of berries, surf creaming, polish of carbon, ku klux klan gauze, pockets of wishes, cracked heirloom, soul-shift, baby crap. Cave of calcium icicles.* The golden bough that tricked me into the underworld. *Acid kisses, blood-caul, a briefcase of tangerines.*

That was the year we dubbed ourselves Dumb Bitches. D.B.s. Joy and I sitting in Pancho's All You Can Eat Mexican Buffet on the west side of San Antonio, just down the road from Randy's Rodeo, where a mob of Texas shit-kicker teens had made headlines for hurling Lone Star Longnecks at Sid Vicious and the Sex Pistols. A man just two red greasy booths away raging.

— Shut the fuck up, you worthless dumb bitch cunt.

— Hey Dumb Bitch, I said to Joy, — pass the salsa.

> Now your head, excuse me, is empty.
> I have a ticket for that.
> Come here, sweetie, out of the closet.
> Well, what do you think of that?
> Naked as paper to start
>
> But in twenty-five years she'll be silver,
> In fifty, gold.
> A living doll, everywhere you look.
> It can sew, it can cook,
> It can talk, talk, talk.

D.B., engraved with ancient glittering sharks' teeth on our mistitled upside-down Texas crowns. And Sylvia Plath, our martyred honey goddess, our Queen D.B. In a town where you could find with ease the Virgin of Guadalupe tattooed across a man's back,

351

Our Lady of Sylvia was emblazoned into our souls' tongues. *Bald and Wild. Not sweet like Mary. Her blue garments unloose small bats and owls.* Her Ariel poems, and especially "Daddy," our sacred text full of high jinks and masks, rage and rebellion, a mirror to behold our self-loathing, our complicity in male authority, our ambivalence about promiscuity and virginity, and our fear.

Plath was teaching us a new way to sing. Besides, we couldn't help but love our Sylvia all dolled up in her achoo giddy-up, red leather saddle, riding English style, her Smith girl voice — *Daddy, daddy you bastard I'm through.* Calling each other D.B. was our way of being smart and satirical, just like Plath. We were taking the way that men looked at us and making fun of it, taking it on, reversing it. Plath was acutely aware of how she was seen. *Ted is a genius. I his wife.* She understood the game and she played for keeps — each round a kind of metaphysical kamikaze mission. No matter how hard she tried to conceal her brilliance and genius it kept coming up to the surface.

So many of our friends, all smart even brilliant women, were in trouble. Edna, gang-raped at the age of thirteen, now drugged on Thorazine and locked in at the Santa Rosa Hospital. Margaret, hiding naked on Christmas Eve behind a carwash, her doctor husband searching for her with army-issue flashlight and weapon. Valerie, stabbed to death in broad daylight while jogging with her baby. Even my mother, one summer night, trying to take herself out of life. So much pain. So much silence. A rage suppressed comes soaring and creeping out in ugly ways.

> The tongue stuck in my jaw.
> It stuck in a barb wire snare.
> Ich, ich, ich, ich,
> I could hardly speak.

That year Joy and I were studying politics and philosophy at St. Mary's. Doc Crane, an Adlai liberal who loved boys from the border, told us stories about Yahoos and morals, the old dirty days of Texas politics, mystification, how deals were made over margaritas at Ma Crosby's down in Ciudad Acuña. The different ways a man and a vote could be bought and sold. After class, at my house, Joy delivering a luminous explanation of Marx and Habermas. My twelve-year-old brother looking up from the table.

— Man, she really laid that out smooth.
— Go for it like a big dog.

> O pardon the one who knocks for pardon at
> Your gate, father — your hound-bitch, daughter, friend.

Big dogs. Dumb Bitches.

> Dirty girl,
> Thumb stump.

Joy practicing her Spanish. — Hey D.B. *no más cabeza sin dolares? Mujer fuerte.* Quit partying down with *muchahos* with *narizes llenas de coke* and condos on the coast. Stay away from gas ovens. Write your poems.

Writing poetry at the time seemed as distant as the moon, as natural as pecan trees and the steering wheel of my blue Nova. I was going to school, waitressing at the Bijou, hanging out, listening hard, Clifford Scott playing bebop at the Sugar Shack, the mariachis at the Esquire after-hours, the Clash. Lessons in poetry. Lessons in swing.

I had an apartment above two Iranian spinster sisters who thought I was possessed by the devil and brewed smelly comfrey teas for me to clear up my complexion. They gave me an old pair of silver high heels. Ricardo Sanchez asked me to read my poems at his bookstore, Paperbacks y Más. My philosophy professor awarded me honors on my "City Planning and Aristotle" paper, telling me later at a party how good I would look nude on a haystack. That was cool, he was taking me seriously as a poet. I wrote my final in rhymed couplets.

Oozing with jammy substance, dead egg, lullaby, a saint's falsetto, body parts swimming with vinegar. The sugar belly. *Black keys, wedding rings, nazi lampshades, tiger pants, potato hiss.* For honey absorbs the taste of everything growing around the hive. That's how I came to understand Plath's poems, as a kind of bitter honey infused with everything going on around her at the time. "Daddy" is not just a poem about her father and her bad marriage; it is a perverse lament for the censoring voices she has killed off, a shrieking assault on our rules for mourning. More than that, the poem is a coup d'état in which, in an effort to find a lineage and a language, Plath dethrones the psyche's *Panzer-man,* i.e., the voices of authority that had empowered her but also who have censored and "dumbed" her.

> So I could never tell where you
> Put your foot, your root,
> I never could talk to you.
> The tongue stuck in my jaw . . .

> So daddy, I'm finally through.
> The black telephone's off at the root,
> The voices just can't worm through.

The poem's central emotion is rage. A rage born from pain. A rage so stylized that it almost becomes a poetic form in itself.

> You do not do, you do not do
> Any more, black shoe
> In which I have lived like a foot
> For thirty years, poor and white,
> Barely daring to breathe or Achoo.

In 1962 she writes to her mother from England:

> Don't talk to me about the world needing cheerful stuff. It is much more help for me, for example, to know that people are divorced and go through hell, than to hear about happy marriages. Let the *Ladies' Home Journal* blither about those. Now stop trying to get me to write about "decent courageous people" . . . It's too bad my poems frighten you. . . . I believe in going through and facing the worst not hiding from it.

I read how Plath's father, a specialist in bees, would begin his college lectures by killing, skinning, cooking and eating a rat in front of the class. Plath shared her father's tastes for breaking taboos and exhibitionism. She has taken a lot of flack from critics and readers for appropriating the imagery of the Holocaust to describe her own pain, but I don't think she is comparing the two, it's more complex. She is not stoking up and sensationalizing her own domestic pain with the news and horrors of the day, but rather searching for a language to understand the censoring powers that controlled her world. She shows how our most private fantasies and obsessions cannot be separated from history and public life. In Plath, I learned to hear a new kind of tune, harsh and sarcastic, a ghastly fugue, that interweaves the nursery rhyme, marriage vows, love cry, goose step and train engine dirge.

> I made a model of you,
> A man in black with a Meinkampf look
>
> And a love of the rack and the screw,
> And I said I do, I do.

Joy and I loved to quote the famous lines to each other:

> Every woman adores a Fascist,
> The boot in the face, the brute
> Brute heart of a brute like you.

We knew that the boot in the poem did not belong to our lovers or fathers but rather it was our own boot that we smacked ourselves hard in the face with doing dazzling high kicks. We were learning all kinds of contortions, and not just in bed.

One night at the Broadway 50/50 we played Marvin Gaye's "Sexual Healing" and Prince's "Little Red Corvette" on the jukebox. Joy grabbed my arm.

— Come on, D. B., let's dance.

We knew that at this longitude and latitude and under this light, we were both supremely D. B. And we danced and laughed. *They will not smell my fear, my fear, my fear.* The way that bees can smell fear. Her words became us. *Ghost column, teacup, silk grits, Hiroshima, babies' bedding, thalidomide, rubber breasts and rubber crotch, bits of burnt paper, balled hedgehog, plato's afterbirth.* A honey that hurt. *Mouth plugs, morning glory pool, earwig biscuits, dead bells, desert prophet, owl cry, some hard stars.* That healed. *Yew tree and moon, wormed rose, Jesus hair, hot salt, eel, widow frizz, blue volt.* That we couldn't stop wanting. That would bear us out. *An earthen womb, the deep throats of night flower.* Sylvia's clove orange honey. *Six jars of it. Six cats' eyes in the wine cellar. The bees are flying. They taste the spring.*

Edward Dahlberg. New York City, 1960. Photograph by Jonathan Williams.

Broaching Difficult Dahlberg
Lydia Davis

BETWEEN *TWO YEARS BEFORE THE MAST* (by Richard Henry Dana, written while still an undergraduate at Harvard, after interrupting his studies for health reasons to spend, in fact, something over two years intermittently before the mast as a common seaman sailing from Boston to California and back) and Robert Creeley's *The Collected Prose* (containing a piece called "Three Fate Tales" that includes a description of a mouse and its shadow moving across the snow under full moon into the storyteller's shadow and thence onto the storyteller's arm as a cat and its shadow wait), on the shelf there are three books together: *Bottom Dogs* (City Lights Books, 1930, 1961), *The Edward Dahlberg Reader* (New Directions, 1967) and *The Leafless American* (McPherson and Co., 1986). Another I thought I had (once I am reminded of it) is missing — where, where, where is it? (*Because I Was Flesh.*) Another shelf in the house? Upstairs? No. Another life, another apartment? See the spine clear as day — somewhere.

I am looking, because of a conversation last night over dinner in a restaurant sitting on a long side of the table across from Ursule Molinaro (whose entire novel *Positions with White Roses* is narrated by a woman who is sitting on a long side of the dinner table with her parents — this is the "normal daughter," the "visiting daughter"), and U. M.'s publisher Bruce McPherson, and next to Matthew Stadler. Also present, but presently out of earshot at the far end of the long table full of people, is Lynne Tillman (*Cast in Doubt, The Madame Realism Complex, The Broad Picture*), who had invited Molinaro out from the city.

L. D. asks U. M. what she thinks of Dahlberg. But that is after she has asked about: Jane Bowles. U. M.: "I *hate* her." (L. D. intensely surprised.) "I hate her work because I love Paul Bowles so much." (L. D. wonders: is this necessary? obviously missing something here.) Well, what authors does she feel close to, has she felt close to? Buzzati, Giorgio Manganelli. But what Americans? (L. D. is persistent.) Well, Paul Bowles is American. Well, besides him?

357

Lydia Davis

Stadler! (*The Sex Offender, The Dissolution of Nicholas Dee, Allan Stein* in progress.) And Jaimy Gordon. She loves Jaimy Gordon. Gordon is also on McPherson & Co.'s list, and that is how Molinaro first met him, some twenty years ago: they both loved Jaimy Gordon and found themselves talking about her somewhere. (L. D. may not be remembering that quite right.)

Also on McPherson & Co.'s list: Frederick Ted Castle. How does U. M. feel about him, whose compendious suitcase of a book, the amazing *Anticipation*, L. D. admires? (U. M.'s answer inconclusive.) Though Castle himself may have been a bit rough-edged when met in a bar and addressed with admiring words by a fan some years ago, *Anticipation* is inviting in the way a journal or a letter is inviting — open, personal, giving the impression of easiness and flexibility and good humor in the writing — and in addition is vast, wide-ranging, informative, opinionated, humorously self-conscious, formally adventurous, exact and written with crystal clarity. In fact, it answers very well to a description of storytelling Creeley gives in his introduction to his *Collected Prose*, a description L. D. discovers when poking around in the book in search of the tale she remembers that included the mouse in moonlight: "that intimate, familiar, localizing, detailing, speculative, emotional, unending talking." As usual, especially in the case of books she admires, L. D. did not finish reading *Anticipation*. One hundred and fifty pages or so, about twelve years ago. Enough to know, though, as in the case of Dahlberg, that it interested her very much.

Now, Molinaro herself is another that L. D. admires (e.g.: "A man with many wives and little money, or perhaps it was: a little wife and much money . . ." — quoting from memory, may not have it quite right and not sure what story it is from). Does she not have certain things in common with Jane Bowles, in fact, as L. D. cautiously suggests, not saying all she is thinking, afraid of offending? But surely, surely not wrong about that? The dry humor. The ladylike characters — as for instance Molinaro's Mrs. Feathergill — with hidden and sometimes criminal or potentially criminal depths. The pitiless eye with which she observes customs, behaviors, foibles. The clear style. The device of repeated epithets, as for instance Molinaro's "the Hispanic-looking boy." The keen irony. ("Just because she has inherited her mother's aquiline nose, does this mean she smells the same rat her mother smells?" Quoting from memory again, from a story she heard Molinaro read out loud.)

"I *hate* Jane Bowles!" she says, though. "*She* is sentimental; *I* am not!" L. D. intends to mull this one over — she has never thought of J. Bowles as sentimental. At a deeper level? Something she has missed? And then more: "*She* is X . . . , *I* am not!" and again: "*She* is X . . . , *I* am not!" — two additional perfectly balanced statements, naming what Bowles is that Molinaro is not. (No one else present can remember what those other two statements were.) Now the two across the table become enthusiastic about Paul Bowles. L. D. has a large place in her heart for Jane Bowles, but agrees with them that P. Bowles's *The Sheltering Sky* is quite admirable as a piece of writing, if horrifying, of course, as a tale. McPherson names other P. Bowles titles, among them (as best L. D. can remember) *Up Above the World*, "A Distant Episode," *A Hundred Camels in the Courtyard* — and Molinaro concurs behind her dark glasses: "My favorite story is 'He of the Assembly.'" She has called for an ashtray immediately, urgently. She smokes Gauloises before and after her plate of gray sliced steak, perhaps even during. ("The mother returns, carrying a second small bowl of Spanish cream. Which she places between the father & the visiting daughter, equidistant from their elbows on the dinner table." — *Positions with White Roses*.) L. D. gives up promoting the case of J. Bowles, but thinks there is more to the story of U. M.'s feelings about J. Bowles: doesn't one often emphatically deny in public what one secretly has to acknowledge?

L. D. continues to think of McP.'s list: what about Dahlberg? U. M. hates him. Can't stand him! Unbearable! Words to that effect, if not exactly those words. McPherson more or less concurs, making exception of certain writings, becoming slightly apologetic — for publishing him? — in the face of her onslaught. (Perhaps merely out of courtesy toward Molinaro.)

L. D. knows Dahlberg interests her though, again, she has read only a little, a long time ago, a few passages from one book or two — that was enough at the time, enough to learn something from, and to know to keep that book, keep it handy. Always intending to read more of it, the rest of it, and more of his other books, as well as the rest of other books not by him, the whole of many other books, later, years later, she thinks, when she retires. (But — retires from what?)

What about Dahlberg, then? Why does she not hear his name often? Was he a grouser also? Brusque in social exchanges like the daring stylist Mr. Castle? Is that why U. M. so emphatically does not like him? Will one be forgotten, no matter how fine a writer, if one is unpleasant or offensive in company? Does McP. publish only nice or at least civil women (though emphatic women — U. M. has spoken out against translating, also: a terrible bore! she says) and cranky, crabby men? No, there's Robert Kelly (*Queen of Terrors, Cat Scratch Fever*) — not in the least a crab! Also on the list is David Matlin (*How the Night Is Divided*), perfectly civil, whom L. D. encounters by chance some days later, in time to ask his view of Dahlberg. What about Dahlberg? she asks Matlin from her seat on a long side of a picnic table by an old hotel, Matlin on the other long side? Matlin's response concerns the importance of Dahlberg's influence on certain American poets, including perhaps Charles Olson. He mentions also how much he admires *Do These Bones Live* (a series of essays on the social and spiritual isolation of American writers first published in 1941), calling it something like "superb."

L. D. knows little about Dahlberg beyond, perhaps, that his handling of language is interesting, that he is an interesting stylist — this is enough for her to want to keep him available on the shelf, even if she has seldom picked up the books. Over dinner, McP. had remarked: underappreciated writer. Here, again. L. D. thinks, comes up this recurring question of underappreciation and, in fact, *overappreciation* of writers, also of other artists. (She has been thinking, lately, of the general underappreciation of Haydn and overappreciation of Mozart that seem beyond correction by now.) P. Bowles also underappreciated, as is J. Bowles. American public may resent expatriate Americans and withhold appreciation from them, as possibly in the case of J. Bowles and P. Bowles. But expatriatism irrelevant to case of Dahlberg, surely. McP. had continued: Dahlberg may be underappreciated because material is so harsh, so difficult. Or did he say: unpalatable. Or painful. But then there's Céline, McP. added. (L. D. thinking, though, Céline is not American.)

Dahlberg (time to go to the shelf, the books — back covers, front matter, back matter; then some reference books): *Bottom Dogs*, introduction by — D. H. Lawrence. Dedication: "For my Friend Jonathan Williams." At least one friend. From Dahlberg's preface, written in Spain, 1961: "When I finished *Bottom Dogs* in Brussels and returned to America, I was quite ill in the hospital at Peterborough, New Hampshire. . . . I was slow in recovering. The real malady was *Bottom Dogs.*"

Lawrence's introduction begins: "When we think of America, and of her huge success, we never realize how many failures have gone, and still go to build up that success. It is not till you live in America, and go a little under the surface, that you begin to see how terrible and brutal is the mass of failure that nourishes the roots of the gigantic tree of dollars." Skimming further, see the word "America" or "American" repeated many times: "savage America . . . American pioneers . . . American position today . . . position of the Red Indian . . . American soil . . . deep psychic change . . . old sympathetic glow . . . The American senses other people by their sweat and their kitchens . . . their repulsive effluvia . . . American 'plumbing,' American sanitation, and American kitchens . . . American nausea . . . American townships . . . repulsion from the physical neighbour . . . *Manhattan Transfer* . . . *Point Counter Point* . . . They stink! My God, they stink! . . . Theodore Dreiser and Sherwood Anderson . . ." Still nothing about Dahlberg himself. What will Lawrence say? Ah: something about Dahlberg's main character, Lorry, and then the conclusion: "The style seems to me excellent, fitting the matter. It is sheer bottom-dog style, the bottom-dog mind expressing itself direct, almost as if it barked. That directness, that unsentimental and non-dramatized thoroughness of setting down the under-dog mind surpasses anything I know. I don't want to read any more books like this. But I am glad to have read this one, just to know what is the last word in repulsive consciousness, consciousness in a state of repulsion. It helps one to understand the world, and saves one the necessity of having to follow out the phenomenon of physical repulsion any further, for the time being." Bandol, 1929. He has also said: "The book is perfectly sane: yet two more strides and it is criminal insanity." That was enough for Lawrence, who was, however, Dahlberg's friend. Repulsion: I think of Céline again.

Dahlberg: an American realist or naturalist preceding the line that stretches from James T. Farrell to Jack Kerouac.

Inside, a biographical note probably written by Dahlberg himself: "Dahlberg was born in 1900 in a charity maternity hospital in Boston and at the age of five committed to a Catholic orphanage. Before reaching his twelfth year he was an inmate of a Jewish orphan asylum, where he remained until he was seventeen." Occupations, after that: Western Union messenger boy, trucker, driver of a laundry wagon, cattle drover, dishwasher, potato peeler, bus-boy, longshoreman, clerk. Education: the University of California and Columbia University. (Though he later, in *Because I Was Flesh*, referred to what he encountered there as "canonized illiteracy" and remarked that "anybody who had read twelve good books knew more than a doctor of philosophy.")

A standard reference book describes him slightly differently, as "the illegitimate son of an itinerant woman-barber" — who is referred to in yet another reference work as "the Junoesque owner of the Star Lady Barbershop of Kansas City."

> She moved from town to town, selling hair switches, giving osteopathic treatments, going on again when she felt the place had been played out. In this way she hoped to save a little money and establish herself in some thriving city. She had taken Lorry with her wherever she went.
>
> — *Bottom Dogs*

Paul Carroll, who edited and introduced the contents of *The Dahlberg Reader*, describes Lawrence's introduction to *Bottom Dogs* as "shrill, chilly." (I would add, keeping more or less to the rhyme scheme, that it seems "unwilling.") In his own introduction he announces: "Three major themes distinguish Mr. Dahlberg's writings: his dialogue with the body; his criticism of other writers; and his condemnation of the modern world."

Carroll goes on to say: "Certainly there is no prose like Dahlberg's prose in all of American literature. At its best, the Dahlberg style is monumental and astonishing," evolving from "hard-bitten, bony, slangy" to "supple, bizarre, a weapon of rage and authority," and peaking after decades with "cadence and dignity . . . and . . . rich, queer erudition." Dahlberg was also described — by Sir Herbert Read, an English poet and champion of the importance of the arts to education and industry — as "a lord of the language, the heir of Sir Thomas Browne, Burton, and the Milton of the great polemical pamphlets." Yet he spent most of his years in poverty, lack of "respectable" recognition. . . .

He despised contemporary America, rigorously hated it and condemned it, hated all that was mechanized and sophisticated that separated people from the natural world. "As for myself," he said in a letter to Sherwood Anderson, "I'm a medievalist, a horse and buggy American, a barbarian, anything, that can bring me back to the communal song of labor, sky, star, field, love."

362

His circle, at various times, included Anderson, Ford Madox Ford (whom he described, before he knew him well, as a "Falstaffian bag of heaving clothes"), Josephine Herbst, Karl Shapiro, Isabella Gardner, Jonathan Williams, Allen Tate, e. e. cummings, William Carlos Williams — the last two of whom Ford wrote about together with Dahlberg as three "neglected" authors. He was also supported by Williams, by Archibald MacLeish and by Robert Duncan.

The *Reader* includes literary essays, personal letters, portions of the novel *The Sorrows of Priapus* and chapters from the autobiographical *Because I Was Flesh*. Jonathan Williams took the cover photograph, and Alfred Kazin contributed a quote to the back cover that calls this "one of the few important American books published in our day." I skim through.

Here is Dahlberg being curmudgeonly about Melville. "*Moby-Dick*, a verbose, tractarian fable on whaling, is a book of monotonous and unrelenting gloom. . . . *Moby-Dick* is gigantology, a tract about a gibbous whale and fifteen or more lawless seamen. . . . In a book of half a millennium of pages, the adjectives alone are heavy enough to sink the Theban Towers . . . 'moody,' 'mad,' 'demonic,' 'mystic,' 'brooding,' 'crazy, 'lunatic,' 'insane,' and 'malicious'. . . . Melville was as luckless with his metaphors. . . . His solecisms and hyperboles are mock fury. . . . This huffing treatise is glutted. . . . Melville's jadish vocabulary is swollen into the Three Furies. . . ."

Who else did he vilify? Where is the list? Here is a partial one, from Paul Carroll's introduction — "What he said [at a party given for him by Isabella Gardner] about Hemingway, Faulkner, Eliot, Edmund Wilson, Pound, and, I believe, the New Critics was univocal, brilliant, sour, erudite, and unanswerable." One of the reference works adds to that list: Fitzgerald. Among the few whom he praised were Thoreau, Sherwood Anderson and Dreiser.

Did he like, in prose, what he did himself? He employed a stout, pungent Anglo-Saxon vocabulary, including unfamiliar words, with beautiful sound: "A low, squab mist hovers over the bay which damps the job-lot stucco houses." — *Because I Was Flesh*. (I look up "squab" to understand this curious way he is using it. I find no adjective form but: fledgling pigeon about four weeks old; short, fat person; couch; cushion for chair or couch.)

Literary and classical allusions combined in vivid descriptions: "The playgrounds in back resembled Milton's sooty flag of Acheron. They extended to the brow of the stiff, cindered gully that bent sheer downwards toward a boggy Tophet overrun with humpback bushes and skinny, sour berries." I enjoy "boggy Tophet" and make a halfhearted attempt to find Milton's sooty flag of Acheron. I find only Acheron — meaning one of the rivers in the infernal region; and Hades itself. As for Tophet, it is a shrine south of ancient Jerusalem where human sacrifices were performed to Moloch.

Opening here and there, I also find an irony, a careful, self-conscious word choice with an edge of humor, that remind me again of J. Bowles. "The sight of the poultry seemed to make him listless."

The preface to *The Leafless American* is by Robert Creeley (written 1986, in Waldoboro, Maine). "The immense loneliness of this country's people. . . . It may be that there is truly no hope for any one of us until we remember, literally, this scarified and dislocated place we presume humanly to come from, whether the body of ground we claim as home or the physical body itself, which we have also all but lost. Dahlberg has made this determined gesture of renewal and recognition again and again in his work, and if he is, as some feel, the necessary Job of our collective American letters, he is also a resourceful friend to any who would attempt their own instruction and survival in the bedlam of contemporary life. . . . Because we have neither a history simply available to us nor the resource of a community underlying our acts, no matter their individual supposition or nature, we work in singular isolation as writers in this country. Unlike our European counterparts who work in modes and with words long established by a communal practice and habit, we have had to invent a syntax and address appropriate to the nature of our situation. . . . Therefore the extraordinary rhetorical resources of Dahlberg's writing are intensively American in nature . . ."

Americans are the subject of the first essay in *The Leafless American*. The other short pieces concern: the decline of souls in America ("May no one assume that these granitic negations comfort me" — I relish the word "granitic"); Kansas City ("a smutty and religious town . . . Homer detested Ithaca, and let me admit, I hate Kansas City"); Spain; Rome and America ("The difference between the Roman and the American empire is that we are now adopting the licentious habits of a Poppaea, or a Commodus, or a Domitian, without having first acquired stable customs, deities, or a civilization"); an unfavorable review; literature's place of low esteem in American culture at the time of writing (but I can find no dates of first publications of these pieces); Stephen Crane; Sherwood Anderson ("We are now in the long, cold night of literature, and most of the poems are composed in the Barren Grounds" — "Barren Grounds": I suspect the reference is to *The Pilgrim's Progress*, and I look through the book, another I have on the shelf and will someday read, but I cannot find the phrase); Oscar Wilde (more or less unsympathetic, which disappoints me); Nietzsche (sympathetic); cats and dogs in what appears to be a parable set in Biblical times; "The Garment of Rā" in a poem of many pages; the problem of governing, or not governing, one's desire.

At the book's end, there is a portrait of Dahlberg consisting of diary entries reporting encounters with him by Gerald Burns. (Who is Gerald Burns? There are few notes in this book, little editorial comment, little explanation of items that are not self-evident, few dates or provenances.) "[1.8.73] . . . His outerworks were hard to breach, but I got through them twice without harm." "[12.29.73] . . . He said a wonderful thing about people who don't like Ruskin." Burns reports that Dahlberg's favorite Pascal quote is: no man fears himself enough. His second favorite: men are always surprised by their characters. "I had heard he was down on blacks," says Burns, and goes on to give some evidence of this. A bigot? Céline again. Hamsun. And that other old question again: Willing to admire the work of a racist or a misogynist? Willing even to read it? How bad does the bigotry have to be before one has to stop reading it? How good does the writing have to be for one to consent to read it?

A few months ago I read a survey of writers organized and written up by an intelligent-seeming academic named Alice Kaplan on the question of Céline and his standing among writers now. Of the sixty-five writers who responded to the survey, thirteen said that Céline's political views had no effect on their reading of him. At the other end of the spectrum some (number not specified) refused to read him at all. Among these, in fact, was Paul Bowles, who said, "I have avoided him for five decades." (Other writers mentioned in the article who have been spurned for political reasons — their work not read because of ideologically unacceptable positions in text or author's life — were: Paul Eluard, Pound, Heidegger, Paul de Man.) One writer who did read Céline, and was excited by the style, the urgency of Céline's writing, felt that the effects of the politics were part of the complexity of the work. He says the politics "deepens an appreciation of the dystopian and repulsive character of this work." In the article, in passing, Edward Dahlberg is mentioned, being defined — along with early James Farrell, Dos Passos and William Saroyan — as a "proletarian lyric writer."

As I explore the question of Dahlberg, I find I am doing my own limited, informal survey in casual conversations as I encounter other writers. Two poets more or less my age (born mid to late forties) did read Dahlberg, but many years ago, in college, and have very remote memories of his work, no particular impression. One essayist and translator my age was very excited about Dahlberg in college, but would not read him now, now reacts against the "eighteenth-century" style. He also says that whereas he used to think Dahlberg was a sweet man who turned into a monster only when he wrote, he later came to believe that Dahlberg was in fact always a monster.

One fiction writer about five years younger knows the name but has never read him, has no impression of him, associates him with the thirties but confesses she may be mixing him up with another writer who writes about cats (possibly in verse form). Another fiction writer ten years younger has or may have (he is away from home and cannot check) a book of Dahlberg's on his shelf, not read, acquired close to ten years ago on the recommendation of another writer he admires, perhaps James Purdy but perhaps another writer, this book being one of the two hundred to three hundred books not yet read that he keeps because they promise to be of value to him eventually. His strong impression, though he has not read Dahlberg, is of a vigorous playfulness in forms both short and long. Another writer still younger has no sense of Dahlberg at all, associates nothing with the name, though he knows the name. He asks when Dahlberg died. In the early eighties, I say incorrectly — the actual date is 1977. The younger writer suggests that age may be a factor — the younger the writer, the less well acquainted with Dahlberg. (And it is true that those City Lights and New Directions books on my shelf appeared before and during the years when I and those two poets were in college.)

There may be something in that, or there may not, but in fact when I question the last writer, who is also the oldest, born in the first decade of the century, she becomes animated. Dahlberg? Oh yes, he was delighted to meet her husband, a literary critic. They met Dahlberg in the midforties on Cape Cod. He offered some sort of practical help to them where they were staying in Wellfleet, which resulted in a misunderstanding concerning some dirty laundry left in front of Dahlberg's door. "He was highly insulted!" she says. "I wish I still had his letter!" She goes on to say more generally: "Crazy fellow, crazy guy!" About his work, however, she is, like the others, vague. "Offbeat, not mainstream, anyway," she says.

> One evening I saw her staggering about in the room, jostling against the sink and the steamer trunk. She turned to me, throwing out her hands; the tears hung upon her sagging face, and I saw there all the rivers of sorrow which are of as many colors as there are precious stones in paradise. She said to me, "I am going to die, Edward. Let me sign over to you what I still have left."
>
> I stood there, incapable of moving. Had it come, the void, the awful and irrevocable chasm between us? What should I do? Instead of taking this shrunken heap of suffering into my arms, I only shook my head. I had already stolen too much from her; I had not the strength either to lift up my guilt or to say more.
>
> Every night after that when she lay on the cot, she continued to grease her face and arms and neck with her lotions, and before going to sleep, I came to her and knelt on the floor beside her cot and kissed her, and then I arose and went to my own bed.
>
> With the money she had given me I purchased an old house on Cape Cod and a secondhand car, and one night my wife and I sat in the car outside the flat saying good-bye to my mother. Then I watched this shamble of loneliness, less than five feet of it, covered with a begrimed and nibbled coat, walk away from me.
>
> — *Because I Was Flesh*

I take a random look at some of the critical works I happen to have on the shelf. In Harry Levin's *The Power of Blackness*, there is no mention of Dahlberg, but Richard Henry Dana is mentioned three times. According to Levin, Melville linked himself with Dana, as he linked Ishmael with Queequeg, by the metaphor of Siamese twins. Melville praised Dana's contribution as a sincere and sympathetic witness to the sailor's way of life — "a voice from the forecastle." Melville admitted to Dana that it was hard to get poetry out of blubber. In this and another book, one about Melville, Dana's "flogging scene" is described as being more forceful, more moving, than Melville's. (I also learn that Melville asked, "Are the green fields gone?" — lamenting that the mystery of unexplored America was vanished — in a spirit not unlike Dahlberg's.)

Dahlberg is not mentioned by contemporary theorists like Terry Eagleton. In a memoir by Alfred Kazin, I am in the right decades, but there is nothing about Dahlberg. I learn, though, that the critic Edmund Wilson (one of those reviled by Dahlberg) saw nothing in Kafka, as he saw nothing in Dickinson or Frost.

In the correspondence of James Laughlin and William Carlos Williams there is a little more: that Dahlberg was a member of the "Friends of William Carlos Williams" formed by Ford Madox Ford in 1939; that Williams thought well enough of Dahlberg's *The Flea of Sodom*, published by New Directions in 1950, to write something about it for the press, saying to Laughlin: "its a unique & valuable book even tho' overpacked with wild metaphor" (Creeley, though, I learn later, found it at the time "dismal . . . unreadable, [a] sick, sick book"); and that New Directions also published Dahlberg's *The Sorrows of Priapus* in 1957 with drawings by Ben Shahn. I also learn that both Dahlberg and Shahn appear in Book 5 of Williams's *Paterson*. Dahlberg's appearance takes the form of a longish letter by him apparently written from Spain. ("Plato took three journeys to Dionysius, the Tyrant of Syracuse, and once was almost killed and on another occasion was nearly sold into slavery because he imagined that he influenced a devil to model his tyranny upon The Republic," he tells "Bill," before talking about his morning shopping excursions with his wife to the *"panadería"* and *"lechería."*) At one stage, before the final revision of Book 5, there was, instead of the letter from Dahlberg, a letter from Cid Corman. Other letters included in Book 5 are from Josephine Herbst, Allen Ginsberg ("I mean to say Paterson is not a task like Milton going down to hell, it's a flower to the mind too") and Ezra Pound. I learn also, since I continue to read backwards and forwards in the letters, that New Directions published Paul Bowles's *The Sheltering Sky* in 1949 and that it sold twenty-five thousand copies, and that such successes (along with successes in the sales of Tennessee Williams and Thomas Merton) made it possible for Laughlin to publish, as he says (in 1950), "kids like Hawkes." Born very close to the same year as Dahlberg were: Ben Shahn, Bennett Cerf (founder of Random House), Josephine Herbst, William Faulkner, F. Scott Fitzgerald. . . .

I suppose I have been trying to answer the question of why, though Dahlberg seems to be considered worth writing about as an American author (his name appears often enough on certain lists), he is so rarely talked about now, his work so unknown to American writers writing today. Is an answer taking shape having to do with: his cantankerous, difficult personality (his "sensitive, touchy and bitter temperament regarded even by friends as somewhere between difficult and impossible," according to Tom Clark's *Charles Olson: The Allegory of a Poet's Life*); his isolation ("Blessed and burdened with one of the great voices in American literature he has long likened himself to Ishmael and Job and lived an eremitic life of writing, caring only to please himself" — introduction to the *Reader*); his offensive degree of bigotry or narrowness ("he dwelt in agreement with Homer and Euripides, neither of whom 'regarded woman as a moral animal'" — Clark's *Olson*); his glorification of rusticity and American roots and landscape, not particularly in fashion nowadays ("Perhaps no American writer since Thoreau has been so enamoured of our natural history, our woodlands, meadows, rivers, and their creatures. These are the gardens we left for lucre's apple . . ." — introduction to the *Reader*); his strong identification in subject matter and to some degree in style with a proletarian literature very identified with its time and thus, perhaps, feeling dated to us; stylistically his heavy use of literary and classical allusion, also not fashionable now?

> There are five trash towns in greater New York, five garbage heaps of Tofeth. A foul, thick wafer of iron and cement covers primeval America, beneath which cry the ghosts of the crane, the mallard, the gray and white brants, the elk and the fallow deer. A broken obelisk at Crocodopolis has stood in one position for thousands of years, but the United States is a transient Golgotha.
> — *Because I Was Flesh*

It occurs to me, before I settle in to read one of Dahlberg's own books, to follow up on what Matlin said about Olson. I read around in a biography I have by Tom Clark and discover that indeed Dahlberg was a father-figure to Olson in the beginning of their relationship, in the midthirties, a Bloom to his Stephen Dedalus, that Dahlberg influenced him in his education, his reading and stylistically. Interestingly, I discover as I browse how Melville was involved in their relationship at every turn — Dahlberg encouraging and helping Olson in the beginnings of the Melville project that

resulted eventually in *Call Me Ishmael;* the severing of their relationship being ostensibly caused by jealousies over certain of what
Olson felt were his own ideas about Melville that appeared in a
Dahlberg essay on Melville; their partial or temporary reconcilia-
tion coming about over the publication of Olson's book. . . .

As I read about Olson, glimpses of Dahlberg's personal and professional life keep appearing, most often dark ones, filled with
difficulties: divorce, child-custody suits, a thankless job teaching
freshman composition at a Brooklyn college; lastly, as Clark puts
it, "latterly descended to the meanest of free-lance wastelands."

I am eventually led to Olson's essay "Projective Verse" and Dahlberg's appearance in it: "Now (3) the *process* of the thing, how the
principle can be made so to shape the energies that the form is
accomplished. And I think it can be boiled down to one statement
(first pounded into my head by Edward Dahlberg): ONE PERCEP-
TION MUST IMMEDIATELY AND DIRECTLY LEAD TO A FUR-
THER PERCEPTION."

Before I desist from my exploration of Dahlberg, under pressure
of time, I am left with a thought about his possible importance
being, for one thing at least, his influence on Olson's development
as a writer and particularly on *Call Me Ishmael:* for Olson, *Do
These Bones Live,* along with William Carlos Williams's *In the
American Grain* and Lawrence's *Studies in Classic American
Literature* served as models of, as Clark says, "a loosely constellated
associative structure from which an unstated central thesis might
be allowed to emerge as a strong cumulative pattern or sense."

Now, an unexpected, eleventh-hour source of opinion: I open
Gilbert Sorrentino's book of essays, *Something Said* (North Point
Press, 1984), looking for something having nothing to do with
Dahlberg, and find three short pieces on Dahlberg, reviews that
were originally published in 1964, 1970 and 1973. Running through
these pieces is a robust indignation: "The neglect accorded him by
the world of fashionable or frivolous criticism is infamous"—and
also an unmitigated admiration. In Sorrentino's opinion, Dahlberg
was shunned because he never "smile[d] at the correct suits and
ties . . . chat[ted] amicably with the proper dentures at the proper
cocktail parties"—he was "not for sale." And he continues: "Let's
get it said immediately: Edward Dahlberg is a great writer . . . His
prose is as sublime as Donne's gold beaten to 'ayery thinnesse' . . .
As with great writers generally, Dahlberg's basic unit is the phrase.
When he has that, he goes on to the next, until the sentence is

fashioned." An interesting question is raised by Sorrentino, one that I will link to something Beckett once said about style: he posits that great writing is *all* in the style, and that "writers have only a fistful of ideas"—his examples being Joyce, Pound and Beckett, for three. He concludes his 1973 essay by saying, about Dahlberg, "The only thing you can do with him is read him. He will repay your least attention with his best, i.e., perfection."

Having situated Dahlberg sufficiently for my purposes, I will go on to read at least *Bottom Dogs*, meanwhile looking for a copy of *Because I Was Flesh*. (And it will be interesting to see what, if any, Dahlberg titles turn up in secondhand bookstores. One friend tells me that Dahlberg's own library was sold, after his death, to a secondhand bookstore now defunct and that my friend bought there Dahlberg's own copy of Ford Madox Ford's *Selected Letters* in which Dahlberg had underlined, he says, every "perfect Dahlberg sentence.")

Then again, I haven't read *Two Years Before the Mast* either, and I like the idea of reading a good adventure book (opening, "The fourteenth of August was the day fixed upon for the sailing of the brig Pilgrim on her voyage from Boston round Cape Horn to the western coast of North America. As she was to get under weigh early in the afternoon, I made my appearance on board at twelve o'clock, in full sea-rig, and with my chest, containing an outfit for a two or three years' voyage . . ."). Especially an adventure book that includes language I will not necessarily understand. (Dana says in his preface: "There may be in some parts a good deal that is unintelligible to the general reader; but I have found from my own experience, and from what I have heard from others, that plain matters of fact in relation to customs and habits of life new to us, and descriptions of life under new aspects, act upon the inexperienced through the imagination, so that we are hardly aware of our want of technical knowledge. Thousands read the escape of the American frigate through the British channel, and the chase and wreck of the Bristol trader in the Red Rover, and follow the minute nautical manoeuvres with breathless interest, who do not know the name of a rope in the ship.") William Cullen Bryant helped to get this book published. Dana went on to become a lawyer, and appeared in important cases defending fugitive slaves (that was around 1848). Late in life he said, "rather sadly": "My great success — my book — was a boy's work . . ." He died in Rome and is buried there in the Protestant cemetery near Shelley and Keats.

Lorine Niedecker. Fort Atkinson, Wisconsin. 1967. Courtesy photographer Gail Roub.

For Lorine Niedecker
Norma Cole

"Guido, I wish that Lapo, thou and I,
   Could be by spells conveyed, as it were now,
Upon a barque, with all the winds that blow. . . ."
Dante to Cavalcanti, trans. Rossetti[1]

"Robin, it would be a great thing if you, me, and Jack Spicer
Were taken up in a sorcery with our mortal head so turnd. . . ."
Robert Duncan, "Sonnet 3, From Dante's Sixth Sonnet"[2]

"I wish you and Louie and Celia and I could sit around a table.
Otherwise, poetry has to do it."
Lorine Niedecker, letter to Cid Corman, October 1964[3]

fly back to it each summer[4]

Tribute, from *tribuere,* to assign, give pay, eventually metaphorizes from actual payment in acknowledgement of submission, or in exchange for the promise of peace, to homage paid, or acknowledgement of esteem, affection. Edmund Spenser's first line of the envoi *"To His Booke"* echoes Chaucer with affection and esteem:

"Goe little booke: thy selfe present"[5]
from
"Goe, litel bok, go litel myn tragedye"[6]

---

[1]*Dante and his Circle,* ed. & trans. Dante Gabriel Rossetti (London, 1874) 143.
[2]Robert Duncan, *Roots & Branches* (NY, 1964) 124.
[3]*"Between Your House and Mine": The Letters of Lorine Niedecker to Cid Corman, 1960 to 1970,* ed. Lisa Pater Faranda (Durham, 1986) 48.
[4]Lorine Niedecker, *My Life By Water: Collected Poems 1968* (UK, 1970) 41. This line is cited in Norma Cole, *My Bird Book* (LA, 1991) 28.
[5]Edmund Spenser, *The Shepheardes Calender* (1579; in *Norton Anthology,* 1962) 530.
[6]Geoffrey Chaucer, *Troilus and Criseyde* (c.1380; NY, 1987) 1.1786.

Norma Cole

Old words make new worlds, place is idea. Think of the forms water takes: Spinoza, Burns, Xenophanes, Blake, Sappho, Dostoevsky, "the James Brothers," William Carlos Williams, the Webbs, Jefferson, Pasternak, Engels, the Brontës, Dickinson, Ovid, Einstein, Pound, Gilbert White, Audubon, Duke Ellington, Reznikoff, Darwin, H. D., Langston Hughes, Plato, Homer, Dante, Shakespeare and of course Zukofsky, and so on — a discreet selection of references describing Niedecker's coordinates, her *locus*, her lost & found.

Without preliminaries, the meticulous unobserved observer enters *in medias res* (like New York photographer Helen Levitt, whose special camera fitted with a right-angle viewfinder permitted her to work unnoticed by those who show up in her work[7]), continues her speculations, her "reflections," as she called them, beyond subjectivity. She speaks of the flood from its midst, for like Cézanne, she has the capacity for repeated defamiliarization of "what is there," and is endlessly occupied by it. Mind, bird, war, sky, street, ". . . a river, impersonally flowing. . . ."[8]

Topologies, dichotomies: "I wonder what the mind will be capable of doing someday without danger to the body?"[9] The structure of particularity whose sound mind names and verbs, notates intervals with tender color, sensuous, passionate intellection in a repertoire of motion, its timing and tension fully motivated, activating space.

Extending by re-membering, meaning surprises event. A life/work is shaped by the equation place = "there is nothing else."[10] The choice to live in one's spot, to restrict one's engagement with the social, is the choice to coexist atemporally with a selected cohort of makers and thinkers. This coexistence extends to Niedecker's recuperative use of found materials imbricated with studied dexterity in the immediate, the vernacular of her present, a complex overlapping creating disjunctive order.

---

[7]Sandra S. Phillips, "Helen Levitt's New York," in SFMOMA Catalogue *HELEN LEVITT* (SF, 1991) 16.
[8]Jesse Redmon Fauset, *Plum Bun*, excerpted in *The Gender of Modernism*, ed. Bonnie Kime Scott (Indiana, 1990) 167.
[9]Jenny Penberthy, *Niedecker and the Correspondence with Zukofsky 1931–1970* (Cambridge, 1993) 198.
[10]*Ibid.*, 217.

Niedecker's choices are not separate from the form they take. *". . . poetry has to do it."*[11] Inexorability of the assumptive prerogatives of a dialogic inner speech shapes her acute attention to formal re(ve)lations, causality, chance, change, a strict complexity. The pivotal nature of apostrophe runs through it. Here is someone remembering someone's remembering in the present. "The *tone* of the thing. And awareness of everything influencing everything."[12]

Language is the body's last symptom. *". . . a rhythm of emergence and secrecy sets in, a kind of watermark of the imaginary."*[13] The poet sits in the "anxious seat."[14] The hand gives up the writing. The person in the poem is someone else. Naming echoes. The nothing, like the magician's hand, conducts the something lost in the flood. Puzzle rejects closure: prosody tells this story. Although words may refer, the poem, like the subject, has no referent, for it does not pre-exist itself. Rather, it predicts itself, calls itself into being by means of calling or being. Indivisible, it cannot be regional.

Lorine Niedecker was born 12 May 1903, Fort Atkinson, Wisconsin. Except for a few brief excursions (to New York, and on driving trips to further her knowledge of Wisconsin and neighboring states) she lived mostly on Blackhawk Island, Jefferson County, Wisconsin. She died 31 December 1970 in a hospital in Madison, Wisconsin.

> *now live in music*
> *now read in peace, Lorine*[15]

---

[11]Faranda, 48.

[12]Lorine Niedecker, letter to Gail Roub, 1967, in "Getting to Know Lorine Niedecker," Gail Roub. *Lorine Niedecker: Woman and Poet,* edited by Jenny Penberthy (Orono, 1996) 86.

[13]Jean Baudrillard, "The Ecstasy of Communication," in Baudrillard, *The Ecstasy of Communication* (NY, 1988) 33.

[14]John Brinkerhoff Jackson, "The Sacred Grove in America," in Jackson, *The Necessity for Ruins* (Amherst, 1980) 85.

[15]Norma Cole, *MARS* (Berkeley, 1994) 19.

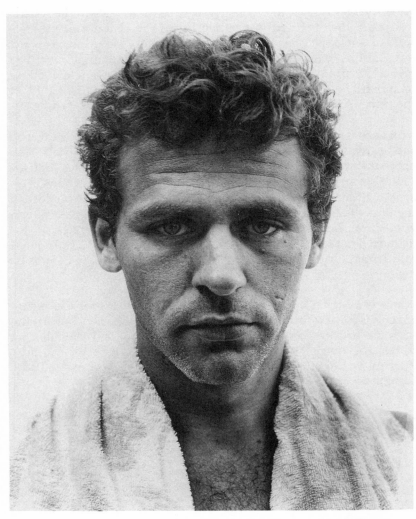

James Agee. Long Island Beach, 1937. Photograph by Walker Evans. Harvard University Art Museums.

Now Let Us Praise James Agee
David Means

SOME WRITERS ARE HEROIC in their ability to write against the odds, in their struggle against the plight of what has been offered up to them in the form of life; others are heroic in their struggles against the word itself — the form and the content and the very gist of their creations. James Agee was both kinds of heroes. The loss of his father at an early age stands as the penultimate event of his early life, and the impetus, one has to suppose, for most of his artist endeavors — including the obvious connection to his great novel, *A Death in the Family*, which, although left unfinished at his death, was pieced together and won the Pulitzer Prize posthumously; his other great creation mirrors his other great heroic state, the battle of the artist with the material: *Let Us Now Praise Famous Men*, a great work of modernism, was his collaboration with photographer Walker Evans in attempting to "document" the plight, or lives, or whatever you want to call the existence of a few southern tenant farm families. After years of struggle (originally the piece was an assignment for *Fortune* magazine), the project ended up being partly a statement, a manifesto, a confession, of Agee's own doubts and fears — a huge sprawling testament (a symphonic collage of brilliantly rendered depictions; some of the best lyric writing we have) to the limitations (in Agee's terms) of art itself, in the examination of a few lives. It is the essence of this doubt, the great humility of the artist before his work — on both the technical front and the deeply probing personal front — that I love about Agee. Great humility. And humility — as the theologian Merton declares — is the only remedy against despair. Maybe it's this humility that keeps Agee partly obscured, partly unsung. He built a bridge of doubt between his modernist sensibilities, which were bebop great, and his deep, profound, religious beliefs (which were always problematic). He drank hard and sinned with great profundity (see his biography by Laurence Bergreen for good juicy details of sexual/domestic escapades), but at the same time he knew that it was possible to hold both sides of his moral being in the same cup; he knew that duplicity and paradox rule contemporary life as they ruled ancient life; and that, like Whitman, one way to honest art is through a declaration of one's self-contradiction. It was no fluke that Agee was picked by Luce to write the *Time* magazine story about the detonation of the atomic bomb over Hiroshima and the end of the war: a piece that slices into the moral complexities, dark and light, of the blast that ended the war.

Today it seems unfashionable — sadly — to love and cherish the forebears of the Western artistic tradition — whoever you want to say those forebears are. Wide, sweeping embraces and deep public confessions of love for dead artists (or your fellow living human kind, for that matter) ring false to many. Better to strike ironic, detached stances and keep said cards of adoration close to the vest. Many avoid real acknowledgment; maintain hard, solemn, unconnected poses. But for Agee, being an artist meant singing love songs to those he held in highest esteem (like Bob Dylan lovingly replicating the intonations of Woody Guthrie): Jesus Christ, of course, but also Beethoven (there's a famous story of Agee playing blasting music in his office), Dostoevsky and Van Gogh, to name a few. The dedication to his collection of poetry, *Permit Me Voyage* (1934), which won the Yale Younger Poets Award, is a fantastic, eight-page song to those artists and thinkers — and others, including God — to whom Agee felt in debt. It is Agee's deep humility and respect, his bowing down, his admission, that one cherishes: "Have mercy upon us therefore, O deep God of the void, spare this race in this your earth still in our free choice: who will turn to you, and again fail you, and once more turn as ever we have done. And make the eyes of our hearts, and the voice of our hearts in speech, honest and lovely within the fences of our nature, and a little clear." Believers and nonbelievers, should, with a willing suspension of nit-picking and overall concern for the canon, be able to see that Agee's dedication is, simply, beautiful in its supplication to the ideals of art.

In the end, Agee's work seems to be about the limits of verbal felicity (as was, say, Beckett's). It isn't enough to be good with words, to sing with exciting dexterity or even to respect the material; without a moral conundrum at the center — that conundrum being what art is — you're only left with interesting fluff. Art is the question, Agee says in his work, not the answer.

Kenneth Patchen: "Hiya, Ken Babe, What's the Bad Word for Today?"

Jonathan Williams

THEY'VE NEVER MADE a movie about Kenneth Patchen (1911–1972). Now they're too late. The only guy who could play him, Robert Mitchum, has just died. He had the voice, the build and the sleepy eyes. He had the laconic barroom style to deliver a poem like "The State of the Nation," whose last line I have altered in the title above.

It's difficult to fathom why he's not read by the young these days. Do the young have enough grounding to read any unconventional poet these days? Basil Bunting always insisted there were still plenty of "unabashed" boys and girls about, but their slovenly teachers had never trained them in the literature that mattered. There were three or four decades when Kenneth Patchen was a poet who mattered a lot to a lot of people. I was having lunch last autumn with J. Laughlin, Patchen's old friend and his publisher at New Directions. He shook his head sadly, "They just don't read Kenneth anymore — how can we understand that?" I don't think we can understand. Each century produces a Blake and a Whitman, a Ryder and a Bruckner. They didn't arrive out of the empyrean with fan clubs and web sites.

Patchen wrote at a time when most writers stayed home and wrote, in places like Rutherford, Old Lyme, Fort Atkinson and Sausalito. The previous generation was into celebrity and reporters followed them to Pamplona, the rue de Fleurus and Rapallo. Patchen had to stay home, and stay in bed — his wrecked back gave him no mercy. Except for a few sessions of poetry-and-jazz with Charles Mingus in New York in the late 1950s, and with the Chamber Jazz Sextet in California, Patchen was a private man, not on stage.

It is instructive, perhaps, to contrast this kind of life with that of two later poets who have recently died: Allen Ginsberg and James Dickey. Both of these men spent early years working in public relations on Madison Avenue and neither stopped jabbering

379

for a single second thereafter. Ginsberg was a mensh. His desire to be the spokesman of his generation was the last thing I could imagine or would want, but we always enjoyed being together on what were rare occasions in San Francisco, New York or here in Dentdale. He upset a lot of squares, he opened up liberating avenues, he put himself on the line; but, may I be excused if I have to say that most of the poetry struck me as hard-sell advertising. I was reminded more of Walter Winchell and Gabriel Heater and Paul Harvey than of the Buddha. . . . Sheriff Dickey, more bubba than mensh, was unbelievably competitive. At a poetry occasion in the White House put on by Rosalynn Carter and Joan Mondale, Jim barely had time to shake my hand. He whispered to his wife, "Come on, honey, we got to go work the crowd." He never forgave me for writing to someone that *Deliverance* was about as accurate about goings-on in Rabun County, Georgia, as Rima the Bird-Girl was in *Green Mansions*, by W.H. Hudson. I also made the mistake of quoting Mr. Ginsberg on *Deliverance:* "What James Dickey doesn't realize is that being fucked in the ass isn't the worse thing that can happen to you in American life." Compared to these public operators, Patchen was as remote as one of the Desert Fathers. (The Desert Fathers is not a rock group.)

I sat in Concourse K at O'Hare Airport in Chicago recently, reading *The New York Times* and *Fanfare* and watching the Passing Parade for about three hours. This is very sobering work. I'm not sure I saw one individual who was dressed individually. Most people looked like mall-crawlers. Most people looked overactive and stressful. They were moving at speed, like the ants in a formicary. Others were merely bland and moved like wizened adolescents. It would be futile to suggest any sign of appetite amongst these citizens for Kenneth Patchen or J. V. Cunningham or Wallace Stevens or James Laughlin. A few people waiting for the evening flight to Manchester were reading paperbacks purchased at the airport. John Grisham and Danielle Steele and Dean Koontz were most in evidence. (One young man was reading Camus, but we must pretend he doesn't exist.) I decided to buy *The Door to December*, by Dean Koontz, "a number one *New York Times* author who currently has more than 100 million copies of his books in print."

Kenneth Patchen. San Francisco, 1954. Photograph by Jonathan Williams.

... Whatever the cause of his crumbling self-control, he was becoming undeniably more frantic by the moment.

Wexlersh.

Manuello.

Why was he suddenly so frightened of them? He had never liked either of them, of course. They were originally vice officers, and word was that they had been among the most corrupt in that division, which was probably why Ross Mondale had arranged for them to transfer under his command in the East Valley; he wanted his right-hand men to be the type who would do what they were told, who wouldn't question any questionable orders, whose allegiance to him would be unshakable as long as he provided for them. Dan knew that they were Mondale's flunkies, opportunists with little or no respect for their work or for concepts like duty and public trust. But they were still cops. . . .

That goes on for 510 pages. So, fellow-stylists, there is hope for us all, whether you like square hamburgers or round hamburgers. I go for the round ones, as I am sure Mr. Koontz does. McDonald's has sold over ninety billion of the little buggers. Here's to LitShit and a kilo of kudzu up the kazoo!

New York publishers calculate the fate of the American novel is in the hands of five thousand readers who will actually purchase new hardback fiction. At the Jargon Society we would be delighted to sell five hundred copies of the latest poetry by Simon Cutts or Thomas Meyer. It might take ten years. Of course, out there in the real world, thousands of verse-scribbling plonkers crank out a ceaseless barrage of what Donald Hall calls the McPoem. Oracles in high places proclaim a Renaissance of Poetry. A distributor tells me of the purchase of twenty thousand hardback copies by a woman poet I have never read nor heard of. The hermits and caitiffs I hang out with don't explore other parts of the literary jungle and just stick to their Lorine Niedecker and Basil Bunting, and even drag out volumes of Kenneth Patchen when the fit is on them. We few, we (occasionally) happy few. . . .

How did we odd readers find our way to Kenneth Patchen? He, of course, would never have been in the curriculum at St. Albans School or at Princeton, my adolescent stomping grounds. I stumbled across a pamphlet by Henry Miller, *Patchen: Man of Anger & Light*. Miller I knew about because evil *Time* magazine had so vilified his book *The Air-Conditioned Nightmare* that I took the next bus to Dupont Circle in Washington, D.C., and bought it at the excellent bookshop run by Franz Bader. By the time I was ten I had the knack of discovering the books important to me beyond those required at school. But I was lucky. I had three good teachers in prep school and I lived in a city with real bookstores. And reading books was something you did. Nowadays, books are a form of retro-delivery-system with no cord to plug in. Way uncool.

By the time I was twenty and had dropped out of Princeton to study painting and printmaking and graphic design, I was into Patchen in a big way. I read him along with Whitman, Poe, H. P. Lovecraft, William Carlos Williams, e. e. cummings, Edith Sitwell, Robinson Jeffers, Hart Crane, Kenneth Rexroth, Thoreau, Randolph Bourne, Kropotkin, Emma Goldman, Henry Miller and Paul Goodman. Before I was twenty-five I owned the manuscripts of *The Journal of Albion Moonlight* and *Sleepers Awake.* I had over forty of Patchen's painted books and a few watercolors. I'd published KP's *Fables & Other Little Tales* during my stay in the medical corps in Germany. What was the attraction?

Patchen was an original. Someone said, equally, of Babe Ruth: "It's like he came down from out of a tree." He was ready to play. Patchen and the Babe were heavy hitters, and nobody struck out more. There is a towering pile of Patchen poems that amounts to not much. But he really does have twenty or twenty-five poems that seem as good as anybody's. He had power, humor, intuitive vision and a kind of primitive nobility. He knew his Blake and Rilke. He loved George Lewis's clarinet and Bunk Johnson's cornet. He drew fabulous animals and painted very well. There was nobody like him.

A few examples. "The State of the Nation" is from *First Will & Testament* (1939):

> Understand that they were sitting just inside the door
> At a little table with two full beers and two empties.
> There were a few dozen people moving around, killing
> Time and getting tight because nothing meant anything
> Anymore
> Somebody looked at a girl and somebody said
>   Great things doing in Spain
> But she didn't even look up, not so much as half an eye.
> Then Jack picked up his beer and Nellie her beer
> And their legs ground together under the table.
> Somebody looked at the clock and somebody said

383

Great things doing in Russia
A cop and two whores came in
And he bought only two drinks
Because one of them had syphilis
No one knew just why it happened or whether
It would happen again on this fretful earth
But Jack picked up his beer and Nellie her beer again
And, as though at signal, a little man hurried in,
Crossed to the bar and said Hello Steve to the bartender.

Painting by Edward Hopper, piano by Hoagy Carmichael — very evocative stuff. The music in the poem is slow, bluesy, uncomplicated. Here's another I like in a similar vein, "Lonesome Boy Blues," from *Orchards, Thrones & Caravans* (1952):

Oh nobody's a long time
Nowhere's a big pocket
To put little
Pieces of nice things that
Have never really happened
To anyone except
Those people who were lucky enough
Not to get born

Oh lonesome's a bad place
To get crowded into
With only
Yourself riding back and forth
On
A blind white horse
Along an empty road meeting
All your
Pals face to face

Oh nobody's a long long time

And then there is the Patchen of social injustice, who keeps asking "I wonder whatever became of human beings?" "The Orange Bears," from *Red Wine & Yellow Hair* (1949) sets you up and asks just what kind of punch you can take:

The orange bears with soft friendly eyes
Who played with me when I was ten,
Christ, before I left home they'd had
Their paws smashed in the rolls, their backs
Seared by hot slag, their soft trusting
Bellies kicked in, their tongues ripped
Out, and I went down through the woods
To the smelly crick with Whitman
In the Haldeman-Julius edition,
And I just sat there worrying my thumbnail
Into the cover — What did he know about
Orange bears with their coats all stunk up with soft coal
And the National Guard coming over
From Wheeling to stand in front of the millgates
With drawn bayonets jeering at the strikers.

I remember you could put daisies
On the windowsill at night and in
The morning they'd be so covered with soot
You couldn't tell what they were anymore.

A hell of a fat chance my orange bears had!

Severity, gravity and wistful sadness. Patchen worked this combination to great effect in *The Famous Boating Party* (1954). He tells the poem like a good shaggy-dog story and he knows how to time and place the punchline just right. Here are two prose-poems, "Soon It Will" and "In Order To":

SOON IT WILL

Be showtime again. Somebody will paint beautiful faces all
over the sky.
Somebody will start bombarding us with really wonderful
letters . . . letters
full of truth, and gentleness, and humility . . . Soon (it says
here) . . .

IN ORDER TO

Apply for the position (I've forgotten now for what) I had to
marry the Second Mayor's daughter by twelve noon. The
order arrived at three minutes of.

385

I already had a wife; the Second Mayor was childless: but I did it.

Next they told me to shave off my father's beard. All right. No matter that he'd been a eunuch, and had succumbed in early childhood: I did it, I shaved him.

Then they told me to burn a village; next, a fair-sized town; then, a city; a small down-at-heels country; then one of "the great powers;" then another (another, another) — In fact, they went right on until they'd told me to burn up every man-made thing on the face of the earth! And I did it, I burned away every last trace, I left nothing, nothing of any kind whatever.

Then they told me to blow it all to hell and gone! And I blew it all to hell and gone (oh, didn't I) . . .

Now, they said, put it back together again; put it all back the way it was when you started.

Well . . . it was my turn to tell *them* something! Shucks, I didn't want any job that bad.

I hope some of you reading this will connect with Kenneth Patchen — he's real good people. New Directions keeps quite a few paperbacks in print. My copy of the *Collected Poems* is inscribed from Kenneth to me, September 1969:

as we were, we are, my friend

If the Lord is willin'
And the creeks don't rise

The Visionary Art of Henry David Thoreau

Joyce Carol Oates

> Life too near paralyzes Art. Long these matters
> refuse to be recorded, except in the invisible colors
> of Memory.
>
> — *Ralph Waldo Emerson*

HENRY DAVID THOREAU WAS MY first love. Insomniac, restless, exhilarated to an almost unbearable degree by late-night sessions of writing, and of reading, when the rest of the household was asleep, I discovered Thoreau at the age of fifteen and found him the very voice of my inarticulate soul. The voice of romance, and of searing common sense. A poet's voice, an artist's eye. The intransigent, abrasive, quarrelsome soul of rebellion. "My arrow aimed at your hearts, my friends!" Ralph Waldo Emerson gloated, anticipating how his young Concord friend would unsettle his Boston literary acquaintances Margaret Fuller and James Russell Lowell, among others. And so Thoreau has been, through the decades, an arrow aimed at the collective heart of America.

There are writers so explosive to the adolescent imagination — Dostoyevsky, Nietzsche, D.H. Lawrence, as well as Thoreau — that to pick up their books is to bring a lighted match to touch flammable material. Many of us have been permanently altered by a single book, and *Walden* is frequently that book. Beyond the almost too exquisitely written sentences of *Walden* we may discover the more spontaneous, vivid and conversational passages of the *Journal*, one of the great, though relatively little-known, of nineteenth-century works. For here is a poet of the near-at-hand. A visionary whose certitude is, if we are honest, our own. Thoreau addresses us with devastating directness. He honors us by setting for us the highest standards of integrity. We can never live up to his expectations. Yet even to fail is to have been illuminated, touched by grace. He is a poet of doubleness, too, warning us against the virtues of youth that are his own: "The scythe that

387

cuts will cut our legs." Perhaps the razor-sharp scythe that Thoreau wielded, flashing in the dullish light of his world, cut him, to a degree. For never has a man so wounded by life (by the repudiation of his first love, Ellen Sewall, by the ghastly, protracted death from lockjaw of his beloved older brother John) so defiantly redefined himself. Born "David Henry Thoreau," he baptized himself "Henry David Thoreau." Out of the rough, seemingly unpromising materials of his background he forged a personality that would in turn write the essays, poems and books, and the great project of his life, the many-volumed journal. We who are writers stand in awe of Thoreau who created "Thoreau" by a continuous exertion of will. We marvel at his confidence that he could, and would, forge a new American prose. A self-proclaimed critic of mere fiction ("one world at a time"), Thoreau was the most inspired of fiction-writers. His gift for language has given us his brilliant prose, and his gift for imagination has given us the man, Thoreau.

This scene follows Thoreau's quarrel with Emerson, who has spoken of his disappointment with Thoreau. Emerson gives the twenty-eight-year-old Thoreau a deed of purchase to land on Walden Pond and commands him to live up to his self-proclaimed promise— "*Go out upon that, build yourself a hut, and there begin the grand process of devouring yourself alive.*"

WALDEN, 1845

(*GREEN-TINCTURED LIGHT. The sound of the "Universal Lyre" in its most ethereal tone. The atmosphere is dream-like but suffused with joy.* THOREAU *appears like a sleep-walker who comes awake, and grows vigorous, purposeful. He is unshaven and his hair disheveled. As he speaks, the light gradually shifts to the subtly golden radiance of indirect sunshine.*)

THOREAU. To go to Walden. To return
  to Walden. The white-pine woods above the cove.
  Deep-emerald water. Floating clouds.
  Sky mirror. Shock of its cold.
  Transparency. Stillness. (*Pause.*)
  To go to Walden at last.
  Earth's eye. You fall and fall forever.
  Geese flying like a tempest overhead.

In the blaze of noon — a thrumming of bright dragonflies.
To go to Walden where the blue iris grows in pure water.
To go to Walden where red foxes run.
To go to Walden where squirrels fly overhead in the scrub-oaks.
To go to Walden where snakes glide invisible through the grass.
To go to Walden to suck life's marrow from the bone.
To go to Walden where the well for my drinking is already dug.
It is no dream of mine but it may be that
I, Henry David Thoreau, am a dream of Walden.

(*A beat. In another voice, more probing, at first skeptical; then rising to euphoria, determination.*)

THOREAU. To throw off "personal history" —
to give birth to myself —
to tear off the clock's damning hands —
to obliterate Memory —
to make myself the man I am not —
to make myself HENRY DAVID THOREAU —
no man's slave, and no woman's lover —
no father's son, and no son's father —
to go to Walden as a pilgrim, as a child —
to worship God in each seed, each raindrop, each rock,
    each heartbeat —
to begin again, in innocence —

(*A beat.*)

THOREAU. I SAY THAT IT IS POSSIBLE!

(THOREAU *constructs his cabin. Perhaps an ax floats, or flies, into his hand. By degrees a "cabin-shape" should emerge, ten feet wide by fifteen feet long, eight feet in height, with one door, one fireplace, two windows. Going through the motions of building the cabin, wielding the ax, perhaps a hammer, nails, saw, etc., in brisk rhythmic movements,* THOREAU *whistles intermittently: we recognize, if he does not, the whistling of his brother* JOHN.)

THOREAU. Near the end of March 1845, I borrowed an ax and went down to the woods by Walden Pond, and began to cut down some tall arrowy pines for timber. I hewed the main timbers six inches square, most of the studs on two sides only, and the rafters and floor timbers on one side, leaving the bark on, so that

389

they were just as straight and much stronger than sawed ones. (*Pause.*) I dug my cellar in the side of a hill sloping to the south. It was but two hours' work. (*Pause.*) By April first, the ice of Walden Pond began cracking. By May first, I set up the frame of my house. By July fourth, Independence Day, it was boarded and roofed, and ready for occupancy. By October first, the chimney was built, the plastering and shingling were completed. (*Pause, proudly.*) *My* house, as fine as any in Concord I think it: ten feet wide by fifteen long, and eight feet in height. The cost? — for such as secondhand boards, bricks, windows, hinges, nails? — $28.12.

(*A beat.*)

THOREAU. If I seem to boast more than is becoming, my excuse is that I brag for humanity rather than myself. (*Pause.*)
I have heard no bad news. (*Pause.*)
I am the first man of creation, the Adam of this shore.
And no rib torn from *my* side! (*Pause.*)

(THOREAU *continues his brisk, matter-of-fact "construction."*)

THOREAU. My first year, I planted two and a half acres of beans, potatoes, corn, peas and turnips. My second year, I planted even less, for I had found I needed less. (*Proudly.*) My townspeople looked upon me askance, as a sort of wild eccentric, or hermit, but I was the only free man of my acquaintance, for I was not anchored to any house or farm. No children's crying disturbed the peace of *my* woods. (*Pause.*) For two years I lived in the woods, and for five years I maintained myself solely by the labor of my hands. I found that I could support myself by working but *six weeks* out of *fifty-two* — devoting the remainder of my time to living. And to writing.

(THOREAU *strides to his desk, takes up his ledger-journal and a pencil.*)

THOREAU. Very few books I carried into the woods. Very few I needed. For it was my own book I was writing — WALDEN. As I lived, I wrote of my experiment in living. As I wrote of my experiment in living, I lived. My words became me: HENRY DAVID THOREAU. I need no other epitaph.

(*A beat.* THOREAU *paces about. There is a tincture of mania in his euphoria which he manages, just barely, to control.*)

THOREAU. (*Gloating.*) I MADE MYSELF THE MAN I WAS NOT. AND, BEING SO MADE, I . . . *WAS.*

(*An echo as of thunder. The RADIANT GOLD LIGHT has been steadily dimming; there is a corresponding sound of thunder. A sudden flash of lightning.* THOREAU *cringes in his cabin. A sound of pelting, drumming rain on the roof.*)

THOREAU. If the damned roof leaks, I shall not record *that.* (*Despondent laugh.*) Am I . . . imprisoned here? (*Pause, looking out the window; as if reasoning with someone.*) TO LIVE ONE LIFE, YOU MUST REJECT ALL OTHERS. (*Shivers; coughs; strikes chest with his fist.*) Am I alone? — it is my CHOICE.

(*The storm continues. A discordant music.* THOREAU *loses confidence.*)

THOREAU. Madness. My secret terror . . .

(ELLEN SEWALL, *as a girl of seventeen, appears at a distance, a taunting apparition. Her hair is loose and the front of her dress partly open.*)

ELLEN. Henry Thoreau . . .

THOREAU. No! I don't know you.

ELLEN. (*Seductive.*) Henry Thoreau. I did love you.

THOREAU. No.

ELLEN. Loved loved LOVED YOU. (*As she strokes her body.*)

THOREAU. NO.

ELLEN. You were not MAN ENOUGH to take me.

THOREAU. NO!

ELLEN. (*Deliciously.*) Animal. Crude. Henry Thoreau. You disgust me.

(THOREAU *kicks a chair across the room.* ELLEN *vanishes.*)

THOREAU. Leave me alone, you — *woman!* All Nature is my bride.

391

(*Rain continues drumming on the roof.* THOREAU *lights a candle at his desk and takes up his journal to write in it, but he's too excited to sit down.*)

THOREAU. (*Determined.*) "I love to be alone. I never found the companion that was so companionable as SOLITUDE." Yes, good! "In my time at Walden, I never felt lonesome, or in the least oppressed by a sense of solitude, but once . . . when, for a dreadful hour, I came near to collapse." (*Pause.*) No: strike that. ". . . when, for an hour, I doubted if the neighborhood of man was not essential to a serene and healthy life." (*Pause.*) ". . . But I was at the same time conscious of a slight insanity in my mood, and seemed to foresee my recovery." Yes, exactly! ". . . In the midst of a gentle rain while these thoughts prevailed, I was suddenly sensible of such sweet and beneficent society in Nature . . ."

(*A lightning flash, and a peal of thunder so loud that* THOREAU *drops his journal.* JOHN THOREAU *appears at a distance, as an apparition.*)

JOHN. Henry! — dear brother . . .

THOREAU. John!

JOHN. Come to me!

THOREAU. (*Shielding his face.*) Am I dreaming? I *am* dreaming —

JOHN. I love you, Henry. I alone have plumbed the depths of your heart.

THOREAU. (*Frightened.*) John, no — leave me alone.

JOHN. Brother, would you deny *me? My* suffering, *your* agony?

THOREAU. (*Guilty, despairing.*) Am I to wallow in grief, forever?

JOHN. Better grief than nothing.

THOREAU. (*Picking up the journal.*) This that I have is NOT NOTHING!

JOHN. (*Tenderly, seductively, opening his arms to* THOREAU.) Brother! No one has loved us as we loved each other. Would you mock my suffering? Recall how I died.

THOREAU. Nature *is* sweet and beneficent. The world *is* good.

JOHN. (*Pleading, raving.*) BROTHER COME TO ME HELP ME BROTHER DON'T ABANDON ME BROTHER —

THOREAU. God help me! —

(THOREAU *drops the journal. He begins to have convulsions; his jaws lock in a grotesque parody of a grin. He tears at his hair and clothes, groaning in terror and anguish.*)

THOREAU. —help HELP ME —

(*A flash of lightning. A peal of thunder.* THOREAU *staggers toward his bed and collapses onto the floor.* JOHN *has vanished. Lights out. Lights up. Next morning: a brilliant radiance, as at the start of the scene. The "Universal Lyre" in its ethereal mode.* THOREAU, *on the floor, wakes, and looks around in apprehension; manages to get up, unsteadily; washes his face in a basin. His clothes are torn and there is a bruise on the side of his face. He has a haggard, dazed look, but the terror has passed. Close outside the cabin, a cardinal sings.* THOREAU *whistles in reply. A beat. The bird answers.*)

THOREAU. (*In the doorway, sunshine on his face.*) That's it, then. I turn my face to — "the world."

(*Lights out.*)

Henry David Thoreau. Concord Free Public Library, Concord, Massachusetts.

Joyful Noise:
The Gospel Sound of Henry D. Thoreau
Donald Revell

Now at Sundown I hear the hooting of an owl—hoohoo hoo—hoorer—hoo . . . I rejoice that there are owls. They represent the stark twilight unsatisfied thoughts I have.
—Journals, November 18, 1851

Some chickadees come flitting close to me, and one utters its spring note, *phe-be*, for which I feel under obligations to him.
—Journals, January 9, 1858

I hear in several places the low dumping notes of awakened bullfrogs, what I call their *pebbly* notes, as if they were cracking pebbles in their mouths; not the plump *dont dont* or *ker dont*, but *kerdle dont dont*.
—Journals, May 10, 1858

When, in doleful dumps, breaking the awful stillness of our wooden sidewalk on a Sunday, or, perchance, a watcher in the house of mourning, I hear a cockerel crow far or near, I think to myself, "There is one of us well, at any rate," and with a sudden gush return to my senses.
—"Walking"

THE POEMS OF A DAY begin presently with sound, and they continue so. Henry David Thoreau, devoted friend of the days, wrote continually, and still the writing makes the sound of poems. Devotion is competent to every art. It pays perfect attention, and in the economy of poetry (anything written attentively is a poem, whatever else befalls), attention offers a presence to all sounds and to what becomes of sound in words. In his *Journals* and in books and essays collected out of them, Thoreau imagines unmediated becoming, effortlessly. Sound becomes sense without even trying. An owl hoots and Thoreau rejoices in the instantaneous and

395

unintended representation of his thought. A chickadee "utters its spring note," and Thoreau is under easy obligations he repays in kind: *"phe-be,"* faithfully inscribed. Nothing is lost or stolen in translation because nothing is translated. Shaped by senses actually present, onomatopoeia makes sense. And when I read, it makes a sense in me. I am awakened with the bullfrogs by a noise Thoreau has somehow made my own. If I have a noise in mind, I must be somewhere, hearing it. And Thoreau is there beside me, untranslating all the while. I write poems because I love the sound of poems. My faith rests there. And Thoreau assures me faith is not misplaced. Every line, even before it is a line, and ever afterwards if it is true, instances the onomatopoeic sense of being somewhere in particular at a particular point in time. In poetry, the particular is good health to me, and saneness. As Thoreau explains, sound returns us to our senses. From doleful spells of inwardness, we are startled awake. The day is well, and it says so.

> But the music is not in the tune; it is in the sound.
> —*Journals*, June 25, 1852

Unscored, unscripted, the sense of the day is the day itself. It makes no references. Its forms transpire, indistinguishable by me from evidence of my senses. Where I put my faith I put myself. I find myself there, in passing, and there my feelings transpire, indistinguishable from the day. Thoreau's devotion to the hale sense of all sounds sets his words in the presence of presences: each is particular, not separate; each is musical, but not recognizable in the easy way of tunes. Always original, a sound declares itself unprecedented. And of course, of course that is what I believe about true feeling. *This has never happened to me before.* Reading a poem I hear a sound unheard until now. Making a poem, I utter sounds whose sense is sudden and particular to the hour. In *Walden*, Thoreau realizes that even an echo is "an original sound" and "not merely a repetition," and it elapses over circumstances of space and time (treetops and sunrises) particular to itself. In tuneless restless sound Thoreau discovers a keener presence of mind. He abandons his faculties to his senses. Poetry, like freedom, like love, should always be unrecognizable, particularly to itself. It abandons poetry to become a poem. In reckless devotion, Thoreau becomes the stranger who is effortless to know.

Where there is sense, experience arrives. And so does death. In

the intervals, effort serves the more to postpone experience —
change of circumstances, change of world — than to pronounce it.
So often, work is the delay of weal and woe. Early in the history
of our Republic, Thoreau upends the work ethic, averring it a dis-
traction from the urgent business of the day: life and death. Habits
of effort, ritual and piecemeal, muffle extraordinary sounds of
transformation. In a wonderful biography, *The Days of Henry
Thoreau*, Walter Harding offers a glimpse of the man in undis-
tracted extremity. The occasion is the death of Helen Thoreau, his
elder sister.

> Helen died on June 14, 1849, aged only thirty-six. The
> funeral was held in the home on the eighteenth with both
> the Unitarian and the Trinitarian ministers in attendance.
> Thoreau sat seemingly unmoved with his family through
> the service, but as the pallbearers prepared to remove the
> bier, he arose and, taking a music box from the table, wound
> it and set it to playing a melody in a minor key that seemed
> to the listeners "like no earthly tune." All sat quietly until
> the music was over.

A moment of true feeling interrupts the inertial motion of
ritual. Grief defies a senseless consolation, and the defiance is a
sound, "a melody like no earthly tune." Helen, departed from Earth,
is sounded no sound of Earth by her attentive brother. The onomatopoeia of extinction is a mechanical minor key. The sound of
grief, whose object only is unearthly, employs no words. To speak
of death, say nothing.

And Thoreau remained sound upon the efforts of speech, even
to the end. Harding relays this telling vignette of a visit from one
Parker Pillsbury to Thoreau only a few days before the writer's
death.

> "Then I spoke only once more to him, and cannot remember
> my exact words. But I think my question was substantially
> this: 'You seem so near the brink of the dark river, that I
> almost wonder how the opposite shore may appear to you.'
> Then he answered, 'One world at a time.'"

Effortlessly, all sounds here. Elsewhere is a work of fiction worrying the minor keys.

> A child loves to strike on a tin pan or other ringing vessel with a stick, because, its ears being fresh, sound, attentive, and percipient, it detects the finest music in the sound, at which all nature assists. Is not the very cope of the heavens the sounding board of the infant drummer? So clear and unprejudiced ears hear the sweetest and most soul-stirring melody in tinkling cowbells and the like (dogs baying the moon), not to be referred to association, but intrinsic in the sound itself; those cheap and simple sounds which men despise because their ears are dull and debauched. Ah, that I were so much a child that I could unfailingly draw music from a quart pot! Its little ears tingle with the melody. To it there is music in sound alone.
>
> —*Journals*, June 9, 1852

Music — sustained, passionate, tenacious — remains innocent of effort. It is a feeling that persists in the act of hands, breath and senses. As melody, persistence makes the action of sound easy and sweet. Every day, Thoreau went out of the house of mourning to meet his senses where the music never stopped. Undebauched, undulled, never so much begun as continuing, the music of the day is ever available: "cheap and simple." From the available music, Thoreau could easily draw a full day's measure of poetry and truth, as above, in the innocent insistence of "sound alone." Our senses make tenacity a mere matter of waking (and of walking) to the world. There, uninterrupted by insensible referral, we find everything to be intrinsic. We find no duplication. Every sound originates with itself. And so, as a passage from *A Week on the Concord and Merrimack Rivers* believes, "The heart is forever inexperienced." Presence is percussion. All being makes a sound and another and then another. The truth and poetry of being are ever present unprepared, all parts particular. Here in the world, hearts hear, and a new heart beats in every sound.

> Far in the night, as we were falling asleep on the bank of the Merrimack, we heard some tyro beating a drum incessantly, in preparation for a country muster, as we learned, and we thought of the line, —
>
> "When the drum beat at dead of night."
>
> We could have assured him that his beat would be answered, and the forces be mustered. Fear not, thou drummer of the

night; we too will be there. And still he drummed on in the silence and the dark. This stray sound from a far-off sphere came to our ears from time to time, far, sweet, and significant, and we listened with such an unprejudiced sense as if for the first time we heard at all. No doubt he was an insignificant drummer enough, but his music afforded us a prime and leisure hour, and we felt that we were in season wholly. These simple sounds related us to the stars. Ay, there was a logic in them so convincing that the combined sense of mankind could never make me doubt their conclusions. I stop my habitual thinking, as if the plow had suddenly run deeper in its furrow through the crust of the world. How can I go on, who have just stepped over such a bottomless skylight in the bog of my life? Suddenly old Time winked at me, — Ah, you know me, you rogue, — and news had come that IT was well. That ancient universe is in such capital health, I think undoubtedly it will never die. Heal yourselves, doctors; by God I live.

—from "Monday," *A Week on
the Concord and Merrimack Rivers*

It really works. A present attention to particular sound realizes a place relating a place of one's own therein: a new world and new words; a poem. Hearing the real, incessant drum-taps straying through the dark, Thoreau is instantly "in season wholly," i.e., alert and fertile, i.e., present for a change. And change comes. The logic of the onomatopoeic instant overturns all convictions and previous logic. It is a wilding of habit. It is a deeper ground. It is a poem, as only poetry could overstep a skylight in a bog. The wink of Time in allegorical rough-and-ready assures us that Time is well. Surely the well-being of Time is news that stays news: i.e., a poem.

It is not words that I wish to hear or to utter — but relations
that I seek to stand in . . .

—*Journals,* December 22, 1851

Sounds occur to our hearing: *to* our hearing. They are immediately related, and we receive them in unique relationship. From Thoreau, I learn that poetry is not words primarily. Not even words are words originally. First comes sound. Standing or walking in his faith, Thoreau was always positioned to hear what Whitman, in a like place, called "the origin of all poems." Poetry is first a relation to the sounds of a day and only subsequently the relating of itself in sentences and lines. And what comes first is, eventually, enough. Composer Charles Ives, the most articulate Thoreauvian of all, once announced "American music is already written." In the moments of days, for anyone standing in good relation to the sounds, American poetry is also already written. Thoreau says so.

> Above all, we cannot afford not to live in the present. He is blessed over all mortals who loses no moment of the passing life in remembering the past. Unless our philosophy hears the cock crow in every barnyard within our horizon, it is belated. That sound commonly reminds us that we are growing rusty and antique in our employments and habits of thought. His philosophy comes down to a more recent time than ours. There is something suggested by it that is a newer testament — the gospel according to this moment.
>
> — "Walking"

By the sound of things, unbelated is eternal. I awaken to no immediate danger. The gospel is right on time.

The editors express gratitude to everyone who offered their time and expertise while we were working on *Tributes,* with special thanks to Nancy Crampton, Rollie McKenna, Jonathan Williams, Gail Roub, Joe LeSueur, George Robert Minkoff, Declan Spring/ New Directions Publishing Corporation, Eleanor W. Traylor/ Howard University, Nancy MacKechnie/Vassar College Libraries, Erick Falkensteen/The Granger Collection, Quincy Troupe, Robert Kelly, Anthony McCall, Thalia Field, Karen Walker, Sadia Talib and, in particular, our managing editor, Michael Bergstein.

Quotations from the work of Sterling Brown are reprinted by permission. "Strong Men," "Frankie and Johnny," "The New Congo," "Mob" (section VII from "Side by Side"), the first two stanzas of "Crispus Attucks McKoy" and the penultimate stanza of "Honey Mah Love" are reprinted from *The Collected Poems of Sterling A. Brown,* copyright © 1980 by Sterling A. Brown. Originally published by Harper & Row Publishers, Inc. in 1980, and reprinted by TriQuarterly Books in 1989 and by Tri-Quarterly Books/Northwestern University Press in 1996 by arrangement with HarperCollins Publishers, Inc. "Frankie and Johnny" was published in *Southern Roads* by Sterling A. Brown; copyright © 1932 by Harcourt, Brace & Co.; copyright renewed 1960 by Sterling A. Brown. All rights reserved; this material is used with permission of Northwestern University Press.

Quotations from Yvor Winters, *Edwin Arlington Robinson,* reprinted by permission of New Directions Publishing Corporation. Copyright © 1971 by New Directions Publishing Corporation.

Quotations from Jack Kerouac, *Mexico City Blues,* reprinted by permission of Sterling Lord Literistic, Inc. Copyright © 1995 by John Sampatakakos, literary representative.

Quotations from Frank Stanford, *You* and *The Battlefield Where the Moon Says I Love You* by permission of C. D. Wright. Copyright © the Estate of Frank Stanford. Material on the horse apple, in C. D. Wright's "Of the Mulberry Family: An Arkansas Epilogue," adapted from *Trees of Arkansas,* by Dwight M. Moore. Reprinted by permission of Arkansas Forestry Commission.

Quotations from Ralph Ellison, *Invisible Man,* reprinted by permission of Random House, Inc. Copyright © 1947, 1948, 1952 by Ralph Ellison.

Quotations from Kenneth Patchen, *First Will & Testament; Orchards, Thrones & Caravans; Red Wine & Yellow Hair;* and *The Famous Boating Party* reprinted by permission of New Directions Publishing Corporation. Copyright © 1939, 1949, 1952, 1954 by New Directions Publishing Corporation.

Quotations from Edward Dahlberg, *The Edward Dahlberg Reader,* reprinted by permission of New Directions Publishing Corporation. Copyright © 1961 by Edward Dahlberg and New Directions Publishing Corporation.

NOTES ON CONTRIBUTORS

WILL ALEXANDER has three books forthcoming: *Towards the Primeval Lightning Field* (O Books), *Above the Human Nerve Domain* (Pavement Saw Press) and *Impulse & Nothingness* (Sun & Moon Press).

AMIRI BARAKA has recently published *Transbluesency: Selected Poems 1961–1995* (Marsilio), *Funk Lore: Recent Poetry* (Littoral Press), *Eulogies* (Marsilio) and *The Autobiography of LeRoi Jones*. He and his wife, the poet Amina Baraka, are co-directors of Kimako's Blues People, a multimedia arts space. He is also artistic director of The Newark Music Project, a research and publishing group working at archiving all the music produced in Newark. The first concert in January 1998 will be the works of Willie "The Lion" Smith.

SVEN BIRKERTS is the author of four books of essays, most recently *The Gutenberg Elegies: The Fate of Reading in an Electronic Age* (Faber & Faber).

CATHERINE BOWMAN is the author of two collections of poems, *1-800-HOT-RIBS* and *Rock Farm*, both published by Gibbs Smith. She teaches at Indiana University.

ANA CASTILLO is a novelist, poet, editor and essayist. Her most recent publications include a book of short stories, *Loverboys* (W. W. Norton), and *Goddess of the Americas: Writings on the Virgin of Guadalupe*, an anthology (Riverhead).

NORMA COLE's most recent books of poetry are *MOIRA* (O Books) and *Contrafact* (Potes & Poets). An active translator of contemporary French writing, she has just (with Stacy Doris) co-edited *Raddle Moon 16*, a special issue of French writers appearing in North America for the first time.

ROBERT CREELEY is presently at work on a collaboration with the German artist Georg Baselitz. New Directions will publish a new collection of his poems, *Life & Death*, in spring of 1998, and a reissue of *Hello, Later* and *Mirrors* in one volume under the title *Later* will be published in fall 1998.

VICTOR HERNÁNDEZ CRUZ writes in English and Spanish and lives in Puerto Rico. His most recent book is *Panoramas*, published by Coffee House Press.

LYDIA DAVIS is the author of *Break It Down* and *The End of the Story* (both published by Farrar, Straus & Giroux) as well as numerous translations from the French including works by Maurice Blanchot and Michel Leiris. A new collection of stories, *Almost No Memory*, has just been issued by Farrar, Straus & Giroux.

ELAINE EQUI is the author of several books of poetry, including *Surface Tension* and *Decoy*, both from Coffee House Press. A new collection, *Voice-Over*, is forthcoming in 1998. She teaches at Rutgers University and The New School.

STEVE ERICKSON is the author of *Days Between Stations, Rubicon Beach, Tours of the Black Clock, Leap Year* and *Arc d'X*, all published by Poseidon Press, and *Amnesiascope* and *American Nomad*, published by Henry Holt.

ELI GOTTLIEB's first novel, *The Boy Who Went Away*, was published by St. Martin's Press in January 1997.

MAUREEN HOWARD is the author of the novels *Natural History* (W.W. Norton) and *Bridgeport Bus* (Penguin) and a memoir, *Facts of Life* (Penguin). Her new novel, *A Lover's Almanac*, will be published by Viking in January 1998.

SIRI HUSTVEDT is the author of a collection of poems, *Reading to You* (Open Book Publications), and the novels *The Blindfold* (Poseidon Press) and *The Enchantment of Lily Dahl* (Henry Holt). A book of essays, *Yonder*, will be published by Holt in the spring of 1998.

ROBERT KELLY's most recent books are *Red Actions: Selected Poems 1960–1993* (Black Sparrow Press), the fictional *Queen of Terrors* (McPherson & Co.) and the long poem *Mont Blanc* (Otherwind Press).

JIM LEWIS is the author of two novels: *Sister* (Graywolf) and *Why the Tree Loves the Ax* (Crown).

PHILLIP LOPATE's most recent essay collection is *Portrait of My Body* (Doubleday/Anchor). He is editor of *The Art of the Personal Essay* (Anchor) and *The Anchor Essay Annual* (Anchor), and teaches at Hofstra University.

NATHANIEL MACKEY's book of poetry *Whatsaid Serif* is due out soon from City Lights. *Bedouin Hornbook*, the first volume of his ongoing epistolary fiction *From a Broken Bottle Traces of Perfume Still Emanate*, was recently reissued by Sun & Moon Press, which also published volume two, *Djbot Baghostus's Run*. A third volume in the series, *Atet A.D.*, is forthcoming.

BEN MARCUS is the author of *The Age of Wire and String* (Knopf). He lives in Providence.

CAROLE MASO is the author of *Ghost Dance* (Ecco), *The Art Lover* (Ecco), *AVA* (Dalkey Archive), *The American Woman in the Chinese Hat* (Plume), *Aureole* (Ecco) and, forthcoming from Dutton, *Defiance*.

ELLEN McLAUGHLIN's plays include *Days and Nights Within, A Narrow Bed, Infinity's House* and *Iphigenia and Other Daughters*, all of which have received American and international productions. Her latest play, *Tongue of a Bird*, premieres at the Intiman Theater in Seattle and will also be produced at the Almeida Theater in London.

DAVID MEANS is the author of *A Quick Kiss of Redemption and Other Stories* (William Morrow). His recent fiction appeared in *Harper's* and *Paris Review*.

PAUL METCALF's *Collected Works* have recently been published as a three-volume set by Coffee House Press.

RICK MOODY is the author of the novels *The Ice Storm* and *Purple America*, both published by Little, Brown and Co.

BRADFORD MORROW's novels are *Come Sunday* (Penguin), *The Almanac Branch* (W. W. Norton), *Trinity Fields* (Penguin) and, most recently, *Giovanni's Gift* (Viking). He is the founding editor of *Conjunctions.*

JOYCE CAROL OATES is the author most recently of the novel *Man Crazy* and the story collection *Will You Always Love Me?* (both published by Dutton). She is the 1996 recipient of the PEN/Malamud Award for Achievement in the Short Story.

LAWRENCE OSBORNE is the author of *Paris Dreambook* and a collection of essays, *The Poisoned Embrace* (Vintage). He is currently writing a book on New York.

DALE PECK is the author of three novels, all from Farrar, Straus & Giroux: *Martin and John*, *The Law of Enclosures* and the forthcoming *Now It's Time to Say Goodbye.*

DONALD REVELL is the author of five collections of poetry, most recently *Beautiful Shirt* (Wesleyan). His translation of Guillaume Apollinaire's *Alcools* was published by Wesleyan in 1995.

JOHN SAYLES is the author of the novels *Pride of the Bimbos, Union Dues* and *Los Gusanos* and the story collection *The Anarchists' Convention*, all published by HarperCollins. Some of the films he has written and directed are *Lone Star, Return of the Secaucus 7, Eight Men Out* and *Matewan.*

JOANNA SCOTT's most recent novel, *The Manikin* (Henry Holt), was a finalist for the Pulitzer Prize. She teaches at the University of Rochester.

NTOZAKE SHANGE is the author of *For Colored Girls Who Have Considered Suicide/When the Rainbow Is Enuf* (MacMillan) as well as the poetry collection *Nappy Edges* (St. Martin's Press) and the novel *Betsey Brown* (Picador USA).

LISA SHEA is the author of *Hula,* a novel (W. W. Norton), and is completing a second novel, *The Free World.* She is the recipient of a Whiting Writer's Award.

MONA SIMPSON is the author of *A Regular Guy* (Knopf). She is working on *My Hollywood,* a novel, and a collection of short stories, *Virginity and Other Fictions.*

PETER STRAUB is the author of many best-selling novels, among them *Ghost Story* (Pocket), *Shadowland* (Berkley), *Koko* (Dutton), *The Throat* (Dutton) and *The Hellfire Club* (Random House). He was selected as grand master at the 1997 World Horror Convention.

COLE SWENSEN's most recent book of poetry is *Noon* (Sun & Moon Press). *Numen* was published in 1995 (Burning Deck) and her translation of *Art Poetic'* by Olivier Cadiot will be out this year from Sun & Moon. She is director of the creative writing program at the University of Denver.

LYNNE TILLMAN's recent books include the novel *Cast in Doubt* (Poseidon Press) and *The Velvet Years: Warhol's Factory 1965–1967* (Thunder's Mouth Press), with photographs by Stephen Shore. *The Broad Picture* (Serpent's Tail), her first collection of essays, just appeared in August. Her new novel, *No Lease on Life* (Harcourt Brace), will be published in January.

QUINCY TROUPE is the author of *Avalanche*, a volume of poems (Coffee House Press). *Miles and Me: A Memoir of Miles Davis* (University of California Press) will be published in the fall of 1998. He teaches literature and creative writing at the University of California, San Diego.

ANNE WALDMAN's most recent works are *Iovis, Book II* (Coffee House Press) and *Songs of the Sons and Daughters of Buddha*, translations with Andrew Schelling (Shambhala). She is editor of *The Beat Book* (Shambhala) and co-editor of *Disembodied Poetics: Annals of the Jack Kerouac School* (University of New Mexico Press).

MAC WELLMAN is a poet and playwright living in New York. He is a recipient of a Lila Wallace–Reader's Digest Writers' Award for 1996. His play *Fnu Lnu* will be produced by Soho Rep in October.

PAUL WEST's novel *The Tent of Orange Mist* (Scribner) was runner-up for the National Book Critics Circle Award for 1996. In the same year, the government of France made him a Chevalier of Arts and Letters. His most recent works of fiction are the novella *Sporting with Amaryllis* (Overlook) and *Terrestrials* (Scribner), both published in 1997.

DIANE WILLIAMS's most recent book is *The Stupefaction*, out from Knopf. She co-edits *StoryQuarterly*.

JONATHAN WILLIAMS's next book of poems will be *Kinnikinnick Brand Kickapoo Joy-Juice* (Turkey Press), with drawings by John Furnival of the Norman church at Kilpeck in Herefordshire.

C. D. WRIGHT's most recent collection of poetry is *Tremble* (Ecco). She co-edits Lost Roads Publishers, a book press, and is on the faculty at Brown University.

KEVIN YOUNG's *Most Way Home* (William Morrow) was selected for the National Poetry Series and won the John C. Zacharis First Book Prize from *Ploughshares*. He recently completed a traveling exhibition and book-length manuscript of poems on the late artist Jean-Michel Basquiat. He is assistant professor of English in African-American studies at the University of Georgia.

To Them, To Their First Conversation

Sunlight: Her pituitary balks at the lack of it
and he's an engraver, so for them

light is not taken for granted. On this day in October
downtown, lunch hour, the sun's acting paternal.

Showing them off to each other. The man
is flushed with the debonair mutiny of blowing off

his day job, of loafing on the sidewalk, flirting with a woman
with bobcat green eyes. Between the edge of her scarf

and the scoop neck of her sweater there's a crescent of her skin,
unprotected. Their first conversation alone.

Blaring noon. People have to step around them.
A southeastern sky tips down to them its light,

half cloudy, like tea dashed with milk,
which, after a long illness, is brought—

slowly now—
           to the lips.

Dalkey Archive Press

Killoyle
by Roger Boylan

"A bucking, snorting horse of a tale that gallops heedlessly through the streets and pubs of one Irish town."
—*Minnesota Daily*

$13.95 paper

The Shutter of Snow
by Emily Holmes Coleman

"Coleman's lyrical rendering of her two-month treatment for post-partum psychosis in 1924 is fresh and immediate and, at the same time, historically revealing."
—*Publishers Weekly*

$12.95 paper

Reader's Block
by David Markson

"A novel often dreamed about by the avant-garde but never seen . . . utterly fascinating."
—*Publishers Weekly*

$12.95 paper

Visit our website at {www.cas.ilstu.edu/english/dalkey/dalkey.html} to find out about titles by Carole Maso, Edward Dahlberg, Paul Metcalf, Gertrude Stein, Paul West and others.

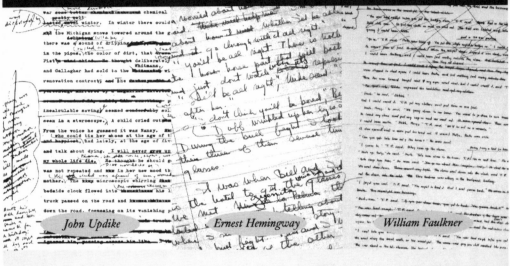

Critical acclaim has been unanimous in declaring PAUL METCALF a newly rediscovered genius.

"The publication of Metcalf's Collected Works . . . is nothing less than an event."
—Library Journal

"Metcalf maps an invaluable literary landscape, unrestrained by any form or geography. At last, it is open to the general public."
—Publishers Weekly (starred review)

"The great-grandson of Herman Melville and [one of the] last of the Black Mountain writers, Metcalf possesses a passionate and dramatic sense of American history."
—ALA Booklist

"[Metcalf] echoes Ezra Pound's facility with disparate sources and William Carlos Williams's fascination with the history of place. "
—CUPS

Paul Metcalf

COLLECTED WORKS, VOLUME I, 1956-1976   CLOTH $35.00
Introduction by Guy Davenport. Includes: *Will West, Genoa, Patagoni, Apalache,* and *The Middle Passage.*

COLLECTED WORKS, VOLUME II, 1976-1986   CLOTH $35.00
This volume is comprised of: *1-57, Zip Odes, Willie's Throw, U.S. Dept. of the Interior, Both, The Island,* and *Waters of Potowmack.*

COLLECTED WORKS, VOLUME III, 1987-1997   CLOTH $35.00
Of particular note to Metcalf collectors is the debut of his latest two significant works—*Huascarán* and *The Wonderful White Whale of Kansas,* available exclusively in this edition. Also included: *Louis the Torch, Firebird, Golden Delicious, ". . . and nobody objected," Araminta and the Coyotes, Mountaineers Are Always Free!, Where Do You Put the Horse?,* and *Three Plays.*

AVAILABLE AT COFFEE HOUSE PRESS: 1-612-338-0125.
DISTRIBUTED BY CONSORTIUM BOOK SALES & DISTRIBUTION: 1-800-283-3572.

THE
EMBROIDERED
SHOES

stories

CAN XUE

 HENRY HOLT AND COMPANY, INC.